George Manvil

C000184389

Menhardoc

George Manville Fenn

Menhardoc

1st Edition | ISBN: 978-3-75231-410-6

Place of Publication: Frankfurt am Main, Germany

Year of Publication: 2020

Outlook Verlag GmbH, Germany.

George Manville Fenn

"Menhardoc"

Chapter One.

Introduces Will and his Henchman, Josh.

"You don't know it, Master Will, lad, but Natur' couldn't ha' done no better for you if she'd tried."

"Why, Josh?"

"Why, lad? There's a queshton to ask! Why? Warn't you born in Co'rn'all, the finest country in all England, and ain't you going to grow into a Cornishman, as all old books says is giants, when you've left off being a poor smooth, soft-roed, gallish-looking creatur', same as you are now?"

The utterer of these words certainly spoke them, but in a musical, sing-song intonation peculiar to the fishermen of the district. He was a fair, short man, somewhat deformed, one arm being excessively short, seeming little more than a hand projecting from one side of his breast; but this in no wise interfered with his activity as he stood there glittering in the bright morning sunshine on the deck of a Cornish lugger, shaking pilchards out of the dark-brown net into the well or hold.

Josh Helston glittered in the morning sunshine like a harlequin in a limelight, for he was spangled from head to foot with the loose silvery scales of the pilchards caught during the night, and on many another night during the past few weeks. There were scales on his yellow south-wester, in his fair closely-curling hair, a couple on his ruddy-brown nose, hundreds upon his indigo-blue home-knit jersey, and his high boots, that were almost trousers and boots in one, were literally burnished with the adherent disks of silvery iridescent horn.

The "poor smooth, gallish-looking creatur'" he addressed was a well-built young fellow of seventeen, with no more effeminacy in his appearance than is visible in a lad balanced by nature just on that edge of life where we rest for a short space uneasily, bidding good-bye to boyhood so eagerly, before stepping boldly forward, and with flushed face and flashing eyes feeling our muscles and the rough hair upon our cheeks and chins, and saying, in all the excitement of the discovery of that El Dorado time of life, "At last I am a man!"

Josh Helston's words did not seem fair, but his way was explained once to Michael Polree as they stood together on the pier; and the latter had expostulated after his fashion, for he never spoke much, by saying:

"Easy, mate, easy."

"Easy it is, Mike," sang rather than said Josh. "I know what I'm about. The old un said I wasn't to spoil him, and I won't. He's one o' them soft sort o' boys as is good stuff, like a new-bred net; but what do you do wi' it, eh?"

"Bile it," growled old Mike, "Cutch or Gambier."

"Toe be sure," said Josh; "and I'm biling young Will in the hot water o' adversitee along with the cutch o' worldly knowledge, and the gambier o' fisherman's gumption, till he be tanned of a good moral, manly, sensible brown. I know."

Then old Mike winked at Josh Helston, and Josh Helston winked solemnly at old Mike Polree, who threw a couple of hake slung on a bit of spun yarn over one shoulder, his strapped-together boots stuffed with coarse worsted stockings, one on each side, over the other shoulder, squirted a little tobacco juice into the harbour, and went off barefoot over the steep stones to the cottage high up the cliff, muttering to himself something about Pilchar' Will being a fine young chap all the same.

"That's all nonsense about the Cornishmen being giants, Josh," said Will, as he rapidly passed the long lengths of net through his hands, so that they should lie smooth in the hold, ready for shooting again that night without twist or tangle. "Old writers were very fond of stretching men."

"Dessay they was," said Josh; "but they never stretched me. I often wish I was ten inches longer."

"It wouldn't have made a better fellow of you, Josh," said Will, with a merry twinkle in his eye.

"I dunno 'bout that," said Josh disparagingly; "I ain't much account," and he rubbed his nose viciously with the back of his hand, the result being that he spread a few more scales upon his face.

"Why, you're the strongest man I know, Josh. You can throw anyone in Peter Churchtown, and I feel like a baby when you grip hold of me."

Josh felt flattered, but he would not show it in the face of such a chance for giving a lesson.

"Babby! And that's just what you are—a big soft, overgrown babby, with no more muscle in you than a squid. I'd be ashamed o' myself, that I would, if I was you."

"Can't help it, Josh," said the young fellow, wrinkling his sun-browned forehead, and still turning the soft nets into filmy ropes by passing them through his hands.

"Can't help it! Why, you ain't got no more spirit in you than a pilchar'— no more'n one o' these as run its head through the net last night, hung on by its gills and let itself die, whar it might ha' wriggled itself out if it had had plenty o' pluck. If you don't take care, my lad, you'll get a name for being a regular soft. I believe if one of the lads o' your own size hit you, you'd cry."

"Perhaps I should, Josh, so I hope no one will hit me."

The lad thrust back his scarlet woollen cap, and bent down over the brown nets so that his companion should not see his face; and as he shook down the soft meshes, with the heap growing bigger and bigger, so did the pile of silvery pilchards grow taller, as Josh growled to himself and shook out the fish easily enough, for though the gills of the herring-like fish acted as barbs to complete their arrowy form as they darted through the sea, and kept them from swimming back, the hold on the net was very frail, and they kept falling pat, pat, upon the deck or in the well.

"After all I've done for you I don't want you to turn out a cur," growled Josh at last.

"Well, was I a cur last night?" cried Will eagerly. "Mike said there was a storm coming on, and that we'd better run in. Didn't I say, 'let's stop and shake out the fish,' as we hauled the nets?"

"Ay, but that's not very plucky," cried Josh, giving his face another rub and placing some spangles under his right eye; "that's being foolhardy and running risks with your craft, as no man ought to do as has charge of a lugger and all her gear. Ah, you're a poor gallish sort o' lad, and it's only a silly job to try and make a man of you."

It was quite early in the morning, and the sun was just showing over the bold headland to play through the soft silvery mist that hung in patches over the sea, which heaved and fell, ruddy orange where the sun glanced upon the swell, and dark misty purple in the hollows. The surface was perfectly smooth, not a breath of air coming from the land to dimple the long gentle heaving of the ebbing tide. Here and there the dark luggers, with their duck-shaped hulls and cinnamon-brown sails, stood out clear in the morning sunshine; while others that had not reached the harbour were fast to the small tub buoys; and again others that had not heeded the warnings of the threatened storm were only now creeping in, looking strange and mysterious, half-hidden as they were by the veil of mist that now opened, now closed and completely blotted them from the sight of those in the harbour.

It was a wild-looking place, the little fishing town nestling on the cliff, with the grey granite rocks piled-up behind and spreading to east and west like cyclopean walls, built in regular layers by the giants of whom Josh Helston had told. The wonder was that in some north-east gale the little fleet of fishing vessels was not dashed to pieces by the huge breakers that came tearing in, to leap against the rocks and fall back with a sullen roar amidst the great boulders. And one storm would have been enough, but for the harbour, into which, like so many sea-birds, the luggers huddled together; while the great granite wall curved round them like a stout protective arm thrust out by the land, and against which the waves beat themselves to spray.

It was a wild but singularly attractive view from Peter Churchtown, for the simple Cornish folk did not trouble themselves to say "Saint," but invariably added to every village that boasted a church the name of churchtown. High above it, perched upon the steepest spots, were the tall engine-houses of the tin and copper mines, one of which could be seen, too, half-way down the cliff, a few hundred yards from the harbour; and here the galleries from whence the ore was blasted and picked ran far below the sea. In fact it was said that in the pursuit of the lode of valuable ore the company would mine their way till they met the work-people of the Great Ruddock Mine over on the other side of the bay, beyond the lighthouse through the curve of the shore.

As the mist lifted from where it had half-hidden the tall lighthouse, with its base of black rocks, against which the sea never ceased breaking in creamy foam, a boat could be seen on its way to a large black, mastless vessel, moored head and stern with heavy chains, and looking quite deserted in the morning light.

"There they go off to work, Josh," exclaimed Will suddenly.

"Well, and you're off to work too," said Josh gruffly, as he picked from the net the half, of a pilchard, the tail portion having been bitten off by some predatory fish, as it hung helplessly by its gills. "Them hake have been having a nice game wi' the fish to-night."

As he spoke he picked out another and another half pilchard, and threw them as far as he could, when, almost as each piece touched the water, a soft-looking grey gull swept down and caught it from the surface with its strong beak, uttering a low peevish-sounding wail as it swept up again, hardly seeming to move its long white-lined wings.

"I should dearly like to go aboard the lighter and see what they are doing," said Will eagerly.

"Paying attention to their work," said Josh sharply, "and that's what you're not doing."

"I'm only a few fathoms behind you, Josh, and I shall be waiting directly. I say, when we're done let's row aboard."

"I don't want to row aboard," said Josh sourly, but watching the progress of the boat the while.

"They've got regular diving things there, Josh, and an air-engine; and the men go down. I should like to have a look."

"What are they going down for?" said Josh; "looking for oyster-beds?"

"No, no. Trelynn Mine is like to be flooded by the water that comes in from one of the galleries under the sea, and the divers go down to try and find the place where it gets in, and stop it with clay and cement."

"Humph! are they going to find it, d'yer think?"

"Yes, I believe so. They measure so exactly that they can put a boat right over the place. I say, Josh, shouldn't you like to go down?"

"What! dive down?"

"Yes."

"I should just think not, indeed. A man's place is in a boat floating atop of the water, and not going underneath. If man was meant to go underneath he'd have gills and fins and scales, same as these here pilchar's."

"Oh, yes, I know all that; but only think of trying on a diver's suit, and being supplied with air from above, through a tube into your helmet."

"This here dress is good enough for me, and my sou'-wester's a sight better than any helmet I know, and the only air as I care about having through a tube's 'bacco smoke."

"But shouldn't you like to go and see the diving?"

6

"Not I," said Josh, staring hard at the great lighter. "'Sides, when we've done here, and the fish is all salted down, I want to row across to the lighthouse."

"That will be going close by, Josh. I'll take an oar with you, and let's stop on the way."

"Just couldn't think o' such a thing. Come, work away, lad," cried Josh; and both he and Will did work away, the latter saying nothing more, for he knew his man, and that there was eager curiosity and also intense longing in the looks directed by the fisherman across the water from time to time.

The result was, that, armed with a couple of good-sized pollack as a present to the skipper in charge of the lighter, Josh Helston and his young companion rowed alongside the well-moored vessel before the morning was much older, and were soon on deck watching the proceedings with the greatest interest.

One of the divers was just preparing to go down as they set foot aboard; and they were in time to see the heavy leaden weights attached to his back and breast, and the great helmet, with its tail-like tube, lifted over his head and screwed on to the gorget. Then with the life-line attached he moved towards the gangway, the air-pump clanking as the crew turned the wheel; and step by step the man went down the ladder lashed to the lighter's side. Josh involuntarily gripped Will's hand as the diver descended lower and lower, to chest, neck, and then the great goggle-eyed helmet was covered, while from the clear depths the air that kept rapidly bubbling up rendered the water confused, so that the descending figure looked distorted and strange.

"Three fathom o' water here, my lad," whispered Josh, as with his companion he leaned over the side and gazed down at the rocks below.

"Three and a half, isn't it, Josh?" said Will in a low tone. "Mike always says there's three and a half here at this time of the tide."

"And I says it's three fathom," growled Josh dogmatically. "My, but it's a gashly sight for a man to go down like that!"

"Why, I wouldn't mind diving down, Josh," said Will excitedly.

"Diving down! Ay, I wouldn't mind diving down. It's being put in prison, and boxed up in them gashly things as makes it so horrid. Here, let's be off. I can't stand it. That there poor chap'll never come up again alive."

"Nonsense, Josh! He's all right. There, you can see him moving about. That pump sends him down plenty of air."

"Lor', what a great soft sort of a chap you are, William Marion!" said Josh. "You'll never larn nothing. The idee of a pump pumping air! They're a-pumping the water from all round him, so as to give the poor chap room to breathe. Can't you see the long soft pipe? Here, I don't like it. I want to go."

"No, no: not yet," cried Will excitedly. "I want to watch the diver."

"An' I don't," said Josh, turning his face away. "I never could abear to see things killed, and I never would go and see it. I can stand fish, but that's enough for me. Here's a human bein' goin' to be as good as murdered, and I won't be one o' them as stands by and sees it done."

"What nonsense, Josh!" cried Will. "This is regular diving apparatus. That's an air-pump; and the man has air pumped down into his helmet through that india-rubber pipe."

"Garlong; don't tell me, boy," cried Josh indignantly. "Into his helmet indeed! Why, you can see all the water bubbling up round him. That's what it is—pumped away. I tell 'ee I'm off. I won't stop and see the gashly work going on."

Just then there was a cry from one of the men by the gangway, for the life-line was jerked.

"More air!" he shouted; and the men spun the wheel round faster; but the line jerked again.

"There's something wrong!" shouted one of the others. "Here, lay hold there—quick! Keep on there with that handle, stupids! Do you want the man to choke? Pump, I tell you. Now, then, haul!"

"There, I told you so, Will," cried Josh, whose ruddy-brown face was looking mottled with white. "I know'd the gashly old job was wrong. Come away, boy, come away."

For answer, in his excitement Will thrust his arm aside and ran to the line to help haul.

"No, no, my lad; stand aside," cried the man who seemed to be captain of the diving-crew, and who was dressed for the work all but his helmet. "Haul away, do you hear?"

The men were hauling hard, but the rope had come taut; and instead of their bringing up the diver it was plain to all that the poor fellow had got the line hitched round a piece of rock, or else one of his legs wedged in some crevice of the rocks he was exploring.

"Shake the rope loose for a moment and haul again," cried the leader.

The men obeyed and then hauled again, but the line came taut once more; and if they had hauled much harder it would have parted.

"Lend a hand here quick with that other helmet. Make fast there! I'll go down and cast him loose. Here, quick, some of you!"

"He'll be a dead un afore you get to him," growled the skipper of the lighter, "if you arn't sharp."

"I knowed it, I knowed it," whispered Josh hoarsely. "I see it all along."

"Screw that on," panted the leader; "and you, Winter, stand by the engine. Be cool. Now, the helmet. Hah!"

There was a loud crash just then as the trembling and excited man who was handing the second helmet let it fall upon an iron bar lying upon the deck, so injuring the delicate piece of mechanism that the men stared at each other aghast, and Will's hands grew wet with horror.

"Is there a man here who can dive?" shouted the skipper coming forward with a thin coil of line. And, amidst a breathless silence Will stepped forward.

"No, no, he can't," shouted Josh excitedly; and then he stood open-mouthed and with one hand clasping the other as he saw Will make a rapid hitch in the line, throw it round his waist, tighten it, and then, after a quick glance round, seize one of the diver's leaden weights lying on an upturned cask. Then stepping to the side he said quickly, "Josh, look to the line!" and with the heavy weight held out at arm's-length he leaped from the gangway, right where the air-bubbles were still rising, and plunged headforemost into the sea.

Note: Net-making in Cornwall is called net-breeding.

Chapter Two.

Josh does not approve of his Pupil's Dive.

As Will made his daring plunge Josh Heist on rushed to the side, and stood with starting eyes gazing at the disturbed water. Then turning fiercely upon the skipper, he caught him by the shoulder, gave him a twist, and dragged him within reach of his deformed arm, the hand of which fastened upon his waist-belt, and held him perfectly helpless, although he seemed to be a much stronger man.

"This was your doing!" cried Josh angrily, but with quite a wail in his intoned words. "You drove him to do that gashly thing!"

"Don't be a fool, Josh! Here, let go! Do you hear, let go!"

"If he don't come I'll send you after him!" cried Josh, with his face flushed with anger.

"Do you want the lad to drown for want of help?" cried the skipper; and his words acted like magic. Josh loosed his hold, and once more ran to the side.

Meanwhile the pumping had been kept up, and a constant stream of air-bubbles could be seen ascending; but the men who had hauled upon the life-line had kept it taut, and were still hauling as those who were gazing down into the clear water, vainly trying to make out the movements of the two divers, suddenly uttered a shout.

"Here he comes!" cried the skipper; and Josh, who had been holding his breath in the agony of suspense, gave a loud expiration as the lad suddenly appeared above the surface, panting for breath, and swam to the ladder, shaking the water from his eyes and hair.

"Slack the line!" he cried; "it's round a rock. Give me one of those leads."

Josh, who had been the first to oppose the descent, was now the first to help, by seizing the back lead left upon the barrel head, and, with cat-like agility, leaping to the ladder and going down to the swimmer.

A dozen voices were shouting words of advice to Will, but the lad paid no heed; he merely drew himself up on the ladder, saw that the life-line was slack, and, clasping the leaden back-piece with both hands, with the life-line running loosely between his arms to act as a guide, he once more plunged into the sea, the weight seeming to take him down with tremendous force.

One instant the ponderous lead struck the water, the next there was a confused foam on the surface, and Will was gone.

The moments that followed seemed prolonged to hours. There was an indistinct movement visible in the disturbed water; the bubbles of air seemed to be lashing up more fiercely as the life-line was drawn rapidly through the hands that held it, and then, once more, Will's head appeared, and he swam towards the ladder.

He could not speak, but made a sign with one hand.

"Haul!" cried Josh; "haul away!" as he reached out, caught Will's arm, and drew him to the ladder; holding him up, for he was utterly exhausted, and could hardly get his breath.

And there they stayed while the line was hauled up, and the diver once more appeared above the surface; the poor fellow being hoisted on deck and his helmet rapidly unfastened and removed.

The men looked helplessly from one to the other as they lifted their eyes from the blackened countenance that one of the lighter's men was supporting on his arm. No one seemed to know what would be best to do, and a couple were ordered into the boat to row ashore for the doctor.

"Why don't you take off them gashly things?" cried Josh, who had now helped Will to the deck, where he stood holding on by a stay, trembling in every limb.

Two men immediately began to take off the heavy india-rubber diving suit, with its copper collar and heavy leaden-soled boots, with the result that when the poor fellow was freed from these encumbrances and once more laid upon the dock, the lifting and moving he had received proved so far beneficial that he uttered a low sigh, and the purple tinge began to die out from his face.

"He's a coming to!" said the skipper eagerly; and his words proved to be right, for at the end of half an hour the poor fellow had recovered consciousness, and was able to say that his life-line had become hitched round a mass of rock, to which was attached some very long grown strands of sea-weed, and these had been swept by the water right over the line. Then when he had tried to free it his hands only came in contact with the loose slimy wrack, and after a trial or two he had become confused and excited.

"And you know I've allus told you as a diver should be as cool as a cucumber," said his chief.

"Yes, I know all about that," said the diver huskily, "and so I meant to be; but when you're shut-up in one o' them soots and are down in three or four fathom o' water, and thinking your life-line's fast, you don't seem as if you could be cool, mate."

"But you ought to be," said the chief severely; "and now, all along o' your getting in a flurry, here's the newest helmet with a great dent in the neck, so as it won't screw down on the collar, and I shall have to pay damages out o' my wage."

"Better than having to pay to keep my wife and weans," said the diver huskily; "and now I want to have a look at that young chap as dived and set free the line."

"Here he be!" cried Josh eagerly, hauling at Will's arm; "here he be, lad. Ain't much of a chap to have done it, be he?"

Josh laughed, and gave Will a thrust forward, much to the lad's discomfort, for there was a low murmur of admiration from the little group around.

"Oh, it's nothing to make such a fuss about!" said Will, whose cheeks were burning now, as he stood there with the sea-water slowly soaking from his clothes, and making a little puddle on the deck.

"No!" said the diver huskily; "it's nothing to make a fuss about; only one man saving another man's life, when nobody else knew what to do!"

"Oh, it was an accident!" said Will kindly; "and they hadn't time to think."

"Yes," said the diver, looking softly up at Will; "an accident, my lad, and nothing to make a fuss about; but there's some one at home as would have made a fuss about it, and you've done more than save me, my lad; you've saved a poor woman from a broken heart, and six bairns from wanting charity; that's all. Let's shake hands!"

He held out his hand to Will in the midst of a strange silence, and held that of the young man with a very strong grip, before sinking back with his head upon a ship's fender, and closing his eyes.

"He arn't a bad sort of chap," said Josh softly, as Will drew back; "but I don't hold with a fellow, even if he have just been drowned, coming to life again and calling a boy like you a man. You're wain enough as it is, and you've no call to be. So come along ashore, and get home and change them wet clothes."

Will said a word to the chief of the divers about where the lead weights lay, and then stepped over the side to Josh, who was already in the lugger's boat, without letting any one know that he was going.

Josh thrust off the boat, let his oar fall with a splash, and Will followed his example; but they were not a dozen yards from the lighter before they were missed, and divers and crew rushed to the side and gave a tremendous cheer.

"Here, come back!" cried the skipper; "come back!"

"Arn't got time," roared Josh, frowning; and then, as the men cheered again: "Well, of all the gashly fuss as was ever made this is about the worst! Pull hard, my lad, and let's get out of it. I want to go home."

"And I want to get warm, Josh," said Will laughing. "I'm glad that poor fellow came round before we left."

"Well, I dunno," said Josh, sourly. "Of course you liked it because he called you a man. He ought to have knowed better, at his time o' life. Lor', Will, what a gashly peacock of a chap you would grow if it warn't for me."

Chapter Three.

Pilchar' Will and the Old Folks at Home.

"Been overboard again? Well, I never did see such a boy in my life; never!"

"What's the matter, Ruth?"

"Matter enough!" came in the same strident voice, in answer to the hoarse gruff inquiry. "There, who spoke to you? Just you get back to your work; and if that pie's burnt again to-day you'll have to leave!"

This last was to a heavy-faced simple-looking girl, who, on hearing her mistress's angry voice, had hurried into the passage of Nor'-nor'-west Cottage, Cliffside, and stood in front of the kitchen door, with one end of her apron in her mouth.

Amanda Trevor, commonly called Betsey, stepped back into the kitchen, just catching the word "dripping" as she closed the door—a word that excited her curiosity again, but she dared not try to gratify it; and if she had tried she would only have been disappointed on finding that it related to a few drops of water from Will Marion's clothes.

"I said—heave ho, there! what's the matter?" was heard again; and this time a very red-faced grey-haired man, with the lower part of his features framed in white bristles, and clad in a blue pea-jacket and buff waistcoat, ornamented with gilt anchor buttons, stood suddenly in the doorway on the right, smoking solemnly a long churchwarden clay pipe, rilling his mouth very full of smoke, and then aggravating the

13

looker-on by puzzling him as to where the smoke would come from next—for sometimes he sent a puff out of one corner of his mouth, sometimes out of the other. Then it would come from a little hole right in the middle, out of which he had taken the waxed pipe stem, but only for him perhaps to press one side of his nose with the pipe, and send the rest out of the left nostril, saving perhaps a little to drive from the right. The result of practice, for the old man had smoked a great deal.

"Collision?" said Abram Marion, ex-purser and pensioner of the British navy.

"No," said Mrs Ruth Marion, his little thin acid wife. "Overboard again, and he's dripping all over the place. It isn't long since he had those clothes."

"Six months," said the old purser, sending a couple of jets of tobacco smoke from his nostrils at once.

"Yes; and what with his growing so horribly, and the common stuff they sell for cloth now, shrinking so shamefully, he's always wanting clothes."

"Oh, these will last a long time yet, aunt!" said Will.

"No, they will not last a long time yet, Will!" cried the little lady, with her face all trouble wrinkles.

"Will," said the old man, stopping to say *pup, pup, pup, pup, pup, pup*, as he emitted half a dozen tiny puffs of smoke, waving his pipe stem the while; "mind what your aunt says and you'll never repent."

"But he don't mind a word I say," cried the little woman, wringing her hands. "Wringing wet! just look at him!"

"Been fishing, my lass; and they brought home a fair haul," said the purser, throwing back his head, and shooting smoke at a fly on the ceiling.

"What's the use of his bringing home fair hauls if he destroys his clothes as he does; and the holes he makes in his stockings are shameful."

"Can't help getting wet at sea," said the ex-purser, solemnly spreading a good mouthful of smoke in a semicircle. "Water's wet, specially salt-water. Here, you, sir! how dare you make holes in your stockings for your aunt to mend? I don't believe your father ever dared to do such a thing in his life."

"It don't matter, Abram," said the old lady in a lachrymose whine; "it's my fate to toil, and I'm not long for this world, so it don't matter. It was my fate to be a toiler; and those clothes of his will be too small for him to wear when they're dry. I don't know what I'm to do."

"Stretch 'em," said the old gentleman, sending a cloud into his waistcoat.

"But they won't stretch," cried the old lady peevishly.

"Put 'em away and save 'em," said the old man. "I may adopt another nevvy—smaller size,"—and here there was a veil spread over his face by his projecting his lower lip and sending the smoke up into his eyes.

"If you ever did such a thing again, I'd have a divorce," cried the old lady sharply. "You go and change your things, sir, and then get a book till dinner's ready."

The old lady stepped into the parlour, and the old purser was in the act of winking solemnly at his nephew when Mrs Marion reappeared.

"Ah, I saw!" she cried. "You are encouraging this boy, Abram. Here; Betsey, bring your flannel and wipe up this mess. And you, go in directly and change your things."

The old lady disappeared again, and the wrinkles stood all over the old purser's face as he growled softly between fancy puffs of smoke.

"Woman's words in house, Will, is like cap'en's orders 'board ship, with the articles over at the back. Must be minded, or it's rank mutiny, and a disrate. *Puff.* Go and get a dry rig."

"Yes, uncle," said Will quietly.

"And—*puff*—you—*puff*—must be more careful of your clothes—*puff*, boy. *Puff, puff, puff.* We all sail through life—*puff*—under orders. *Puff.* —Few of us is cap'ens—*puff.* Very few of us is admirals—*puff*; and what with admiralty and the gov'ment—*puff, puff*, and the people's opinion—*puff*, and the queen—*puff*; they can't do so much as they like, as a regular tar. *Puff, puff.*"

The way in which the ex-purser distributed his tobacco smoke during this oracular lecture to his brother's orphan son was something astounding; and he had smoked so heavily that it seemed at last as if he were trying to veil himself from the lad's gaze lest he should see the weakness exhibited with regard to Mrs Marion's rule; while he kept glancing uneasily at the lad, as if feeling that he was read by heart.

"All right, uncle, I understand," said Will, turning to go.

"That's right—*puff*, Will. Good lad. Your aunt means well, and if she pitches into us both—rams us, as you may say, Will, why, we know, eh?"

"Oh yes, uncle, we know."

"It don't hurt us, lad. She says lots about what you cost for food, and what an expense you've been to her, and she calls you lazy."

"Yes, uncle," said Will, sadly.

"But what do it amount to, eh? Only tongue, and tongue's only tongue after all."

"No, uncle."

The last puff of smoke had been sucked out of the pipe, and the old gentleman kept on gesticulating with it as he spoke.

"Only tongue, lad. Your aunt's one o' the finest and best and truest women under the sun. See how clean she's always kept you ever since you first come to us."

"No, uncle, since you came and fetched me from that miserable school, and said, 'don't cry, my man; you're my own brother's boy, and as long as I live I'll be a father to you.'"

"Did I say them words, Will? Was they the very words?"

"Yes, uncle," cried the lad, flushing; "the very words;" and he laid his hand affectionately on the old man's shoulder.

"Ah! well, and very proper words too, I suppose," said the old man; "and I did mean to be, lad; but you see I never had no experience of being a father, and I'm afraid I've made a mess of it."

"You've always been like the kindest of fathers to me, uncle," said Will warmly.

"And she's always been the kindest of mothers, like, my lad. Lor' bless you, Will, my boy, it's only tongue. Splendid craft your aunt is, only she's overweighted with engine, and her bilers is a bit too big. Tongue's safety-valve, Will, and I never sit on it, my lad. Make things worse. Burst."

"Yes, uncle, I see," said Will, with a sad smile.

"You're all right, my lad. I didn't care to send you in the Ryle Navee, so I did the next best thing, made a sailor of you in a lugger. She's mine now with all her craft of nets—leastwise she's aunt's, for she keeps the accounts; but some day when I'm sewn up and dropped overboard out of the world, the lugger'll all be yours; only if I go first, Will," he whispered, drawing the lad closer to him, "never mind the bit of a safety-valve as fizzles and whistles and snorts; be kind, lad, to your aunt."

"I don't want the lugger," cried Will, laying his hands on the old man's shoulders. "I want my dear old uncle to stop, and see him enjoy his pipe, and I won't take a hit of notice—"

"Of the safety-valve, Will?"

"No, uncle; but I want to get on," cried the lad excitedly. "I'm tired of being a burden to you, uncle, and—"

"Hasn't that boy changed his things yet?"

"Right, Ruth, my dear," cried the old purser loudly, assuming his old sea lingo. "Here, you, sir, how much longer are you going to stand jawing there. Heave ahead and get into a fresh rig with you."

Here he winked and frowned tremendously at Will, giving one of his hands a tremendous squeeze, and the lad ran upstairs.

The lugger was not to put out again till evening, when the soft breeze would be blowing, and the last rays of the sun be ready to glorify sea, sky, and the sails and cordage of the fishing-boats as they stole softly out to the fishing-ground for the night, so that as Mrs Marion had gone up to lie down after dinner, according to custom, and the old purser was in the little summer-house having his after-dinner pipe, as he called it, one which he invariably enjoyed without lighting the tobacco and with a handkerchief over his head, Will was at liberty to go out unquestioned. Accordingly he hurried down to the harbour, where the tide was out, the gulls were squealing and wailing, and apparently playing a miniature game of King of the Castle upon a little bit of black rock which appeared above the sea a couple of hundred yards out.

In the harbour the water was so low that the *Pretty Ruth*, Abram Marion's lugger—named, for some reason that no one could see, after the old man's wife—was lying over nearly on her beam-ends, so that, as Josh Helston, who was on board, went to and fro along the deck with a swab in his hands it was impossible to help thinking that if nature had made his legs like his arms, one very much shorter than the other, he would have found locomotion far easier.

As it was, he had to walk with one knee very much, bent, so greatly was the deck inclined; but it did not trouble him, his feet being bare and his toes spreading out widely and sticking to the clean narrow planks as if they were, like the cuttle-fish, provided with suckers.

Josh was swabbing away at the clinging fish-scales and singing in a sweet musical voice an old west-country ditty in which a lady was upbraiding someone for trying "to persuade a maiden to forsake the jacket blue," of course the blue jacket containing some smart young sailor.

"Hi, Josh!"

"Oh, it's you, is it?" said Josh, rubbing his nose with the mop handle. "No, I'm busy. I sha'n't come."

"Yes, do come, Josh," said Will, crossing three or four luggers and sitting on the rail of the *Pretty Ruth.*

"What's the good, lad?"

"Good, Josh? Why, I've told you before. I can't bear this life."

"Fisherman's a good honest life," said Josh sententiously.

"Not when a lad feels that he's a dependant and a burden on his friends," cried Will excitedly. "I want to get on, Josh. I want to succeed, and—there, I knew you'd come."

For Josh had thrown away the mop with an angry movement, and then dragging on a pair of great blue stockings he put on shoes and followed Will without a word.

Out along the beach and away from the village, and in and out among the rocks for quite two miles, till they were where the cliff went sheer up like a vast wall of rugged granite, at a part of which, where a mass of broken stone had either fallen or been thrown down, Will stopped and looked round to see if they were observed. As they were alone with no other watchers than a swarthy-looking cormorant sitting on a sunny lodge drying his wings, and a shag or two perched with outstretched neck, narrowly observing them, Will climbed up, followed by Josh, till they were upon a broad shelf a hundred and fifty feet above the sea—a wild solitary place, where the heap of débris, lichened and wave-beaten, was explained, for mining operations had once gone on hero, and a great square hole yawned black and awful at their feet.

They had evidently been there before, for Will stepped close to a spot where the rock overhung, and reaching in, drew out some pieces of granite, and then from where it was hidden a large coil of stout rope, and threw it on the broken fragments around.

"It's your doing, mind, you know," said Josh. "I don't like the gashly job at all."

"Yes, it's my doing," said Will.

"And you mean to go down?"

"I do, Josh, for certain."

"It be a gashly unked hole, and you'd best give it up. Look here."

As he spoke he stooped and picked up a piece of rock weighing quite a hundredweight, poised it in his hands for a moment or two, and then, with a wonderful display of strength, tossed it from him right over the middle of the disused mine-shaft. The mica flashed in the sun for a moment, and then the great piece plunged down into the darkness, Josh and Will involuntarily darting to the side and craning over the awesome place to try and follow it with their eyes and catch the reverberations when it struck the sides and finally plunged into the black collected waters far enough below.

Chapter Four.

A Foolhardy Venture for a Goodly End.

It seemed as if that stone would never reach the bottom, and a curious expression was upon the eager faces that peered down, a strained look almost of pain, till all at once there was a start as of relief, as a hollow heavy plash was heard that came hissing, and echoing, and reverberating up the rocky sides of the shaft past them and into the sunny air.

"Ugh!" growled Josh, "who knows what gashly creatures lives down there. P'r'aps its harnted with them as tumbled down and was killed."

"Don't talk nonsense, Josh," said Will, in a voice full of contempt; "I never heard of anybody falling down here."

"Looks as if lots had. Ugh! I wouldn't go down for the price of a new boat and all her gear."

"If everybody felt like you do, Josh, what should we have done for tin and copper?"

"I d'now," growled Josh. "Why can't you leave it alone and 'tend to the fishing. Arn't catching pilchar' and mack'rel good 'nough for you? Yah! I shall never make nothing of you."

"No, Josh; catching pilchard and mackerel is not good enough for me."

"Then why not get aboard the smack and larn to trawl for sole and turbot? There arn't no better paying fishing than that, so long as you don't get among the rocks."

"No, Josh; nor trawling won't do," said Will, who ashore seemed to take the lead that he yielded to his companion and old Michael Polree on board the lugger. "I want to make my way in the world, and do you hear, I will."

He said the last word so emphatically that the fisherman stared, and then said in an ill-used tone:

"Then why don't you try in a reasonable way, and get to be master of a lugger? and if that arn't enough for you, have your share o' nets in another; not come poking about these gashly holes. What's the good?"

"Good!" cried Will, with his eyes flashing. "Hasn't a fortune been got out of Gwavas mine year after year till the water began to pour in?"

"Oh, yes! out o' that."

"And I'm sure one might be got out of this," cried Will, pointing down into the black void.

"What, out o' this gashly pit? Yah! Why didn't the captain and 'venturers get it, then, when they dug it fifty year 'fore I was born?"

"Because they missed the vein."

"And how are you going to find it, lad?"

"By looking," said Will. "There's Retack Mine over yonder, and Carn Rean over there, and they're both rich; and I think the old people who dug down here went too far, and missed what they ought to have found."

"And so you're going to find it, are you, my lad?"

"I don't know," said Will quietly; "but I'm going to try."

As he said those last words he set his teeth and knit his brow, looking so calmly determined that Josh picked up a little bit of granite, turned it over in his fingers a few times as if finding a suitable part, and then began to rub his nose with it softly.

"Well, you do cap me, lad, you do," he said at last. "Look ye here, now," he cried, as if about to deliver a poser, and he seated himself on the rock and crossed his legs, "you don't expect to find coal, do you?"

"No," said Will, "there is no coal in Cornwall."

"Nor yet gold and silver?"

"No: not much."

"Then it's tin you're after, and it won't pay for getting."

"You are wrong, Josh," said the lad smiling.

"Not copper?"

"Yes: copper."

"Yah! Now is it likely?"

"Yes," said Will. "Come here."

Josh rose reluctantly, and the lad began to descend again, climbing quickly down the old mine débris till they reached the shore, and then walking a dozen yards or so he climbed in and out among the great masses of rock to where there was a deep crevice or chink just large enough for a full-grown man to force himself through to where the light came down from above.

"What's the good o' coming into a gashly place like this?" growled Josh, whose breast-bone and elbows had been a little rubbed.

"I wanted to show you that," said Will, pointing to a little crack through which a thread of water made its way running over a few inches of rock, and then disappearing amongst the shingly stones.

"Well, I can see it, can't I?"

"Yes; but don't you see that the rock where that, water runs is all covered with a fine green powder?"

"Yes, it's sea-weed," said Josh contemptuously.

"No; it's copper," cried Will excitedly; "that's a salt of copper dissolved in the water that comes out there, and some of it is deposited on the stones."

"Yah! nonsense, lad! That arn't copper. Think I don't know copper when I see it? That arn't copper."

"I tell you it is," said Will; "and it proves that there's copper in the rock about that old mine if anybody could find it; and the man who discovers it will make his way in the world."

"You do cap me, you do indeed, lad. I shall never make anything of you. Well, and do you mean to go down that gashly hole."

"I do; and you are going to manage the rope!"

"And s'pose you falls in and gets drowned, what am I to say to your uncle?"

"I'm not going to fall in, and I'm not going to be drowned," said Will quietly. "I'm going to try and find that copper; so now come along."

There was not a nice suitable piece of stone for Josh to use in polishing his nose, so he contented himself with a rub of the back of his hand before squeezing himself through the narrow passage between the masses of rock, and following his companion to the ledge where the old adventurers had spent their capital in sinking the shaft, and had given up at last, perhaps on the very eve of success.

"It's all gashly nonsense," cried Josh as they reached the mouth of the shaft once more; "if there'd been copper worth finding, don't you think those did chaps would have found it?"

"They might or they might not," said Will quietly; "we're going to see."

He went to another crevice in the face of the cliff and drew out a good-sized iron bar shaped like a marlinspike but about double the size, and throwing it down with a clang upon the rock he startled a cormorant from the ledge above their heads, and the great swarthy bird flew out to sea.

"Lay out that line, Josh," said Will, who, after a little selection of a spot, took up the bar and began to make a hole between two huge blocks of granite, working it to and fro so as to bury it firmly half its length.

The crevice between the stones helped him in this; and he soon had it in and wedged tightly with a few sharp fragments that had been dug from the shaft.

"Going to fasten one end o' the line to that?" sang Josh.

"Yes."

"What's the good? I could hold it right enough with a couple such as you on the end."

"But I want the rope to be round that, Josh, and for you to lower me down or haul me up as I give signals."

"Oh yes!" growled Josh; "only we might as well have had a block and fall."

"If we had brought a block and fall up, Josh, it would have been like telling all Peter Churchtown what we were going to do; and you're the only man I want to know anything about it till I've found the copper lode."

"Ho!" ejaculated Josh, rubbing his nose meditatively with the line. "How much is there here—five-and-thirty fathom?"

"Thirty," said Will, smiling, as his companion passed the cord through his hands with the skilful ease of a seaman. "Will it bear me?"

"Two of you," said Josh gruffly.

"Well, I'm going to trust you to take care of me, Josh," said Will, taking a box of matches from his pocket, and lighting a piece of candle, which he stuck upon one of those little points known as a save-all, and then, bending down, he thrust it into a square niche about a foot below the surface of the mine-shaft—one of several carefully chiselled-out holes evidently intended for the woodwork of a platform.

"Oh! I'll take care of you."

"Lower me down quite slowly, and stop whenever I shout. You're sure you can haul me up?"

"Ha, ha! haw, haw!" laughed Josh. "Can I haul you? What do you take me for—a babby?"

As he spoke he caught the lad by the waistband with one hand, lifted him from the ground, and stiffening his muscles held him out at arm's-length for a few seconds before setting him down.

"That will do, Josh," said Will quietly; and taking the end of the line he made a good-sized loop, round part of which he twisted a piece of sailcloth to make it thicker; then stepping through the loop as though it had been one prepared for an ordinary swing, he turned to Josh:

"Ready?"

"Ay, ay!" was the laconic answer as the fisherman passed the line over the round iron bar, which seemed perfectly safe, took a good grip of the rope, and then stood looking at his young companion.

"I tried to stop you when you wanted to dive down," he said, "and I s'pose I ought to try and stop you now. It looks a gashly sort of a hole. S'pose I was to let go?"

"But you would not, Josh," said Will confidently, as he lowered himself slowly over the edge as calmly as if only about to descend a few feet,

23

with perfect safety in the shape of solid earth beneath him, though, as he moved, he set free a little avalanche of fragments of granite, that seemed to go down into the shaft with a hiss, which was succeeded by the strange echoing splashes—weird whispers of splashes—as they reached, the water below.

It would have daunted many a strong man; but so intent was the lad upon his task that he paid no heed to the sounds, and directly after, taking the candle from its niche, he began to scan the walls of the shaft.

"Lower away, Josh, steadily and slowly," he said, as his head disappeared from the fisherman's sight. "I'll shout to you when I want to stop."

The face of the fisherman seemed to undergo a change as his companion passed out of his sight—from looking stolid and soured it suddenly became animated and full of excitement; the perspiration stood out upon it in a heavy dew, and muttering to himself, "I sha'n't let him go down far," he slowly lowered away.

For the first few yards of his descent Will could easily scrutinise the walls of the carefully-cut square hole by the light of clay, the flame of his candle looking pale and feeble; but as he sank lower, swinging to and fro with a pendulum-like motion, which now took him to one side of the shaft, now to the other, so that it needed little effort on his part to be able to carefully examine fully half of the cutting, the light from the candle grew more clear and bright, and he thrust it here and there wherever there was a glitter in the time-darkened stone.

Lower and lower, with now his elbow chafing against the rough wall, now his boots, but nothing to reward his search. There was a bright glitter here, but it was only the large flakes of mica in the stone. Lower down there was a sign of ore—of little black granules bedded in deep-red stone, and before this he paused for a minute, for he knew that there was here a vein of tin; but as far as he could tell it looked poor, and not so good as some that miners had told him hardly paid for crushing.

"All right, Josh; lower away!" he cried; and his words went echoing up to where the fisherman slowly allowed the strong line to glide through his hands.

Some twenty feet lower Will shouted to his companion to halt, for there was a broad band of glittering-yellow metallic stone crossing the shaft-wall diagonally.

The lad's heart beat wildly for a few moments, but he calmed down as he felt that had this been of any value the old adventurers would not have passed it by.

"Only mundic," he said, as he inspected it more closely. "Lower away, Josh!" and the band of sulphuret of iron was left behind.

Lower and lower, with the top of the shaft looking a comparatively small square hole, and as the lad glanced up at it for a moment the first symptom of fear that he had felt attacked him. For as he saw how frail was the cord by which he hung, and realised that he was depending entirely upon his companion's strength of arm, his brain swam, his eyes closed, and he clung tightly with both hands to the rope.

The attack passed off directly.

"Josh thinks I'm a coward," he muttered, "and I suppose I am; but I won't show it;" and shouting a cheery order to the fisherman to lower away, the lad descended farther and farther, with the right of his candle flashing now from the walls, which were wet and shining with the oozings of the surrounding rock. This moisture had gone on coating the walls in patches for many a long year, so that in these places it was impossible without scraping for the keenest of eyes to detect even the composition of the stones, and with a sigh of dissatisfaction the searcher shouted to Josh to lower away.

"Here, you've gone down far enough," cried Josh. "I'm going to haul you up now."

"No, no!" shouted Will, the excitement of being in antagonism with his helpmate driving away the last particle of nervousness. "Lower away!"

Josh hesitated for a moment, and made a movement as if to rub his nose, but his hands were engaged, and he got over the difficulty by bending down his head and applying the itching organ to the rope, after which he shook his head fiercely, but went on lowering.

"He's getting too much for me a gashly sight, this boy," he growled.

There was ample line to lower Will right down to the surface of the water, though he was unaware of the fact, as he swung gently to and fro, eagerly scanning every clear space of the rock through which the shaft had been cut; and where the wall was dry, in spite of the time that had elapsed since the work was done the marks of the miners' picks and hammers were as clear as if the blows had fallen only a few months before. As the lad looked, too, he could, in his own disappointment, realise how great must have been that of the adventurers whose capital was being expended day after day cutting on and finding nothing but grey, hard granite, with here and there bands of ruddy stone suggestive of the presence of tin, but in such minute quantities that it would not pay for the labour of lifting out and crushing the stone.

Granite, granite, nothing but granite; and now the rope seemed to cut harshly into his legs, and a curious aching sensation set in, half numbing the arm that clung to the rope, for the lad had been so deeply interested in his search that he had not once altered his position.

"Look out, Josh!" he said, "I'm going to change hands."

"Here, I'm a-going to haul you up now," replied Josh, the great shaft acting like a speaking-tube, so that conversation was easy enough.

"Not yet," shouted back Will; and as the rope seemed to glide down he changed his position a little, taking the candle in the numbed hand, a fresh grip with his right, and altering his seat so that the line did not cut so harshly.

As he did so another slight touch of nervousness came over him; and in spite of himself he began to glance at the knot he had made in the rope, and then at the candle to see how much longer it would last, to find that it was half burned down and that the length of time it would keep burning must guide his descent. He was a little disheartened too, for it had not entered much into his calculations that clever men must have well examined that shaft when it was being cut, and that they would have made the discovery if it was to be made.

In fact, the idea had come to him when climbing up the cliff in search of sea-birds' eggs. He had reached this shelf and found the forgotten mine, and to him it had seemed like the entrance to a matter-of-fact, everyday-life Aladdin's cave, where, after a little search, he was going to hit upon a vein of copper and become an independent man. And now that he was making his first bold venture into the region where the precious metal was to be found, all was darkness, nothing but stone walls, now wet and slimy, now cold, and hard, and grey.

"Here, now you are coming up," shouted Josh; and the descent was once more checked.

"No, no. Just a few more fathoms, Josh," shouted back Will. "The candle's nearly done."

There was a grumbling response, and the descent continued once

26

more, till, as he swung to and fro, the lad gave his feet a thrust against the wall, turned right round, and then uttered an eager ejaculation:

"Stop, Josh!" he said, and then, "Hold fast!"

"Right!" came from above; and as Will found himself opposite to an opening in the wall he swung himself backwards and forwards two or three times, till, gaining sufficient impetus, he could have landed right in a low arch, evidently the mouth of a gallery following a lode.

"Half a fathom lower, Josh," shouted Will; and the rope ran down a trifle here, and then, swinging himself to and fro again, he finally gave himself a good urge through the air and his feet rested on the rough floor.

He turned cold, and the wet dew of horror stood upon his face as he grasped at the rough wall, sending the candle flying forwards to lie burning sidewise upon the stones, for the rebound of the rope as it struck the crown of the arch nearly dragged him back just as he had released his hold.

It was a narrow escape, but forgotten directly in the excitement of his discovery; and freeing himself from the rope he picked up the candle carefully, to find that he had only about an inch left, and perhaps a mile of galleries to explore.

"There must be abundance of metal here," he said aloud, as he held the candle above his head and gazed before him. "I shall be the discoverer and—"

"Here, hoy! Will Marion! ahoy!" shouted Josh, who was kneeling down at the edge of the shaft, his face drawn with horror and strangely mottled, as he stared down into the pit. For, without warning, Will had freed himself from the rope, the tension upon which was gone; and as Josh drew a few feet up, and let the line run down again, his eyes seemed starting from his head, and he listened for the awful splash he expected to hear.

He listened for quite a minute, and then rousing himself from his half cataleptic state, he uttered a stentorian hail.

"Right, Josh, right!" shouted Will. "I've found it at last."

"He's found it at last!" growled Josh, wiping his wet brow. "Why, he must have got to the bottom then. Are you all right?"

"All right!" came back faintly; and Josh gave his hands a rub, his arms a stretch, and then leaving the rope, he seated himself on the stones, thrust his hands into his pockets, and out of one he drew forth a heavy clasp-knife, from the other a steel tobacco-box, which he opened, took out some roll tobacco, and proceeded to cut himself off a piece to chew.

As he was thus occupied a strange, sharp, rustling noise fell upon his ear, and then stopped.

He listened, and looked round, but saw nothing.

"Can't be snakes up here!" he muttered, and then he became all alert once more, for there was a noise from below, as of a small stone having fallen.

"What's he doing of now?" growled Josh. "Here, I wish I hadn't come. Eh! What!"

Just at the same time, after carefully groping his way for a very short distance along the gallery, Will was warned by his expiring candle to return to the mouth, which he reached just in time to hear a curious whistling sound and then a long-drawn splash.

"What's that?" he exclaimed, and then his blood ran cold as, in a hoarse voice that he hardly knew as his own, he shouted up the shaft:

"Josh, Josh! The rope!"

It was in a frantic hope that his idea was wrong, and that it was not the rope which he had heard *whish* through the air, and then fall below.

Just then the candle wick toppled over on one side in a little pool of molten composition, sputtered for an instant, sent up a blue flash or two, and went out.

Chapter Five.

Will finds himself in a Painful Position.

It was a position perilous enough to alarm the stoutest-hearted man, and awkward enough without the danger to puzzle any schemer, and for a few minutes the lad stood with one hand resting on the rock, and the cold perspiration gathering on his forehead, trying to think what he had better do.

As he stood, there was a low whispering noise that came up the shaft —a noise that puzzled him as to what it could be, for he did not realise that the water down below had, when set in motion by the fall of the rope, kept on lapping at the side, and that this lapping sound echoed and repeated itself strangely from the shaft-walls.

"Say, my lad—below there!" came now from above.

"Ahoy!" answered Will, the call acting like an electric shock and bringing him to himself.

"Where are you?" shouted Josh.

"Here, in a gallery of the old mine," replied Will.

"That's right!" came back. "I thought perhaps you had fallen."

"No, I'm all right," cried Will through the great granite speaking-tube; and then he listened for some words of comfort from his companion.

"Below!" shouted Josh again.

"Hullo!"

"Say, my lad, the rope's gone down."

"Yes, I know."

"Well, what's to be done?" cried Josh.

Will turned cold. He had expected to get a few words of comfort from his companion, and to hear that he was about to propose some plan for his rescue, and all he seemed ready to do was to ask for advice.

"How came you to let the rope go?" cried Will, forcing himself into an angry fit so as to keep from feeling alarmed at his position.

"Dunno! It kind o' went all of itself like," Josh shouted back. "What's to be done? Can't jump down into the water and swim out by the adit,

29

can you?"

"No," cried Will angrily. "Here, go back and get a rope."

"Where?" shouted back Josh. "I say, I knowed you'd be getting into some mess or another going down there."

Will was equable enough in temper, but a remark like this from the man he had trusted with his life made him grind his teeth in a fit of anger, and wish he were beside Josh for a moment, to give him a bit of his mind.

"Go up to any of the fishermen, never mind where, and borrow a line."

"All right!"

"And, Josh."

"Hullo!"

"Don't make any fuss; don't alarm anybody. I don't want them to know at home."

"But suppose we never get you out again?" shouted Josh, in a tone of voice that startled a shag which was about to settle on a shelf of rock hard by, and sent it hurrying away to sea.

Will stamped his foot at this, and mentally vowed that he would never trust Josh again.

"Go and borrow a line," he cried, "and look sharp. I don't want any one to know."

"All right!" cried Josh; and directly after Will knew that he was alone.

The place was not absolutely dark, for he could plainly make out the edge of the gallery, seen as it were against a faint twilight that came from above; and this was sufficient to guide him as to how far he dare go towards the shaft if he wished to move.

For the first few minutes, though, he felt no disposition that way, and seating himself on the stony floor, with hundreds of loose fragments of granite beneath him, he tried to be calm and cool, and to come to a conclusion as to how he should escape.

If Josh came back soon with a rope it would be easy enough; and possibly they might be able to rig up a grappling-iron or "creeper," as the fishermen called it, for the line that was lost; but a little consideration told him that in all probability the line had sunk before now and was right at the bottom of the shaft.

Then he wondered how long Josh would be, and whether he would have much difficulty in borrowing a rope.

If Josh said at once what was the matter, there would be a crowd up at the head of the shaft directly with a score of lines; but he did not wish for that. Even in his awkward, if not perilous, position he did not want the village to be aware of his investigations. He had been carrying them on in secret for some time, and he hoped when they were made known to have something worth talking about.

How long Josh seemed, and how dark it was! Perhaps he was being asked for at home, and he would be in disgrace.

That was not likely, though. He had chosen his time too well.

"I wonder how far it is down to the water?" he said at last; and feeling about, his hand came in contact with a large thin piece of stone, as big as an ordinary tile.

He hesitated for a moment or two, and then threw it from him with such force that it struck the far side of the shaft and sent up a series of echoes before, from far below, there came a dull sullen plash, with a succession of whishing, lapping sounds, such as might have been given out if some monster had come to the top and were swimming round, disappointed by what had fallen not being food.

"It's all nonsense!" said Will. "I don't believe any fish or eel would be living in an old shaft."

Some of the mining people were in the habit of saying that each water-filled pit, deep, mysterious, and dark, held strange creatures, of what kind no one knew, for individually they had never seen anything; but "some one" had told them that there were such creatures, and "some one else" had been "some one's" authority: for the lower orders of Cornish folk, with all their honest simplicity and religious feeling, are exceedingly superstitious, and much given to a belief in old women's tales.

Chapter Six.

A Case of Lost Nerve, and the Help that came.

It must have been quite an hour of painful waiting before Josh's voice was heard from above.

Will had been sitting there in the dark passage listening to every noise, though scarcely anything met his ear but the incessant drip and trickle of the water that oozed from the shaft sides, when all at once there was a faint sound from above, and his heart leapt with excitement.

Was it Josh at last?

"Bellow—er!" came down the shaft.

"Ahoy!" shouted back Will. "Got a rope?"

"Ay, lad; I've got un, a strong noo un as'll hold us both, a good thirty fathom!"

"Make it fast to the iron bar, Josh!" cried Will, whose hands now felt hot with excitement.

"Ay, I won't lose this gashly thing!" cried Josh, whose words came down the shaft-hole wonderfully distinctly, as if a giant were whispering near the lad's ear.

Will listened, and fancied he could hear his companion knotting the end of the rope and fastening it round the iron bar; but he could not be sure, and he waited as patiently as he could, but with a curious sensation of dread coming over him. He had felt courageous enough when he came down, indifferent, or thoughtless perhaps, as to the danger; but this accident with the rope had, though he did not realise it, shaken his confidence in Josh; and in addition, the long waiting in that horrible hole had unnerved him more than he knew, full proof of which he had ere long.

"There, she's fast enough now," came down the great granite speaking-tube. "I'm going to send the line down, lad. She's a gashly stiff un, but she was the best I could get. Make a good knot and hitch in her, and sit in it; I'll soon have you up."

"All right!" shouted Will; but his voice sounded a little hoarse, and his hands grew moister than before.

"Below there! down she comes!" said Josh; and, taking the ring of new hempen rope, freshly stained with cutch to tan it and make it water-resisting, he planted one foot upon the loop he had secured over the iron bar, and threw the coil down into the pit, so that the weight might tighten out the stiff hemp, uncoil the rings, and make it hang straight.

The rope fell with a curious whistling crackling noise, tightening against the fisherman's foot; and the knot would have jumped off but for his precaution. Then it stopped with a jerk, and Josh shouted again:

"There you are, lad! See her?"

"Ye–es," came up faintly.

"Well; lay hold and make her fast round you. Hold hard a minute till I've hauled up a fathom or two."

He stooped down, keeping his foot on the bar the while, took hold of the rope, and hauled it up a little way.

"There you are, my lad; and now look sharp. I want you out of this unked place."

There was no answer, and Josh waited listening.

"Haven't you got her?" he shouted.

"No; I can't reach. I'm on the other side," came up.

"Oh, I see!" said Josh; and stooping down so as to keep the rope tight to the iron bar, he crept round to the opposite side of the shaft-hole, and held the rope close to the edge.

"There you are, lad," he said. "Got her?"

No answer.

"Have you got her?"

"N–no! I can't reach."

Josh Helston uttered a low whistle, and the skin of his forehead was full of wrinkles and puckers.

"Look out, then!" he shouted; "I'll make her sway. Look out and catch her as she comes to you."

He altered his position and began swinging the rope to and fro, so that as he looked down the void he could see that it struck first one side and then the other of the rocky hole; but there was no sudden tug from below, and he snouted down again:

"Haven't you got her, lad?"

"N–no," came up hoarsely; "I can't reach."

Josh Helston wiped the perspiration from his forehead, and uttered the low whistle once again.

Then an idea struck him.

"Wait a bit, lad," he cried; "I'll make her come."

He began to haul the rope up again rapidly, fathom after fathom, till it began to come up wet; and soon after there was the end, which he took, and after looking round for a suitable piece he pounced upon a squarish piece of granite, which he secured to the rope by an ingenious hitch or two, such as are used by fishermen to make fast a killick—the name they give to the stone they use for anchoring a lobster-pot, or the end of a fishing-line in the sea.

This done he began to lower it rapidly down.

"Here's a stone!" he shouted; "say when she's level with where you are."

There was no answer, but there was the harsh grating noise made by the descending stone as it kept chipping up against the granite wall; and Will sat about two yards from the mouth of the gallery, dripping with cold perspiration, clinging almost convulsively to the rough wall against which he leaned, and waiting for the stone to be swung so low that Josh could give it a regular pendulum motion, and pretty well land it in the gallery.

It seemed darker than ever, and to Will it was as if some horrible sensation of dread was creeping up his limbs to his brain, unnerving him more and more. For he had been already somewhat unnerved, and, in a manner quite different to his usual habit, he had stepped quite close to the mouth of his prison, felt about with his left hand till he found a niche, into which he could partly insert his fingers. Then, leaning forward, he was able to get his head clear, turn it, and glance upwards towards the light.

It was so risky a thing to do that he shrank back directly with a shudder, and closed his eyes for a moment or two, seeming to realise for the first time the terrible danger of his venture.

He collected himself a little, though, and waited, seeing the rope at last very faintly, after hearing its descent and splash in the water at the bottom.

But though he could see it, as he said it was beyond his reach.

Then it seemed to disappear, and come into sight again like a dark thread or the shadow of a cord. Now it seemed near, now afar off, and after waiting a few moments he made a snatch at it. As he did so he felt the fingers of his left hand gliding from the wet slippery niche into which he had driven them, and but for a violent spasmodic jerk of his body he would have been plunged headlong down to the bottom of the shaft.

Shivering like one in an ague he half threw himself upon the rock, and crept back from the entrance to the gallery, hardly able to answer the demands of his companion at the mouth above.

He forced himself, though, to answer, fighting all the time with the nervous dread that was growing upon him; and at last he knew, though he could hardly see it, that the great stone was being swung to and fro.

"Now, lad, can't you get it?" cried Josh; and once more the hoarse reply "*No,*" came up to him.

"Try now!" cried Josh; and the stone was agitated more and more, striking the sides of the shaft, sometimes swinging into the gallery a foot as it seemed, but Will was as if in a nightmare—he could not stir.

"Are you trying?" came down the shaft now in quite a sharp tone, to echo strangely from the sides.

"No," said Will faintly; and just then the stone struck against the opposite wall, the rope hung loose, and at the end of a moment or two there was once more the hollow sullen splash in the water at the bottom.

"Here! hullo there!" cried Josh; "what's up with you, lad?"

"I—I don't know!" cried Will hoarsely. "I shall be better soon."

"Better!" shouted Josh. "What! aren't you all right?"

Will did not answer, but sat there chained, as it were, to his place.

Josh let fall the rope and stood upright, giving vent to a loud expiration of the breath, and then wiping the perspiration from his face.

He was thinking, and when Josh thought he closed his eyes tightly, as if he could think better in the dark. He was not quick of imagination, but when he had caught at an idea he was ready to act upon it.

The idea came pretty quickly now, and opening his eyes he looked sharply round, picked up a great stone, and drove the iron bar a little more tightly into the crevice of the rock.

Then he threw down the stone, stooped and tried the bar to find it perfectly fast, and once more stopped to think.

An idea came again, and he pulled off his black silk neckerchief, a very old weather-beaten affair, but tolerably strong, and kneeling down he bound it firmly round the bar above the rope, passing it through the loop at last, and knotting it securely below, so that the rope should not be likely to slip off the smooth iron.

This done, Josh stood upright once more, gazing down into the black shaft.

"Phew!" he said, with a fresh expiration of the breath; "it's a gashly unked place, and the more you look the unkeder it gets, so here goes."

He went down on his hands and knees, took hold of the iron bar with one hand, then with the other, and shuffled his legs over the shaft, an act of daring ten times greater than that of Will, for he had no friend to leave who had strength of arm to drag him up.

He held on by both hands for a few moments, then by one, as he took fast hold of the rope with, his short deformed hand, and twisted one leg in the rope, pressing his foot against it to have an additional hold; and then, without the slightest hesitation he loosed his grasp of the iron bar, placed the free hand above the other, and began to slide slowly down.

If Josh Helston felt nervous he did not show it, but slid gently down, his hands being too horny from constant handling of ropes to be injured by the friction; neither did the task on hand seem difficult, as he went down and down, swaying more and more as the length of rope between him and the iron bar increased, and gradually beginning to turn as the hard rope showed a disposition to unwind.

"He said she were strong enough to bear anything," he muttered; "and I hope she be, for p'r'aps she'll have to carry two."

How this was to happen did not seem very clear; but the idea was in Josh Helston's not over clear head that it might be so, and the fact was that it took all his powers of brain to originate the idea of going down to help his companion—he had not got so far as the question of how they were to get out. Even if he had thought of it, there was the rope, and he would have said, "If you can climb down you can climb up."

Down lower and lower, with the water dripping upon him here, spurting out from between two blocks of granite there; but Josh's mind was fixed upon one thing only, and that was to reach the spot where Will was waiting to be helped.

For some distance he descended in silence. Then he began to shout:

"Coming down," he said. "Look out!"

Will started and stared towards the mouth of the gallery, but he did not answer. He could not utter a word.

"Coming down!" shouted Josh again at the end of a few seconds.

"Where are you, lad?"

There was no response for a few moments, and then, hoarse and strange from many feet below, came up the word:

"Here!"

"Right!" shouted back Josh quietly enough; "and that's where I'll be soon. I wish I had one o' the boat's lanterns here all the same."

The rope slipped slowly through his hands, checked as it was by the twist round his right leg, and he dropped lower and lower, turning gently round the while.

"Now, then! Where?" he shouted again.

"Here!" was the answer from close below now; and Josh took one look upwards, to see that the square mouth of the shaft seemed very small.

"I'm 'bout with you now, my lad," he said as he still glided down. "Now, where are you?"

"Here!" came from below him: and he tightened his grasp, while the rope slowly turned till his face was opposite to the mouth of the shaft.

"Right, lad!" he cried, striking his feet against the side of the shaft. "I can't see very well," he added as he swung to and fro more and more, "but I'm 'bout doing it, ain't I?"

"Yes—I think so," faltered Will. "Take care."

"Sha'n't let go o' the rope, lad," said Josh, striking his feet again on the shaft-wall, and giving himself such impetus that they rested, as he swung across, on the floor of the gallery, into which he was projected a foot; but the rope, of course, caught on the roof of the place, and he was jerked back and swept over to the opposite wall.

The next time he approached the gallery backwards, and his feet barely touched; but he swung round again, gave himself a fresh impetus, shot himself forward, and as he entered the opening he let the rope slide through his hands for a few feet, the result being that when he tightened his grasp he was landed safely, and he drew a long breath.

"Where are you?" he said sharply as he drew up more of the rope; and, making a running loop, passed it over his head and round his waist, so as there should be no danger of its getting free.

"Here!" cried Will, whose nerve seemed to return now that he had a companion in his perilous position; and, starting up, he caught the rough fisherman tightly by the arm.

Chapter Seven.

"I say, my lad, what's going to be done?"

"Why, what's the matter with you?" cried Josh angrily.

"I don't know. Nothing," replied Will. "I could not reach the rope."

"Ah! well, you've got it now," said Josh gruffly; "and the sooner we get out of this the better."

"Get out of it?" said Will hoarsely.

"Get out of it! To be sure. You didn't mean to come here to live, did you?"

"No," said Will, "but—"

He paused, for his nervous feeling was returning, and shame kept him from saying that he was afraid.

He might have spoken out frankly, though, for Josh Helston, blunt of perception as he was over many things, saw through him now, and in a gruff voice he said:

"Well, if anybody had told me that you could have got yourself skeered like this, Master Will, I should have told him he was a fool. But there, you couldn't help it, I s'pose. It was that diving as upset you, lad."

"Yes, yes; perhaps it was," cried Will, eagerly grasping at the excuse. "I'm not myself, Josh, just now."

Josh began to whistle a dreary old minor tune as they stood there in the dark, to the accompaniment of the dripping water, and for some few minutes no word was spoken.

"Hadn't we better get back?" said Josh at last.

"But how?" said Will despairingly.

"Rope," replied Josh laconically. "Swarm up!"

Will laid his hand upon the slight cord his companion had knotted round his waist.

"I could not climb up that," he said, "at any time. It's impossible now."

Josh whistled again and remained silent.

"Well, it is gashly thin to swarm up," he said. "I never thought of that till now."

"You did not think of getting back?" cried Will.

Josh rubbed the side of his nose with a bit of the rope.

"Well, no," he said slowly; "can't say as I did, lad. Seemed to me as you was in trouble, and I'd better come to you, and so I come."

"Josh!" cried the lad.

"Yes, my son. Well, what's going to be done? We can't stop down here. We shall be wanted aboard, and there ain't a bit o' anything to eat."

"Do you think when we are missed that they will come and look for us?"

"Well," said Josh slowly, "they might or they mightn't; but if they did they wouldn't find us."

"I don't know," said Will thoughtfully.

"Well, I think I do, lad," said Josh, after another scrub at his nose. "I don't s'pose anybody in Peter Churchtown knows that this gashly old hole is here, and it ain't likely they'd come up here to look for us."

"But they would hunt for us surely, Josh."

"Dunno. When they missed us they'd say we'd took a boat and gone out somewheres to fish, and happened on something—upset or took out to sea by the current."

"Yes," said Will thoughtfully.

"Seems to me, lad, as it's something like a lobster-pot—easy enough to get in, and no way out."

"Shall we shout for help?"

"You can if you like," said Josh quietly. "I sha'n't. It makes your throat sore, and don't do no good."

"Don't be cross with me, Josh," cried Will excitedly.

"Oh! I arn't cross with you, lad; I'm cross with myself. It's allus my way: I never did have no head. Think o' me walking straight into a corner like this, and no way hardly out. Well, anyhow, it's being mate-like to you, my lad, and it won't be so dull."

"But, Josh, you could climb out and go for help."

"Why, of course I could," he replied. "I never thought of that."

"Then go at once. Bring a couple of men; and then if you left me the rope you could haul me up."

"Why I could haul you up myself, couldn't I? and then nobody need know anything about it. Here goes."

Will could not help a shudder as his companion proceeded to haul up the portion of the rope that hung down in the shaft, coiling it in rings in the gallery till it was all there.

"Now, then, you mind as that don't fall while I go up again," said Josh. "I wish it warn't so gashly dark."

As he spoke he untied the loop from about his waist and drew the rope tight from above.

"Just like me," he grumbled. "If I'd had any head I should have made knots all down the rope, and then it would have been easy to climb; but here goes; and mind when I'm up you make a good hitch and sit in it, I'll soon have you up."

"Yes, I see," said Will, who was fighting hard against the nervous dread that began once more to assail him; "pray take care."

"Take care! why, of course I shall. Don't catch me letting go of the rope in a place like this. Here goes!"

He reached up as high as he could, holding the rope firmly, and then swung himself out of the gallery over the black void, becoming visible to Will as the faint light from above fell upon his upturned face. Then with legs twined round the rope, Josh began to draw himself up a little bit at a time, the work being evidently very laborious, while Will held the rope and saw him disappear as he ascended beyond the gallery; but the rope the lad held was like an electric communication, the efforts of the climber being felt through the strong fibres as he went up and up.

Then there was a pause, and as Josh rested it was evident that he could not keep himself quite stationary, but slipped a few inches at a time.

Then he started once more, and as the cord jerked and swung, the loud expirations of the climber's breath kept coming down to where, with moist palms and dewy forehead, Will listened.

How high was he now? How much farther had he got by this? Josh's arms were like iron, and the strength in that deformed wrist and hand was tremendous.

Up he went; Will could feel it; and he longed to gaze up and see how he progressed; but somehow that horrible shrinking sensation came over him, and he could only wait.

How long it seemed, and how the rope jerked! Was it quite strong enough? Suppose Josh were to fall headlong into the black water below!

Will shuddered, and tried to keep all these coward fancies out of his mind; but they would come as he stood listening and holding the rope just tight enough to feel the action of his friend.

What a tremendous effort it seemed; and how long he was! Surely he must be at the top by now.

"Nearly up, Josh?" he shouted.

"Up! No: not half-ways," replied the fisherman. "She's too thin, and as wet as wet. I can't get a hold."

Will's heart sank, for he felt that there was failure in his companion's words; and with parched lips and dry throat he listened to the climber's pantings and gaspings as he toiled on, paused, climbed again, and then there was a strange hissing noise that made Will hold his breath. The rope, too, was curiously agitated, not in a series of jerks, but in a continuous vibrating manner, and before Will could realise what it all meant Josh was level with the gallery once more, swinging to and fro in the faint light.

"Haul away, young un, and let's come in," he panted; and somehow he managed to scramble in as Will held the rope taut.

"It ain't to be done," said Josh, sitting down and panting like a dog. "If it were a cable I could go up it like a fly, but that there rope runs through your legs and you can't get no stay."

"How far did you get, Josh?" whispered Will.

"Not above half-ways," grumbled Josh, "and I might have gone on trying; but it was no good, I couldn't have reached. I say, my lad, what's going to be done?"

Chapter Eight.

How Will would not promise not to do the "gashly" thing again.

It seemed that all they could do was to sit and think of there being any likelihood of their being found, and Will asked at last whether anyone knew where Josh was about to take the new rope.

"Nobody," he said gruffly. "I knowed you didn't want it known, so I held my tongue."

"But who lent you the rope, Josh?"

"Nobody."

"Nobody?"

"Nobody. Folk won't lend noo ropes to a fellow without knowing what they're going to do with 'em. I bought it."

"You bought it, Josh—with your own money?"

"Ain't got anybody else's money, have I?" growled Josh. "Here, I know. What stoopids we are!"

"You know what?" cried Will.

"Why, how to get out o' this here squabble."

"Can you—find a way along this gallery, Josh?" said Will eagerly.

"Not likely; but we can get down to the water and go along the adit."

"Adit!" said Will; "is there one?"

"Sure to be, else the water would be up here ever so high. They didn't bring all the earth and stones and water up past here, I know, when they could get rid of 'em by cutting an adit to the shore."

Will caught the fisherman's arm in his hands. "I—I never saw it," he cried.

"Well, what o' that? Pr'aps it's half hid among the stones. I dunno: but there allus is one where they make a shaft along on the cliff."

"But what will you do?"

"Do, lad? Why, go down and see—or I s'pose I must feel; it'll be so dark."

As Josh spoke he rose and got hold of the rope once more.

"No, no!" panted Will. "It is too dangerous, Josh, I can't let you go."

"I say, don't be stoopid, lad. We can't stop here; you know. Nobody won't bring us cake and loaves o' bread and pilchard and tea, will they?"

"But, Josh!"

"Look here, lad, it's easy enough going down, ain't it?"

"Yes, yes," cried Will; "but suppose there is no adit; suppose there is no way out to the shore: how will you get back?"

"There I am again," growled Josh in an ill-used tone. "I never thought of that. I've got a good big head, but it never seems to hold enough to make me think like other men."

"You could not climb up to the mouth, so how could you climb up again here?"

Josh remained silent for a few minutes, and then he gave a stamp with his foot.

"Why," he cried, "you're never so much more clever than me. Why didn't you think o' this here?"

"What? What are you going to do, Josh?"

"Do, lad!" he cried, suiting the action to the word by running the rope through his hands sailor-fashion till he got hold of the end; "why, I'm going to make a knot every half fathom as nigh as I can guess it, and then it'll be easy enough to climb up or down."

Will breathed more freely, and stood listening to his companion's work, for it was a task for only one.

"There you are," cried Josh at the end of a few minutes' knotting. "Now, then, who'll go down first—you or me?"

"I will," said Will. "I'm better now."

"Glad to hear it, lad; but you ain't going first into that gashly hole while I'm here. Stand aside."

Catching hold of the rope again he gradually tightened it to feel whether it was all right and had not left its place over the iron bar; and then, swinging himself off, he descended quickly about fifty feet till Will could hear his feet splash into the water, and then he shouted:

"Hooray, lad!"

"Is there an adit, Josh?"

"Dunno yet, but there's a big stick o' wood floating here as someone's pitched down, and our old rope's lying across it. I shall make it fast to the end here before I go any farther."

A good deal of splashing ensued, and then as Will listened it seemed to him that his companion must have lowered himself partly into the adit, for the rope swung to and fro. Then his heart leaped, for Josh sang out cheerily:

"All right, lad! here's the adit just at the bottom here, and the water dribbling out over it, I think. Come on down."

"Come on down!" echoed Will.

"To be sure, lad. Here I'm in the hole all right. Lay hold o' the rope. It's all slack now."

He set it swinging as he spoke, and at the end of a few moments Will caught it, drew in a long breath, and let himself hang over the black gulf, which seemed far less awful now that there was a friendly voice below.

"Steady it is, lad, steady. There, they knots make her easy, don't they?" Josh kept on saying as his young companion lowered himself rapidly down into the darkness, till he could see the water with the light from above reflected upon it; and the next moment he was seized and drawn aside, his feet resting on solid stone. "Stoop your head, lad, mind."

He bent down, and Josh drew him into a gallery similar to that which they had just left, only there was a little stream of water trickling about their feet.

"Come along, lad. I'll go first," said Josh. "Never mind the ropes: we'll go up and haul them to the top when we get out."

Then creeping cautiously forward in the total darkness, and with Will following, Josh went slowly, feeling his way step by step for about fifty yards, when a faint ray of light sent joy into their breasts; and on pushing forward they found their way stopped by what seemed to be a heap of fallen rock and earth, at whose feet the little stream that ran from the mine trickled gently forth.

The light came through several interstices, which seemed to be overgrown with ferns and rough seagrass and hanging brambles; but it needed no great effort to force some of them aside, sufficient for Josh to creep out, and the next minute they were standing in the broad sunshine, the reason of the mouth of the adit being closed evident before them, the earth and stones from the cliff above having gone on falling for perhaps a century, and plants of various kinds common to the cliff covering the débris, till all trace of the opening but that, where

44

a spring seemed to be trickling forth was gone.

Will drew a long breath and gazed with delight at the sail-dotted sea. Then, without a word he led the way up the cliff, till, after an arduous climb, they stood once more by the open shaft.

"I—say!" cried Josh, staring; and Will looked down with horror to see that the iron bar had so given way that the rope had gradually been dragged to the top, passed over, and probably both Josh and Will had made their last descent depending upon the strength of the former's old silk neck-tie.

"What an escape, Josh!" cried Will.

"Well," said Josh smiling, "I didn't think the old bit had it in her. Well, she is a good un, any way."

Stooping down he undid the knots, handed the rope to Will to haul, while he smilingly replaced his kerchief about his neck with a loose sailor's knot, tucking the ends afterwards inside his blue jersey, and then helped with the rope, taking hold of the old one, as it came up at last dripping wet, and soon forming it also into a coil.

The next thing was to drag out the iron bar, which came out easily enough, making Will shake his head at it reproachfully, as if he thought what an untrustworthy servant it was.

This and the ropes were hidden at last; and they turned to descend, when Josh exclaimed:—

"Well, lad, I s'pose you won't try any o' them games again?"

"Not try?" said Will. "I mean to try till I succeed."

Chapter Nine.

The young "Gent" in the Eton Jacket and him in the flannel Suit.

"Here!"

This was said in a loud, imperious tone by a well-dressed boy—at least if it is being well-dressed at the sea-side to be wearing a very tight Eton jacket and vest, an uncomfortably stiff lie-down collar, and a tall glossy black hat, of the kind called by some people chimney-pot, by the Americans stove-pipe.

He was a good-looking lad of fifteen or sixteen, with rather aquiline features and dark eyes, closely-cut hair, that sat well on a shapely head; but there was a sickly whiteness of complexion and thinness of cheek that gave him the look of a plant that had been forced in a place where there was not enough light.

He was standing on the pier at Peter Churchtown intently watching what was going on beneath him on the deck of the *Pretty Ruth*, where our friend Will was busy at work over a brown fishing-line contained in two baskets, in one of which, coiled round and round, was the line with a hook at every six feet distance, and each hook stuck in the edge of the basket; in the other the line was being carefully coiled; but as Will took a hook from the edge of one basket, he deftly baited it with a bit of curiously tough gelatinous-looking half transparent gristle, and laid it in the other basket, so that all the baits were in regular sequence, and there was no chance of the hooks being caught.

Close by Will sat Josh, busy at work upon an instrument or weapon which consisted of a large hook about as big as that used for meat; and this he had inserted in a strong staff of wood some four feet long, while, to secure it more tightly, he was binding the staff just below the hook most neatly with fine copper wire.

Sailors and fishermen generally do things neatly, from the fact that they pay great attention to their work, and do it in a very slow, deliberate fashion, the fashion in which Josh on that sunny afternoon was working, with one end of the copper wire made fast to a bolt, to keep it straight while he slowly turned the staff round and round.

No one paid any heed to the imperious "Here!" so the lad shouted again:

"Hi! Here! You, sir!"

Josh looked up very deliberately, saw that the eyes of the stranger were fixed upon Will, and looked down again.

"He's hailing o' you, my lad," he said in a gruff voice, just as the stranger shouted again:

"Hi! Do you hear?"

Will looked up, took in the new-comer's appearance at a glance, and said:

"Well, what is it?"

The new-comer frowned at this cool reply from a lad in canvas trousers and blue jersey, which glittered with scales. The fisher-boy ought to have said "Yes, sir," and touched his straw hat. Consequently his voice was a little more imperious of tone as he saidsharply:

"What are you doing?"

Will looked amused, and there was a slight depression at each corner of his mouth as he said quietly:

"Baiting the line."

No "sir" this time, but the new-comer's curiosity was aroused, and he said eagerly:

"Where's your rod?"

"Rod!" said Will, looking up once more, half puzzled. "Rod! Oh, you mean fishing-rod, do you?"

"Of course—" *stupid* the stranger was about to say, but he refrained. "You don't suppose I mean birch rod, do you?"

"No," said Will, and he went on baiting his hooks. "We don't use fishing-rods."

"Why don't you?"

"Why don't we!" said Will, with the dimples getting a little deeper on either side of his mouth. "Why, because this line's about quarter of a mile long, and it would want a rod as long, and we couldn't use it."

"Hor—hor—hor!" laughed Josh, letting his head go down between his knees, and so disgusting the stranger that he turned sharply upon his heel and strutted off, swinging a black cane with a silver top and silk tassels to and fro, and then stopping in a very nonchalant manner to take out a silver hunting watch and look at the time, at the same moment taking care that Will should have a good view of the watch, and feel envious if enviously inclined.

He walked along the pier to the very end, and Josh went on slowly turning the staff, while Will kept baiting his hooks.

The next minute the boy was back, looking on in an extremely supercilious way, but all the while his eyes were bright with interest; and at last he spoke again in a consequential manner:

"What's that nasty stuff?"

"What nasty stuff?" replied Will, looking up again.

"That!" cried the stranger, pointing with his cane at the small box containing Will's bait.

Before the latter could answer there was a shout at the end of the pier.

"Ahoy! Ar—thur! Taff!" and a boy of the age and height of the first stranger came tearing along the stones panting loudly, and pulling up short to give Will's questioner a hearty slap on the back.

"Here, I've had a job to find you, Taff. I've been looking everywhere."

"I wish you would not be so rough, Richard," said the one addressed, divine his shoulders a hitch, and frowning angrily as he saw that Will was watching them intently. "There's no need to be so boisterous."

"No, my lord. Beg pardon, my lord," said the other boy with mock humility; and then, with his eyes twinkling mirthfully, he thrust his stiff straw hat on to the back of his head, and plumped himself down in a sitting position on the edge of the pier, with his legs dangling down towards the bulwark of the lugger, and his heels softly drubbing the stone wall.

For though to a certainty twin brother of the first stranger, he was very differently dressed, having on a suit of white boating flannels and a loose blue handkerchief knotted about his neck.

"Why, Taff," he cried, "this chap's going fishing."

"I wish you wouldn't call me out of my name before this sort of people," said his brother, flushing and speaking in a low voice.

"All right, old chap, I won't, if you'll go back to the inn and take off those old brush-me-ups. You look as if you'd come out of a glass case."

The other was about to retort angrily and walk away, but his curiosity got the better of him, for just then the boy in the flannels exclaimed in a brisk way:

"I say: going fishing?"

"Yes," said Will, looking up, with the smile at the corner of his lips deepening; and as the eyes of the two lads met they seemed to approve of each other at once.

"May I come aboard?"

"Yes, if you like," said Will; and the boy leaped down in an instant, greatly to his brother's disgust, for he wanted to go on board as well, but held aloof, and whisked his cane about viciously, listening to all that was going on.

"How are you?" said the second lad, nodding in a friendly way to Josh.

"Hearty, thanky," said the latter in his sing-song way; "and how may you be?"

"Hearty," said the boy, laughing. "I'm always all right. He isn't," he added, with a backward nod of his head, which nearly made him lose his straw hat; but he caught it as it fell, clapped it on the back of his head again, and laughingly gave his trousers a hitch up in front and another behind, about the waist, kicking out one leg as he did so. "That's salt-water sort, isn't it? I say," he added quickly, "are you the skipper?"

"Me!" cried Josh, showing two rows of beautifully white teeth. "Nay, my lad, I'm the crew. Who may you be?"

"What? my name? Dick—Richard Temple. This is my brother Arthur. We've come down to stay."

"Have you, though?" said Josh, looking from one to the other as if it was an announcement full of interest, while the lad on the pier frowned a little at his brother's free-and-easy way.

"Yes, we've come down," said Dick dreamily, for he was watching Will's busy fingers as he baited hook after hook. "I say," he cried, "what's that stuff—those bits?"

"These?" said Will. "Squid."

"Squid? What's squid?"

Josh ceased winding the wire round his staff.

"Here's a lad as don't know what squid is," he said in a tone of wondering pity.

"Well, how should I know? Just you be always shut-up in London and school and see if you would."

"What? Don't they teach you at school what squid is?" said Josh sharply.

"No," cried the boy.

"A mussy me!" said Josh in tones of disgust. "Then they ought to be ashamed of themselves."

"But they don't know," said the boy impatiently. "I say, what is it?"

"Cuttle-fish," said Will.

"Cut-tle-fish!" cried Dick. "Oh! I know what that is—all long legs and suckers, and got an ink-bag and a pen in its body."

49

"Yes, that's it," said Will, laughing. "We call it squid. It makes a good tough bait, that don't come off, and the fish like it."

"Well, it is rum stuff," cried Dick, picking up a piece and turning it over in his fingers. "Here, Taff, look!"

His brother screwed up his face with an aspect of disgust, and declined to touch the fishes' *bonne-bouche*; but he looked at it eagerly all the same.

"I say, what do you catch?" said Dick, seating himself tailor-fashion on the deck opposite Will.

"What? on this line? Nothing sometimes."

"Oh! of course. I often go fishing up the river when we're at home, and catch nothing. But what do you catch when you have any luck?"

"Lots o' things," said Josh; "skates, rays, plaice, brill, soles, john-dories, gurnets—lots of 'em—small conger, and when we're very lucky p'r'aps a turbot."

"Oh! I say," cried the boy, with his eyes sparkling, "shouldn't I like to see conger too! They're whopping great chaps, arn't they, like cod-fish pulled out long?"

"Well, no," said Will, "they're more like long ling; but we can't catch big ones on a line like this—only small."

"But there are big ones here, arn't there?"

"Oh, yes!" said Will; "off there among the rocks sometimes, six and seven foot long."

"But why don't you catch big ones on a line like that?"

"Line like that!" broke in Josh; "why, a conger would put his teeth through it in a moment. You're obliged to have a single line for a conger, with a wire-snooded hook and swivels, big hooks bound with wire, something like this here."

As he spoke he held out the hook, just finished as to its binding on.

"And what's that for?" cried the boy, taking the hook.

"Gaffing of 'em," said Josh; but he pronounced it *"gahfin' of 'em."*

"Oh, I do want to go fishing!" cried the boy eagerly. "What are you going to do with that long-line?"

"Lay it out in the bay," said Will, "with a creeper at each end."

"A what?"

"A creeper."

"What's a creeper?"

"I say, young gentleman, where do you go to school?" said Josh in indignant tones.

"London University," said the boy quickly. "Why?"

"And you don't know what a creeper is?"

"No," said the boy, laughing. "What is it?"

"Oh! we call a small kind of grapnel, or four-armed anchor, a creeper," said Will.

"Oh!"

"Then when we've let down the line with one creeper we pay out the rest."

"Pay out the rest?"

"A mussy me!" said Josh to himself.

"Well, run it out over the side of the boat we're in, and row away till we've got all the line with the baited hooks in."

"Yes," said the boy eagerly; "and then you put down the other anchor. I see."

"That's her," said Josh approvingly.

"Well," said the boy excitedly, "and how do you know when you've got a bite?"

"Oh! we don't know."

"Then how do you catch your fish?"

"They catch themselves," said Will. "We row then to the other end of the line and draw it up."

"How do you know where it is?"

"Why, by the buoy, of course," said Josh. "We always have a buoy, and you think that's a boy like you, I know."

"Oh no! I don't," said Dick, shaking his head and laughing. "Come, I'm not such a Cockney as not to know what a b-u-o-y is. But, I say, what do you do then?"

"Why, we get up the end of the line, and put fresh baits on when they're taken off, and take the fish into the boat when there are any."

"Oh, I say, what fun! Here, when are you going to put in that line?"

"Sundown," said Josh.

"Here, I want to go," said our friend on the pier. "I'll give you a shilling if you'll take me."

"No; we can't take you," said Josh grimly. "We should make you in such a mess you'd have to be washed."

"There, Taff, I told you so," cried Dick. "Why don't you put on your flannels. I hate being dressed up at the sea-side!" he added to himself as his brother stalked impatiently away.

"There, now, he's chuffy," said Dick, half to himself. "Oh! I do wish he wasn't so soon upset! Hi, Taff, old man, don't go, I'm coming soon. He had a bad illness once, you know," he said confidentially to Will; but his brother did not stop, walking slowly away along the pier, to be met by a tall, dark, keen-looking man of about forty who was coming from the inn.

"I say," said Dick, who did not see the encounter at the shore end of the pier, "I *should* like to come with you to-night."

"Why, you'd be sea-sick," said Josh, laughing.

"Oh, no! I shouldn't. I've been across the Channel eight times and not ill. I say, you'll let me come?"

Will looked at Josh, who was turning the new wire binding of the gaff-hook into a file for the gentle rubbing of his nose.

"Shall we take him, Josh?" said Will.

"I don't mind," replied that worthy, "only he'll get in a gashly mess."

"I don't mind," said Dick. "Flannels will wash. I'll put on my old ones, and—"

"Why, Dick, what are you doing there?" cried the keen-looking man, who had come down the pier.

"Talking to the fishermen, father," cried the boy, starting up. "I say, they're going out to lay this line. May I go with them?"

His father hesitated a moment and glanced quickly to seaward before turning to Josh.

"Weather going to be fine?" he said in a quick way that indicated business more than command, though there was enough of the latter in his speech to make Josh answer readily:

"Going to be fine for a week;" and then confidentially, "We'll take care on him."

The stranger smiled.

"Yes, you can go, Dick; but take care of yourself. It does not take you long to make friends, young man. Come, Arthur, I'm going for a walk along the beach."

"Can't I go with Dick, papa?" said the boy addressed, in an ill-used tone.

"No; I should think three will be enough in a small boat; and besides—"

He said no more, but glanced in a half-amused way at his son's costume, being himself in a loose suit of tweeds.

Arthur coloured and tightened his lips, walking off with his father, too much hurt to say more to his brother, whom he left talking to Will.

"There," said the latter, impaling the last bit of squid on a hook and then laying it in its place, "that's ready. Now you'd better do as I do: go home and get some tea and then come back."

"But it's too soon," replied Dick, "I can't get tea yet—"

"Come home and have some with me then," said Will.

"All right!" said Dick. "I say, does he live with you? Is he your brother?"

"Hor—hor—hor—hor!" laughed Josh. "That is a good one. Me his brother! Hor—hor—hor!"

"Well, I didn't know," said Dick colouring. "I only thought he might be, you know."

"Oh, no, youngster! I ain't no brother o' him," said Josh, shaking his head. "There, don't you mind," he continued, clapping his strong hand on the boy's shoulder, and then catching hold of him with his short deformed limb, an act that looked so startling and strange that the boy leaped back and stared at him.

Josh's deformity was his weakest as well as his strongest point, and he looked reproachfully, half angrily, at the boy and then turned away.

With the quick instinct of a frank, generous nature, Dick saw the wound he had inflicted upon the rough fisherman, and glanced first at

Will, who was also touched on his companion's account. Then stepping quickly up to Josh he touched him on the arm and held out his hand.

"I—I beg your pardon," he said. "I didn't know. I was surprised. I'm very sorry—"

Josh's weather-tanned face lit up directly with a pleasant smile, and grasping the boy's hand he wrung it so hard that Dick had hard work to keep from wincing.

"It's all right, my lad," he said. "Of course you didn't know! It be gashly ugly, bean't it? Fell off the cliff when I was quite a babby, you know, and soft. Fifty foot. Yonder, you know;" and he pointed to the steep cliff and its thin iron railing at the end of the village.

"How shocking!" said Dick.

"Oh! I dunno," said Josh cheerily. "I was such a little un, soft as one of our bladder buoys, you see, and I never knowed anything about it. Bent it like, and stopped it from growing; but thank the Lord, it grew strong, and I never mind. There, you be off along o' Will there and get your tea, and we'll have such a night's fishing, see if we don't!"

Chapter Ten.

Uncle Abram always has a bit of Salt Provision in Cut.

The two lads went off towards the village, Dick in the highest of glee, and chattering and questioning about everything he saw, Will getting more and more quiet and lower of spirit as he thought of the ordeal that he had to face.

For he had asked this young stranger, whom he had never seen before, to come home and share his meal, and all in the frankness of his young hospitable feelings. In fact, he would have given him his own meal with the greatest of pleasure; but it had all been done without a thought of Aunt Ruth and Uncle Abram.

"Where do you live?" said Dick suddenly.

"Up at the end there; the white cottage."

"What! with the pretty garden and the flowers?" cried the boy. "I know Nor'-nor'-west Cottage. Father said he wished we could have it when we looked round."

"Yes, that's my home," said Will. "Uncle is very fond of his garden, and takes great pains with it."

"Uncle?" said Dick. "Do you live with your uncle?"

"And aunt," replied Will quietly; and there was so much meaning in his tone that his companion did not ask the question upon his lips about father and mother.

"I like gardens," said Dick; "but we can't grow anything in our back garden in town. I did try some vegetable-marrows, but the cats scratched up some, and the smoke and blacks killed the others. Anything will grow down here, I suppose?"

"Oh, yes, if you don't plant it just where the west wind cuts. It is so fierce sometimes. Let's go round by the back, and I can take you through our garden."

"All right!" cried Dick eagerly, and he did not notice the deepening of the colour in his new friend's face, for Will felt guilty of a subterfuge. He was really alarmed as to the result of his invitation, and its effect upon his aunt, so he hoped by going round by the back to find his old uncle in the garden, according to his custom, planting, weeding, and fumigating his plants, whether they needed it or no.

Fortune favoured Will, for after a climb round by the narrow alley he let his companion in by the little top gate into the rough terrace garden on the steep slope of the cliff—a quaint little place full of rocks and patches of rich earth, and narrowed stony paths, but one blaze of bright colour, and full of promise of fruit.

"Why, how comical!" said Dick. "We're higher than the roof of your house!"

"Yes; it's all so steep here," replied Will. "Oh! here's uncle."

He turned down a narrow path, where, pipe in mouth, and emitting puffs of smoke, the old gentleman was busy with some strips of matting tying up the heavy blossoms of carnations to some neatly cut sticks. So intent was he upon his occupation that the two lads stood gazing at him for a few minutes before he rose up, emitting a long puff of smoke, and turned round to nod shortly at Will, and stare severely at the new-comer in a stolid manner peculiarly his own.

"What cheer?" he said slowly.

"Uncle, this is a young gentleman just come down from town."

"To Peter Churchtown, eh?" said the old gentleman, pulling down his buff waistcoat with the brass crown-and-anchor buttons, and passing one hand over his chin to make sure whether his grey beard did not look stubbly.

"Yes, sir; my father has come down on mining business," said the lad eagerly, "and we're going to stay."

"Glad to see you, sir, glad to see you," said the old gentleman, holding out an enormous gnarled hand, whose back was covered with great veins, and faintly showed through its ruddy-brown a blue tattooed figure of a mermaid.

"He's going fishing with Josh and me this evening; we're going to lay the bolter from the boat."

"Quite right!" said the old gentleman, nodding. "Nice evening for fishing. You'll get some flat-fish, I daresay."

"And," said Will, making an effort, and speaking hoarsely in his eagerness to make a clean breast, "I asked him if he'd come home and have tea with me before we go."

The old gentleman winced for a moment, as he might have winced in the old days when, as purser, he inspected his stores on a long voyage, and feared that they were running short. It was but for a moment, and then he recovered himself.

"Asked him to tea? that's well, that's right, my lad. I'm glad to see you, sir. Do you like flowers?"

"I love them," cried the boy, who was gazing half wonderingly at the old man's florid face, and its frame of stiff grey hairs.

"Then you shall have one of my best clove-pinks," he went on, taking his great pruning-knife from his pocket. "Let me see," he continued, opening the blade slowly, "which is the best? Ah! that's a good one— that's a beauty—there!"

He stooped down, and after a good deal of selection cut a splendid aromatic clove-pink, and handed it smiling to the boy, who smelt it and placed it in the button-hole of his loose flannel jacket.

"It's a beauty," he cried.

"Yes, isn't it?" said the old man proudly. "Don't get such flowers as that in London, eh?"

"Only in Covent Garden," replied the visitor.

"What garden?—oh! ah! yes, I recollect, Covent Garden Market. Marrows growing well, sir, arn't they?" he continued, pointing to the great succulent plants trailing over the rocks. "My bees;" he pointed to five straw hives. "You shall taste our honey. Wild thyme honey off the cliff and moor. Very glad you've come, sir. But, I say," he added, stopping short in the middle of the path, taking his pipe from his lips, and sending a puff down first one nostril and then the other, "never mind him, I'm master. You shall be my visitor to-day, eh?"

He chuckled and clapped Dick on the shoulder, pushing him half before him down the stony, steppy path, and as he did so he turned his great grey head and gave a most prodigious wink, accompanied by a screw up of the face at Will, a look full of secrecy and scheming, all of which, however, Will fully understood and felt relieved.

"It's very kind of you to a stranger," said the visitor.

"Not at all, my lad, not at all. You've come to live among us, and we're very glad to see you. Here we are, here's my good lady—Mrs Marion. I've got a visitor, my dear: Mr—Mr—what's your name?" he whispered hastily.

"Richard Temple," said the lad, in the same tone.

"Ah, to be sure! my memory's getting bad. Mr Richard Temple, my dear. Young gentleman from London. Come to have a cup of tea with us to-night."

Aunt Ruth's first feeling was that it was a liberty to ask anyone to tea without first obtaining her consent; her second, one of annoyance that she had not put on her black silk that afternoon; her next, one of pleasure, for the lad went up to her in a pleasant, frank, gentlemanly way, and held out his hand, behaving towards the old lady with that natural chivalry and courtesy that you always see in a boy who has been much with a good mother and grown-up sisters.

"It's very kind of you to welcome me like this," he said; and, to Will's great relief, Aunt Ruth smiled and felt ready to purr, and as if she really had been welcoming the visitor very warmly. "Don't think me rude," continued the lad, whose eager eyes kept wandering about, "but I've just come from London, where everything seems so dark and grim; and your cottage does look so beautiful, and clean, and snug."

"Well said, youngster!" cried Uncle Abram; "so it does. Our skipper won't have a spot on anything or a bit of dust anywhere; eh, Will?"

"Oh no! aunt likes the place to look nice," echoed Will.

"Don't you listen to them, my dear," said Aunt Ruth; "but I'm very glad to see you, and you must excuse me now."

She slipped out of the room, and Uncle Abram gave his nephew another look full of intelligence before proceeding to show his young guest his collection in the best room while the tea was being prepared.

For the best room was quite a museum of trophies brought by Uncle Abram's own hands from what he called "furren lands;" and Dick was excitement itself over the inspection.

"This here's the grains," said the old gentleman, pointing to a five-pronged spear, on a long slight pole, with a cord attached to the shaft. "We uses this to take bonito and dolphin out in the hot seas. Strikes 'em as they play under the bobstay, you know."

"And what's this?" said Dick eagerly.

"Backbone of a shark, twelve foot long, as we hooked and drew aboard o' the *Princess* off Barbadoes, Jennywury sixteen, eighteen hundred forty-nine."

"You caught it with a hook?" cried Dick.

"Baited with a bit o' very bad salt pork," said the old man. Then, pointing with the stem of his pipe: "His jaws."

Then from the lancet-toothed jaws to a sea-snake in a large bottle of spirits—an unpleasant looking little serpent, said to be poisonous. In a glass case was the complete shell of a lobster, out of which the crustacean had crawled; and beside this were some South Sea bows and arrows, pieces of coral from all parts of the world, a New Zealand paddle on the wall, opposite to a couple of Australian spears. Hanks of sea-weed hung from nails. There was a caulking hammer that had been fished up from the bottom of some dock, all covered with acorn barnacles, and an old bottle incrusted with oyster-shells, the glass having begun to imitate the iridescent lining of the oyster. Under the side-table was a giant oyster from off the coast of Java. Over the chimney-glass the snout of a sword-fish. A cannon-ball—a thirty-two pounder—rested in a wooden cup, a ball that had no history; and close by it, in a glass case, was a very ill-shaped cannon-ball, about one-fourth its size, which had a history, having been picked out of the wall of Saint Anthony's Church on the cliff, into which it had been fired by the Spaniards in the days of "good Queen Bess."

There were curiosities enough to have taken the young visitor hours more to see, only while they were in the midst of them Aunt Ruth came in smiling, and in a state of compromise—that is to say, there had been no time to change her dress, but she had mounted her best cap and put on her black watered-silk apron, two pieces of confectionery that it would take half a chapter to properly describe, so they may go with the simple announcement that they were wonders.

"Tea is ready," said the old lady; and she smiled more graciously still when Dick stepped forward and offered his arm to walk the four steps across to the second best room, where meals were always spread.

Everything was very homely and simple, but to the boy fresh from London the table was a delight. Right in the centre there was a blue jug full of the old purser's choicest flowers scenting the room. The best tea-tray covered one end, with its paraphernalia of best china, the battered old silver pot and very much worn silver tea-spoons; while at the other end was a ham in cut, a piece of ornamental preservation, all pinky fat and crimson lean, marbled throughout. A noble-looking home-baked loaf, a pat of yellow butter—real cow's butter—ornamented with a bas-relief of the swing-tailed horned lady who presumably was its author, and on either side a dish of raspberry jam, and another containing a piece of virgin honey-comb, from which trickled forth the pale golden sweetness.

"Allus make it a rule here, sir," said the old purser, "o' having a good bit o' salt provision in cut. Let me give you a bit o' 'am."

Dick raised no objection, and then, as soon as he was helped, and saw the cup of tea with a veined pattern of rich lumpy cream running over it, he sighed involuntarily.

"There, I am sorry," cried Aunt Ruth, "it isn't to your liking. I knew that ham would be too salt."

Dick Temple flushed like a girl.

"Oh no!" he cried; "it wasn't that."

"Then it's the butter!" cried the old lady, in mortified tones.

"Butter!" cried Dick, who had already eaten two semicircles out of a slice; "why, it's glorious! We never get such butter in London."

"But you sighed," said the old lady, bridling, while Uncle Abram wrinkled his forehead and shook his head at Will.

"Did I?" said Dick, colouring a little more deeply. "Well, it was because I wished Taff was here."

"What, is that your dog?" said the old lady, smiling again.

"No!" cried Dick, laughing; "it's my brother Arthur. I always call him Taff, because—because—I don't know why, but I generally call him Taff."

"I'm sure we should be very pleased to see the young gentleman," said Aunt Ruth in the most stately manner; and then poor Taff was forgotten, from the fact that, after well assisting the guest, Uncle Abram and Will set such an example in the way of eating that it proved contagious, and Dick was soon proving himself no mean trencherman, while he fully realised the wisdom of the old sailor in always having "a good bit o' salt provision in cut."

When they rose from the table Aunt Ruth was quite sure that her visitor had not had half a tea, which words were comforting to Dick, whose conscience, now that he had eaten, was beginning to smite him for behaving so voraciously at these strangers' table—unnecessary qualms, for his performance had been very mild compared to that of the purser, who shook hands warmly when his guest took leave, Mrs Marion supplementing her good-bye with a warm invitation to come again.

Chapter Eleven.

Dick Temple takes a Lesson in finding his Bearings before the Bolter is laid.

"So your father has to do with mines, has he?" said Will rather eagerly, as the two lads walked down towards the little harbour.

"Yes, and I'm going to be a mining engineer," said Dick. "I say, I wish I was a fisherman—boy, I mean!"

"And I wish I was going to be a mining engineer," said Will, smiling sadly.

"Why, it isn't half such fun!" cried Dick. "You have to learn all sorts of stuff about rocks and strata, and chemistry, and mechanics, and hydro-all-sorts-of-things. I say, do you ever see sharks down here?"

"Not very often," said Will. "I never did see one. Josh hooked one once with his gaff, after it had taken a conger bait."

"Oh, did he? Tell me all about it."

"There isn't much all to tell," replied Will. "Josh was out in the boat, fishing off the rocks with a mate—out yonder, where you can see the cliff with the white patch on the top—Poldee."

"Yes, I see."

"Well, they couldn't catch a single conger, and they were going to give it up, when Josh's mate had a bite; and when he began to pull up, he thought it was a conger, but only a very small one; and then, when they got it to the top of the water they stared, for it was—how much do you think?"

"Forty feet!" cried Will eagerly.

"No, no!" said Will smiling; "they thought it was about six."

"Oh, that isn't big!" said Dick in disappointed tones.

"Not big! What, a fish the size of a tall man, and ten times as strong in the water! Not big! We think it very big down here."

"Well, go on," said Dick.

"Oh, there's no more to tell; only that Josh took up the gaff and got hold of the shark, which gave one flash with his tail and went down again, taking with it Josh's gaff-hook and the conger-line, and thatwas all."

"Oh!" said Dick in a disappointed tone. "They ought to have caught it."

"Yes," said Will dryly; "they ought to have caught it, but they did not. There's Josh already in the boat. I wonder whether he thought of a line to whiff."

"To whiff? what's that—to make cigars?"

"No, no!" said Will as they went along the pier. "I'll show you when we get on board.—Think of a line to whiff, Josh?"

"Ay, lad; I thought young master there might like to try as we went out."

"This way," said Will, pausing in front of the lugger, which was now very little below the edge of the pier, as the tide was flowing fast. "Shall I help you?"

"Oh no!" cried Dick, leaping aboard; and then actively lowering himself into the lugger's boat, a short, broad, heavy affair, wherein sat Josh, with the long-line and box of bait.

"You sit down there—aft," said Josh, "and we'll soon row you out."

"Is it far?" cried Dick.

"'Bout three mile," replied Josh, taking up an oar and pushing the boat away from the side of the lugger, Will following his example, and getting an oar over the side.

"Stop! Look, look, look!" cried Dick, pointing out in front of them, where, through the water, there about eighteen inches deep, he could see what seemed to be a long white worm or serpent dashing here and there in a curious way. "There's another and another!"

"That's only the cleanings of the fish," said Will; "intestines, don't you call 'em? That's a shoal of small fish come into the harbour, only they're so clear you can't make 'em out; and first one lays hold of one end and runs off with it, and then another. Looks just like little snakes darting about, don't it?"

"Why, so it is," said Dick. "I can see the little rascals swimming about, and drawing the long white strings after them. Oh, I say, I wish Taff were here!"

"Look there!" said Will, eager to show the stranger all the peculiarities of the place; "do you see that?"

He was pointing to a shallow part, close inshore, just after they had left the harbour, where a drain ran down, and the smooth black water-polished rock was veined with white spar.

"I can see something shadowy-like in the water. Why, there was a fish went over that white place—two—three—there's a whole shoal of them!"

"Grey mullet, nearly as long as your arm!" said Will.

"Got a line? Oh, I wish I had my fishing-rod! Let's try forthem."

"No use," said Will; "they very seldom take a bait. I don't like them; they're nasty fish. They come up to feed off the mouth of that dirty drain."

"We'll ketch something better than them as soon as we get outside," said Josh, bending to his oar, Will following suit, and the water began to rattle under the blunt bow of the heavy boat as they sent it speedily along.

"What are all those little tubs for?" said Dick as they threaded their way amongst a number lying a short distance outside the harbour. "Buoys?"

"Yes," said Will; "anchor buoys, to make fast the luggers to when they have been out fishing, and are coming into the harbour in fine weather."

They were now leaving the village behind, and it looked like a panoramic picture lit up by the sinking sun, with the tall cliff to left and right, and the hills rising in a steep slope behind. Eight away over the bay the rippling water was stained with the reflection of the western sky, and the sides of the waves glistened with orange, and blue, and gold.

"Oh, you are lucky to live down here!" cried Dick, who was in ecstasies with the beauty of the scene. "I say, though, I wish we'd brought poor old Taff!"

"We'll bring him another time," said Will smiling.

"Will you?" cried Dick joyfully. "Oh, then, I don't mind."

"I thought London was a very beautiful place!" said Will as he tugged at his oar.

"Beautiful!" cried Dick; "why, it's horrid. You can't play a game of cricket without going out by rail; and as for seeing a bird, why, there isn't anything but the old chiswicks—the sparrows, you know. Why, this is worth a hundred Londons. I say, what a big buoy!"

"Yes; that's a dangerous rock there."

"Can you see?"

"Oh, yes!" said Josh; "she's only about five foot under water now," and, giving an extra tug at his oar, he turned the boat's head to a huge tub that was anchored close by the rock, and which looked like the cork-float likely to be used by the giant who bobbed for whales.

"Give's your oar, Will, lad, and I'll take her over the rock while you get ready a whiffing-line."

He rowed close up to the great buoy, and then bade the visitor look down through the clear water.

"See her?" he said.

"Yes, quite plain," cried Dick; "why, it's all covered with long waving sea-weed, and—oh! quick! give me a fishing-line! I can see lots of fish!"

"Oh, they're only wraaghs," said Josh contemptuously. "Here, you wait till he's got the whiff ready, and you shall ketch something better than that."

"Shall I?" said Dick, and he turned to Will, who was unwinding a stout cord from a square wood frame. "Why, you're not going to fish with that piece of rope, are you?" he added, laughing.

"Yes; but I shall put on a fine snood. We're obliged to have strong tackle out here."

"Why, we fish with fine silk lines, and hooks tied on single horse-hairs in the Thames."

"Do you?" said Will quietly.

"Yes, and little tiny hooks. Why, you'll never catch anything with that great coarse thing; it would be too big for a jack."

"We do catch fish with them, though, sometimes," said Will coolly, as he deftly tied the hook on to a fine piece of cord by making a couple of peculiar hitches round the shank, the end of which was flattened out. This thinner cord, or snooding, he tied to the stout line, and on this latter he fastened a good-sized piece of lead formed like a sugar-loaf cut down the middle so as to leave one half.

"Why, you'll frighten all the fish away with that!" cried Dick. "See how clear the water is!"

"Wait a bit," said Will good-humouredly. "This is salt-water fishing, not fresh. We don't fish like the gentlemen who go up on the moor for trout. But you'll see."

"Well, but," cried Dick, in tones of remonstrance, "if you're going to use that great hook you must hide it in the bait. Don't put your bait on like that."

"I showed him how, and that's the right way," said Josh with authority; and then to himself, speaking right into his blue jersey as he bent his head, "Mussy me, how gashly ignorant the boy be!"

"Yes, this is the best way to fish out here," said Will. "We try all sorts of ways, and this is one of the best, only I'm obliged to use this bait till I get a better. It's the end of a squid's arm, and the fish will take it for a worm."

"But do bury the hook in it!" said Dick earnestly.

"No; let's try my way first," said Will, "but let's see yours."

He handed the hook and piece of grey gristly squid to Dick, who, after a fashion, buried the hook in it right over the shank, making a clumsy knob, which he held up with a triumphant—"There!"

"Won't do," said Will smiling, as he let it fall over into the water. "That don't look like anything that lives in the water, does it?"

"I d'know," said Dick, who was disappointed.

"I do!" growled Josh to himself.

"Look here, sir," said Will, tearing the hook out of the piece of squid and throwing it away before picking a similar piece about five inches long from his basket. "I shall just hook it through like that on the end. Now, look here! watch it as we go through the water."

He threw a yard or two of line in the water, the bait going in with a little splash; and as it was drawn along close to the surface by the progress of the boat it had a curious wavy motion, while, when Will snatched the line a little now and then, the bait seemed to be making darts.

"Why, it looks like a little eel!" cried Dick.

"Yes, like a sand-eel! See that!"

"Oh!" said Dick excitedly, as there was a splash astern, and something flashed like silver through the water.

"Little tiny mackerel," said Will calmly. "There you are. Let it go; pitch the lead over, and that will keep the bait down, and you can let out twenty or thirty yards of line, and then hold on."

"But won't that lead sink it to the bottom?" said Dick, as he obeyed his companion.

"It would if we kept still; but rowing like this, it will only keep it down a few feet. If you had no weight, you'd only have the long noses after it, for the bait would be skipping along the top of the water."

"Long noses!" cried Dick eagerly; "what are they?"

"A-mussy me!" sighed Josh to himself, as he looked pityingly at the young visitor.

"We call the gar-fish long noses," said Will. "They are long silvery fish with bodies like eels."

"I've seen them at the fishmongers'," cried Dick. "They've regular beaks something like a bird's."

"But full of sharp teeth," said Will. "Those are the fellows, and they're very hard to catch."

"Why?"

"Because there is so little for the hook to hold on by."

"Oh! I say! look here!"

During the above conversation the line had been allowed to run out forty or fifty yards, the lad holding it in his left hand, with his arm hanging over the stern. Then all at once there was a sharp snatch, and Dick turned over on to his knees, holding the line with both hands.

"I've got him!" he cried. "Such a big one! Oh, don't he pull!"

"Well, why don't you pull?" cried Will laughing at his new friend's excitement.

"I'm going to play him first."

"Pull him in sharp, hand over hand, or you'll lose him!" cried Josh.

The boy obeyed, and drew away at the cord till he could see what looked like a great silver shuttle darting about in the quivering water, and then, panting still, he drew out a fine mackerel, with its rippled sides, glorious with pearly tints, and its body bending and springing like so much animated steel.

"Oh, you beauty!" cried Dick in a state of excitement. "But I thought it must have been four times as big; it pulled so."

Will had been rowing, but he now handed the oar to Josh, unhooked the mackerel, killed it by a blow or two on the head, and then, to Dick's astonishment and horror, took out his sharp jack-knife and sliced off a long narrow piece of the silvery-skinned fish close to the tail.

"Oh, what a pity!" cried Dick. "I say!"

"You must have a good bait," said Will quietly, "and a lask from a mackerel's tail—"

"A what?"

"A long thin piece like this—we call it a lask—is one of the best baits you can have."

"But it seemed such a pity to cut that beautiful fish."

"Catch another," said Will laughing; and he threw the newly-baited hook over the side, where, as the lead dragged it down into the clear water, Dick could see it dart out of sight, looking like a small silvery fish.

"Why, how quick a mackerel must be to catch that as it goes through the water!" he said.

"Quick as lightning," said Josh. "There, you've got him again."

"So I have," cried Dick, hauling in rapidly now, as the result of his teaching, and bringing in another mackerel larger than the first.

"I'll take it off for you," said Will.

"No, no, I will. Get me another bait."

"All right!" cried Will.

"Ugh! you nasty cannibal, eating bits of your own brother!" cried Dick, apostrophising the lovely fish as it lay beating the bottom of the boat with its tail.

"Hor! hor! hor! hor!" laughed Josh heartily, the idea of the fish being a cannibal tickling him immensely. "They'll eat their own fathers and mothers and children too, when they get a chance."

"Mind, or he'll tangle the line," said Will; and he pounced upon the fish just as it was going to play shuttle in the boat, and weave the line into a task that it would take long to undo.

Then another bait was hooked on, the line thrown over, and Will resumed his oar.

"Put her along, Josh," he said.

"Ay, ay, lad," cried the sturdy fellow; and the water began to patter beneath the bows of the boat, when all at once there was a sharp crack, and Josh went backwards with his heels in the air.

"Look at that," he said sourly. "That comes o' having bad thole-pins;" and he began to knock out the remains of the pin that formed the rowlock and which had broken short off.

This brought the boat nearly to a standstill, and consequently down went the lead to the bottom; but only to be dragged up again, Dick hauling away excitedly as he felt a good tug, tug at his bait.

"I've got him again!" he cried.

"Then you can catch fish with such tackle as ours!" said Will, who looked on highly amused at his friend's excitement.

"Oh, yes!" said Dick. "You see I didn't know. Why, what's this? Look at him how he's going. Here, I've seen these chaps in the fishmongers' in London too. I know: it's a gurnard."

"Gunnet," said Josh correctively.

"Why, you might catch these with a great meat hook," cried Dick. "Oho! what a mouth!"

"Look sharp and put in again, and you may get a red one: this is a grey," said Will. "Some of the red ones are beauties, and you'll hear them grunt when you take them out of the water."

"Go along," cried Dick laughing. "None of your nonsense!"

"A mussy me!" muttered Josh to himself as he knocked in a fresh thole-pin; "what a gashly little these Londoners do know!"

"They do make a grunting noise really," said Will; "just when you pull them out of the water. You'll see."

The hook was already speeding towards the bottom, but no grunting red gurnard took the bait, the boat being once more going easily along; and for the next quarter of an hour Dick did not get a bite; but at last, as they were rowing along by a rugged part of the coast where the waves foamed and roared among the rocks, tossing the olive-brown sea-weed up and dragging it back, Will bade him look out.

"You'll get a pollack along here perhaps."

For another five minutes, though, there was no sign, and Dick suggested that the bait must be gone.

"Pull it in and see," said Josh.

The lad began to haul, but at the second pull there was a tremendous snatch, the line was dragged from his fingers, and began to run rapidly over the stern.

"Look out!" cried Will.

"I've got him!" cried Dick, snatching at the line again, and holding on though it threatened to cut into his soft white hands. "My! don't he pull! Oh! this is a monster."

"Pull! haul at him! get his nose this way!" roared Josh; and Dick pulled, with the fish darting to right and left, sixty yards away from the boat's stern; but the stress soon began to tell, and it came easier after a time, nearer and nearer, till it was drawn close up, and then Dick, who was boiling over with excitement as he gazed at the great prize he had hooked, became aware that the boat was motionless and that Will was leaning over him ready to deftly insert the new gaff-hook in the fish's gills, and lift it over the side.

"What a beauty!" cried Dick. "Is it the setting sun makes it look like that?"

"No, it's the natural colours," replied Will, taking out the hook and then laying the magnificent fish down upon its side to be admired.

"What is it?" cried Dick.

"A rock pollack," replied Will.

"And she weighs ten pound if she weighs an ounce," cried Josh.

"No, not more than nine, Josh," said Will.

"Ah! well, you've handled her, my lad. Glad you've got such a good un, squire. You see we want strong lines and snooding out here."

"I didn't know you got such beauties as this close to the shore. Oh! I wish father and Taff were here to see it!"

"You must take it home and show them," said Will.

"May I?"

"Why not? You caught it."

"Oh!" cried Dick, who could say no more, and he even failed to think of having a fresh bait put on, as he knelt in the bottom of the boat gazing at his prize, whose sides were gorgeous with golden orange and bronze, darkening off on the back to a deep olive-brown, like sea-weed, while the lower parts of the fish seemed to have been rubbed with burnished brass.

"Is it good to eat?" he cried at last.

"Almost as good as any fish that swims," said Will.

"But it's as beautiful as a gold-fish almost," cried Dick; "quite as beautiful as a carp—more, I think—like those golden tench I once saw. Why, where are you going now?"

"Right out," said Will; "you don't mind, do you? It won't be rough."

"No, I don't mind," said Dick stoutly. "I should not mind if it was rough. At least I wouldn't say I did."

"Hor! hor! hor!" laughed Josh again. "That's right. But it won't be rough. We're going out about two miles straight away now. We ought to have been there by now on the ground."

"But how can you tell where the ground is?" said Dick innocently. "Does it come above water?"

"Do what come above water?" said Josh.

"The ground."

"What ground?"

"Didn't you say you ought to be on the ground?" said Dick. "Of course you mean the bottom of the boat."

"Get out!" said Josh. "The fishing-ground's five fathom under water."

"Then how can you tell when you get there?"

"Bearin's," growled Josh.

Dick looked helplessly at Will, while Josh muttered to himself about "gashly ignorance."

"What are bearings?" said Dick at last.

"I'll show you," said Will, "when we get out there by and by. We have to guide ourselves, you know, out at sea by—"

"Compass. I know," cried Dick.

"Ah! that's out of sight of land," said Will quietly. "Along shore we sail by bearings that we take—hills and points and trees, so as to lay the boat where we like."

"But I don't see how you can," cried Dick.

"Don't you?" said Will good-humouredly, while Josh went on growling to himself and looking disgusted down between his knees. "Well, I'll try and show you. Now, you look right behind you and you can see that we're opening out that old chimney on the top of Toll Pen."

"Opening out!" said Dick. "I don't know what you mean."

"Well, beginning to see it come into sight."

"Oh! now I know," cried Dick. "I say, is there anything the matter with him?" he added, for Josh was rumbling with indignation at their visitor's "gashly ignorance."

"No, there arn't," growled Josh roughly. "Only they did ought to teach you something at school."

"They do," said Dick, laughing merrily; "but they don't know anything about bearings and openings out, and such things. It's all Latin, and Greek, and algebra, and Euclid."

"And none o' them won't teach you how to lay a boat to her bearin's on a bit o' good fishing-ground," said Josh; "and it's a good job for you, my lad, as you've run acrost us. We will teach you something afore we've done."

"Why, you have already," cried Dick. "I say, are you tired? Shall I help you now?"

"Tired? No, lad, not us. No. There, you keep your eye on that old chimney. Tell him, Will, how to find the ground."

"All right!" said Will. "Well, you see that pile of stones on the top of the hill behind the chimney to the right?"

"What, a rough bit like a lump of sugar on a loaf of bread?"

"That's it!" said Will. "Now, you see those, as we row out, seem to grow closer together?"

"Yes, I see, because you're getting them more in a straight line."

"To be sure!" said Will. "Well, then, when we get them exactly one in front of the other, they give us our bearings one way."

"Oh!" said Dick.

"Now, look yonder at that church tower at Gullick," said Will.

"Yes, I see it."

"There's a big tree on the hill to the left of it."

"Six," said Dick.

"No, no, not that clump; but that one standing by itself."

"Yes, I see."

"Well, when the church is right before that tree it gives us the bearings the other way."

"I think I see," said Dick dubiously; "but I'm not sure."

"It's easy enough," said Will. "You'll soon see. Now look out—the mine chimney over the cairn, and Gullick church in front of the big tree, and there we are right on our fishing-ground."

They rowed on for another quarter of an hour, watching the chimney and church, which seemed to glide more and more over the distant points till, full of excitement as he began to comprehend more fully the little simple problem learned by fishermen without instruments or books, he waited till he thought that the various points must be exactly coinciding, and called out to those who were rowing behind him as he looked over the stern:

"It's now, isn't it—now?"

"Now it is," said Josh, as there was a splash in the water and the rattling of a rope over the gunwale.

Dick had well learned his first lesson in taking bearings, and called out at the exact moment, just as Josh was in the act of throwing over the little anchor and buoy, to which the long-line, or "bolter," was to be made fast.

Here is the problem in mathematical lines:

Which being explained is that A represents the old mine chimney, B the cairn, C Gullick Church, and D the tree. The boat was rowed till A and B were in a straight line, and C and D were also in a straight line. This would place the boat at E, the fishing-ground, which they could always find by these simple means.

Chapter Twelve.

The Catching of many Fish, and the Getting Caught themselves.

It was a glorious evening, the aspect of the bay being grand, lit up as it was by the golden light of the setting sun. Distant windows glowed like fire; the rugged Cornish hills were like amber; and sea and sky were gorgeous with brilliant hues.

"Oh! I do like this!" cried Dick. "I wish poor old—but you will bring him next time. Now, then, what shall I do?"

"Sit still," said Josh gruffly, "and see him pay out the line."

Dick felt snubbed; but on glancing at Will he was met by a friendly nod as the lad busied himself in making fast one end of the line, coiled up in the basket, to the buoy-rope, and then, as Josh took both oars, fixed his eyes upon a point on land, and began to row slowly due south, Will let the line run over the side.

It was no easy task, and it required co-operation on the part of him at the oars, for every now and then, in spite of the care with which the line had been coiled, and the hooks regularly baited and laid in place, there would be a disposition to kink, and for hooks to catch and go down tangled with each other. But Josh always had an eye for this, and was ready to ease the boat's progress, or in a bad case to back water, while Will's quick clever fingers pounced upon every hitch, shook out the line, and sent it down fathom after fathom with its hooks and baits clear to lie upon the bottom.

"Shall I—shall I hinder you if I talk?" said Dick at last, when about half the line was out.

"Hinder! No," cried Will; "talk away."

"Why didn't you put the line down there where we caught that beautiful —what was it—pollack?"

"Because the bottom was all rocks, and we should have lost the line. Besides, it isn't a good place for long-line fish."

"Oh!" said Dick; and he was silent, watching the line go over, and the baits seem to dart down through the dark clear water and disappear, while Josh rowed on and on, with his eyes now on the line-basket, now on the land, his forehead wrinkled, and his countenance as solemn as if this were the most serious venture of his life.

And what a wonderful sight it was! The waters of that great bay turning to topaz, and then to ruby, as if the oars were plashing up wine, which bubbled and foamed as the boat went slowly on, while close down in the shadow, where Will lowered the line, all was of a dark transparent slate.

Down went bait after bait, coil after coil of the line, till the uneven rings in the basket grew fewer—fewer still—then there were only three or four—two—one.

"Avast!" shouted Josh, throwing in his oars and dropping another little grapnel anchor overboard, which ran out so much rope. Then a little tub buoy was passed after it, and Josh held on by the ring, while Will fastened the line to the rope, dropped it, and as the last bait rested on the bottom, turned with satisfied face to the visitor.

"There!" he said; "that's done."

"But you did not tell me why you came here to lay the line," said Dick.

"'Cause it's a good place," growled Josh.

"Yes; it's a long even bank of sand, all about the same depth, five or six fathoms; and the flat-fish lie here a good deal."

"And the trawler can't touch 'em, 'cause there's a rock here and there as would stop their net."

"I see," said Dick dubiously. Then, determined to know all—"No, I don't quite see," he said. "I don't know what you mean by the crawler."

"Trawler, lad—trawler. I didn't say crawler," cried Josh. "A mussy me!" he added softly.

"Well, trawler, then. What's a trawler?"

"Fore-an'-aft rig boat."

"Oh, I say!" cried Dick merrily, "it's all like Dutch to me. How am I to know what a fore-an'-aft rig boat is?"

"A mussy me!" groaned Josh, to Will's great delight; "how your eddication have been neglected! Don't you know what rig means?"

"Yes; the rigging of a ship."

"Or a boat," said Josh. "Well, don't you know what fore-and-aft means?"

"Not unless it's before and after, or behind."

"It ain't no before and no after; it's fore-and-aft," growled Josh.

"He's quite right, Josh," said Will, taking his new friend's side; "fore means before, or forward, and aft means after, or behind."

"Oh! very well; have it your own way," said Josh, putting a pellet of tobacco in his mouth. "I call it fore-and-aft."

"That's right too, Josh. Look here, sir, we call the rig of a boat or ship fore-and-aft when the sails are flat, like they are in a cutter or sloop or schooner. When I say flat I mean stretching from the front of the vessel to the stern; and we call it square-rigged when the sails are put across."

"Then there's lug-sails like them," said Josh, pointing to some fishing-boats, whose brown sails stood out against the amber sky; "and there's lots of other rigs as well."

"Yes; but what's a trawler?" cried Dick.

"It's a fore-and-aft rigged boat that trawls," said Will. "She has a great net like a big night-cap stretched over on a spar, which we call a trawl-beam, and this is lowered down, and as the boat sails it is dragged along the bottom, and catches soles, and turbot, and plaice and sometimes john-dory, and gurnet, and brill. They like sandy banks, such as this is; and if there were no rocks the trawler would soon sweep this clean."

"On'y, they can't run their trawl along here a-cause o' the rocks," said Josh.

"Which would catch the net, and they'd p'r'aps lose it."

"But they might fish it up again."

"Oh, yes! I daresay they would," replied Will with a smile.

"I say," cried Dick, "I wish you wouldn't call things by such names. What's a creeper?"

"These are creepers that we've just put down; grapnels."

"Ah, we call them drags in London," said Dick. "I say, I should like to go in a trawler."

"Well, you easily can," replied Will, "if you are going to stay here."

"Think you've got a bite yet?"

"What, at the baits? Let's try."

Josh was already putting the boat about, and was beginning to row back over the same ground towards the first buoy.

75

"Oh, you're going to try there first!" said Dick.

"Of course, where the line has been down longest," said Will. "See how the tide flows."

"Does it?" responded Dick, staring.

"Yes; can you see that Josh has to pull harder with one oar than with the other, or else we should be carried right away from the buoy? The line's set right across the tide."

"Is it? Why?"

"So as to be ready for the fish that come up with the tide to feed. Look at that."

"Why, it rains," cried Dick. "No, it don't. Why, the water's all of a patter. It's fish rising."

"Little school o' mack'rel," said Josh. "They'll be seeing o' them from up the cliff bime-by."

"And does a *school* of mackerel always play about on the top like that?" said Dick, watching the dappled water where the fish were swimming close to the surface.

"Not it, lad. They're oftener down below. Look at the mews coming after 'em."

He nodded in the direction of half a dozen grey gulls which came flapping towards them, and as the school passed off to the left and the boat bore to the right Dick could see the flap-winged birds keep dipping down with a querulous cry, splash the water, and ascend again.

"They're after the brill," said Will.

"Brill!"

"Yes; the small fish that the mackerel are feeding on. They keep snatching them up from the top of the water. Little fish about half as big as sprats. Look at them, you can almost see the little fish they catch. There, that fellow has got a good one."

And so they watched the evolutions of the gulls for a few minutes, till Josh called out "*Avast!*" and Dick turned, to find that they were back at the first buoy.

"Now, then, are you ready?" said Will.

"Yes," cried Dick.

"Take Josh's gaff then, and you shall hook in the first big one."

Will's sleeves were rolled up above the elbow, and the line was drawn up over the boat, which was so placed that the line was across it, Josh helping with one oar, while Will hauled at the line, drawing it up one side and letting it go down again on the other.

First bait untouched, and passed on to descend on the other side. Second bait gone, and replaced by a fresh piece of squid from the basket. Third bait gone, and replaced, to descend on the other side. Then four baits untouched, six more gone, taken off.

"Why, if you'd been ready to strike, you might have had all these fish when they began to bite," cried Dick.

"P'r'aps so," said Will. "Maybe it was only the crabs that bit the baits off."

And all the time he kept on hauling in the line and examining the hook till they were a long way on towards the farther buoy.

"Oh, I say," cried Dick at last, "this isn't half such good sport as—what do you call it?—whiffing."

"Think not?" said Will.

"Yes, that I do. I should have thought you would have caught lots of fish with a line like this."

"So we do," cried Josh, "sometimes."

"I wish you'd catch something now," said Dick in a disappointed tone.

"Here you are then," cried Will, laughing as he hauled on at the line; "a big one."

"Where, where?" cried Dick, ready with the hook.

"Down below here; I can feel him."

"Let me haul him in."

"No, no," said Will. "You'd better let me. You'll get too wet. Be ready with the hook."

"Yes, yes, I am," cried Dick, more excitedly than ever.

But he began to look disappointed as he saw three bare hooks drawn out, all of which Will baited and passed on, to fall into the sea on the other side.

"Why, there can't be," began Dick. "Yes, there he is; I can see him."

"Yes, here he comes," said Will, hauling strongly now as a great quivering grey object changing to white could be seen below. "Ready with the hook! slip it into him anywhere, and haul him aboard. Never mind a bit of splashing."

But Dick did flinch for a few moments as something came to the surface, beating, flapping, and sending the water flying; while before the lad had recovered from his surprise, Josh had bent forward, taken the hook, and lifted the great fish on board just as it freed itself from the hook, and lay floundering at the bottom of the boat.

"Skate," cried Dick. "What a monster!"

"No," cried Will, coolly rebaiting the hook; "it's his first cousin. That's a thornback. Mind his prickles."

The great ugly sharky fish was hooked forward by Josh and placed in a great basket, where it lay writhing its eely tail, and flapping its wing-like fins as the boat slowly progressed, and bait after bait was replaced, many being untouched, the thornback, skate, or ray being the only fish taken.

"But he's a very big one," said Dick, seeking to make up for the disappointment.

"Yes, she's big enough," said Josh; "but they don't pay for taking."

"Better luck next run down," said Will, as they rowed back to the first buoy, he helping this time with an oar. "The fish feed better when it begins to be dusk; they can't see the line."

"But they would not be able to see the bait."

"Then they would smell it," said Will. "Fish generally feed best in the dark."

The buoy was reached, and the line once more hauled aboard, this time with a grey gurnard on the first hook. The second was bare. The third and fourth both had gurnards upon them. Then there was an untouched bait, and then a very large plaice, dotted with orange spots, whose appearance made Josh grunt with satisfaction. Next came a large sole, then a small one, and again a large sole, after which there was a long array of empty hooks, and Dick began to feel dissatisfied, for there was no work for the gaff-hook.

"Here's a conger, I think," said Will suddenly.

"A conger!" cried Dick excitedly, as he began to think of gigantic creatures like sea-serpents.

"Yes, a small one. Get your knife, Josh."

The latter opened his big knife, and as a great eel about three feet long was drawn over the side they did not trouble to extract the hook which was swallowed right down; but Josh cut the string of the snooding close to the living creature's jaws, and let it drop in the boat, about which it began to travel serpent-fashion to Dick's great discomfort.

"She won't hurt you," said Josh, "unless you put your finger in her mouth. She can bite, but not like the big ones."

"But is this a conger?" said Dick, watching the slimy creature as it sought for a hiding-place, and strove to get under the grating in the bottom of the boat.

"Conger! To be sure it is," said Will.

"But I thought congers were very big."

"They grow big, of course," said Will smiling.

"But this may be only a large eel. They do go in the sea, you know."

"Oh, yes! I know they do; but river eels don't have eyes like this. Look at them," he said, pointing to the creature's huge eyes. "Sea fish nearly all have very large eyes, so as to see deep down at the bottom. Here's something better. Now try and gaff this."

"Why, it's another skate," cried Dick, determined this time not to give up the hook; and as the large round white fish came up fighting hard against capture he made a dash at it and hooked it firmly, drawing it over the side, to lie flapping in the bottom of the boat.

"That's better," cried Will.

"Cheerily ho, my lad; well done," cried Josh. "That's the way to gawf 'em."

"But it's a turbot," said Dick excitedly. "Why, you don't catch turbots here, and like this?"

"Seems as if we did," said Will laughing, "when we can. We don't often have a bit of luck like this. He's worth seven or eight shillings."

"My father will buy it," cried Dick. "I say, let him have it."

"Oh, he shall have it if he likes," cried Will, as the turbot was thrown into the basket to set the skate flapping, and the gurnards curling their heads round towards their tails like cleaned whiting, and a regular scuffle took place.

Meanwhile the boat was forced on beneath the line and a whiting and a couple of small plaice were taken off. Then more bait had disappeared, and then the last hook was being hauled up when Will snatched at the hook, made a sharp stroke with it, twisted it round, and held it under water for a minute before dragging out a nasty grey-looking bag, all tentacles, and with a couple of ugly eyes, which dropped from the hook as Will gave it a twist.

"Cuttle-fish," he said. "Did you see him squirt out his ink?"

"And make that cloud in the water?" said Dick. "Yes, I saw."

This curious object with its suckers took his attention as they rowed back once more to the first buoy, where once more the line was overrun, the first fish caught being a dog-fish—a long, thin, sharky-looking creature, with its mouth right underneath and back from its snout, and its tail not like that of an ordinary fish, but unequal in the fork, that is to say, with a little lobe and a very large one.

"Game's over," said Josh. "Let's go back and get in the buoy and creeper."

"Yes," assented Will; "it's of no more use to-night."

"Why?" asked Dick.

"Drove of dogs on the bank, my lad," said Josh. "They'll eat every bait we put down. No use to fish any more to-night."

Dick did not believe it, but he said nothing as the first buoy was taken on board, and the little creeper anchor hauled in. Then the oars were laid in, and Josh set to work hauling in the line, leaving the boat to drift, the line being strong enough for them to work it up towards the second buoy, while both took off the baits and the fish—twelve of them, and all dog-fish, to be killed and thrown overboard.

At last the boat was drawn right up to the last buoy, the hooks being all cleaned and laid in place, and the line coiled in its basket, the evening growing dark the while, and the lights twinkling on the shore, when, all at once, as Josh was hauling in the little anchor, Will happened to look up.

"Quick, Josh! oars! pull!"

Dick started and looked up, and as he did so it seemed as if a great black cloud were coming to crush them down.

Chapter Thirteen.

How to bale out a Boat when she's much too full.

Accidents generally happen instantaneously; people are in safety one moment, the next there is a sudden awakening to the fact that something dreadful has happened. It was so here in the coming darkness of night. Almost before the two lads had realised more than the fact that something black was approaching there was a loud rushing noise, a crash, and shock, as the boat was struck a tremendous blow on the side, whirled round, sucked under water, and then all was blackness, choking, strangling sensations, and a horrible sense of dread.

Dick, fresh from London, did not understand what was the matter. For one moment he had an idea that the boat had been attacked by a monstrous whale; the next moment that and every other idea was washed out of him by the dark waters, which ran up his nose and thundered in his ears, as they made him gasp for breath.

How long this lasted he could not tell, before he found himself on the surface, confused and helpless, amidst a sheet of foaming, swirling waters.

"Can you swim?" some one shouted in his ear.

"Ye–es—a—lit-tle," panted Dick.

"Steady then, steady, lad. Slow—slow—take in a reef. You'll drown yourself like a pup if you beat the water that how."

Influenced by the stronger will and the stern order, Dick, who had been striking out with all his might, calmed down and began to swim steadily, but with a great dread seeming to paralyse his limbs, while Josh, who was by him, shouted, "*Ahoy!*"

"Ahoy!" came faintly from a distance, in the direction where the black cloud had resolved itself into the form of a great screw steamer with star-like lights visible here and there.

"Here away, lad," shouted back Josh. "They haven't seen us," he added to Dick.

"What—what was it?" panted Dick, who was swimming more steadily now.

"Big steamer—run us down—ain't seen us—no good to shout," cried Josh. "Steady, lad, steady. We've got to swim ashore."

"Josh, ahoy! Where's young master?" came out of the darkness. And now as Dick grew a little calmer, he fancied he saw pale lambent flashes of light on the water a little distance away.

"Here he be," shouted back Josh. "Steady, boy, steady! Don't tire yourself like that," he added again to Dick.

The latter tried hard to obey, as he now became aware that at every stroke he made the water flashed into pale golden light; tiny dots of cold fire ran hither and thither beneath the surface, and ripples of lambent phosphorescent glow fell off to right and left.

At the same moment almost, he saw, beyond the star-like lanthorns of the steamer, the twinkling lights of the village, apparently at a tremendous distance away, while one strong bright star shed a long ray of light across the water, being the big lamp in the wooden cage at the end of the harbour pier.

"Avast there, Will!" shouted Josh again; "let's overhaul you, and keep together. Seen either o' the buoys?"

"No."

"Why don't they swim ashore?" thought Dick. "Never mind the buoys. Oh! I shall never do it."

A cold chilly feeling of despair came over him, and he began to beat the water more rapidly as his eyes fixed themselves wildly on the far-off lights, and he thought of his father and brother, perhaps waiting for him on the pier.

"Swim slowly," cried another voice close by; and Dick's heart gave a leap. "It's a long way, but we can do it."

"Can you?" panted poor Dick, who was nearly exhausted. "How far is it?"

"About two miles, but the tide's with us."

"I can't do it," panted Dick, "not a hundred yards."

"Yes, you can," said Will firmly. "Only just move your arms steady, and let the tide carry you along. Josh," he said more loudly, "keep close here."

"Ay, lad, I will," replied the fisherman; and the calm, confident tones of his companions, who spoke as if it were a matter of course to swim a couple of miles, encouraged the lad a little; but his powers and his confidence were fast ebbing away, and it was not a matter of many minutes before he would have been helpless.

For even if the sea had been perfectly smooth, he was no experienced swimmer, his efforts in this direction having been confined to a dip in the river when out on fishing excursions, or a bit of a practice in some swimming-bath at home. But the sea was not perfectly smooth, for the swift tide was steadily raising the water into long, gently heaving waves, which carried the swimmers, as it were, up one minute to the top of a little ridge, and then sank them the next down, down, out of sight, into what seemed to be profound darkness whenever the pier light was blotted out.

"I—I—can't keep on," panted Dick at last, with a piteous cry. "Tell father—"

He could say no more, for, striking out feebly, he had allowed his mouth to sink beneath the surface, and breathing in a quantity of strangling water he began to beat the surface, and then felt himself seized.

Involuntarily, and with that natural instinct that prompts the drowning to cling to anything they touch, Dick's hands clutched despairing at the stout arm that came to his help, but only to feel himself shaken off and snatched back, so that his face was turned towards the stars.

"Float! Hold still! Hands under water!" a voice yelled in his ear; and half stunned, half insensible, he obeyed, getting his breath better at times, at others feeling the strangling water sweep over his face.

It was a time of great peril, but there was aid such as neither Josh nor Will had counted upon close at hand.

"I'll keep him afloat till I'm tired," Josh had said hoarsely, "and then you must have a turn. You can manage to make the shore, can't you?"

"Yes," said Will; "but we—we mustn't leave him, Josh."

"Who's going to?" growled Josh fiercely. "You keep aside me."

They swam on, every stroke making the water flash, and the phosphorescence, like pale golden oil, sweep aside and ripple and flow upon the surface. The sky was now almost black but quite ablaze with stars, and the big lamp at the pierhead sent its cheery rays out, as if to show them the way to go, but in the transparent darkness it seemed to be miles upon miles away, while the sturdy swimmers felt as if they got no nearer, toil as they might.

"I'm going to give him over to you, lad," said Josh in his sing-song voice, for he had calmed down now. "I'll soon take him again, lad, but —"

"Hooray, Josh!" cried back Will; and he struck off to the left.

"What is it, lad?"

"Boat! the boat!"

Josh wrenched himself up in the water, and looked over Dick, to see, dimly illumined by the golden ripples of the water, the outline of the boat, flush with the surface, its shape just seen by the phosphorescence, and he bore towards it.

"T'other side, Will, lad," cried Josh as he swam vigorously over the few intervening yards, half drowning Dick by forcing his head under water again and again; but as he reached the boat's side, which was now an inch or two above, now the same distance below, he drew the lad flat on the surface, passed his hands beneath him, got hold of the gunwale, and half rolled Dick in, half drew the boat beneath him.

"Mind he don't come out that side, lad," shouted Josh.

"Ay, ay!" And then Will held on by one side of the sunken boat, while Josh held on the other.

So slight was the buoyancy of the filled boat that the slightest touch in the way of pressure sent it down, and Dick could have drowned as easily there as in the open sea, but that, feeling something hard beneath him, a spark of hope shot to his brain, and he began to struggle once more.

"Keep still," shouted Will. "Lie back with your head on the gunwale;" and Dick obeyed, content to keep his face just above water so that he might breathe.

"It arn't much help, but it are a bit of help, eh, lad?" panted Josh. "Way oh! Steady!"

"Yes, it is a rest, Josh," panted back Will, whose spirits rose from somewhere about despair-point to three degrees above hope; but in his effort to get a little too much support from that which was not prepared to give any, he pressed on the gunwale at his side, and sent it far below the surface, drawing from Josh the warning shout, "Way oh! Steady!"

The slightest thing sent the gunwale under—in fact, the pressure of a baby's hand would have been sufficient to keep it below the surface; but the experienced swimmers on either side knew what they were about, and after seeing that Dick's face was above water, and without any consultation, both being moved by the same impulse, they threw themselves on their backs beside the sunken boat, one with, his head towards her stem, the other head to stern, and after a moment's pause each took hold of the gunwale lightly with his left hand, his right being free, and then they waited till they began to float upward.

"Ready, lad?" said Josh.

"Ready," cried Will.

"Both together, then."

Then there was a tremendous splashing as each turned his right-hand into a scoop and began to throw out the water with a skilful rapid motion somewhat similar to the waving of the fin of a fish; and this they kept up for quite five minutes, when Josh shouted again:

"Easy!"

There was not much result. They had dashed out a tremendous quantity of water, but nearly as much had flowed in again over the sides, as in their efforts they had sometimes dragged down the gunwale a little. Besides which a little wave had now and then broken against one or the other and sent gallons of water into the boat.

Still they had done something, and after a rest Josh cried again:

"Ready? Go ahead."

Once more the splashing began, the water flying out of the boat like showers of liquid gold; and just when the hand-paddles were in full play the boat began to move slightly, then a little more. Neither Josh nor Will knew why, for they could not see that it sank a little lower for a few minutes and then began to rise.

"Hooray!" cried Josh hoarsely. "Well done, young un; out with it. Hooray! Oh, look at that!"

He had just awakened to the fact that Dick had come to himself sufficiently to alter his position, and was lending his aid by scooping out the water with both hands till a wave came with a slight wash and half demolished all their work.

"Keep on," shouted Will; and once more the splashing went forward at a tremendous rate.

A handful of water, or as much as it will throw, out of a full boat is not much; but when three hands are busy ladling with all their might a tremendous amount of water can be baled out, and so it was, that when the balers rested again there were three inches of freeboard, as sailors call it, and the next wave did not lessen it a quarter of an inch.

"Ready again?" cried Josh. "Go ahead, youngster."

The splashing went on once more; and now both Will and Josh could support themselves easily by holding on to the gunwale, the boat increasing in buoyancy every moment, while three hands scooped out the water with long and vigorous well-laden throws.

It became easier for Dick too now, for he found that he could sit astride one of the thwarts, holding on in position by twisting his legs beneath; and this gave him power to use both hands, which he joined together and scooped out the water in pints that became quarts, gallons, and bucketsfull.

"Hooray!" cried Josh with a cheer, and there was a few minutes' rest. "A mussy me! it's child's play now. Look here; s'pose you roll out now and take my place. No: go out on Will's side and hold on by him while I get in."

Dick shivered at the idea. It seemed so horrible to give up his safe position and trust to the sea once more. But he did not hesitate long.

Taking tight hold of the bulwark, he literally rolled over the side and let himself down into the sea, with the phosphorescence making his body, limbs, and feet even, visible like those of his companion. But there was no time to study the wonders of Nature then, or even look at the way in which the keel of the boat was illumined by myriads of golden points.

"Hold on! Steady! Keep her down!" cried Josh; and then, as the two lads clung to the gunwale they were raised right up, as there was a wallow and a splash; the opposite side went down so low that it began to ship water, but only for a moment; Josh had given a spring, and rolled in over the side.

"Now, then, leave him there, Will, lad, and work round, by her starn. I'll soon have some of the water out now."

He began feeling about as he spoke with his hands beneath the thwarts forward, and directly after he uttered a cry of joy.

"Here she be," he said, tearing out the half of a tin bucket that had held the bait. "Now we'll do some work."

86

As he spoke he began dipping and emptying, pouring nearly a gallon of water over the side at every turn; and in ten minutes, during which he had laboured incessantly, he had made such a change that he bade Will come in.

"Now you can bale a bit," he said. "My arms are about dead."

Will climbed in and took the bucket, scooping out the water with all his might, while Josh bent over Dick.

"You're 'bout perished, my lad. Come along."

He placed his hands under Dick's arm-pits, and though he said that his own arms were about dead he hoisted the boy in almost without an effort, and then left him to help himself, while he resumed baling with his hands, scooping out the water pretty fast, and each moment lightening the little craft.

"Good job we'd no stone killicks aboard, Will," he said, "or down she'd have gone."

"There's the buoys too wedged forward," said Will; "they have helped to keep her up."

"'Bout balanced the creepers," said Josh. "It's a question of a pound weight at a time like this. There, take it steadily, my lads. We're safe now, and can see that the tide's carrying of us in. Lights look bigger, eh?"

"Yes," said Will, who was working hard with his baler. "Where shall we drive ashore?"

"Oh! pretty close to the point," cried Josh. "I say, youngster, this is coming fishing, eh?"

"Oh! it is horrible," said Dick, piteously.

"Not it, lad," cried Josh. "It's grand. Why, we might ha' been drownded, and, what's wuss, never washed ashore."

Dick shivered as much from cold as misery, and gazed in the direction of the lights.

"Wonder what steamer that was as run us down!" said Josh, as the vessel he used to bale began now to scrape the wood at the bottom of the boat.

"French screw," replied Will. "An English boat would have kept a better look-out. Why, you are cold!" he added, as he laid his hand on Dick.

"Ye–es," said the latter with a shudder. "It is horribly cold. Shall we ever get ashore?"

"Ashore! yes," cried Josh. "Why, they'd be able, 'most to hear us now. Let's try."

Taking a long breath, he placed both hands to his cheeks, and then gave vent to a dismal hail—a hail in a minor key—the cry of the sailor in dire peril, when he appeals to those on shore to come to his help, and save him from the devouring storm-beaten sea.

"Ahoy—ah!" the last syllable in a sinking inflexion of the voice a few seconds after the first.

Then again:

"Ahoy—ah!"

He went on baling till no more water could be thrown out, and the boat drifted slowly on with the tide.

Away to their left there rose the lamp-lit windows and the pier light. Lower down, too, were a couple of dim red lamps, one above the other, telling of the little dock; but no answer came from the shore.

"There's sure to be some one on the cliff, Josh; hail again," said Will.

"Ay, if we had a flare now, we should bring out the life-boat to fetch us in," cried Josh. "Why, Will lad, we shall be taken a mile away from the town, and perhaps out to sea again. I wish I had an oar."

"Ahoy—ah!"

Then again and again; and still there was no response, while they drifted slowly on over the sea, which looked to Dick, as he gazed down into its depths, alive with tiny stars, and these not the reflections of those above.

"Ahoy—ah!" shouted Josh again, with all the power of his stentorian lungs.

"They're all asleep," he growled; "we shall have to drift ashore and walk home. If I only had one oar I'd scull her back in no time. Ahoy—ah!"

Still no response, and the boat floated on beneath the wondrous starry sky, while every time those in the boat made the slightest movement a golden rippling film seemed to run from her sides, and die away upon the surface of the sea.

"She brimes a deal," said Josh, in allusion to the golden water; and then, leaping up, he began to beat his breast with his arms; "I'm a-cold!" he exclaimed. "Now, then; let's have a try;" and, placing his hands to his face once more, he uttered a tremendous hail.

"Ahoy—ah!"

Long drawn out and dismal; and then Dick's heart gave a quick hopeful leap, for, from far away, and sounding faint and strange, came an answering hail, but not like Josh's dismal appeal. It was a sharp, short, cheery "*Ahoy!*" full of promise of action.

"They've heard us at last!" cried Will eagerly. "That's the coastguard, and they'll come off in their gig, as it's so smooth."

"I say," said Josh, in his low sing-song way; "haven't I put it too strong? They'll think somethin' 'orrid's wrong—that it's a wreck, or somethin' worse."

"Let them!" cried Will. "It's horrible enough to be afloat in an open boat in the dark without oar or sail. Hail again, Josh."

"Ahoy—ah!" cried the fisherman once more, and an answer came back at once. Then another and another.

"They'll soon get a boat," cried Will. "You listen."

"But they'll never find us in the dark!" cried Dick dismally.

"Oh, won't they!" cried Josh; "they'd find us if we was only out in a pork tub. Lor'a mussy me, youngster, you don't know our Cornish lads!"

"We shall keep on hailing now and then," said Will, whose teeth were chattering in spite of his cheery tones.

"Ahoy—oy—oy!"

Very distinct but very distant the shouting of a numerous crowd of people; and now, like the tiniest and faintest of specks, lights could be seen dancing about on the shore, while all at once, one star, a vivid blue star, burst out, burning clear and bright for a few minutes, making Dick gaze wonderingly ashore.

"Blue light," said Will.

"To hearten us up a bit, and say the boat's coming!" cried Josh. "Ahoy —ah! Let 'em know which way to row."

Josh shouted from time to time, and then Will gave a shout or two; and there were answering shouts that seemed to come nearer, and at last plain enough there was the light of a lanthorn rising and falling slowly, telling of its being in a boat that was being propelled by stout rowers.

"Why, my father's sure to be in that boat!" cried Dick suddenly. "He'll have been frightened about me, and have come off to see."

"Shouldn't wonder," said Josh. "I should if I had a boy."

"You shall hail when they get nearer," said Will. "They couldn't hear you yet."

"I wish he could!" cried Dick. "He'll have been in such trouble. Oh, I know!"

He had suddenly remembered a little silver whistle that was attached to his chain, and placing it to his lips he blew upon it a shrill ear-piercing scream.

"There, I knew he would be!" cried Dick joyously; and he gave Will a hearty clap upon the shoulder in the eagerness of his delight. For from far away, where the dim light rose and fell upon the waters, there came an answering shrill chirruping whistle.

Then Dick gave two short whistles.

Two exactly similar came in response.

"I knew he would be," cried Dick; "but he'll be very angry, I suppose."

"Uncle Abram will be there too, I should say," said Will quietly.

"Why, your father won't be angry, my lad," said Josh after a few minutes' thought. "If he be it'll be with Josh, which is me, for not keeping a bright lookout. He can't row you for being run down, for you wasn't neither captain nor the crew. Hillo! ahoy—ah!" he answered in return to a hail.

"I say!" said Dick suddenly; "the lights are going the other way."

"Right, my lad; and so they have been this quarter hour past."

"Why's that?" said Dick.

"Because the tide's ebbing fast."

"And what does that mean?" cried Dick.

"As if they didn't overhaul us we should be carried out to sea."

"But will they find us, Will?"

"No fear of that. See how plain the light's getting. Ahoy—ah! ahoy—ah!

They're not above a quarter of a mile away."

Soon after the dipping of the oars could be seen as they threw up the lambent light in flashes, while an ever-widening track of sparkling water was plain to the eyes. Then the voices came asking questions.

"Ahoy! Who's aboard there?"

"Young gent Dick!" yelled Josh back.

"Who else?"

"Will Marion!"

"Who else? Is that Josh?"

"Ahoy, lad!"

"Hurrah!" came from the boat three times, and the oars made the water flash again as they were more vigorously plied.

"That's your sort, Master Dick!" cried Josh. "That's Cornish, that is! They chaps is as glad at finding us as—as—as—"

"We should be at finding them," said Will.

"Ay; that's it!"

And so it seemed, for a few minutes more and the boat was alongside, and the wet and shivering fishers were seated in the stern-sheets, wrapped in oilskins and great-coats, their boat made fast behind, and Dick's hand tight in that of his father, who said no word of reproach; while, after a long pull against tide, with the boat towing behind, they were landed at the head of the little harbour, where a crowd of the simple-hearted folk, many having lanthorns, saluted them with a hearty cheer, and any amount of hospitality bright have been theirs.

For these dwellers by the sea, who follow their daily toil upon the treacherous waters, are always ready with their help, to give or take in the brotherly way that has long been known in the fishing villages upon the Cornish shores.

Chapter Fourteen.

Dick Temple finds it unpleasant for another to learn to smoke.

There was too much to do in seeing that Dick was not likely to suffer from his long exposure for his father to say much to him that night. But there was a little conversation between Dick and Arthur, who slept in the same room.

It was after the candle was out, Arthur having received strict injunctions to go quietly to bed and not disturb his brother, who was said to be in a nice sleep and perspiring well.

This is what the doctor said, for he had been fetched and had felt Dick's pulse. He had looked very grave and shaken his head, saying that fever might supervene, and ended by prescribing a stimulus under another name, and a hot bath.

"Just as if I hadn't sucked up water enough to last me for a month!" Dick had said.

The people at the little hotel thought it unnecessary to send for a doctor, and when he came the doctor thought so too; but he omitted to make any remarks to that effect, contenting himself with looking very grave, and treating Dick as if his was a very serious case indeed.

And now the patient was lying snugly tucked up in bed, with only his nose and one eye visible, with the exception of a tuft of his hair, and Arthur was undressing in the dark, and very carefully folding up his clothes.

He had been deliberately undressing himself, brushing his hair, and going generally through a very niggling performance for nearly half an hour before Dick spoke, for the latter was enjoying the fun, as he called it, "of listening to old Taff muddling about in the dark, instead of jumping into bed at once."

At last, however, he spoke:

"I'm not asleep, Taff."

"Not asleep!" cried his brother. "What! haven't you been asleep?"

"No."

"What! not all the time I've been undressing?"

"No."

"Then it was very deceitful of you to lie there shamming."

"Didn't sham," said Dick.

"Yes, you did, and pretended that you were very ill."

"No, I didn't. I didn't want the doctor fetched."

"But why did you pretend to be asleep?"

"I didn't, I tell you. I only lay still and watched you fumbling about and taking so long to undress."

"Oh, did you?" said Arthur haughtily. "Well, now lie still, sir, and go to sleep. You are ill."

"No, I'm not," cried Dick cheerily; "only precious hot."

"Then if you are not ill you ought to be ashamed of yourself," said Arthur pettishly; "causing papa so much anxiety."

"Why, I think I behaved well," said Dick, chuckling to himself. "If I had taken you with me I should have given father twice as much trouble and worry."

"Taken me! Why, I should not have gone," said Arthur haughtily; "and if you had not been so fond of getting into low company all this would not have happened."

"Get out with your low company! There was nothing low about those two fishermen."

"I only call one of them a boy," said Arthur, yawning.

"Oh, very well: boy then. But I say, Taff, I wish you had been there."

"Thank you. I was much better at home."

"I mean while we were fishing. I caught such lovely mackerel, and a magnificent Polly something—I forget its name—all orange and gold and bronze, nine or ten pound weight."

"Stuff!" said Arthur contemptuously.

"But I did, I tell you."

"Then where is it?"

"Where is it? Oh, I don't know. When the steamer ran us down the fish and the tackle and all went overboard, I suppose. I never saw it again."

"Then you lost all the sprats," said Arthur sneeringly.

"Sprats! Get out, you sneering old Taff! You are disappointed because you didn't go with us. Why, there was a big turbot, and a sole or two, and a great skate with a prickly back, and gurnards and dog-fish."

"And cats?" sneered Arthur.

"No, there were no cats, Taff. I say, though, I wish you had been there, only not when we got into trouble. I'll get Josh and Will to take you next time we go."

"Next time you go!" echoed Arthur. "Why, you don't suppose that papa will let you go again?"

"Oh, yes, I do," said Dick, yawning and speaking drowsily. "Because a chap falls off a horse once, nobody says he isn't to ride any more. You'll see: father will let me go. I don't suppose—we should—should—what say?"

"I didn't speak," said Arthur haughtily. "There, go to sleep."

"Go to sleep!" said Dick. "No—not bit sleepy. I—I'm—very comfortable, though, and—and—Ah!"

That last was a heavy sigh, and Arthur Temple lay listening to his brother's deep regular breathing for some minutes, feeling bitter and hurt at all that had taken place that day, and as if he had been thrust into a very secondary place. Then he, too, dropped asleep, and he was still sleeping soundly when Dick awoke, to jump out of bed and pull up the blind, so that he could look out on the calm sea, which looked pearly and grey and rosy in the morning sunshine. Great patches of mist were floating here and there, hiding the luggers and shutting out headlands, and everywhere the shores looked so beautiful that the lad dressed hurriedly, donning an old suit of tweed, the flannels he had worn the day before being somewhere in the kitchen, where they were hung up to dry.

"I'd forgotten all about that," said Dick to himself. "I wonder where Will Marion is, and whether he'd go for a bathe."

Dick looked out on the calm sea, and wondered how anything could have been so awful looking as it seemed the night before.

"It must have been out there," he thought, as he looked at the sun-lit bay, then at the engine-houses far up on the hills and near the cliff, and these set him thinking about his father's mission in Cornwall.

"I wonder whether father will begin looking at the mines to-day!" he said to himself. "I should like to know what time it is! I wonder whether Will Marion is up yet, and—Hallo! what's this?"

Dick had caught sight of something lying on the table beside his brother's neat little dressing-case—a small leather affair containing brush, comb, pomatum, and scent-bottles, tooth-brushes, nail-brushes, and the usual paraphernalia used by gentlemen who shave, though

Arthur Temple's face was as smooth as that of a little girl of nine.

Dick took up the something, which was of leather, and in the shape of a porte-monnaie with gilt metal edges, and on one side a gilt shield upon which was engraved, in flourishing letters, "AT."

"Old Taffs started a cigar-case," said Dick, bursting into a guffaw. "I wonder whether—yes—five!" he added, as he opened the case and saw five cigars tucked in side by side and kept in their places by a leather band. "What a game! I'll smug it and keep it for ever so long. He ought not to smoke."

Just then the handle of the door rattled faintly, the door was thrust open, and as Dick scuffled the cigar-case into his breast-pocket Mr Temple appeared, coming in very cautiously so as not to disturb his sick son.

Dick did not know it, but his father had been in four times during the night to lay a hand upon his forehead and listen to his breathing, and he started now in astonishment.

"What, up, Dick?" he said in a low voice, after a glance at the bed, where Arthur was sleeping soundly.

"Yes, father; I was going to have a bathe."

"But—do you feel well?"

"Yes, quite well, father. I'm all right."

Mr Temple looked puzzled for a few minutes, and then rubbed his ear, half-amused, half vexed.

"Don't wake Arthur," he said. "Come along down and we'll have a walk before breakfast."

"All right, father!" cried Dick smiling, and he followed his father out of the room and down-stairs, where they met the landlord.

"All right again then, sir?" said the latter cheerily. "Ah! I thought our salt-water wouldn't hurt him. Rather a rough ride for him, though, first time. When would you like breakfast, sir?"

"At eight," said Mr Temple; and after a few more words he and Dick strolled out upon the cliff.

"Now are you sure, Dick, that you are quite well?" said his father. "Have you any feverish sensations?"

"No, father."

"You don't feel anything at all?"

"No, father. Yes, I do," cried Dick sharply.

"Indeed! what?" cried Mr Temple.

"So precious hungry."

"Oh!" said his father, smiling. "Well, here is one who will find us some refreshment."

He pointed to a man with a large can, and they were willingly supplied each with a draught of milk, after which they bent their steps towards the pier.

"I have my glass, Dick," said Mr Temple, "and I can have a good look at the shore from out there."

"Lend it to me, father," cried Dick eagerly; and quickly focussing it, he directed it at a group of fishermen on their way down to the harbour.

"Yes, there they are," cried Dick eagerly. "There's Josh, and there's Will. I say, father, I don't believe they had the doctor to them last night," he added laughingly. "You were too frightened about me, you know."

"The danger is behind you now, and so you laugh at it, my boy," replied Mr Temple quietly; "but you did not feel disposed to laugh last night when you were drifting in the boat. And, Dick, my boy, some day you may understand better the meaning of the word anxiety."

"Were you very anxious about me last night, father?" said Dick eagerly.

"I was in agony, my boy," said Mr Temple quietly.

Dick's lips parted, and he was about to say something, but the words would not come. His lip quivered, and the tears rose to his eyes, but he turned away his head, thrust his hands down into his pockets, and began to whistle, while his father's brow wrinkled, and, not seeing his boy's face, nor reading the emotion the lad was trying to hide, his face grew more and more stern, while a sensation of mingled bitterness and pain made him silent for some little time.

They walked on in silence, till suddenly Mr Temple's eyes lit upon the top of the gilt-edged cigar-case sticking out of Dick's pocket.

"What have you there, Dick?" he said rather sternly.

"Where, father?"

"In your pocket."

"Nothing, father. My knife and things are in the other clothes. Oh, this!" he said, suddenly remembering the case, and turning scarlet.

"Yes," said Mr Temple severely, "that! Open it."

Dick took the case from his pocket slowly and opened it.

"I thought so," said Mr Temple sternly. "Cigars for a boy not sixteen! Are you aware, sir, that what may be perfectly correct in a man is often in a boy nothing better than a vice."

"Yes, father," said Dick humbly.

"So you have taken to smoking?"

"No, father."

"Don't tell me a falsehood, sir!" cried Mr Temple hotly. "How dare you deny it when you have that case in your hand. Now, look here, sir: I want to treat my boys as lads who are growing into men. I am not going to talk to you about punishment—I don't believe in coarse punishments. I want there to be a manly feeling of confidence between me and my boys."

Dick winced at that word confidence, and he wanted to say frankly that the case belonged to Arthur; but it seemed to him so mean to get out of a scrape by laying the blame upon another; and, besides, he knew how particular his father was about Arthur, and how he would be hurt and annoyed if he knew that his brother smoked.

"I am more angry than I could say," continued Mr Temple; "and I suppose I ought to take away that case, in which you have been foolish enough to spend your pocket-money; but I will not treat my boys as if I were a schoolmaster confiscating their playthings. Don't let me see that again."

"No, father," said Dick, with a sigh of relief, though he felt very miserable, and in momentary dread lest his father should ask him some pointed question to which he would be bound to reply.

They walked on in silence for some minutes, and the beautiful morning and grand Cornish scenery were losing half their charms, when Mr Temple finished his remarks about the cigar-case with:

"Did you smoke yesterday, Dick?"

"No, father?"

"Were you going to smoke to-day?"

"No, father."

"Honour, Dick?"

"Honour, father, and I won't smoke till you tell me I may."

Mr Temple looked at him for a moment, and then nodded his satisfaction.

By this time they were close to the harbour, where, being recognised by several of the fishermen, there was a friendly nod or two, and a smile from first one and then another, and a hearty sing-song "Good-morning!" before they reached the middle of the pier, close up to which the lugger was moored. Josh and Will were upon deck discussing what was to be done to the boat, partly stove in by the steamer on the previous evening; whether to try and patch her up themselves or to let her go to the boat hospital just beyond the harbour head, where old Isaac Pentreath, the boat-builder, put in new linings and put out new skins, and supplied schooners and brigs with knees or sheathing or tree-nail or copper bolt. He could furnish a stranger with boat or yacht to purchase or on hire.

"Mornin', sir!" sang out Josh. "Mornin', Master Richard, sir! None the worse for last night's work, eh?"

"No, I'm all right, Josh," said Dick. "Good-morning, Will! I say, you lost all the fish and the tackle last night, didn't you?"

"We lost all the fish, sir; but the tackle was all right; a bit tangled up, that's all."

"Oars is the worst of it," said Josh, "only they was old uns. Will and me's got a good pair, though, from up at Pentreath's. Game out of a French lugger as was wrecked."

"I want to have a look round at some of the old mine-shafts, my man," said Mr Temple. "Who can you tell me of as a good guide?"

"Josh, sir," said Will.

"Will, sir," said Josh.

"Josh knows all of them for three or four miles round."

"Not half so well as Will, sir. He's always 'vestigatin' of 'em," cried Josh.

"You, my lad?" said Mr Temple, turning sharply on Will, whose brown face grew red.

"Yes, sir; I have a look at them sometimes."

"Prospecting, eh?" said Mr Temple, smiling.

"We could both go if you like, sir," said Josh. "We could row you to Blee Vor, and to Oldman's Wheal and Blackbay Consols and Dynan Reor, and take you over the cliff to Revack and Rendullow and Saint Grant's."

"Why, Dick," said Mr Temple, "we have hit upon the right guides. When will you be at liberty, my lad?"

"Any time, sir, you like. We ain't going out with, our boots for the next few days."

"Not going out with your boots?" said Dick.

"Boots, not boots," said Josh, grinning. "I don't mean boots as you put on your foots, but boots that you sail in—luggers, like this."

"Oh! I see," said Dick.

"A mussy me!" muttered Josh. "The ignoramusness of these here London folk, to *be* sure."

"Could you row me and—say, my two sons—to one of the old mining shafts after breakfast this morning?"

"Think your uncle would mind, Will?" said Josh.

"No," replied Will.

"Of course you will charge me for the hire of the boat," said Mr Temple; "and here, my son ought to pay his share of the damage you met with last night;" and he slipped half a sovereign in Dick's hand—a coin he was about to transfer to Josh, but this worthy waved him off.

"No, no!" he said; "give it to young Will here. It ain't my boot, and they warn't my oars; and very bad ones they were."

"Here, Will, take it," said Dick.

"What for? No, I sha'n't take it," said Will. "The old oars were good for nothing, and we should have cut them up to burn next week. Give Josh a shilling to make himself a new gaff, and buy a shilling's worth of snooding and hooks for yourself. Uncle Abram wouldn't like me to take anything, I'm sure."

Mr Temple did not press the matter, but making a final appointment for the boat to be ready, he returned with Dick to the inn, where they had hardly entered the sitting-room with its table invitingly spread for breakfast, when Arthur came down, red-eyed, ill-used looking, and yawning.

"Oh, you're down first," he said. "Is breakfast ready? I've got such a bad headache."

"Then you had better go and lie down again, my boy," said his father; "nothing like bed for a headache."

"Oh, but it will be better when I have had some breakfast. It often aches like this when I come down first."

"Try getting up a little earlier, Arthur," said Mr Temple. "There, sit down."

The coffee and some hot fried fish were brought in just then, and Arthur forgot his headache, while Dick seemed almost ravenous, his father laughing at the state of his healthy young appetite, which treated slices of bread and butter in a wonderfully mechanical manner.

"Your walk seems to have sharpened you, Dick," he said.

"Oh, yes, I was so hungry."

"Have you been for a walk?" said Arthur, with his mouth full, and one finger on an awkward starchy point of his carefully spread collar.

"Walk? Yes. We've been down to the harbour."

"Making arrangements for a boat to take us to two or three of the old mines."

"You won't go in a boat again—after that accident?" said Arthur, staring.

"Oh, yes! Such accidents are common at the sea-side, and people do not heed them," said Mr Temple. "I'm sorry you will not be well enough to come, Arthur."

Dick looked across the table at him and laughed, emphasising the laugh by giving his brother a kick on the leg; while Arthur frowned and went on with his breakfast, clinging a little to a fancied or very slight headache, feeling that it would be a capital excuse for not going in the boat, and yet disposed to throw over the idea at once, for he was, in spite of a few shrinking sensations, exceedingly anxious to go.

"Oh, by the way, Dick," continued Mr Temple, "I am just going to say a few words more to you before letting the matter drop; and I say them for your brother to hear as well."

Dick felt what was coming, and after a quick glance at Arthur, he hung his head.

"I am taking your word about that cigar-case and its contents, and I sincerely hope that you will always keep your promise in mind. A boy at your age should not even dream of using tobacco. You hear what I am saying, Arthur?"

"Yes, papa," said the latter, who was scarlet.

"Bear it in mind, then, too. I found Dick with a cigar-case in his pocket this morning. I don't ask whether you were aware of it, for I do not want to say more about the matter than to express my entire disapproval of my boys indulging in such a habit."

"Now if Taff's half a fellow he'll speak up and say it was his cigar-case," thought Dick.

But Arthur remained silently intent upon his coffee, while Mr Temple dismissed the subject, and looked smilingly at his boys as the meal progressed.

"Ten minutes, and I shall be ready to start, Dick," said Mr Temple, rising from the table.

"I—I think I'm well enough to go, papa," said Arthur.

"Well enough! But your head?"

"Oh! it's better, much better now."

"But won't you be alarmed as soon as you get on the water? It may be a little rough."

"Oh, I'm not afraid of the water!" said Arthur boldly; and then he winced, for Dick gave him a kick under the table.

"Very well, then," said Mr Temple, "you shall go. But you can't go like that, Arthur. I did not see to your clothes. Haven't you a suit of flannels or tweeds?"

"No, papa."

"How absurd of you to come down dressed like that!"

Arthur coloured.

"You can't go in boats and climbing up and down rocks in an Eton jacket and white collar. Here, Dick, lend him a suit of yours."

"Yes, father," said Dick, who was enjoying what he called the fun.

"Let me see; you have a cap, have you not?"

"No, papa; only my hat."

"What! no straw hat?"

"No, papa."

"My good boy, how can you be so absurd? Now, ask your own common sense—is a tall silk-napped hat a suitable thing to wear boating and inspecting mines?"

"It—it's a very good one, papa," replied Arthur, for want of something better to say.

"Good one! Absurd! Velvet is good, but who would go clambering up cliffs in velvet!"

"Taff would if he might," said Dick to himself, as he recalled his brother's intense longing for a brown silk-velvet jacket, such as he had seen worn by one of his father's friends.

"Dick, go with your brother to the little shop there round the corner. I saw straw hats hanging up. Buy him one. I'm going to write a letter. There, I'll give you a quarter of an hour."

Mr Temple left the room, and as Arthur jumped up, scarlet with indignation, to pace up and down, Dick laid his face upon his arm in a clear place and began to laugh.

"It's absurd," said Arthur in indignant tones. "Your clothes will not fit me properly, and I hate straw hats."

"I wouldn't go," said Dick, lifting his merry face.

"Yes," cried Arthur furiously, "that's just what you want, but I shall go."

"All right! I should like you to come. Go and slip on my flannels; they're sure to be dry by now."

"Slip on your rubbishy old flannels!" cried Arthur contemptuously; "and a pretty guy I shall look. I shall be ashamed to walk along the cliff."

"Nobody will notice you, Taff," said Dick. "Come, I say, look sharp, here's nearly five minutes gone."

"And what's that about the cigars?" said Arthur furiously. "You stole my case."

"I only took it for a bit of fun," said Dick humbly. "I did not think father would have noticed it. You see he thinks it is me who smokes."

"And a good job too! Serve you right for stealing my case."

"But you might have spoken up and said it was yours," said Dick.

"I daresay I should," said Arthur, loftily, "if you had behaved fairly; but now—"

"I say, boys," cried Mr Temple, "I shall not wait."

"Here, you go and slip on my flannels," said Dick. "I'll go and buy you a hat. If it fits me it will fit you."

"Get a black-and-white straw," said Arthur. "I won't wear a white. Such absurd nonsense of papa!"

"Not to let you go boating in a chimney-pot!" said Dick, half to himself, as he hurried off. "What a rum fellow Taff is!"

Unfortunately for the particular young gentleman there were no black-and-white hats, so Dick bought a coarse white straw with black ribbon round it, and then seized the opportunity—as they sold everything at the little shop, from treacle to thread, and from bacon and big boots to hardware and hats—to buy some fishing-hooks and string, finding fault with the hooks as being soft and coarse, but the man assured him that they were the very best for the sea, so he was content.

"See what a disgusting fit these things are!" cried Arthur, as his brother entered.

"Yes; you do look an old guy, Taff," cried Dick maliciously. "Ha! ha! ha! why, they've shrunk with being dried. Here, let's pull the legs down. You've put your legs through too far."

"There! Now what did I tell you?" cried Arthur, angrily. "Look at that now. I distinctly told you to bring a black-and-white straw; I can't wear a thing like that."

"But they had no black and whites," said Dick.

"Stuff and nonsense!" cried Arthur; "they've plenty, and you didn't remember."

"Now, are you ready?" said Mr Temple.

"Yes, papa; but look here," began Arthur in a depressing voice.

"I was looking," said Mr Temple; "I congratulate you upon looking so comfortable and at your ease. Now you can fish, or climb, or do anything. Mind you write home to-night for some things to be sent down. Come away."

Mr Temple went out of the room, and Dick executed a sort of triumphant war-dance round his brother, who frowned pityingly and stalked to the corner of the room, with his nose in the air, to take up his tasselled, silver-mounted cane.

"No, you don't," said Dick, snatching the cane away and putting it back in the corner. "No canes to-day, Dandy Taff, and no gloves. Come along."

He caught his brother's arm, thrust his own through, and half dragged, half thrust him out of the place to where his father was waiting.

"Never mind your gloves, Arthur," said the latter dryly, "or if you particularly wish to keep your hands white, perhaps you had better take care of your face as well, and borrow a parasol."

Arthur reddened and thrust his gloves back into his pockets, as he followed his father down to the little pier; but he was obliged to raise his straw hat from time to time, and smooth his well pomatumed hair, ignorant of the fact that his every act was watched by his brother, who could not refrain from laughing at the little bits of foppishness he displayed.

Chapter Fifteen.

An Exploring Trip along beneath the Cliffs of the Rocky Shore.

Josh and Will were in waiting with the boat, not the one that had been used on the previous night, for it had been determined to send that in to hospital, but a rather larger and lighter boat, belonging to Uncle Abram; and this had been carefully mopped out, with the result that there were not quite so many fish-scales visible, though even now they were sticking tenaciously as acorn barnacles to every level spot.

"All ready, sir," said Will, coming forward; "and my uncle says you're welcome to a boat whenever there's one in, and that as to payment, you're to please give our man Josh a trifle, and that's all."

Mr Temple was about to make an objection, but he determined to see Uncle Abram, as he was called, himself, and he at once went down the steps and into the boat.

"Dick," said Arthur, plucking at his brother's sleeve, "what's that fisher-fellow grinning at? Is there anything particular about my clothes?"

"No. He was only smiling because he was glad to see you. There, go along down."

Josh, who had been spoken of as "that fisher-fellow," endorsed Dick's words by singing just as if it was a Gregorian chant:

"Glad to see you, sir. Nice morning for a row. Give's your hand, sir. Mine looks mucky, but it don't come off. It's only tar."

"I can get down, thank you," said Arthur haughtily, and he began to descend the perpendicular steps to where the boat slowly rose and fell, some six feet below.

But though Arthur descended backwards like a bear, it was without that animal's deliberate caution. He wanted experience too, and the knowledge that the steps, that were washed by every tide, were covered with a peculiar green weedy growth that was very slippery. He was in a hurry lest he should be helped—aid being exceedingly offensive to his dignity, and the consequence was, that when he was half-way down there was a slip and a bang, caused by Arthur finishing his descent most rapidly, and going down in a sitting position upon the bottom of the boat.

"I say," said Josh, "if that had been your foots you'd ha' gone through."

Arthur leaped up red as a turkey-cock, and in answer to his father's inquiry whether he was hurt, shook his head violently.

"Don't laugh, Will, don't look at him," said Dick, stifling his own mirth and turning his back, pretending to draw Will's attention to the fishing cord and hooks he had bought.

"All right, Master Dick!" said Will cordially; and he began to examine the hooks; but Arthur could see through the device and, kindly as it was meant, he chafed all the more. In fact, he had hurt himself a good deal, but his dignity was injured more.

"Yes, they're the best," said Will; "but I've got a whiffing-line ready, and some bait, and laid it for you in the stern. I thought you'd like to fish."

"So I should," cried Dick, looking his thanks, and thinking what a frank, manly-looking fellow his new companion was; "but we must let my brother fish to-day. He'll pretend that he don't care for it, but he wants to try horribly, and you must coax him a bit. Then he will."

"What's the use of begging him?" said Will, who was rather taken aback.

"Oh! because I want him to have a turn, and I hope he'll get some luck. If he don't he'll be so disappointed."

"All ready?" cried Mr Temple just then, and Dick proceeded to scuffle down the steps, Arthur watching him eagerly to see him slip on the worst step. But Dick was not going to slip, and he stepped lightly on to one of the thwarts, closely followed by Will with the painter, and the next minute they were on their way to the mouth of the harbour, where there was a gentle swell.

Mr Temple and Dick were smiling as they looked back at the fishing village so picturesquely nestling in the slope of the steep cliff, and they paid no heed to Arthur, who suddenly snatched at his father on one side, at the boat on the other.

"What's the matter, my boy?" cried Mr Temple.

"Is—is anything wrong?" gasped Arthur. "The boat seemed sinking!"

"Hor—hor!" began Josh; but Arthur turned upon him so angrily, that the fisherman changed his hoarse laugh into a grotesque cough, screwing his face up till it resembled the countenance of a wooden South Sea image, such as the Polynesians place in the prow of their canoes.

106

"Gettin' so wet lars night, I think," he said in a good-tempered, apologetic growl, as he addressed himself to Will. "Sea-water don't hurt you though."

"There we are sinking again, Arthur," said Mr Temple, for the boat mounted the swell, as the wave came lapping the stone wall, raising them up a couple of feet, and letting them glide down four. "Let go!" he whispered. "Don't be a coward."

Arthur snatched his hands away, and from being very white he turned red.

"I suppose the sea comes in pretty rough sometimes," said Mr Temple to Josh.

"Tidyish, sir, but not bad. She gives a pretty good swish at the face o' the harbour when the weather's rough from the south-east, and flies over on to the boats; but Bar Lea Point yonder takes all the rough of it and shelters us like. If the young gent looks down now, he can see Tom Dodder's Rock."

Mr Temple looked over the side.

"Yes, here it is, Arthur," he exclaimed, "about six feet beneath us."

"Five an' half at this time o' the tide," said Josh correctively.

"Oh! five and a half, is it?" said Mr Temple, smiling. "Can you see, Arthur?"

"Yes, papa," said the boy, looking quickly over the side and sitting up again as if he did not approve of it. "Do you mean that great rough thing?"

"That's her," said Josh. "Tom Dodder, as used to live long ago, wouldn't keep a good look-out, and he used to say as his boat would ride over any rock as there was on the coast. He went right over that rock to get into the harbour lots of times out of sheer impudence, and to show his mates as he wouldn't take advice from nobody; but one morning as he was running in, heavy loaded with pilchar's, after being out all night, and getting the biggest haul ever known, such a haul as they never get nowadays, he was coming right in, and a chap on the pier there shouts to him, 'luff, Tom, luff! She won't do it this tide.' 'Then she shall jump it,' says Tom, who wouldn't luff a bit, but rams his tiller so as to drive right at the rock. You see there was lots o' room at the sides, but he wouldn't go one way nor yet the other, out o' cheek like. He was one o' these sort of chaps as wouldn't be helped, you see; and as soon as the lads on the pier heared him say as his boat should jump over the rock—lep it, you know—they began to stare, as if they expected something was coming."

"And was something coming?" said Dick, who was deeply interested, though he could not help thinking about his brother's refusal of help.

"Coming! I should think there was, for just as the boat comes up to the rock, she acts just like a Chrishtun dog, or a horse might when her master wanted her to—what does she do but rises at the rock to lep right over her, but the water seemed to fail just then, and down she come sodge!"

"How?" said Arthur, who had become interested, and had not understood the comparison.

"Sodge, sir, sodge; breaks her back, melts all to pieces like a tub with the hoops shook off; and the sea was covered with pilchar's right and left, and they all went scoopin' 'em off the bay."

"And was any one drowned?" said Arthur.

"Well, sir, you see the story don't say," said Josh, moistening first one hand and then the other as he rowed; "but that's why she were called Tom Dodder's Rock; and there's the rock, as you see, so it must be true."

As soon as they were clear of the bar at the mouth of the harbour the sea had become smoother, and in the interest he had taken in Josh's narrative about Tom Dodder's Rock, Arthur had forgotten a little of his discomfort and dread; but now that the boat was getting farther from land and the story was at an end, he began to show his nervousness in various ways, the more that nobody but Josh seemed to be noticing him, for his father was busy with a small glass, inspecting the various headlands and points, and looking long and earnestly at the old mines, whose position was indicated by the crumbling stone engine-houses.

"Is the sea very deep here?" said Arthur to his brother, who did not answer; he was too intent upon the preparation of a fishing-line with Will.

"Deep? No," said Josh, "not here."

"But it looks deep," said Arthur, gazing over the side.

"Ah! but it ar'n't. 'Bout three fathom, p'r'aps."

"Three fathoms!" cried Arthur. "Why, that's eighteen feet, and over my head!"

"Well, yes, you ar'n't quite so tall as that!" cried Josh, with a bit of a chuckle.

"But suppose the boat was overset?" said Arthur.

"Oh, she won't overset, my lad. You couldn't overset her; and if she did —can you swim?"

"A little—not much. I'm not very fond of the water."

"Ah! that's a pity," said Josh; "everybody ought to be able to swim. You'd better come down to me every morning, and I'll take you out in the boat here and you can jump in and have a good swim round, and then come in again and dress."

Arthur looked at him in horror. The idea seemed frightful. To come out away from land, and plunge into water eighteen feet deep, where he might go to the bottom and perhaps never come up again, was enough to stun him mentally for the moment, and he turned away from Josh with a shudder.

"Here you are, Taff!" said Dick just then. "Now have a try for a fish. Come and sit here; change places."

Dick jumped up and stepped over the thwarts, vacating his seat right in the stern. In fact he looked as if he could have run all round the boat easily enough on the narrow gunwale had there been any need, while, in spite of his call and the sight of the fishing-line, Arthur sat fast.

"Well, why don't you get up?"

"I—I prefer staying here," said Arthur, who looked rather white.

"But you said you would like to fish!" cried Dick in a disappointed tone.

"Did I? Oh yes, I remember. But I don't wish to fish to-day. You can go on."

"Oh, all right!" said Dick lightly. "I daresay I can soon get something;" and he set the line dragging behind.

"Like to be rowed over to yon mine, sir, on the cliff?" said Josh, nodding in the direction of the old shaft, the scene of his adventures with Will.

"Where, my man? I can see no remains. Oh yes, I can," he continued, as he brought his glass to bear on the regular bank-slope formed by the material that had been dug and blasted out. "I see; that's a very old place. Yes; I should like to inspect that first."

"Me and him went down it lass week," said Josh, as he tugged at the oar, Will having now joined him in forcing the boat along.

"It's not a deep one, then," said Mr Temple carelessly.

"Dunno how deep she be," said Josh, "because she's full o' water up to the adit."

"Oh, there is an adit then?"

"Yes, as was most covered over. She begins up on that level nigh the cliff top, where you can see the bit o' brown rock with the blackberry bushes in it, and she comes out down in that creek place there where the bank's green."

"I see!" said Mr Temple eagerly. "Ah! that must be an old place. When was it given up?"

"Oh, long before we was born, or our grandfathers, I expect!" said Josh.

"The more reason why I should examine it," said Mr Temple. "I suppose," he added aloud, "we can land here?"

"Oh yes, while the sea's like this! You couldn't if she was rough. The rocks would come through her bottom before you knowed where you were."

"Is it going to be rough, did you say?" said Arthur eagerly.

"Yes, some day," said Josh. "Not while the wind's off the shore."

"Taff, Taff! Here! I've got him!" cried Dick excitedly; and his words had such an effect upon Arthur that he started up and was nearly pitched overboard; only saving himself by making a snatch at his father, one hand knocking off Mr Temple's hat, the other seizing his collar.

"You had better practise getting your sea-legs, Master Arthur," said his father. "There, give me your hand."

Arthur longed to refuse the proffered help, for he knew that both Josh and Will were smiling; but he felt as if the boat kept running away from beneath him, and then, out of a sheer teasing spirit, rose up again to give the soles of his feet a good push, and when it did this there was a curious giddy feeling in his head.

So he held tightly by his father's hand while he stepped over the seat, and then hurriedly went down upon his knees by where Dick was holding the line, at the end of which some fish was tugging and straining furiously.

"Here you are!" cried Dick, handing the line to his brother. "He's a beauty! A pollack, I know; and when you get him he's all orange, and green, and gold!"

"But it's dragging the line out of my hands!" said Arthur.

"Don't let it! Hold tight!" cried Dick, whose cheeks were flushed with excitement.

"But it cuts my hands," said Arthur pettishly.

"Never mind that! All the better! It's a big one! Let a little more line out."

Arthur obeyed, and the fish darted off so vigorously that it would have carried off all there was had not Dick checked it.

"Now, hold tight!" cried Dick. "Play him. Now begin to haul in."

"But the line's all messy," said Arthur, in tones full of disgust.

"Oh, what a fellow you are! Now, then, never mind the line being messy; haul away!"

"What, pull?" said Arthur feebly.

"To be sure! Pull away hand over hand. I know he's a monster."

Mr Temple and the little crew of two were so intent upon the old mine that they paid no heed to the boys. Hence it was that Dick took the lead and gave his directions to his brother how to catch fish, in a manner that would have been heartily condemned by both Josh and Will, whose ideas of playing a fish consisted in hauling it aboard as soon as they could.

"Oh, you're not half hauling it in!" cried Dick, as he grew out of patience with his brother's fumbling ways. "You'll lose it."

"You be quiet and let me alone," said Arthur quickly. "I daresay I know as much about sea-fishing as you do."

"Then why don't you haul in the line?"

"Because the fish won't come, stupid! There, you see, he will now!" continued Arthur, hauling pretty fast, as the captive began to give way. "Oh, how nasty! I'm getting my knees quite wet."

Quite! For he had remained kneeling in the bottom of the boat, too much excited to notice that he was drawing the dripping line over his legs, and making a little pool about his knees.

"Never mind the wet—haul!" cried Dick; and he hardly keep his fingers off the line.

Urged in this way by his brother, Arthur went on pulling the line in feebly enough, till the fish made a fresh dash for liberty.

"Oh!" cried Arthur; "it's cutting my hands horribly. There—he's gone!"

Not quite, for Dick made a dash at the flying line, which was rushing over the gunwale, caught it in time, and began a steady pull at it till the fish was more exhausted, and he could turn its head, when he pulled the line in rapidly, and the boys could soon after see the bright silvery fish darting here and there.

"Got a gaff, Will?" shouted Dick.

"There's the old one stuck in the side, sir," replied the lad; and, holding on with one hand, Dick reached the gaff-hook with the other; but though he got his fish close up to the stern two or three times, he found that he was not experienced fisherman enough to hold the line with his left hand and gaff it with the other.

"Here!" he cried at last, for Arthur was looking on helplessly. "You catch hold of the line while I gaff him!"

Arthur obeyed with a grimace indicative of disgust as he felt the wet and slippery line; and, in obedience to his brother's orders, he dragged the fish close in; but just as Dick made a lunge at it with the big hook it darted off again, cutting Arthur's hands horribly. The next time it was dragged in Dick was successful, getting his hook in its gills, and hoisting it on board, flapping and bounding about as if filled with so much steel spring.

"Hallo! you've got one then, Dick!" cried his father, turning round; Josh and Will having been quietly observant the while.

"Yes, father!" cried Dick in the most disinterested way; "Arthur held him and I gaffed him. Isn't it a beauty? What is it, Josh—a silver pollack?"

"A-mussy me, no!" cried Josh, who had ceased rowing. "That be no pollack; that be a bass. Dessay there be a shoal out there."

"Mind his back tin, Master Dick!" cried Will excitedly, as he saw Dick take hold of his prize.

"Yes, I'll mind," said Dick. "Here, never mind, it being wet," he went on; "catch hold of him with both hands, Arthur, I'll get out the hook."

"Oh—oh—oh!" shouted Arthur, snatching back his hands. "It pricks!"

"What pricks?" cried Dick, seizing the fish and throwing it down again sharply. "Oh, I say, it's like a knife."

"Shall I take it off, sir?" said Will.

"No, I'm not going to be beaten!" cried Dick, whose hand was bleeding. "I didn't know what you meant. Why, it's a big stickleback!"

He took hold of the prize more cautiously, disengaged the hook, and then laid the fish before his father—a fine salmon bass of eight or nine pounds.

"Bravo, my boy!" said Mr Temple; "but is your hand much cut?"

"Oh, no! it's nothing," said Dick, hastily twisting his handkerchief round his hurt. "I say, isn't it a beauty? But what is the use of that fin?"

"Means of defence, I suppose," said his father, raising the keen perch-like back fin of the fish.—"But there, we are close inshore now. Run her in, my men."

The next minute the boat was grating upon the rocks. Will leaped out and held it steady, for the waves rocked it about a good deal; and the party landed close to the adit, the boat being moored with a grapnel; and then they all walked up to the hole in the foot of the rock, through which Josh and Will had made their escape after their adventure in the mine-shaft a short time before.

Chapter Sixteen.

Arthur Temple catches his Largest Fish—An odd one—And even then is not at rest.

Mr Temple took a small flat lantern from his pocket, struck a match inside, and lit the lamp, which burned with a clear, bright flame.

"Is the shaft belonging to this open at the top?" he said to Will.

"Yes, sir—quite."

"Ah! then there's no foul air. Now, Arthur, come along and you shall see what a mine adit is like."

"I—er—I'd rather not come this time, papa," said Arthur in a rather off-hand way; "the knees of my trousers are so wet."

"Oh! are they?" said Mr Temple quietly. "You will come, I suppose, Dick?"

"Yes, father. May I carry the lamp?"

"Yes; and go first. Slowly, now. Rather hard to get through;" and after a little squeezing the whole party, save Arthur, crept into the low gallery, the light showing the roof and sides to be covered with wet moss of a glittering metallic green.

There was not much to reward the seekers,—nothing but this narrow passage leading to a black square pool of water, upon which the light of the lamp played, and seemed to be battling with a patch of reflected daylight, the image of the square opening, a hundred and fifty feet above.

"Hah!" said Mr Temple after a few minutes' inspection of the adit and the shaft, whose walls, as far as he could reach, he chipped with a sharp-pointed little hammer formed almost like a wedge of steel. "A good hundred years since this was worked, if ever it got beyond the search. Copper decidedly."

"And you think it is very rich?" said Will excitedly, for he had been watching Mr Temple with the greatest eagerness.

"Rich! No, my lad. What, have you got the Cornish complaint?"

"Cornish complaint, sir?" said Will wonderingly.

"The longing to search for mineral treasures?"

"Yes, sir," said Will bluntly after a few moments' pause.

"Then you need not waste time here, my lad."

"But there's copper here. I proved it; and now you say there is."

"Yes; tons of it," said Mr Temple.

"There, Josh!" cried Will triumphantly.

"But," continued Mr Temple as they all stood there half-crouching in the narrow adit, "it is in quantities and in a bed that would be hard to work, and every hundredweight you got out and smelted would have cost more in wages than you could obtain when you sold your copper."

"There, lad, what did I gashly say?" cried Josh eagerly. "Didn't I say as the true mining was for silver in the sea—ketching fish with boats and nets."

"No, you did not," cried Will hotly; "and you meant nothing of the kind in what you did say."

"Ah! there's nought like the sea for making a living," said Josh in an ill-used tone. "I wouldn't work in one of these gashly places on no account; not for two pound a week, I wouldn't."

"Well, let's get out in the open air at all events, now," said Mr Temple. "I should like to see the mouth of the shaft."

"I'll show you, sir," said Will eagerly; and Mr Temple watched him closely as they stood once more out in the bright sunshine, and, lithe and strong, he began to climb up the rocks, Dick following him almost as quickly, but without his cleverness in making his way from block to block.

Mr Temple followed, then Josh, lastly Arthur, who got on very badly, but indignantly refused Josh's rough tarry hand when he good-naturedly offered to help him up the rough cliff.

"Here's where Josh and I went down," said Will, as they all stood at the shaft mouth.

"And did you go down there, my lad?"

"Yes, sir."

"Swinging on a rope?"

"Yes, sir."

"Then you've a good nerve, my lad. It wants a cool head to do that."

Will winced and glanced at Josh, who wrinkled up his forehead in a curious way.

"A tremendous nerve," continued Mr Temple. "You wouldn't care to go down, Dick?"

"No, father; but I'd go if you told me, and the rope was safe."

"That's right," said Mr Temple, smiling; "but, as I said before, it would require tremendous nerve—like that of our friend here."

Will looked from one to the other uneasily, and turned his cap first to right, and then to left. Suddenly he drew a long breath.

"I felt when I got out of the shaft, sir, as if I never dared try to do it again," he said hastily.

"Indeed!"

"Yes, sir; I wasn't at all brave over it."

"Steady, my lad—steady!" said Josh in a reproving tone. "I think you did well. P'raps the gentleman would like to go now to Blee Vor."

"Yes, I should," said Mr Temple, "so let's go at once. There is nothing to be done here."

Josh led the way down the cliff—rather a dangerous road, but one which seemed easy enough to him, while Arthur shuddered and stopped two or three times on the way down, as if the descent made him giddy. He was always well enough, though, to resent any offer of assistance, even into the boat when it was hauled close up to the rock. Josh would have lifted him in; Will was ready to lay a back for him and porter him in like a sack; but the sensitive London boy looked upon these offers of aid as insulting; and the consequence was that he got on board with one of his shoes full of water, and a very small piece of skin taken off his shin.

"Shall we row you on to Blee Vor," said Josh.

Mr Temple nodded in a short business-like way, and taking out his glass, he began to examine the rock as they went along.

All of a sudden, though, he turned to Dick.

"Go and take that oar," he said sharply; and then to Will—"Come here, my lad."

Will coloured a little as he gave up his oar to Dick, who began rowing with a great deal of vigour and a great deal of splash, but with little effect upon the progress of the boat.

"And so you are spending your spare time hunting for metals, are you, my lad?" said Mr Temple, gazing sharply at Will.

"Yes, sir."

"Why?"

Will hesitated for a moment and then said frankly:

"I want to get on, sir, and make myself independent."

"Capital idea!" said Mr Temple; "but what knowledge have you on the subject? Have you studied mineralogy?"

"Not from books, sir. Only what the miners about here could teach me."

"But you know a little about these things?"

"Very little, sir; but I'm trying to learn more."

"Ah! that's what we are all trying to do," said Mr Temple quickly. "That will do. Perhaps we shall see a little more of each other."

116

He took up his glass once more; and feeling himself to be dismissed, Will went back to his seat, and would have taken the oar, but Dick wanted to learn how to row, and would not give it up.

"Go and help my brother catch another bass," he said; so rather unwillingly the lad went to where Arthur was diligently dragging the whiffing-line through the water.

"Don't you get any bites, sir?" said Will.

"No. I don't think there are many fish hero now," said Arthur haughtily.

"But there are a few," said Will smiling. "Did you put on a good bait?"

"Good bait!" said Arthur, looking at his questioner in a half-offended tone.

"Yes, you must have a good lask on your hook, or the fish will not rise at it."

"Why, I've got the same hook on that my brother used when he caught that fish."

"Let me look," said Will quietly.

Arthur frowned, and would have declined, but Will did not wait for permission, and drew in the line till he came to the lead, lifted it carefully inboard, and then hauled up the hook.

"You might have kept on trying all day," said Will. "There's no bait."

"Oh, indeed! then some fish must have bitten it off," said Arthur in the most nonchalant way. "I thought I felt a tug."

Will had his back turned to the fisherman, so that he could smile unobserved, for he knew that there had been no bait left on the hook, and that Arthur would not have soiled his fingers to put one on.

"There," he said as he hooked on a good bright lask; "now try."

He threw the bait over and then dropped in the lead, when the bait seemed to dart away astern, drawing out the line; but to Arthur's surprise Will checked it instantly, caught the line from the gunwale and handed it to him, Will's quick eyes having detected the dash of a fish at the flying bait.

"Why, there's one on!" cried Arthur excitedly.

"Small pollack," said Will smiling. "Haul him in."

Arthur forgot all about the wetness of the line this time, and soon drew one of the brightly coloured fish inboard and called to his brother.

"Here, look!" he cried, "you never saw anything so beautiful as this."

"Just like mine," cried Dick, "only it was ten times as big."

"Oh!" said Arthur in a disappointed tone. Then, in a whisper to Will, "I say, boy, put on a big bait this time. I want to catch a large one."

Will felt amused at the other's dictatorial importance, but he said nothing: placing a bait on the hook, and the line was once more trailed behind, but this time without success, and at the end of a few minutes the boat was guided into a narrow passage amongst the rocks, below a high forbidding headland where the long slimy sea-weed that clung to the granite was washing to and fro, as the waves rushed foaming in and out among the huge blocks of stone, some of which were every now and then invisible, and then seemed to rise out of the sea like the backs of huge shaggy sea-monsters playing in the nook.

Josh had taken the oar from Dick, and had now assumed the sole guidance of the boat, rowing slowly with his head turned towards the shore, and once or twice there was a scraping, bumping noise and a jerk or two, which made Arthur seize hold of the side.

"Is it safe to go in here?" said Mr Temple.

"Oh! you may trust Josh, sir," exclaimed Will. "It wouldn't be safe at high water, but there's no danger now."

"Not of getting a hole through the boat?" "Boomp—

craunch!"

Arthur turned quite white, while Dick laughed.

"That's only her iron keel, sir," said Will, for Josh was too intent upon his work to turn his head for answer. "The wave dropped us on that rock, and we slid off, you see, on the keel. Now we're in deep water again."

The action of the waves close inshore on that rugged coast, even in that calm weather, was sufficient to raise them up three or four feet and then let them down, while the water was so clear that they could see the weeds waving and streaming here and there over the tinted rock, patches of which, where they were washed bare, were of the most brilliant crimsons, purples, and greens.

Josh was guiding the boat in and out along a most intricate channel, now almost doubling back, but always the next minute getting nearer to a beautiful white patch of strand, beyond which was a dark forbidding clump of rocks piled-up in picturesque confusion, and above which the gaunt cliff ran up perpendicularly in places till it was at least three hundred feet above their heads, and everywhere seeming to be built up in great blocks like rugged ashlar work, the joints fitting closely, but all plainly marked and worn by the weather.

"Sit fast all!" said Josh; "here's a wave coming!"

He gave one oar a sharp tug to set the boat's head a little farther round, and Arthur sprang up and with a sort of bound leaped to his father's side, clinging to him tightly, as a loud rushing, hissing sound rose from behind, and a good-sized wave came foaming in and out among the great blocks of stone, as if bent on leaping into and swamping the boat; but instead of this, as it reached them it lifted the boat, bore it forward, bumping and scraping two or three rocks below the keel, and then letting it glide over the surface of a good-sized rock-pool, swirling and dancing with the newly coming water.

Josh then rowed steadily on for a few strokes, pausing by some glistening rocks that, after lying dry for a few hours, were being covered again by the title.

"Your young gents like to look at the dollygobs, master?" said Josh.

"Look at the what!" exclaimed Mr Temple.

"Them there gashly things," said Josh, pointing to a number of round patches of what seemed to be deep-red jelly, with here and there one of an olive green.

"Sea-anemones, boys," said Mr Temple. Then to Josh, "No, they must hunt them out another time; I want to land. I suppose we can climb up to that shelf?"

He pointed to a flat place about a hundred feet above them.

"Dessay we can, if it arn't too gashly orkard," growled Josh. "If she be, we'll bring the rope another time and let you down. Sit fast again!"

For another wave came rushing in, seeming to gather force as it ran, while Josh so cleverly managed the boat that he made it ride on the surface of the wave right over a low ridge of rocks, and then rowed close in and ran her head upon what looked to be coarse sand. Then in went the oars, Josh and Will leaped out, waited a few moments, and then, another smaller wave helping them, they drew the boat higher, so that she was left half dry, and her passengers were able to step out on the dry patch beneath the rocks.

"Why, it isn't sand, but little broken shells," cried Dick excitedly, as Mr Temple casually picked up a handful to examine.

"Yes, Dick, broken shells, and not siliceous," said Mr Temple.

"What are those red and green rocks, father?" asked Dick.

"Serpentine; and that white vein running through is soapstone. Ah! now we shall get to know a little about what is inside."

"But why have we come here?" asked Arthur.

"Because there has been a working here. Some one must have dug down and thrown out all that mass of broken rock. Part has been washed away; but all this, you see, though worn and rounded by the waves washing it about, has been dug out of the rock."

He had walked to a long slope of wave-worn fragments of rock as he spoke, forming a steep ascent that ran up into a rift in the great cliff; and he drew Dick's attention to the fact that what seemed like a level place a hundred feet above was so situated that anything thrown down would have fallen in the niche or combe of the cliff just beyond them.

"Now, my fine fellow," said Mr Temple, as he picked up a piece of wave-polished stone, "what's that?"

"Serpentine," said Will quietly.

"And this?" said Mr Temple.

"Granite, sir."

"Eight; and this?"

"Gneiss," replied Will.

"Quite correct. Now this," he continued, breaking a piece of stone in two with his hammer.

"Cop—no, only mundic," cried Will, who had nearly been caught tripping.

"Right again. Now this?"

He picked up a reddish piece of stone which, when broken, showed bright clear crystals, and close to the ruddy stone a number of little black grains.

"Tin," cried Will eagerly; "and a rich piece."

"Let me look at the tin," cried Arthur eagerly; and the piece being handed to him, "where?" he cried; "there's no tin here."

"Tin ore, my boy," said Mr Temple quietly. "Those black grains are rich tin."

"Well, I shouldn't have thought that," said Arthur; "and I should have thought that was gold or brass."

"Then you would have thought wrong," said Mr Temple sharply. "All is not gold that glitters, my boy; and you can't find brass in the earth. What can you find, my lad?" he continued, turning sharply to Will.

"Copper, sir, and tin and zinc."

"Then what is brass?" said Mr Temple.

"Copper and zinc mixed."

"Not copper and tin?"

"Copper and tin, sir, make fine bronze, same as the ancient people used to hammer for swords and spears; but I can't understand, sir, why two soft metals like copper and tin should make a hard one when they are mixed."

"And I cannot explain it to you," said Mr Temple smiling.

"Are we going to stop here long?" said Arthur impatiently.

"Oh? don't go yet," cried Dick, laughing; "I want to hear Will say his miner's catechism."

"Oh! very well," said Mr Temple, smiling. "What is mundic, then, my lad?"

"A mussy me! as if every lad here didn't know what mundic was!" cried Josh to himself; but he spoke loud enough for the others to hear.

"Well, what is mundic, then?" said Mr Temple quickly to Josh.

"What's mundic?" growled Josh, picking up a yellow metallic-looking piece of rock; "why, that is, and that is, and that is. There's tons of it everywhere."

"To be sure there is, my man; but what is it?" said Mr Temple.

"Well, ain't I showing of you!" growled Josh. "This here's mundic."

"The gentleman means what is it made of?" whispered Will, and then he added two or three words.

"Why, how should I know? Made of! 'Tain't made of anything, nor more ar'n't tin. I suppose it grows."

"Do you know?" said Mr Temple.

"I think so, sir," said Will modestly; "sulphur and iron."

"Let's go on now," said Arthur; "I want to fish."

"Stop and learn something, my boy," said Mr Temple sternly.

"Oh! go on, please," cried Dick, who was delighted to find so much knowledge in his new friend.

"What is this, then?" said Mr Temple, picking up a whitish metallic-looking piece of mineral.

"I don't know exactly, sir," said Will eagerly; "but I think it is partly antimony and partly silver."

"Quite right again, my lad," cried Mr Temple, clapping Will upon the shoulder of his fish-scaly blue jersey; "a great deal of antimony, and there is sulphur and iron too, I think, in this piece."

"This must have come out of the working above there," cried Will eagerly.

"Undoubtedly, my lad."

"I didn't know that there had been a mine here," said Will.

"Or you would have had a look at it before now, eh?"

"Yes, sir," said Will, colouring.

"We'll go and have a look at it now," said Mr Temple; "but I don't think we shall find anything of much good."

"Here, papa, what's this?" cried Arthur eagerly. "This must be gold."

"Copper," cried Will. "Then there is copper here too!"

"Yes, that is copper," said Mr Temple, examining and re-fracturing a glistening piece of stone full of purple and gold reflections, with touches of blue and crimson. "Peacock ore some people call it. Now, let's have a climb. Or stop, let's have a look at that cave. I should not wonder if the adit is there."

"Beggin' yer pardon, sir," said Josh respectfully, "I don't think as I'd go in there, if I was you."

"Why not?" said Mr Temple, as he stood just inside the rugged cavern, whose mouth was fringed with sea-ferns.

"Well, you see, sir, they say gashly things about these here old zorns."

"What sort of things, Josh?" cried Dick. "Wild beasts in 'em?"

"Well, no, Master Ditchard, sir," said Josh, who was confused as to the proper way of using the names Dick and Richard; "not wild beasts here."

"You must go two miles farther," said Will, "and we can show you the seal-caves."

"With seals in them?" cried Richard.

"Oh, yes, plenty," said Will. "Josh thinks there is something unpleasant lives in these zorns."

"No, not exactly lives," said Josh, hesitating; "and don't you get making game of 'em, young fellow," he added, turning to Will. "Them as is a deal older than us wouldn't go in 'em to save their lives."

"Why, what is there in the cave, my man?" said Mr Temple.

"Oh! I shouldn't like to say, sir," said Josh, gazing furtively into the darksome hole in the rock.

"But you are not afraid?"

"Afraid, sir! Oh, no, I'm not afraid; but I don't think it's right to go in and disturb what's there."

"Ah, well, Dick, we'll go," said Mr Temple; "and we must apologise if the occupants object."

"I wouldn't go, really, sir," protested Josh.

"You can stay behind, my man," said Mr Temple.

"Then don't take Master Dick, sir. You see he's so young."

"My son can stay outside if he likes," said Mr Temple in a tone of voice that made Dick tighten himself up and fasten the lower, button of his jacket.

"There," said Mr Temple as he closed his lanthorn and held it up; "now we shall see."

He stepped in over the shelly sand which filled up the vacancies between the rocks that strewed the floor, and Dick stepped in after him.

Will turned and looked half-mockingly at Josh as he stepped in next.

"Oh! well, I can't stand that," growled Josh. "Here goes."

He moistened both of his hands as if he were going to get a grip of some rope or spar, and then hurried in, leaving Arthur alone at the mouth of the zorn, peering in at the dancing light and the strange shadows cast upon the glistening stone of roof and wall.

"Shall I go in?" he said to himself. "I know Dick will laugh at me if I don't."

Then he hesitated: the place looked so dark and cold and forbidding, while without it was so light and bright and sunshiny.

"I sha'n't go," he muttered. "Let him laugh if he likes, and that Cornish fisher-boy as well. I don't see why I should go into the nasty old cellar."

Then he peered in, and thought that he would like to go in just a little way; and stretching out one leg he was about to set his foot down when there was a black shadow cast at his feet, a rushing noise, and something came quite close, uttered a harsh cry, and dashed off.

Arthur Temple bounded back into the broad sunshine with his heart beating painfully; and even when he saw that it was one of the great black fishing-birds that had dipped down and dashed off again he was not much better.

"I wish I were not so nervous!" he muttered; and he looked about hastily.

"I'm glad no one was here, though," he added. "How Dick would have laughed! Now I'll follow them in. No, I won't. I'll say I wanted to fish;" and snatching at this idea he ran down to the boat, got in, and arranging the line, gave the lead a swing and threw it seaward, so that it should fall in the deep channel among the rocks, where there was not the slightest likelihood of his getting a fish.

But it requires some skill to throw out lead attached to a fishing-line, especially when there are ten or twelve feet of line between the lead and the hook.

Hence it was then that when Arthur Temple swung the lead to and fro, and finally let it go seaward, there was a sharp tug and a splash, the lead falling into the water about a couple of yards from the stern, and the hook sticking tightly in the gunwale of the boat.

"Bother!" exclaimed Arthur angrily as he proceeded to haul the lead in, and then to extricate the hook, whose bait wanted rearranging, while the hook itself was a good deal opened out in drawing it from the wood.

He got all right at last, screwing up his face a good deal at having to replace the bait, and then stopping to wash his hands very carefully and wipe them upon his pocket-handkerchief. This done, he smelt his fingers.

"Pah!" he ejaculated; and he proceeded to wash and wipe them again before rearranging the line; and then after swinging the lead to and fro four or five times, he let it go, giving it a tremendous jerk, which recoiled so upon his frame, and caused the boat to swerve so much, that he nearly fell overboard, and only saved himself by throwing himself down and catching at the thwarts.

"Bother the beastly, abominable old boat!" he cried angrily as he scrambled up, and with all the pettishness of a spoiled child, kicked the side with all his might, a satisfactory proceeding which resulted in the wood giving forth a hollow sound, and a painful sensation arising from an injured toe.

He felt a little better, though, after getting rid of this touch of spite, and he smiled with satisfaction, too, for the lead had descended some distance off in the water, and with a self-complacent smile Arthur Temple sat down on the edge of the boat and waited for a bite.

"This is better than getting wet and dirty in that cavern," he said. "It's warm and sunshiny, and old Dick will be as savage as savage if he finds that I've caught three or four good fish before he comes. Was that a touch?"

It did not seem to be, so Arthur sat patiently on waiting for the bite, and sometimes looking over the side, where, in the clear water, half-hidden by a shelf of rock, he could see what at first made him start, for it looked like an enormous flat spider lying about three feet down, watching him with a couple of eyes like small peas, mounted, mushroom-fashion, on a stalk.

"Why, it's an old crab," he said; "only a small one, though. Ugh! what a disgusting-looking beast!"

He remained watching the crab for some few minutes, and then looked straight along the line, which washed up and down on a piece of rock as the waves came softly in, bearing that peculiar sea-weedy scent from the shore. Then he had another look at the crab, and could distinctly see its peculiar water-breathing apparatus at work, playing like some piece of mechanism about its mouth, while sometimes one claw would be raised a little way, then another, as if the mollusc were sparring at Arthur, and asking him to come on.

"Ugh! the ridiculous-looking little monster!" he muttered. "I wonder how long they'll be! What a while it is before I get a bite!"

But he did not get a bite all the same. For, in the first place, there were none but very small fish in and about the rocks—little wrasse, and blennies wherever the bottom was sandy, and tiny crabs scuffling in and out among the stones, where jelly-fish were opening and shutting and expanding their tentacles in search of minute food.

In the second place, Arthur sat on fishing, happily unconscious of the fact that he was in a similar position to the short-sighted old man in the caricature. This individual is by a river side comfortably seated beneath a tree, his rod horizontally held above the water, but his line and float, where he has jerked them, four or five feet above his head in an overhanging bough.

There were no overhanging boughs near Arthur, and no trees; but when he threw in his line the lead had gone into a rock-pool, the hook had stopped in a patch of sea-weed on a rock high and dry, and the bait of squid was being nicely cooked and frizzled in the sun.

"I think it wants a new bait," said our fisherman at last very importantly; and, drawing in the line, the lead came with a bump up against the side of the boat, while the bait was dragged through the water, and came in thoroughly wet once more.

"I thought so," said Arthur complacently as he examined the shrunken bait. "Something has been at it and sucked all the goodness away. I wish that fisher-boy was here to put on a fresh one."

But that fisher-boy was right in the cavern, so Arthur had to put on a fresh bait himself. This done, and very badly too, he took the line in hand once more, stood up on the thwart, spreading his legs wide apart to steady himself, because the boat rocked; and then, after giving the heavy lead a good swing, sent it off with a thrill of triumph, which rapidly changed to a look of horror, accompanied by a yell of pain.

"Oh! oh! oh! oh!" cried Arthur. "My leg! my leg! my leg! Oh! help! help! help!" and sitting down in the boat he began to drag in the line rapidly, as he thoroughly realised the fact that he had caught a very large and a very odd fish this time.

Note: Zorn, the Cornish name for a sea-cave.

Chapter Seventeen.

Pilchar' Will performs a surgical operation; which is followed by a wet walk home.

While Arthur had been amusing himself by fishing, with the result just told, his father had penetrated into the cave, closely followed by Dick, Will, and lastly by Josh.

"I'll see fair for 'em anyhow," Josh said; and wetting his hands once more, he followed the dancing light, closing up directly after Will.

"Shall we find anything here, father?" said Dick as his eyes wandered over the dimly-seen masses of rugged rock above his head.

"Perhaps," said his father—"perhaps not. I want to find traces of some good vein of ore; I don't care what, so long as it is well worth working. Of course this place has been thoroughly explored before,—at least I should expect so,—but changes are always taking place. Rock shells off in time; great pieces fall and lay bare treasures that have never before been seen."

"Treasures, father?" cried Dick eagerly.

"Yes, treasures. Not buried treasures—Spanish doubloons or ingots, my boy, but nature's own treasures. We may as well hunt in all sorts of places, for I mean to find something worth working before I have done."

"I say, father, isn't it all stuff and nonsense about anything living in a cave like this?"

"What—of the hobgoblin kind, Dick?"

"Yes, father."

Mr Temple did not answer for a few moments, and then he replied in the same low tone as that in which his son had asked the question.

"For shame, Dick!" he said softly.

That was all.

Dick felt it as a severe rebuke, and did not speak for a minute or two as they went on winding in and out among the rocks, with the roof rapidly curving down, and the floor, which was sandy no longer, seeming to rise as the sides of the cave contracted and the travelling had become an awkward climb.

"I don't believe any of that stuff, father," said Dick softly.

"That's right," replied Mr Temple. "Hah: yes!" he said holding the lantern so that the light shone on the roof—"tin!"

"Tin, father?" cried Dick joyfully. "Have you found tin?"

"Yes, but too poor to be worth working;" and Mr Temple went on a little, and stopped to chip the side with his hammer. "Traces of copper here," he said. "Look: peacock ore; very pretty to look at, but ruinous to work, Dick. Ah! we seem to be coming to the end now."

"Would seals be likely to live in a cave like this?" said Dick.

"I should think not," replied Mr Temple. "The entrance is not near enough to the water. I think they like a place where they can swim right in and out at all times of the tide."

"That's so," said Josh, who had overheard the remark.

"The cave we know, Master Dick," said Will, "is one where you can row right in."

"Can't we go now?" cried Dick excitedly.

"Wait, wait," said Mr Temple, "don't be impatient, my lad. All in good time. Ah! here is the end; and look here, my man, here are some of your strange creatures' drinking vessels."

As he spoke he stepped forward and let the light play upon some pieces of wood, beyond which were five or six very old empty tubs that were a little less than ordinary wooden pails, but narrow at each end like a barrel.

Josh came forward with Will to stare at the half-rotten fragments, which were black and slimy with the drippings from the roof, and the iron hoops were so eaten away that upon Mr Temple touching one of the tubs with his foot it crumbled down into a heap of black-looking earth.

"Fishermen's buoys," said Will, looking at the heap wonderingly.

"No, my lad; smugglers' brandy-tubs," said Mr Temple. "And you, Josh, here's the explanation of your cock-and-bull story. Some fishermen once saw the smugglers stealing in here by night, and at once set them down as being supernatural. There, let's get out and climb up the rock to the old working. No. Stop; just as I thought; here is the adit."

For they had suddenly come upon the narrow passage that led into the shaft—a low square tunnel, not so carefully-cut as the one they had previously explored.

"Is this likely to be an adit, father?" said Dick, who had caught the term. "Isn't it the natural cave hole?"

"Yes—enlarged," said Mr Temple, letting the light play on the wet sides. "Here are the marks of the pick and hammer, looking pretty fresh still. But we shall gain nothing by going in there except wet jackets. How the water drips!"

For, as they listened, they could hear it musically trickling down, and in another part falling with a regular *pat, pat, pat* on the rocky floor.

"But where does the water go?" asked Dick. "It ran out of the other in a little stream."

"Far behind us somewhere, I daresay," replied his father. "Don't you see how this floor upon which we stand has been covered with great pieces of rock that have fallen from above? All, Dick, since men worked here. Perhaps this place was worked as a mine a hundred years before the smugglers used the cave, and they have not been here, I should say, for two or three generations. Now let's get out into daylight once more. You would not be scared again about entering a dark cave, eh, Dick?"

"No, father—Oh! the light!"

"I'm glad of that," replied Mr Temple, "for the lamp has gone out. The wick was too small," he added, "and it has slipped through into the oil."

"A mussy me!" groaned Josh. "And in this gashly place!"

"Now, then, who'll lead the way out?" said Mr Temple sharply.

"Let me," cried Dick.

"Go on then, my boy. There's nothing to be afraid of but broken shins. No. Let Will guide, or—pooh! what nonsense! there's the light. We shall almost be able to see as soon as our eyes grow accustomed to the place."

Will went to the front, slowly feeling his way along with outstretched hands towards a faint reflection before them; and, the others following slowly, they were about half-way back, with the task growing easier each moment, when all at once they heard Arthur's cry for help. Forgetting his caution, Will began to run, and Dick after him, stumbling and nearly falling two or three times, Mr Temple and Josh hastening after him as eagerly, but with more care, till they rounded a huge mass of stone which shut out the sight of the sea, when they also ran, and joined Dick and Will.

"There isn't much the matter, father," said Dick, as Mr Temple came running to the boat, "he has only got the hook in his leg."

"Why, I thought he was 'bout killed," grumbled Josh.

"Let me look," said Mr Temple; and Arthur, as his leg was lifted, uttered a piteous moan, and looked round for sympathy.

Mr Temple drew out his knife, and as he opened the sharp blade Arthur shrieked.

"Oh, don't, don't!" he cried, "I couldn't bear it."

"Why, they're not your trousers, Taff, they're mine," cried Dick; and Mr Temple laughed heartily.

"Don't be a coward, Arthur," he said sternly. "I was only going to slit the flannel."

"Oh!" sighed Arthur, "I thought you were going to cut my leg to get out the hook."

"Well, perhaps I shall have to," said Mr Temple quietly; "but you are too much of a man to mind that."

"Oh!" moaned Arthur again.

"Be quiet, sir," said Mr Temple more sternly. "Take away your hands. You are acting like a child."

"But it hurts so!" moaned Arthur. "Oh! don't touch it. I can't bear it touched. Oh! oh! oh!"

"Tut! tut! tut!" ejaculated Mr Temple, as Dick caught his brother's hand.

"I say, do have some pluck, Taff," he whispered. "Of course it hurts, but it will soon be over."

"Yes; it will soon be over," assented Mr Temple, as with his sharp penknife he cut away the thin cord to which the hook was attached, and with it the remains of the bait.

"No, no! let it stop in till it comes out."

"But it will not come out, you stupid fellow," cried Dick.

"Of course not, my boy. It will only fester in your leg, and make it bad," said Mr Temple.

"Oh! oh! oh!" moaned Arthur. "Don't touch it. How it hurts! Couldn't I take some medicine to make it come out?"

"Yes," said Mr Temple quietly. "Three grains of courage and determination and it will be out. There, hold still, and I won't hurt you much. Catch hold of your brother's hands."

"A mussy me!" grumbled Josh as he looked on, scrubbing and scratching at his head with his great fingers all the time.

"Why, you are always talking about going in the army, Arthur," said Mr Temple, hesitating about extracting the hook, which was buried in the boy's leg, for he felt that he would have to make a deep cut to get it out —it being impossible to draw it back on account of the barb. "How would it be with you if the surgeon had to take off an arm or leg?"

"I don't want to be a soldier if it's to hurt like this," moaned Arthur piteously. "Oh, how unlucky I am!"

Mr Temple hesitated for a moment or two longer, thinking of going back and letting a doctor extract the hook; but the next moment his countenance assumed a determined look, and he said firmly:

"I will not hurt you more than I can help, my boy; but I must get out that hook."

"No, no, no!" cried Arthur. "We'll put on a poultice when we get back."

"Poultice won't suck that out," growled Josh. "We often gets hooks in ourselves, sir. Let me do it. I'll have it out in a minute."

"How?" said Mr Temple as he saw Josh pull out his great jack-knife, at the sight of which Arthur shrieked.

"Oh! I'll show you, sir," said Josh, "if he'll give over shouting."

"No," said Mr Temple. "I have a small keen knife here. I can cut it out better than you."

"Cut it out!" roared Josh, completely drowning Arthur's cry of horror. "You mustn't cut it out. Here, let Will do it. His fingers is handier than mine."

"Yes, sir, I can get it out very quickly," said Will eagerly.

"Do it, then," said Mr Temple. "I'll hold him."

"No, no, no!" shrieked Arthur.

"Be silent, sir," said his father sternly; and Arthur was cowed by the angry look and words.

"Poor old Taff!" said Dick to him softly as he held his hand. "I wish it was in my leg instead;" and the tears stood in his eyes, bespeaking his sincerity as he spoke.

"Give me that old marlinspike, Josh, and your knife," said Will quickly; and he took the iron bar and great jack-knife that were handed to him.

"My good lad, what are you going to do?" said Mr Temple. "You must not dig it out with that."

"Oh, no, sir!" said Will, smiling confidently. "I'm going to cut the shank in two so as to get rid of the flattened end. Here, you hold his leg on the gunwale. That's it. Pinch the hook with your fingers. I won't cut 'em, sir."

"I see!" exclaimed Mr Temple quietly; and as Arthur moaned piteously, afraid now more of his father's anger than of the pain, Mr Temple held the injured leg against the side of the boat, pinching the shank of the hook with his fingers.

Will did not hesitate a moment, but placed the edge of the great jack-knife on the soft tinned-iron hook, gave the back of the blade a sharp tap with the iron bar, and cut clean through the shank.

Arthur winced as he watched the descent of the marlinspike, but he was held too tightly by his father for him to move away, had he wished; and this he did not attempt, for fear of greater pain.

What followed was almost like a conjuring trick, it was so quickly done. For, thrusting Mr Temple's hands on one side, Will seized Arthur's leg with his strong young hands, there was a squeak—at least Dick said afterwards that it was a squeak, though it sounded like a shrill "Oh!" and then Will stood up smiling.

"Don't let him, papa—don't let him!" cried Arthur. "I could not bear it. He hurt me then horribly! I will not have it out! I'll bear the pain. He shall not do it! He sha'n't touch—"

Arthur stopped, stared, and dragged up the leg of his flannel trousers to examine his leg, where there were two red spots, one of which had a tiny bead of blood oozing from it, but the hook was gone.

"Why—where—where's the hook?" he cried in a querulous tone.

"Here it is!" said Will, holding it out, for with a quick turn he had forced it on, sending the barb right through where the point nearly touched the surface, and drawn it out—the shank, of course, easily following the barb now that the flattened part had gone.

133

"Hor! hor! hor! hor!" croaked Josh, indulging in a hoarse laugh. "I taught him how to do that, sir. It'll only prick a bit now, and heal up in a day or two."

"But—but is it all out?" said Arthur, feeling his leg.

"Yes, it's all out, my boy," said Mr Temple. "Now what do you say? Shall we bandage your leg and make you a bed at the bottom of the boat?"

Arthur looked up at him inquiringly, and then, seeing the amused glances of all around, he said sharply:

"I don't like to be laughed at."

"Then you must learn to be more of a man," said his father in a low tone, so that no one else could hear. "Arthur, my boy, I felt quite ashamed of your want of courage."

"But it hurt so, papa."

"I daresay it did, and I have no doubt that it hurts a little now; but for goodness' sake recollect what you are—an English boy, growing to be an English man, and afraid of a little pain! There, jump ashore and forget all about it."

Arthur stood up and obeyed, and then the little party proceeded to climb the cliff, Will leading and selecting the easiest path, till once more they stood beside an open mine-shaft, situated in a nook between two masses of cliff which nearly joined, as it seemed from below, but were quite twenty feet apart when the opening was reached.

"No," said Mr Temple after turning over a little of the *débris* that had been once dug out of the mine; "there would be nothing here worthy of capital and labour."

He busied himself examining the different pieces of stone with his lens, breaking first one fragment and then another, while Dick tried the depth of the shaft by throwing down a stone, then a larger one, the noise of its fall in the water below coming up with a dull echoing plash. The noise made Arthur shrink away and sit down on a piece of rock that was half covered with pink stonecrop, feeling that it would be dangerous to go too near, and conjuring up in his mind thoughts of how horrible it would be to fall into such a place as this.

Mr Temple seemed to grow more interested in the place as he went on examining the stones which Will kept picking out from the heap

134

beneath their feet.

Then he looked down at the steep slope to the shore, and he could now see why the bank of broken stone was so small, for the waves must have been beating upon it perhaps for a couple of hundred years, sweeping the fragments away, to drive them on along the coast, rolling them over and over till they were ground together or against the rocks and made into the rounded pebbles that strewed the shore.

"That will do," said Mr Temple at last; and as the others descended, he signed to Will to stop, and as soon as they were alone he held out half a crown to him.

"You did that very well, my lad," he said. "You have often taken out hooks before?"

"Dozens of times, sir," said Will quietly, and without offering to take the half-crown. "I don't want paying for doing such a thing as that, sir."

"Just as you like, my lad," said Mr Temple, looking at him curiously. "Go on down."

Will began descending the path, and as soon as his head had disappeared Mr Temple picked up a scrap or two more of the stone, examined them carefully, and then, selecting one special piece, he placed it in his pocket and followed Will.

There was plenty to interest them as they embarked once more, to find that the tide had risen so much that the boat was rowed over rocks that had previously been out of water.

Then on they went, along by the rugged cliffs, Josh keeping them at a sufficient distance from the rocks for them to be in smooth water, while only some twenty or thirty yards away the tide was beating and foaming amongst the great masses of stone, making whirlpools and eddies, swishing up the tangled bladder-wrack and long-fronded sea-weed, and then pouncing upon it and tearing it back, to once more throw it up again.

"Bad place for a ship to go ashore, eh?" said Mr Temple to Josh.

"Bad place, sir? Ay! There was a big three-master did go on the rocks just about here three years ago, and the next morning there was nothing but matchwood and timber torn into rags. Sea's wonderful strong when she's in a rage."

"Yes; it must be an awful coast in a storm."

"Ay, it be!" said Josh. "See yon island, sir?" he continued, pointing to a

135

long black reef standing up out of the sea about half a mile from shore. "Why, I've known that covered by the waves. They'll wash right over it, and send their tops clean over them highest rocks."

"And how high are they?" said Mr Temple, examining the ragged pile, upon which were perched half a dozen beautiful grey gulls, apparently watching their fellows, who were slowly wheeling about over the surface in search of food.

"Good fifty feet, sir; and I've seen the waves come rolling in like great walls, and when they reached the rocks they've seemed to run right up 'em and go clean over."

"That's what you call the sea running mountains high, eh, my man?" said Mr Temple, rather dryly.

"No, sir, I don't," said Josh quietly; "'cause the sea don't run mountains high. Out in the middle of the bay there, where the water's deep, I dunno as ever I see a wave that would be more than say fifteen foot high. It's when it comes on the rocks and strikes that the water's thrown up so far. Look at that, sir," he said, pointing towards a wave that came along apparently higher than the boat, as if it would swamp them, but over which they rode easily. "See where she breaks!"

They watched the wave seem to gather force till it rose up, curled over like a glistening arc of water, striking the rocks, and then rushing up, to come back in a dazzling cascade of foam.

"How high did she go?" said Josh quietly.

"Why, it must have dashed up nine or ten feet, my man," replied Mr Temple.

"Things look small out here, sir," said Josh. "If you was to measure that you'd find it all two fathom, and this is a fine day. Sea leaps pretty high in a storm, as maybe you'll see if you're going to stop down here."

"I hope I shall," said Mr Temple. "Now, then, where are you going to land next?"

"Will and me thought p'r'aps you'd like to see the white rock as he found one day?"

"White rock? what is it—quartz?" said Mr Temple.

"No, sir, I don't think it is," said Will; "it's too soft for that."

"You know what quartz is, then," said Mr Temple quickly.

"Oh, yes, sir! all the mining lads down here know what that is. Pull steady, Josh. Somewhere about here, wasn't it?"

"Nay, nay, my lad. I should have thought you'd knowed. Second cove beyond the seal-cave."

"Seal-cave!" cried Dick. "Are we going by the seal-cave?"

"Yes," said Will; "but the sea is too high to go in to-day. There's the seal-cave," he continued, pointing to a small hole into which the waves kept dashing and foaming out again. From where they were it did not seem to be above half a yard across, and not more above the sea to the jagged arch, while at times a wave raced in and it was out of sight —completely covered by the foaming water.

"I don't think much of that," said Arthur; "it looks more like a rough dog kennel."

"Yes, sir; sea-dog's kennel," said Will, who always addressed Arthur as "sir," while he dropped that title of respect with Dick.

"Ah! well, you must examine the seal-cave another day," said Mr Temple. "Let's see this vein of white stone that you say you found, my lad."

Five minutes' rowing brought them abreast of a split in the cliff, which was divided from top to bottom; and here, after a little manoeuvring, Josh took the boat in, but the sea was so rough that every now and then, to Dick's delight, they were splashed, and Arthur held on tightly by the thwart.

"I shall have to stop aboard, sir," said Josh, "and keep the boat off the rocks, or we shall have a hole in her. I'll back in astern, and then perhaps you wouldn't mind jumping off when I take you close to that flat rock."

Mr Temple nodded, and as the boat was turned and backed in, he stood up and followed Will, who lightly leaped on to the rock, while before they knew it, Dick was beside them, and the boat a dozen feet away.

"Be careful," was all he said, and then he smiled as his eyes rested upon Arthur, who was holding on to the thwart with both hands looking the image of dismay. For the boat was in troubled water, rising and falling pretty quickly, and requiring all Josh's attention to keep it from bumping on the rocks.

Will started forward at once, clambering into the narrow rift, which was not very easy of access on account of the number of brambles that ran in all directions, but by carefully pressing them down, the trio got on till they were some fifty feet up the rift. Then, stooping down, Will bent some rough growth aside so as to lay bare the rock and show that, nearly hidden by grey lichen and stonecrop which was growing very abundantly, the rock seemed to be of a pinky cream instead of the prevailing grey and black.

Mr Temple examined it closely without a word. Then taking out his hammer he was about to strike off a fragment, but he refrained and rose up once more.

"That will do for to-day," he said, to Will's disappointment; and for the time it seemed as if the white vein of soft rock was not worthy of notice; but Will noted one thing, and so did Dick. It was that Mr Temple carefully replaced the brambles and overgrowth before climbing higher to the very top of the rift, where he could look out on the open country before he descended and joined the two boys again.

"Now," he said shortly, "back to the boat."

It needed no little skill to get aboard the boat, but Josh handled her so well that he sent her stern close up to the rock upon which they had landed; but just as Mr Temple was about to step on to the rock, in came a wave, and it was flooded two feet deep.

"Little quicker next time, sir," shouted Josh.

"Will you go first, Dick?" said Mr Temple. "Or no; I will," he added; and this time he managed so well that he stepped on to the rock as it was left dry, and from it to the gunwale of the boat as it came towards him, and thence on board.

"Now, Dick, watch your time," said Mr Temple as he sat down.

"All right, father!" shouted back Dick. "I can do it."

"Don't hurry, master," said Josh, as the stone was once more flooded. "Now!" he cried, as the wave sank again.

"One, two, three warning!" shouted Dick, and he jumped on to the rock as it was left bare again, and then found himself sliding on a piece of slimy sea-weed rapidly towards the edge. He made a tremendous effort to recover himself; but it had the contrary effect, and as the next wave came in poor Dick went into it head over heels, and down into deep water.

Arthur uttered a cry, and Mr Temple started up in the boat.

"Sit down!" roared Josh; "he'll come up, and I'll put you alongside him."

Almost as he spoke Dick's head popped up out of the water, and he shook the hair out of his eyes and swam towards the boat, into which he half climbed, was half dragged, and there stood dripping and looking astonished.

"I say, how was that?" he said, staring from one to the other. "I couldn't stop myself. It was like being on ice."

"Sea-weed," said Josh gruffly. "Steady, Will, lad. Don't *you* come aboard that way."

Will did not, but stepped lightly from rock to rock and then into the boat, hardly wetting his feet.

"If I was you, Master Dick," said Josh, "I'd take an oar and row going back—leastwise if we be going back. Then you won't hurt a bit."

"I was going to propose walking home," said Mr Temple, "and I think that will be best."

So they were set ashore at the nearest point to the cliff pathway, where a tramp over the hot rocks with the sunshine streaming down upon his head, half dried Dick before he got back to their rooms, where the dinner he ate after a change fully proved that he was none the worse for this second dip.

"I say, father," he said, "one ought to get used to the sea down here."

"I think so too," said his father smiling; "but, Dick, you must not go on like this."

"No," said Dick; "it's Taff's turn now;" and he said it in so quietly serious a manner that his brother half rose from his seat.

"Oh! by the way, Arthur," said Mr Temple, "Dick's accident made me forget yours. How is the wounded leg?"

"Better, I think," said Arthur, for he had forgotten its existence all through the walk home.

Chapter Eighteen.

Mack'rel in the bay—And the seine fairplay—And a haul for our wives and bairns.

If you want to go to a place where the air you breathe seems to till your veins with joy, and you begin to tingle with a desire to be up and doing something, go down into Cornwall, where the breeze seems to sparkle and effervesce like the waves that beat upon the rocky shore, and from whose crests it bears off the health-giving ozone to mix with the fragrant scent of the wild thyme and heather of the hills and barren moors. The sea never looks two days alike: now it is glistening like frosted silver, now it is as liquid gold. At one time it is ruddy like wine, at another time rich orange or amber, and a few hours after intensely blue, as if the sky had fallen or joined it then and there. Only in storm time is it thick and muddy, as it is in other parts of our coast, and even then it is not long before it settles down once more to its crystal purity.

"Ahoy-ay! Ahoy-ay!"

A musical chorus, softened by distance as it came off the sea, awakened Dick Temple from dreams of boats and mines, and rocks, and caves full of cuttle-fish, crabs, and seals, so big that they seemed monsters of the deep.

The window was open, for he had left it so when he had scrambled out of his clothes and jumped into bed.

Then Arthur, who was calmly folding his garments, or rather his brother's, had quietly gone across the room and shut the window.

"The night air is dangerous," he said.

"No, it isn't," said Dick. "It's all fancy."

"I wish the window to be shut," said Arthur with dignity.

"Oh, very well!" said Dick drowsily; and his brother went on talking.

"Papa has sent for a suit of flannels and a suit of tweeds for me, for I suppose I must wear them while we are down amongst these savages."

The bed creaked and squeaked a little, consequent upon Dick rolling about and laughing; but Arthur was at work with two hair-brushes upon his head, and did not hear.

"I have sent word that the tailor is to make an outside breast-pocket for my handkerchief, and that the flannels are to be edged and bound with black."

Dick's head had been half under the clothes, but he popped it out now to raise himself up a little and say:

"Oh, won't you look lovely!"

Then the bed creaked again as Dick dropped down, his brother not condescending to notice his frivolous remark.

A few minutes later and Arthur had deliberately climbed into bed, yawned, dropped asleep, and Dick had rolled out on his side.

"I don't mean to be smothered when there's such lots of beautiful air outside," he muttered; and he softly opened the window once more, jumped into bed, fell asleep directly, and was awakened by the musical chorus off the sea.

"Oh, I say, what a morning!" he cried as he drew up the blind and saw that about a dozen luggers were coming in from the fishing-ground, where they had been all night, while the sun was turning the bay into one sparkling sheet of glory. "Here! Ahoy! Hi! Rouse up, Arthur. Come and have a bathe."

He made a bound at his brother, and punched and shook him, with the result that Arthur shut his eyes more tightly and hit out at him savagely.

"Get up, or you sha'n't have any clothes," cried Dick, trying to drag them off; but—*Whuff, huff, bang*! down came one of the pillows upon his head, and Arthur rolled himself in the clothes and settled himself for another sleep.

"Oh, sleep away, then!" cried Dick. "Here, hi! Will! Where are you going?"

"To bathe," said Will. "Come!"

"Down in a minute," cried Dick; and deferring all washing till he could get plenty of water out in the bay, he thrust a comb in his pocket, a towel under his arm, and ran down-stairs.

"A nasty old nuisance!" grumbled Arthur, getting out of bed like a badly made parcel, with sheet, blanket, and patchwork quilt rolled round him; and as he shut the window with a bang he could see his brother and Will trudging towards the harbour.

"I'll just have another five minutes, and then I'll get up and dress, and go and meet them," yawned Arthur; then he rolled on to the bed and went off fast asleep.

"Goin' to have a bathe?" said Josh, who was mopping out the boat.

"Yes. Good-morning! How are you?" cried Dick.

"Just nicely, lad," sang Josh. "Here, I don't mind rowing you out if you'll promise to bring me half ounce o' the best 'bacco next time you come."

141

"I'll bring it," said Dick eagerly; and jumping into the boat, Josh rowed the boys out half a mile or so, and then in they went with a plunge off the boat's side, and down into the invigorating clear cool water, to come up again and swim steadily off side by side, Dick being a pretty fair swimmer, though in his modesty he had disclaimed the accomplishment. And as the boys swam, Josh had steadily rowed after them, so that when they had had enough the boat was at hand for them to climb in, have a good towel, scrub, and dress.

"Why don't you have a bathe, Josh?" cried Dick, panting with his exertions. "It's lovely."

"Yes, a good bathe be lovely," said Josh; "but I don't bathe much. I be delicate."

He said it so seriously that Dick never thought of laughing, though Josh seemed solid and hard as wood, which in truth he was.

"Look yonder, lad!" he cried; "see him on the cliff;" and putting the handle of one oar under his leg, he pointed towards the shore west of the village.

"Yes, I can see him: what's he doing?"

"Signalling," cried Josh excitedly; "it's mack'rel."

"What—up there?" cried Dick.

"No, no, lad; in the bay. He can see fish, and he's signalling."

"But he can't see fish in the bay up there."

"Oh, yes! he can. Colour of the water, my lad. He can see a school, and—All right! The lads have seen. There goes the seine-boat."

He pointed to a large boat that seemed laden with something brown. There were several men in her, and they had pushed off, and were rowing steadily out towards the middle of the bay, the water that they lifted with their oars flashing like silver in the sunshine.

"I can see the school, Josh," said Will. "There, just beyond Dallow buoy;" and he stood up pointing with his hand, while the man on the cliff seemed to have a bunch of something in each hand, and to be turning himself into a human semaphore.

"Right, lad! There's the school," said Josh, who had also risen in the boat, and was shading his eyes with his hand. "See, Master Dick?"

"No, I can't see anything."

"What—not out yonder, to left of that buoy?"

"I can see the water looks dark and rippled," said Dick.

"That's them, lad. That's the school o' mack'rel, and I shouldn't wonder if they come right on the flat rock sand."

"What—out of the water?"

"Out of the water? No. Not unless they are catched, and then they'll come out of the water fast enough."

"Look at that chap on the cliff!" cried Dick, as the man began waving what really were boughs of heather up and down.

"Yes, he's signalling away to them in the boat. He can see the school. P'r'aps they can't; and he's telling 'em which way to row."

"But what are they going to do?" cried Dick.

"Do? Why, try and catch that school of mack'rel. Can't you see the seine?"

"What—the net?" said Dick.

"Yes; that's it—hundreds of yards of it. Can you see which way the school's going?"

"Right up to the head of the bay," replied Will.

"Then they are going over the sands, and the lads'll get them. Can't shoot a seine if there's rocks anywhere near," added Josh for the visitor's information. "Get the net torn, and the mack'rel would get out of the hole or under the bottom, where it rests on the rocks. You'd like to stop and see them shoot?"

"What—the mackerel?" said Dick.

"Yah! No; the net."

"Shoot it?" said Dick.

"Yes; shoot it over into the sea."

"Oh! I understand," said Dick; "but they shoot rubbish."

"Oh, they shoot rubbish, do they?" said Josh.

"Yes, about London," replied Dick. "Look how he's waving his arms about."

"Yes. School's going off another way. P'r'aps they mayn't get a chance to shoot, for the school may go out to sea."

143

"Let's row close up. I want to see," cried Dick.

"Nay, nay; we might be frightening the fish. Let's wait and see first, and if they surround 'em then we'll go close up. You sit still andwatch."

The scene was worth watching on that bright morning, with the blue sky above, the glittering sea below, the village nestling in the cliffs, with its chimneys sending up their columns of smoke into the clear air; and at the foot of the cliff, as if seeking its protection, lay the little fishing fleet, with its brown sails giving warmth and colour to as bonny an English landscape as could well be seen. There up aloft, where the hill cliff was purple and gold and grey with heath and furze and crag, was the man with the bushes, signalling to his comrades in the boat, which seemed to be crawling slowly along, the piled-up filmy brown net, lying in a clumsy heap, so it seemed, but really in carefully laid-out folds, with every rope in place ready for the work to be done.

Uncle Abram's boat was allowed to drift with the current as its three occupants watched the proceedings, Will with the more interest that his uncle had a share in the seine, that is to say, he found so many score yards of which its length was composed, and consequently would take his proportion of the profits if the mackerel were caught.

"She's going right for the sands," cried Josh excitedly. "They'll have a fine haul. See 'em, lad—see 'em?"

"Yes, I can see the dark ripple of the water gradually going along," said Dick eagerly. "Oh, I do wish we were nearer!"

"You'll be near enough, lad, when the seine gets to work. Perhaps we shall have to be farther away. Look at 'em; how pretty they come! And you, Will, are always thinking about mines, and stones, and holes in the earth, when you've got a sight like that before you, boy. Eh! but I'm ashamed of you!"

Will laughed and stood watching the school, and answering Dick's questions.

"What are they going to do? Wait and you'll see."

"Oh, no! the fish don't run their heads through these nets and get caught by the gills. Those are drift-nets. This is a seine, and made with smaller meshes. It's stronger, too, and has a rope top and bottom. Now, look, they're getting close enough in. They daren't go any nearer for fear of frightening the fish. Now, see, they're beginning to shoot the net."

For the first time Dick saw that there was a little boat with the big one, and that this little boat had two men in it, who seemed to be stopping in one place, while the big boat was being rowed away from them. Then over the stern a couple of men were passing what seemed to be an enormous brown rope, which they kept shaking as it went over and down into the sea, sinking at once all but what looked like a row of dots on the water right away to the little boat, which now seemed to be connected with the big one by the row of dots.

"That's the seine-net they're shooting overboard," said Will. "It has corks all along the top, and these keep the top edge level with the water, while all the rest sinks right down to the bottom. It's shallow enough over the sands here for the net to touch the bottom."

"I see!" cried Dick excitedly. "And they are going to row right round the shoal of fish and make a regular fence of net about them, so as they can't get away."

"A mussy me!" cried Josh smiling. "Why, I'm getting quite proud o' you, Master Dick. You might ha' been born a fisherman."

"But will the net be long enough to go right round?" said Dick.

"No, perhaps not; but they'll manage that if they're lucky."

The scene was exciting enough to chain the interest of those in the boat, while quite a crowd gathered on the cliff to witness the capture— one which meant money and support to a good many families; for there would be basketing and carting to the far-off station, to send the take to the big towns, if a take it should prove to be. And so all watched as the large boat was rowed steadily, its heap of net growing lower, and the row of dot-like corks that trailed from behind getting longer and longer, and gradually taking the shape of a half-moon.

The little boat remained nearly stationary, only drawing a trifle towards where Dick and his companions were; but the big boat continued its course, and so did the shoal of mackerel, making a beautiful ripple on the surface, that seemed as changeful as the ripple marks on their own backs, and in happy unconsciousness of the fact that their way back to sea was being steadily shut off, and that there were baskets getting ready, and horses being fed to bear them to the train, so that the next morning they would be glittering on stalls in busy towns both far and near.

It was a long but carefully-executed piece of work, the large boat making a very wide circuit, so as not to alarm the fish, now about the centre of a semicircle of net.

"But suppose the net should be twisted," said Dick excitedly, "and not reach the bottom—what then?"

"Then when the mackerel were scared they'd swim about and find the hole, and go through it like the tide between a couple of rocks," replied Will. "But the men wouldn't let the net go down twisted; they're too used to shooting it."

"All out now," said Josh at last. "They'll lose the school if they don't mind. Look yonder."

Dick glanced in the direction indicated, and saw that the man on the cliff was now telegraphing wildly with his boughs, and the men in the seine-boat seemed to let out a long rope, for there was a good space between them and the row of corks.

The two men in the little boat seemed to do the same, and as the two boats were some distance to right and left of Dick and his companions, it seemed as if they meant to come up close with them.

"Josh! Josh! the school's heading this way," cried Will; "they'll lose 'em."

Josh jumped down into the seat, seized the oars, and began to row steadily right across the head of the ripple, just as a hail came first from the big boat and then from the small.

Josh rowed about twenty or thirty yards, and then began to back water, going over the ground again, while the big and little boats steadily rowed on.

"They're gone, Josh!" cried Will, as the ripple on the surface suddenly ceased.

"Maybe they'll come up again, my lad," said Josh. "I'll keep on," and he went on rowing first towards the large boat, then towards the small, as they slowly toiled on, trying to get nearer to each other and Uncle Abram's boat, which was just about intermediate.

If they could once join and form a circle, even if part of it were only the net ropes, the fish would be inclosed, and instead of making for the unfinished part of the circle where there was only rope, they would avoid it and the boats, and make for the other side.

"All right, Josh! they're showing again," cried Will, for the dreaded catastrophe had not taken place—the fish had not gone down and swum away beneath the boats.

146

"Keep wi' us, lad!" came a musical hail to Josh, "and we shall do it yet."

"Ay, ay!" shouted back Josh; and like a sentry he kept going to and fro, with the boats closing up, yard by yard, but slowly, for they had the weight of the widely-spread net to check their progress.

They were forty yards from Uncle Abram's boat on either side, and it seemed a long time before they were twenty, and all the while this was the most dangerous time, for the alarmed shoal was beginning to swim to and fro. Then all at once they disappeared from the surface again, and Dick thought they were gone.

But the fishermen pulled steadily still, and their companions in the stern of each boat kept the line tighter, and just as they were now getting closer the mackerel showed again, making the water flicker as if a violent storm of rain were falling.

"Back out, lad, and go to port," said the captain of the seine-boat; and Josh rowed steadily along close to the line, pausing half-way between the seine-boat and the beginning of the corks, that is, of the net.

The men in the little boat just at the same time passed their rope on board to their friends, and then went off to the right, to pause half-way, as Josh had done to the left.

Meanwhile the men on the seine-boat began to haul steadily at the ropes at each end, drawing the great circle narrower.

"Why, how big is this net round?" said Dick in a whisper, as if he feared alarming the fish.

"Mile," said Josh laconically, "ropes and all."

"But they are drawing the ropes in fast now," said Will, "and when they get the spreaders together it will be seven hundred yards."

"What are the spreaders?"

"Long poles to keep the ends of the net stretched. They've got lead at the bottom, like the net, to keep them on the sand."

"Look out!" shouted the captain of the seine. "Here they come!"

The men hauled the harder, and oars were splashed in all three boats, the smaller rowing to and fro, with the result that the surface of the water became calm once more, not the sign of a ripple to betoken the presence of a fish; but no one ceased his efforts.

"Are they gone, Will?" asked Dick.

"No, they've only gone below; they're hunting all about the seine for a hole to escape, and the thing is now whether they follow it on to one of the ends: if they do, it's only follow my leader, not one will be left."

It was a long job, but the men worked with all their might, keeping up their steady strain at the ropes, and gradually reducing the circle, till at last the two ends of the net were brought together and made to overlap safely, but there was not a sign of the fish.

"They've got away," said Dick.

"I'm afraid so," said Will, for there was an ominous silence among the fishermen, who had been at work all this while apparently for nothing. Then all at once there was a loud cheer, for the shoal, a very large one, suddenly appeared at the top again, fretting the water as the fish swam here and there, shut-up as they were in an irregular circle about two hundred yards across, and hopelessly entangled, for if there had been a loophole of escape they would have found it now.

"There won't be no storm to-day," said Josh, looking round, "so they've got them safe, and now, my lads, what do you say to a bit o' brexfass?"

"Breakfast!" cried Dick. "Oh! I had forgotten all about that. I must go ashore; but I should have liked to see them get the mackerel out."

"Oh! you'll have plenty of time for that," said Josh, beginning to row for the harbour and going close by the seine-boat, whose captain hailed them.

"Thank ye, lads," he cried. "You, Will Marion, tell your uncle we've got as pretty a school as has been took this year."

"Ay, ay!" shouted Will. Then taking one oar he rowed hard, and in a few minutes they were at the harbour, the pier being covered with the fisher folk.

"Best take this year," sang Josh in answer to a storm of inquiries; and then Will sprang up the steps, to run home with a shield of good news to ward off the angry points that Aunt Ruth was waiting to discharge at him for not coming home to his meals in time.

The first faces Dick saw on the pier were those of his father and Arthur.

"I am so sorry, father!" began Dick.

"You've not kept me waiting, my boy," said Mr Temple kindly. "I've been watching the fishing from the cliff."

148

"You might have told me that you were going to see some seine-fishing," said Arthur in an ill-used tone, as they entered the inn parlour, where breakfast was waiting.

"Didn't know myself," cried Dick. "Why, it's ten o'clock! Oh! I am so hungry!"

Chapter Nineteen.

"A gashly great Fish in the Net."

There was quite enough interesting business to see after breakfast to make Mr Temple disposed to go out to the great seine, so that when, about eleven, Will came to the inn to say that he was just going out to the men, if Master Dick or Master Arthur would like to come, their father readily accepted the invitation for all three. So they were rowed out, to find the men very busy at work in boats beside the great circle of corks, shooting a smaller seine inside the big one; and this being at last completed, the small seine was drawn close, the lower rope contracted, and the fish huddled together so closely that a small boat was at work amongst them, the men literally dipping the struggling fish out of the water with huge landing-nets and baskets, the water flying, and the silvery, pearly fish sparkling in the sun.

It was a most animated scene, for as a boat was loaded she went ashore, and the fish were rapidly counted, thrust into small stout hampers, tied down, and loaded on to carts waiting for their freight, and then off and away to the railway-station almost before the fish were dead.

Josh and Will stood high in the good graces of the seine men for their help that morning, so that there was quite a welcome for the party in the boat as the corked line was pressed down, and Josh took the boat right into the charmed circle where the fish were darting to and fro in wild efforts to escape through the frail yielding wall of net that held them so securely.

"I've got a net ready for you," said Will, drawing a strong landing-net from under a piece of sail and handing it to Dick, who was soon after busily at work dashing it in and capturing the lovely arrowy fish in ones and twos and threes. Once he caught five at once, and drew them inboard for his father to admire the brilliancy of the colours upon the live fish, and the lovely purple ripple marks that died away on the sides in a sheen of pink and silver and gold.

Now and then other fish were netted, but fish that had been surrounded with the mackerel. Several times over little stumpy red mullet were seen—brilliant little fish, and then grey mullet—large-scaled silvery fish with tiny mouths and something the aspect, on a large scale, of a river dace.

The fishermen found time to good-naturedly call Josh when any particular prize of this kind was found, and the Temples had not been there long before, flapping, gasping, and staring, a very monster of ugliness was taken out in a landing-net, along with a score of mackerel.

This flat-sided, great-eyed, big-headed creature, with a huge back fin, and general ugliness painted in it everywhere, had a dark mark on either side of the body; and though arrayed and burnished here and there with metallic colours, the fish was so grotesque that its beauties were quite ignored.

"Ah! our friend John-Dory—Jean Doré, as the French call him—gilded John," said Mr Temple. "A delicacy, but not a handsome fish. Look at the thumb and finger marks upon his side."

"Oh! but those are not finger marks," cried Dick.

"No," said his father, "but they are quite near enough in appearance to make people say that this is the fish Peter caught, and held between his finger and thumb while he opened its mouth."

"Here y'are, sir!" shouted a fisherman. "Young gents like to see this?"

Josh rowed the boat alongside and Dick held his net, while the fisherman laughingly turned into it from his own a great jelly-fish, as clear as crystal and glistening in the sun with iridescent colours of the loveliest hue.

"Oh, what a beauty!" cried Dick. "Look, father, look!"

"Yes; keep it in the water, you will see it to the best advantage there."

Dick doused the jelly-fish down into the sun-lit waters, and then they could see its wonderful nature.

In size it was as big as a skittle-ball or a flat Dutch cheese, though a better idea of its shape may be obtained by comparing it to a half-opened mushroom whose stalk had been removed, and where beautifully cut leafy transparencies took the place of the mushroom gills.

No sooner was it in the water than it began to swim, by expanding, and contracting itself with such facility that, but for the meshes of the net, it would soon have taken its wondrous hanging fringes and delicate soap-bubble hues out of sight.

"Better not touch it," said Will, as Dick was about to place his hand beneath the curious object.

"Why not?" asked Arthur sharply.

"Because they sting," replied Will. "Some sting more than others. Perhaps that does, sir."

Arthur glanced at his father, who nodded his head.

"Yes; I believe he is right," said Mr Temple. "It is a curious fact in natural history. We need not test it to see if it is correct."

"Look, look!" cried Dick; "here's a pollack like I caught. Oh! do look at its bright colours, father; but what shall we do with the jelly-fish?"

"Let it go. We cannot save it. In an hour or two there would be nothing left but some dirty film."

The pollack was then examined, with all its glories of gold, bronze, and orange. Then there was a skipping, twining, silvery, long-nose that could hardly be kept in the net, a fish that looked remarkably like an eel, save for its regularly shaped mackerel tail, and long beak-like nose. Sea-bream were the next—ruddy looking, large-eyed fish, not much like their fellows of the fresh water, even what were called the black bream—dark, silvery fellows, similar in shape, bearing but a small resemblance to the fish the brothers had often caught in some river or stream in a far-off home county.

Dick's eyes glistened with pleasure; and waking up more and more to the fact that the finding of fresh kinds of fish gave the boy intense delight, Will kept eagerly on the look-out.

"Here, hi! Throw that over here, Michael Pollard," cried Will.

"It be only a gashly scad," said the great, black-bearded fisherman; and he turned the fish good-humouredly into Dick's landing-net.

"Why, it's a kind of mackerel-looking fish," said Dick, as he examined his fresh prize.

"Ah! mind how you touch it!" cried Will, "it is very sharp and prickly."

"All right!" said Dick. "Oh! I say, though, it is sharp."

"Well, you were warned," said Mr Temple, as Dick applied a bleeding finger to his mouth.

"Yes, but I did not know it was so sharp as that," said Dick. "Don't you touch it, Taff;" and this time he turned the fish over more carefully, to see that it was much the same shape as an ordinary mackerel, but broader of body and tail, and less graceful of outline, while its markings and tints would not compare with those of the ordinary mackerel, and it was provided, as Dick had found, with some very keen spines.

"What do you call this?" said Arthur, rather importantly.

"Scad, sir—horse-mackerel," cried Will.

"Are they good to eat?" said Arthur.

Will shook his head.

"They taste strong, and they say they're not wholesome, sir," replied Will. "Look, they've just caught a bass."

The beautiful silvery fish was passed on by one of the fishermen, and the brilliant scales and sharp, perch-like fin of this favourite fish were being examined, when a violent splashing and commotion told of the presence of something larger in the net.

Whatever it was it escaped for the time; but ten minutes later it was caught in another net, a large, vigorous-looking fish, which made a bold effort to escape, but instead of leaping back into the sea fell into the bottom of one of the boats, where one of the fishermen gave it three or four vigorous blows with a club before he passed it on to Josh, who ladled it into his own boat with the net borrowed from Dick.

"Hake, sir," he said to Mr Temple. "Right good fish, sir, cooked anyhow; and I say as good as cod."

"How came that to be in a mackerel shoal?" said Mr Temple.

"Hungry, sir, *I* should say," replied Josh. "They generally follows the herring and pilchards, and snatch 'em as they're coming into the nets. I s'pose this one wanted a bit o' mackerel for a treat."

"About nine pounds, sir, I should say," said Will. "You'd like to keep it for dinner?"

"Is it good enough?" said Mr Temple smiling.

"Good enough, sir!" cried Will. "Oh, yes! People don't know what a good fish hake is, or they'd oftener want it in London. There's another fish that isn't a mackerel, Master Dick. What should you say that is?"

"Don't know," said Dick, looking at a curious pale-green mottled fish of two or three pounds weight. It was something like a perch in shape, but longer and more regular, and unprovided with the sharp back fin.

"Do you know what it is, papa?" asked Arthur.

"No, my boy, I am not learned in these west-country fishes. What is it, my man?"

"It's a rock-fish, sir, that must have lost its way, for they are not often caught away from the rock," replied Will. "It's the wrasse, sir; some of them are very brightly coloured."

"'Tain't," said Josh gruffly. "What do you want to tell the gentleman wrong for? It's a wraagh, sir—a curner."

"They call them *wraaghs* or *curners*, sir," explained Will, colouring a little; "but the name in the natural history's wrasse."

"Then nat'ral history's wrong," said Josh, in an ill-used way. "A mussy me! as if I didn't know what a wraagh was."

"Want any squid, Josh?" cried one of the fishermen.

"Ay, hand 'em over," said Josh. "They'll do for bait."

"Got three of 'em," said the man, dashing his great landing-net about in the water for some reason that Dick did not understand, and directly after three curious looking, long, slender creatures of the cuttle-fish tribe were in Dick's net, and he was just drawing them in when —*spatter*!—one of them discharged a shower of black inky fluid, a good deal of which fell upon Arthur's trousers, and filled him with disgust.

"Bang 'em 'bout a bit in the water, Master Richard, sir," cried Josh. "He didn't half give it 'em; p'r'aps neither of the others arn't made their cloud."

Instructed by Will, Dick splashed the net down in the water, with the result that it became discoloured with a black cloud, another of these curious looking creatures not having discharged its ink.

"Penanink fish, we calls 'em," said Josh laughing, and turning away his face, for he could not help enjoying the disgust shown by Arthur.

"Make capital bait, Master Richard," said Will, carefully storing the squid away in the locker of the boat.

"Here's some cuttle for you too," shouted Pollard; and this time a couple of cuttle-fish were passed on; but before they reached the boat, taught by experience, Arthur carefully got behind his father, making him a shield against the inky shower which did not come.

As soon as it was safe he emerged, though, and eagerly stood looking on as Dick and his father examined the curious creatures, which looked like soft bags, with so many sucker-covered arms hanging out all ready to seize upon the first hapless fish that came their way, and drag them to their mouths.

"What! is that its mouth?" cried Arthur. "It looks just like a parrot's beak."

It was a good comparison, for there is great similarity between them.

The short tentacles and the two longer ones, with which the cuttle is provided, were duly examined, and then they, murderers as they were of all things that came to their net, were condemned to be eaten in turn.

"Which is only fair, is it, father?" said Dick laughing.

"Quite fair, Dick," he replied. "It seems to be the law of the sea; every fish eats those less than itself and gets eaten in its turn. The only thing with them is, that each one has some chance for its life, and lives as long as it can."

"I see once a very rum kind of a squid," said Josh, who, while the mackerel catching went on and no more curiosities were turned out, seemed disposed to be communicative. "Reg'lar great one he was, at low water out Lizard way."

"Octopus, perhaps," said Mr Temple.

"No, sir—sort o' squid-like, only very different. He was just like a dirty bag with eight arms hanging away from it, all covered like with suckers, and there was two great ugly eyes."

"It was an octopus from your description, my man," said Mr Temple.

"Was it now?" said Josh. "Well, I shouldn't wonder, for it was a horrid gashly thing, and when I saw it first it was sitting in a pool of clear water, with a rock hanging over it, looking at me with its big eyes, and filling itself full of water and blowing it out."

"How large was it?"

"'Bout as big as a bladder buoy, sir, with long arms all round twissening and twining about like snakes; and when I made up my mind that whether it come out and bit me or whether it didn't, I'd stir it up, and I poked at it with a stick, if it didn't shut itself up like and shoot through the water like an umbrella."

"Undoubtedly an octopus," said Mr Temple; "that is its habit."

"Is it now?" said Josh. "Well, I shouldn't have thought it. Seemed queer like for a thing with eight long legs to go zizzling through the water like a shut-up umbrella."

"Did you catch it?" said Dick.

"No, Master Ritchard, sir, I didn't ketch it, only poked at it like with a stick, for it didn't seem good to eat, and it wasn't the sort of thing you'd care to put in your pocket, even if you'd got one big enough, so I left it alone."

"I've heard that they grow very large in the neighbourhood of Jersey," said Mr Temple.

"Do they, though?" said Josh. "Well, they're gashly things, and I don't want to know any more of 'em. Squid and cuttle do very well for us 'bout here."

"Squid, as you call them, are found of immense size in the cold seas towards and in the Arctic circle, large enough, they say, to upset a boat."

"Then I'm glad this is not the Arctic circle," cried Dick. "Only fancy having one of those things picking you out of a boat! Ugh!"

He glanced at his brother and then laughed, for Arthur was looking rather white.

"What say?" roared Josh as loud as he could to a man in a boat close by.

"Gashly great fish in the net," shouted back the man.

"Gashly great fish in the net?" roared Josh.

"Ay; gashly great fish in the net. Mick Polynack see um while ago."

After a few inquiries it was found that the men believed that the great seine had been drawn round some large fish, possibly a shark, and the excitement was great when, after emptying the tuck net, it was gathered in and the great seine drawn closer.

This took a long time, but it was effected at last, the space inclosed being reduced to less than half the former size, and once more the busy scene went on, the mackerel being caught by hundreds, counted into baskets, tied down, and sent off; but though its appearance was eagerly looked for, no sign was given of the presence of the big fish, whatever it might be. More bass were found, and scad, and gurnard, and a long, thin, cod-fish-looking fellow was drawn napping and splashing from the sea, proving to be a ling. Then there was quite a sight of a little shoal of gar-fish or long-nose, which played about the top of the water for some time here and there in a state of excitement; and then there was a splashing and flashing, and one after the other they threw themselves over the cork-line and escaped to the open bay.

"What a pity!" cried Arthur.

"Oh! not much, sir. We don't care a very great deal for 'em down here."

More squid, a cuttle or two, and several other fish of the varieties previously taken; and still, as if the supply was inexhaustible, the mackerel were ladled out as if from a huge basin with the great landing-nets.

"There don't seem to be any big fish here," said Dick at last in disappointed tones, for he had lost all interest in smaller fry since he had heard the announcement of there being something larger inclosed in the net.

"I should say it was a shark," said Josh quietly, "he lies so quiet at the bottom."

The word shark was electrical, and sent a thrill of excitement through the little party.

"But have you sharks off this coast, my man?" asked Mr Temple.

"Not a great few, sir; but we sees one now and then, and times we hear of one being ketched."

"You mean dog-fish," said Mr Temple.

"Oh no! I don't, sir," cried Josh. "Real sharks."

"But only small ones."

"Yes, sir, small ones, big as Will there, and big ones, great as me, and three foot longer. Shouldn't wonder if there was a big one in the net."

"But a large fish such as you speak of would go through the net as if it were a cobweb."

Will shook his head.

"If the net was tight, sir, and the shark swam right at it, the meshes would give way; but they don't seem to swim right at them, and the net goes with the fish like—yields to it—and does not break. It does sometimes, of course; but we've seen a big fish, a porpoise, regularly rolled up in a net and tied in so that it couldn't move."

"Like a conger in a trammel," assented Josh. "Fish is very stoopid, sir, and never thinks of getting out the way they go in."

All this while the seine was being contracted and drawn into the boat, where it was laid up like some gigantic brown skein, the men who were gathering it in shaking out the sea-weed and small fish that had enmeshed themselves and had forced their unfortunate heads in beyond the gills.

"Here she be," shouted one of the men, as there was a tremendous swirl in the water close by a boat.

"All right!" said the captain of the seine, "we'll have her bime-by;" and once more the collecting of the mackerel went on till the tremendous shoal that had been inclosed had exchanged places, and was pretty well all in the baskets that were still being rapidly despatched. And all this time the net had been more and more contracted, the bottom worked by the ropes, so that it was drawn closer and closer, and at last it was decided that the next thing to be done was to capture the large fish, whatever it was, and this they set about, as shall be told.

Chapter Twenty.

Unpleasant Times for a big blue Shark.

Long usage had made the principal fishermen who lived by seine-fishing and trawling as thoroughly acquainted with the bottom of the bay as if they could see it like a piece of land. Every rock and its position was in their mind's eye, every patch of sand and bed of stone, so that they had no difficulty in getting the net in closer and closer towards one side of the bay, where it formed a broad sandy slope, up which it was determined to draw the net, gradually opening the ends, or rather one end, the other being packed deeply down in the seine-boat.

This was done, the small boats being rowed out of the circle of corks, and one going to the free end of the net, while the others, with Uncle Abram's and its load, going to the back of the net, about the middle, so that the visitors might have a good view.

All this took time; but at last the net was so managed that the two seine-boats were ashore, their stems run right on the sands, and the net between them formed a bow towards the coast, the ends being about eighty or ninety yards apart.

There was no mistake now about there being some large fish inclosed; and the excitement of the boys grew intense when they saw Josh take hold of the hitcher, and hold it, spear-fashion, ready to attack the great fish should he see a chance.

"Don't strike at her, Josh," shouted Pollard, "unless she be coming over. I think we can manage her easy enough now."

He was quite right, for long custom had made these men wonderfully clever in the management of a net, which, fragile in its single threads, becomes, in its combination of thousands of meshes, an engine of tremendous power.

The way the men managed was as follows:—

After getting, as it were, the two ends of the net to the shore, they drew on the lower rope, bringing it in, and in, over the sand, till the bow it made was less bent. Then they served the upper rope the same. Then they drew both together, with the result that at last the tremendously extensive net was folded longwise right over upon itself, the top-line was drawn right down upon the foot-line, and at last the fish left in the net were completely shut in what seemed like an enormous old-fashioned purse.

This done, the ends were taken by plenty of willing hands right into shallow water, and as the men hauled, the great purse came closer and closer, and every now and then there was a tremendous agitation towards the middle.

"Let's go ashore, now," said Arthur, as Josh urged the boat on, and the water swirled up tremendously not four yards away.

"Is there any danger—any risk?" said Mr Temple quietly to Josh.

"A mussy me! no, sir; not a bit!" said Josh; and then laughing, he added, "only for shark, sir, of having his liver boiled down for oil."

"Oh! don't I wish I had a spear, or a harpoon!" cried Dick excitedly, as once more the water was churned up and the net came to the surface.

"We'll get her without any o' that tackle, Master Dick, sir," cried Josh, keeping steadily advancing after the cork-line, but not so quickly as to go over the net.

"Are they going to draw the net right ashore, Will?" said Dick.

"Right ashore, Master Dick, on to the sands, and it won't be long now."

"Take care, Dick, or you'll be overboard!" said Mr Temple.

"I should like to be, father; it isn't deep here?"

"Fathom!" said Josh shortly; "soon be half."

There was a regular sing-song kept up by the men who were hauling, and the sands presented quite an exciting scene, for some sixty or seventy of the men who had finished their task, with others who were ashore and not busy, had collected to see the big fish taken in the seine.

"Why, there must be lots of fish in it yet," said Dick.

"Yes; plenty of mackerel left, and a many fish perhaps such as you never saw before."

"Is she heavy, lads?" shouted the captain of the seine-boat.

"Ay, there be a sag o' fish in her yet aside the great un," was shouted back.

"Steady, then! steady! and don't break the seine. Take your time!"

"Hadn't we better get ashore?" cried Dick; "we shall see better."

"No!" said Mr Temple; "I think our friend Josh is right. We are out of the way of the men here and dry. Look, boys, look! there is something big in the net indeed!"

For as he was speaking there was a tremendous commotion, the water was splashed up, and for a moment it seemed as if whatever caused the disturbance had escaped.

But it was not so, though the limits of its prison were growing narrower minute by minute as the ends of the net were gathered on to the sand, and laid at the water's edge like a great soft ridge of brown sea-weed.

The curve of the net was now reduced to fifty feet, and soon it was not above forty; and at this stage of the proceedings what with the weight being collected in such narrow limits, and the water being so shallow, the captain became doubtful of its bearing so tremendous a strain as would be caused by its being hauled bodily ashore, so about twenty men waded in behind the great bag that it formed, and at the word of command as two parties hauled at either end they stooped down, and gathering up a fair quantity of the tightened net in their hands, they too helped, and the thirty or forty feet of shallow water was soon covered, the seine being dragged so that the lead or bottom-line was drawn right on to dry land, and the cork-line raised so that there was a fence of net some three feet above the top of the water, and in the long shallow pool, whose bottom was net, there were the fish by the thousand, rushing to and fro, leaping over each other, and showing flashes of silver, gold, blue, and green, in the bright sun as it shone on the animated scene.

"Bring up some more pads!" cried the captain of the seine; "here be five or six hundred more mackerel. Hand me that boat-hook, my lad, and stand aside. Keep off the net there, you boys!"

Dick realised now the advantage of his position as Josh thrust the boat right up to the net, and he could look down at the crowded fish, some of which began to turn up fast now, killed by the pressure, and the sandy thickness of the water.

But the sight of sights was a long bluish-grey fish that kept slowly forcing itself here and there amongst the silvery crowd, keeping its head well beneath the water, and now and then showing a long, thin, unequally-lobed tail.

"Shark she be, sure enough," said Josh.

"Ay, shark!" said the captain, advancing, boat-hook in hand; "time her mischief was stopped."

"Do they do mischief?" whispered Dick to Will. "No; never mind now; I can't listen to you!"

The scene was too full of interest, for it was evident that the captain meant to hook hold of the shark, and draw it on to the sands before anything else was done.

But this did not prove a very easy task, for the great fish kept diving under the companions of its adversity, and keeping its head boring down towards the bottom.

If it had been a question of catching it by the tail there would have been no difficulty in getting a chance. In fact, several times over a thin line with a noose might have been thrown over the lobes and the fish drawn out; but the captain had made up his mind to get the boat-hook well in the creature's jaws or gills and drag it ashore that fashion, while, when at last he did get a chance he missed, the hook gliding over the shining skin without taking hold.

Twice he missed like this, and it took some time before he could get another chance; but at last it came, and as, full of excitement, the occupants of the boat bent over the side, there was a quick lunge, and a tremendous splashing as the captain ran nimbly up the sands, dragging after him the long bluish fish, which was immediately attacked as it lay on the sands lashing about with its tail, and throwing its head from side to side till the knife-thrusts it received, and the violent blows across the back of the head, disabled it, and its course was at an end.

"I only wonder, sir, as she didn't bite her way out of the net," said the captain of the seine, as Mr Temple and his sons landed to have a look at the take:

"It is a shark, then?" said Mr Temple.

"Ay, sir, she be a blue shark, sure enough. Look at her teeth! Mischievous brutes; they follow the drift-nets, and bite the herring and pilchard out of 'em. I've known 'em swallow a conger when it's been hooked, and I've seen small ones caught that way, but they generally bite through the line and go off. Look, sir, there's teeth—sharp as lancets."

As he spoke he thrust the end of the boat-hook between the shark's jaws, and wrenched them open for the party to see.

"I say, though, Mr Pollard," said Dick.

"Cap'n Pollard, if you wouldn't mind, young gentleman," said the great bluff Cornishman, smiling at Dick.

"Captain Pollard," said Dick, "do these sharks ever attack a man or a boy when bathing?"

"Never heerd o' such a thing," said the captain; "but the mischief they do to a fisherman's craft, sir, is something terrible—lines, nets, fish—they destroy everything. Like to take the shark home with you, sir?"

"No, thank you!" cried Mr Temple, shaking his head; "no sharks, thank you!"

"You're welcome, if you like, sir," said the captain; "but if you don't care for her, I'll send her to London to my salesman, and he'll show her as a cur'osity."

"Eight feet long exactly," said Mr Temple, who had been measuring it.

"Be she, though?" said the captain, "well, it be eight foot o' mischief well put out of the way, and that's a good day's work."

They stopped looking at the long thin shark for some minutes, Dick thinking that it was not so very much unlike a dog-fish after all, and then they turned back to the net, which was being rapidly emptied, the mackerel that were left being quickly counted out into baskets and tied down, those obtained now forming what Dick would have considered quite a good take.

But there were plenty of other fish, though none were very small, the size of the meshes being sufficiently large to allow of their escape. There was one more large hake, and quite a little shoal of red bream, *chad*, as Will called them. Several dog-fish were there too, and some more squid. The fish, however, that most took the attention of the boys now were about a score of red mullet, and half as many more of the grey, very different fish, though, the one being as gorgeous in its scarlet tints as the other was plain, silvery, and grey.

At last, after a most interesting examination of the different captures, the net was declared and proved to be empty, the damaged fish it contained being thrown out upon the sands, where the waves of the flowing tide kept curling over them, and sweeping the refuse away, to be snapped up by the shoals of hungry fish that came up the bay, the thousands that had been captured that morning being as nothing in the immensity of the ocean population.

"Home?" said Dick suddenly, as Mr Temple said something about going. "Of course. Why, we haven't had our dinner!"

"What is for dinner, I wonder?" said Arthur.

"For one thing, fish," said Mr Temple, "for your friend Will went to the inn an hour ago with a basket of the best; so let's go and see if they are done."

Chapter Twenty One.

Mr Arthur Temple is not in the least alarmed.

"Father," cried Dick, bursting into the room where Mr Temple was busy with weights, scales, test-tubes, a lamp, and blow-pipe, trying the quality of some metals—"father, here's Will Marion and Mr Marion's man Josh come to see if we'd like to go with them to-night conger-fishing."

"To-night?"

"Yes; they won't bite very well of a day. He knows a place where—"

"Who is *he*?" said Mr Temple.

"I mean Will, father; he knows of a place where the congers are plentiful, and Josh says he'll take the greatest care of us."

"Whom do you mean by us?" said Mr Temple.

"Arthur and me, father. Taff wants to go very badly."

"I hardly know what to say, Dick," said Mr Temple thoughtfully. "Last time you came to grief, and had a narrow escape."

"Oh, but that isn't likely to occur again, father!" said Dick. "It would be such a treat, too."

"Humph! what am I to do, my boy—coddle you up, and keep you always under my eye; or give you a little latitude, and trust to your discretion to take care of yourself and your brother?"

"Give me a little latitude, father—and longitude too," added Dick with a laugh in his eye.

"Well, I will, Dick; but you must be very careful, my lad, especially of Arthur."

"Oh, but Taff is such a solemn old gentleman with his stick-up collar and his cane that he ought to take care of me, father!"

"Perhaps he ought," said Mr Temple; "but I tell you to take care of him."

"All right, father! I will."

"By the way, Dick, that lad Marion seems a very decent fellow."

"Decent, father! Why, he's a splendid chap. He has rough hands and wears fisherman's clothes and does hard work, but he has been to a big grammar-school in Devonshire somewhere, and he knows a deal more Greek than I do, and quite as much Latin."

"Indeed!"

"Yes, that he does. It made Arthur stare, for he was coming the great man over Will Marion, and being very condescending."

"Yes, it is a way Master Arthur has," muttered Mr Temple frowning.

"I said to Taff that he ought not to, but he would. I like Will Marion. Josh says he'll be owner of a lot of fishing-boats and nets some day when his uncle dies; but he says Will thinks he would like to make his own way in the world, and that it is very foolish of him."

"Oh, that's what Josh thinks, is it?"

164

"Yes, father."

"And what do you think?"

"That a lad ought to be independent and try and fight his own way in the world. I mean to."

"That's right, my boy. Keep to that text and you will succeed. You may have a good many downfalls first, but sooner or later you will get on. There, go away now. I'm busy testing ere."

"Can I help you, father?"

"No, my lad, no. Not now. There, be off, and don't get into any mischief."

"No, father. And about the conger-fishing?"

"If you will take great care you may go."

"Hooray!"

"But stop. Tell that man Josh that I hold him responsible for taking care of you."

"Yes, father," cried Dick. "Hooray!" he whispered as he darted out of the room, and came so suddenly upon Arthur that he sent him backwards into a sitting position.

Arthur sat looking petrified with pain and astonishment, cane in one hand, a book in the other. Then starting up as Dick offered him his hand laughingly, saying, "I'm very sorry, Taff!" Arthur raised his cane and struck his brother viciously across the shoulder a regular stinging cut, while, smarting with the pain, Dick struck back at him, and gave him so severe a blow in the cheek that Arthur this time measured his length on the floor.

"Quiet, you boys, quiet!" said Mr Temple angrily, as he opened his door. "Go and play down on the shore."

Dick's anger evaporated on the instant, and was succeeded by a feeling of mingled shame and sorrow.

"Oh, I am sorry, Taff!" he said, helping his brother to rise. "You shouldn't have hit me, though. If anybody hurts me like that I'm sure to hit out again."

Arthur did not answer till they were outside, and then he turned viciously upon his brother.

"You're a regular coward," he cried, "to strike a blow like that."

"I didn't say you were a coward for beginning it," said Dick sharply. "You struck the first blow. Never mind, let's shake hands. It's all over now."

Arthur turned his back and went away, switching his cane as he walked towards the upper part of the village, while, after stopping to gaze after him for a few minutes, Dick sighed, and strolled down to his favourite post, the pier, to tell Will Marion that he had obtained leave for the fishing, and to ask what time they were to start.

"I wish I hadn't hit Taff," he said to himself dolefully; "but he knows how savage it makes me if I'm hurt. I wish I hadn't hit him, though, all the same."

The regret was vain: he could not take back the blow, and his forehead wrinkled up and his spirit felt depressed as he went on.

"Poor old Taff!" he said to himself. "I don't think he's so strong as I am, and that makes him ill-tempered. And I'd been promising father that I'd take care of him; and then I've got such a brutal temper that I go and begin knocking him about.—Oh, I wish I wasn't so hot and peppery! It's too bad, that it is.

"I suppose we sha'n't go conger-fishing now," he said gloomily. "Taff won't care to go.

"Yes, he will," he said after a few minutes' pause. "I'll tell him at dinner-time I'm very sorry; and then we shall make it up, and it will be all right! Why, hallo! there he is going down to the boats. He must have been round the other way. I'll bet a penny he heard what I said to father about the fishing, or else he has seen Will."

The latter was the more correct surmise, though Arthur had also heard his father give his consent.

"Hi! Taff!" shouted Dick; but his brother did not turn his head, stalking straight down to the pier and getting to where Will and Josh were at work preparing their tackle for the night's fishing.

"I'm very sorry, Taff," said Dick humbly. "I hope I did not hurt you much."

Arthur made no reply, but began to speak to Will.

"Papa has given me leave to go with you," he said; "but I don't think I should care about being out so late."

"Better come, sir," said Josh. "It will be rare sport. I know about the best place along our bay, and it hasn't been fished for six months, has

166

it, Will?"

"Nine months, quite," said Will. "Yes, you had better come, sir."

"He's hoping I won't go," said Arthur to himself; "and Dick hopes I won't go; but I will go just out of spite, to let them see that I'm not going to let them have all their own way."

"Oh, he'll come," said Dick, "and you'll give him some good sport, won't you? He hasn't had any fishing since we've been down here. And I say, Josh, my father says he shall hold you responsible. No getting us run down this time."

"Not I," said Josh. "I'll have a lantern hoisted as we row back, and no boats will come where we are fishing; it's too rocky."

"Let's see the lines," said Dick eagerly. "Oh, I say, what a hook! It's too big."

"Not it," said Will. "Congers have big mouths, and they're very strong."

"What time shall we get back?"

"'Bout ten, sir," said Josh, "and start at half-past five. We'll have everything ready."

Arthur turned to go directly after; and though Dick was anxious to stay he was more eager to make friends with his brother, and he followed him, to have his apology accepted at last, but not in the most amiable of ways.

The fact is Arthur would have held out longer, but he could not do so without jeopardising the evening trip, upon which he had set his mind.

His was a singular state of mind, for although filled with an intense longing, this was balanced by a curious sensation of dread, consequent upon his somewhat nervous temperament, which is a roundabout way of saying that he was afraid.

The idea of going right away, as it seemed to him, at night over the dark water to fish by the light of a lanthorn was startling, and sent a curious shiver through him; but at the same time it attracted him with a strange fascination that forced him to keep to his determination of being one of the party, as often as his old timidity made him disposed to say he would stay at home.

"And if I did, Dick would laugh at me. But he shall not this time."

So he kept up a distant manner towards his brother for the rest of the day, playing grand and pardoning him, as he said to himself, by degrees, so that after an early tea, when they had started together they were pretty good friends.

"I am glad you are going, Taff," said Dick in his buoyant way. "I shall ask Josh to take special care of you."

"I beg that you will do nothing of the sort," said Arthur haughtily. "I daresay I can take care of myself."

Arthur drew himself up as he said this, and stalked along rather grandly; and of course he might dare to say that he could take care of himself: but saying and doing are two very different things, and the probabilities are that if he had known what conger-fishing meant, he would not have gone.

Chapter Twenty Two.

Over the Bay in the Eventide, when the Sun goes down in the West.

It was close upon half-past five, and all Will's preparations had been made. Lines of strong cord with hooks bound up the snooding with brass wire were on their winders. There was a tub half full of tasty pilchards—damaged ones fresh out of a late boat that had come in that afternoon. There was another tub full of much more damaged pilchards—all pounded up for ground bait.

In fact nothing had been forgotten; even three oilskins had been lashed, in the stern ready for the visitors in case it should rain.

"I say," said Josh, "how about the young gent? I mean him Master Dick calls Taff?"

"Well, what about him?" said Will.

"Won't he be scared when we gets a conger over the side."

"I never thought of that," said Will musingly. "Oh! I should think not."

"'Cause we shall be in a gashly pickle if we haul in a big one, and she scares the youngster out of the boat."

"We must kill them at once," said Will.

"Yes; it's all very well to say kill 'em at once," grumbled Josh; "but you know what a gashly thing a big conger is to kill."

"Yes; he won't lie still and be killed sometimes," said Will laughing. "Ah! well, perhaps we sha'n't catch any at all."

"Oh, yes! we shall, and gashly big uns too. Hadn't we better leave young Arthur behind—'tother won't be feared?"

"No; it's too late now," said Will. "Here they are;" for just then the brothers came along the pier, and after Arthur had stepped in rather a dignified way down into the boat, Dick leaped in and insisted upon taking an oar.

The boat was pushed off at once, and while Will and Dick were rowing Josh had to answer Arthur Temple's questions.

"Are those the lines?" he said, gazing at them curiously.

"Yes, sir; and we've got some oilskin aprons for you to put on, so as you sha'n't get wet."

"Aprons!" cried Arthur aghast.

"Yes, sir; they be good uns too."

"I shall not put on an apron," was upon Arthur's lips, but he did not say it; and just then his attention was taken by a short thick truncheon, with a curious notch or fork at the handle end.

"What's that for?"

"Little end's disgorger," said Josh; "t'other's to knock the congers down with."

"To knock the congers down!" cried Arthur aghast.

"Yes, when we get hold of a big one. They're gashly strong, sir."

"Why, how big are they?" cried Arthur.

"Five foot, six foot, seven foot sometimes," said Josh coolly.

Arthur's first thought was to say, "Here, take me back;" but he caught his brother's eye, and suppressed the words.

"I—I did not know they were so big as that," he faltered, though he tried to say it with firmness and a show of resolve.

"They run big, sir, off our coast, and we get some gashly fellows, often," said Josh innocently; "but you see, big as they are, men's stronger, and boys too. Why, our Will would tackle any conger as ever swam about a rock. Takes hold of disgorger like this, you know, and gives one on the head, and that quiets 'em while we get the hook out."

169

"With—with the disgorger?" said Arthur.

"That's it, Master Taff," said Josh.

"My name is Arthur—Arthur Temple," said the boy haughtily.

"'Course it is, sir; I ought to have known," said Josh. "It was along of Master Dick, there, calling you by t'other name. As I was saying," he continued hastily, "Will there gives them a tap with the disgorger, and then holds them under his boot, runs this here down till it touches the hook where they've swallowed it, takes a turn or two of the line round the handle and twists the hook out."

"Why don't you take the hook out properly—the same as I should from a fish?"

"What—with your fingers, sir?"

"Of course."

"A mussy me!" said Josh. "Why, don't you know how a conger can bite?"

"Bite! No," said Arthur, turning pale. "Can they bite?"

"Bite!" cried Josh. "Why, love your heart, young gentleman, look ye here. See this?"

He held up one of the hooks at the end of the conger-line and showed the boy that not only was it very large, and tied on strong cord with a swivel or two, but it was bound from the shank some distance up the line with brass wire.

"Yes, I can see it," said Arthur, "of course. Isn't it too big? A fish would not take a great awkward thing like that in its mouth."

"Won't it?" said Josh laughing. "But it will if you put a pilchar' on it. That there wire as is run round the line is to keep the congers from biting it in two."

"Oh! but, Josh, a conger wouldn't bite through a line like that, would he?" cried Dick as he tugged at his oar.

"Just as easy, sir, as you would through a bit o' cotton after you'd sewed a button on your shirt."

"Why, they must be regular nippers!" cried Dick.

"Nippers, sir? Why, they go at a big dead fish if it's lying in the water, take a good mouthful, and then set their long bodies and tails to work, and spin round and round like a gimlet or a ship augur, and bore the piece right out."

"Oh! I say, Josh, don't you know! He's making that story up, isn't he, Will?"

"No," said Will seriously; "it is quite true. Congers have a way of spinning themselves round like that. Don't you see those swivels on the line?"

"Yes," said Dick, "I see 'em."

"That's because the congers spin round so. If we did not use swivels they'd twist the line all in a tangle before you could get them out."

"Why, they're regular sea-serpents," said Dick.

"Well, no," said Josh; "they ain't so big as sea-sarpents, because they say they're hundreds o' yards long. I never see one, but I've heerd say so; but congers will bite and no mistake. I had one ketch me by the boot once, and he bit right through the leather."

All this while they were rowing farther and farther from the shore, on about as lovely an evening as it was possible to imagine, and the warm glow of the sunshine prevented Arthur's face from looking ghastly white.

He felt that he must beg of them to turn back directly—that he dared not go farther; and yet there was a greater fear still to keep him silent. If he begged of them to row back they would laugh at him for a coward, and he could not bear this.

"Fishing!" he thought; why, it was like going to attack some horrible pack of sea-monsters in their rocky fastnesses; and instead of being dressed in flannels, he felt that he ought to be clothed in complete armour. Why, if a conger could bite through a line, what would he think of flannel trousers? And if one got tight hold of his flesh, what would be the consequences?

Arthur sat there with his mouth dry and his eyes staring as, in imagination, he saw one of the great slimy creatures twisting itself round and round, and cutting a great piece out of one of his legs; and it was all he could do to keep from shuddering with fear.

And all the while there was Dick with a red face, and his hat stuck right at the back of his head, tugging away at his oar, and smiling at all Josh said.

"I must try and be as brave as Dick is," Arthur said to himself; and forcing his teeth firmly together, he began to plan in his own mind what he would do if Dick caught a conger. He would have his penknife ready in his hand, and pretend to help pull in the line; and while he was doing this he would cut it and the monster would swim away.

"Don't you be scared about the congers, Master Taffarthur, sir," said Josh kindly. "They be gashly ugly things to tackle sometimes, but—"

"I'm not afraid," said Arthur indignantly.

"Not you, sir. Why should you be?" said Josh. "We can manage them. A big one has a nasty way of his own of getting loose in the boat and wriggling himself all about under the thwarts—"

Arthur involuntarily began to draw up his legs, as he felt as if one were already loose in the bottom of the boat.

"But just you look ye here," continued Josh, opening the little locker in the stern of the boat. "This is how I serves the big jockeys who'd be likely to give any trouble. I just give them a cut behind the head with this little fellow, and then they lie quiet enough."

As he spoke he showed Arthur a little axe with a very small head, and an edge as keen as a knife.

"That's too much for congers," added Josh.

"I say, how cruel to the poor things!" said Dick laughingly; but Josh took it in the most serious way.

"Well, I have thought that 'bout the gashly conger, Master Dick, sir," said Josh; "but I don't know as it be. You see, they're caught, and it puts 'em out of their misery, like, at once."

"But it's cruel to catch them," said Dick.

Josh scratched his head.

"A mussy me, Master Dick, sir! that's a thing as has puzzled me lots o' times when I've been hooking and killing fish; but then, you see, it's for victuals, and everybody's got to live."

"So have the fish," laughed Dick.

"So they have, sir; but you see here, I catches and kills a conger, or a pollack, or a gurnet, or a bass. Suppose I hadn't killed it—what then?"

"Why, it would be swimming about in the sea as happy as could be."

"Yes, Master Dick, sir; but what else would it be doing?"

"Basking in the sunshine, Josh."

"P'r'aps so, sir; but, a mussy me! he'd be chasing and hunting and eating hundreds of little fish every day; so you see if I catches one big one, I saves hundreds of little ones' lives."

"I never thought of that," said Dick.

"Josh and I have often talked about it," said Will seriously. "It seems cruel to catch and kill things; but they are always catching and killing others, and every bird and fish you see here is as cruel as can be. There goes a cormorant; he'll be swimming and diving all day long catching fish, so will the shags; and all those beautiful grey-and-white gulls you can see on the rock there, live upon the fish they catch on the surface of the water."

"Then if we keep the congers from catching and killing other fishes and eating them, why, it's being very kind, and isn't cruel at all," said Dick merrily; and then he sent a cold chill down his brother's spine by saying, "Let's look sharp and catch all the big ones we can."

"Now, you two take a rest," said Josh, "and I'll put her along a bit;" and changing places with the rowers, Josh handled the oars with such effect that in about half an hour they were approaching a tall mass of rock that had seemed at a distance to be part of the cliff-line, but which the visitors could now see to be quite a quarter of a mile from where the waves were beating the shore.

Chapter Twenty Three.

Dick catches his first Conger.

"Why, Will," cried Dick, "it is quite an island. Oh, Taff, look at the birds!"

"We don't call a rock like that an island," said Will quietly, as the boys watched a cloud of gulls that had been disturbed by their approach, and new screaming and uttering peevish querulous cries above their heads. The top of the rock, which was sixty or seventy feet above the water, was quite white with guano, and every ledge of the perpendicular mass seemed to be the home of the sea-birds which had been perched there in rows, looking almost like pigeons till the near approach of the boat had sent them off.

"How long would it take to row round?" said Arthur, who, in the novelty of the scene, forgot all about the conger.

"Two minutes if you could go close in," said Josh; "ten minutes, because you have to dodge in and out among the rocks which lie out all round."

"And from the Mew Rock to the shore yonder," added Will.

"Yes," said Josh; "it's all rock about here, just a fathom or two under water, and a bad place for boots."

"Then why did you come in your boat?" cried Arthur excitedly.

"I don't mean little boots in fine weather, sir, I mean big boots in foul," replied Josh, rowing steadily away. "This here's the place where we wanted to come, and I'm going to take you to a hole like with rocks all round it, a hole as goes down seven or eight fathom, and the congers swarm in the holes all about here, as you'll see."

Arthur's hand tightened on the boat, and his dread made him feel almost ill; but he struggled with the nervous feeling manfully, though he dared not trust himself to speak.

And all the while Josh rowed steadily on till he was skirting round the edge of the perpendicular mass of rock about whose base the waves foamed and fretted, as if weary with their efforts at trying to wash it down. The birds squealed and hissed, and now and then one uttered a doleful wail as it swept here and there, showing its pearly grey breast and the delicate white feathers beneath its wings.

"Do you ever shoot these birds, Will?" said Dick, lying back so as to stare up at the gulls as they floated so easily by.

"Shoot them! Oh, no! The fishermen here never harm them; they're such good friends."

"Why?" said Arthur.

"They show us where the fish are," replied Will. "We can see them with the glass miles away, flapping about over a shoal of little ones, and darting down and feeding on them; and where they are feeding, big fish are sure to be feeding on the shoal as well."

"Then I shouldn't like to be a shoal of little fish," cried Dick. "Why, as the clown said in the pantomime, 'it would be dangerous to be safe.' I wonder there are any small fish left."

"There are so many of them," said Will laughing; "thousands and millions of them; so many sometimes in a shoal that they could not be counted, and—"

"Stand by with the killick, m'lad," cried Josh, as he paddled slowly now, with his eyes fixed first on one landmark, then on another.

"Ready," said Will, clearing the line, and raising a great stone, to which the rope was fast, on to the edge of the boat.

"Drop her atop of the little rock as I say when," growled Josh.

"Right," answered back Will.

Josh backed the boat a few yards; and as Dick and his brother gazed over the stem they were looking down into black water one moment and then they glided over a pale-green rock flecked with brown waving weeds.

"When!" cried Josh.

Plash!

The big stone went over the side on to the rock, which seemed pretty level, and then as the line ran over the stern Josh began to row once more, and the boat glided over the sharp edge of the rock and into black water once more that seemed of tremendous depth.

"Now, forrard, my lad," said Josh; and Will passed him and took his place right in the bows.

Here a similar process was gone through.

After rowing slowly about thirty yards Josh stopped.

"That ought to do it," he said. "She won't come no further. Over with it."

Will was standing up now in the bows swinging a grapnel to and fro, and after letting it sway three or four times he launched it from him, and it fell with a splash a score of yards away, taking with it another line, upon which when Dick hauled he found that the grapnel was fast in a rugged mass of rock like that which they had just left; and with grapnel and killick at either end of the boat, they were anchored, as Josh pointed out, right in the middle of the deep hole.

"You can find rocks all round us," he said, "on which you could have pitched the killick, and they all go straight down like the side of house or like that there Mew Rock where the birds are."

There was something awe-inspiring in the place, for the boat was in the shadow of the Mew Rock, behind which lay the sun, hastening to his rest, his ruddy beams streaming now on either side of what looked like a rugged black tower standing against a blazing sky, and for the moment even Dick felt oppressed by the solemnity and beauty of the scene.

Away across the head of the bay lay the fishing village from which they had come, with its lattice-windows glittering and flashing in the sunshine, which gilded the luggers that were slowly stealing out to the fishing-ground miles away. Some of them were urged forward by long oars so as to get them beyond the shelter of the land, and into the range of the soft breeze that was rippling the bay far out, though where the fishing party lay the heaving sea, save where it broke upon the rocks, was as smooth as glass.

"Now, young gentlemen," said Josh quietly, "congers is queer customers; sometimes they'll bite."

Arthur shivered.

"Sometimes they won't. I think to-night we shall ketch some."

"Two lines out, eh, Josh?" said Will.

"Ay, two's enough," replied the fisherman; "let the young gents ketch 'em, and we'll do the gawfing and unhooking. You 'tend Master Dickard there; I'll 'tend Master Taffarthur, and let's see who'll get first fish. Starboard's our side, port's yourn."

As he spoke he nodded knowingly to Arthur and took out his knife, seized a pilchard, cut off its head, and split the fish partly up towards the tail and extracted the backbone, so that it was in two flaps. Then taking the large hook, he passed it in at the tail, drew the pilchard carefully up the shank, and then held up the hook for Arthur to see, with the broad flaps hanging down on either side of the curve and barbed point.

"There," he said, "Mr Conger Eel, Esquire, won't notice that there's a hook in that nice tasty bit of pilchar'. He'll take it for his supper, and to-morrow he'll make conger pie. Now, are you ready?"

"Yes," cried Arthur, making an effort to master his dread.

"Right, then," cried Josh; "lift the lead there over the side, and I'll drop in the bait, and we shall have no tangle."

Arthur lifted a heavy piece of lead of the shape of a long egg cut down through its long diameter and attached by wire rings to the line, and lowered it over the side, Josh dropping in the silvery bait of pilchard at the same moment, and as the lead sank the bait seemed to dart down as if alive, disappearing in the dark clear water as the line ran rapidly over the side.

"Let your line run, lad; there's good seven fathom o' water just here. That's the way," said Josh. "Now she's at the bottom."

Plash, plash! came from the other side of the boat, and Dick shouted, "Hooray, Taff! here goes for first fish."

"Never you mind him," said Josh to Arthur. "Now, then, hold hard; haul up a fathom o' line—that's the way: now your bait's just by the bottom, and you'll know when you've got a bite."

Arthur obeyed, and sat in the boat holding the line with both hands as rigid as a wax image, and gazing hopelessly at the rough fisherman, whose one short arm seemed horribly clever and deft, but he fancied it would be awkward if he had to deal with a large eel.

"Hadn't you better get the chopper ready?" said Arthur hoarsely.

"Oh, that's all ready," said Josh laughing; "but you ain't had a touch yet."

"N–no—I'm not sure," said Arthur; "something seemed heavy at the end of the line."

"Four pound o' lead, my lad, is heavy," said Josh, smiling. "You'll know when you get a conger."

"Hadn't—hadn't we better fish for something else, as the congers don't bite?"

"How do you know as they don't bite?" said Josh good-humouredly.

"They—they don't seem to," said Arthur. "Perhaps the bait's off. Had we better see?"

"Oh, no; that bait isn't off," said Josh quietly. "You bide a bit, my lad. Congers don't care about light when they're feeding. You'll see when the sun's well down."

"But I'd rather fish for mackerel, I think," said Arthur as he gazed down into the dark water, and seemed to see twining monsters coming up to pluck him out of the boat.

"Couldn't ketch mack'rel here, my lad. This is a conger hole. Reg'lar home for 'em among these rocks. Will and me found 'em out: nobody else comes and fishes here. We found this hole."

"Ahoy! here's a game. Oh, don't he pull! Oh, my hands!" cried Dick.

"Let me take him," said Will.

"No, no, I'll catch him!" cried Dick excitedly. "I've got such a big one, Taff; he's trying to pull my arms out of the sockets!"

Tug—pull—jerk—drag—the line was running here and there; and if Dick had not twisted it round his hands it would have been drawn through them. As it was, it cut into them, but he held on like a hero.

"Let the line go!" Will kept saying—"let the line go!" but Dick did not seem to understand. If he did, he was not disposed to let it run, and, as he thought, lose the fish; and so he dragged and hauled hand over hand, with Arthur shivering and ready, but for sheer shame, to get right away in the bows, as the struggle went on.

"Here he is!" cried Dick at last. "Oh, what a monster! and how he pulls!"

Arthur did not turn his head, and so he saw nothing of what followed, for he felt sick with dread; but there was a scuffling and a splashing, then a beating and flapping in the boat.

"Keep him clear of the line, Will, lad!" said Josh.

"Right!" was the laconic reply; and then there were two or three heavy dull blows, as if some one were striking something soft. And now Arthur turned round to see that Will had the great head of an eel between his knees, out of which he cleverly twisted the hook, and held the slowly writhing creature up at arm's-length.

"Oh, what a monster!" cried Dick.

"Only a little one," said Will, laughing. "It is not above fifteen or sixteen pounds."

"Why, how big do they grow, then?" cried Dick, as the eel was thrown into the locker and the lid shut down.

"I've seen them ninety pounds!" said Will. "Josh, there, saw one a hundred. Didn't you, Josh?"

"Hundred and three pounds and an half!" said Josh. "We shall have some sport to-night!"

Chapter Twenty Four.

Arthur catches his first Conger, and takes a Lesson in something else.

"Oh!" shouted Arthur; "oh! something's pulling me out of the—"

Boat he would have said, for he had turned the line round his right-hand to keep the lead from the bottom; and all at once it had seemed to him that there was a slight quiver of the line; then it was drawn softly a little way, and then there was a heavy sustained pull that took his arm over the side, and he seemed as if he were about to follow it, only Josh leaned towards him, and took hold of the line beyond his hand.

"Untwist it, my lad; don't turn it round your fingers like that. That's right. Now, take hold with both hands."

"But I can't hold it!" cried Arthur, who was shivering with excitement.

"Oh, yes! you can, my lad," said Josh coolly. "I'll show you. Now, hold tight."

Arthur clung to the line with both hands in desperation; and it seemed to him that the great fish at the end of it was trying to draw his shoulders out of their sockets.

"It's too hard. It cuts my hands. It's horrible!"

"Let him go, then," said Josh laughing; "there's plenty of line. Let it run through your hands."

"It burns them," cried Arthur desperately. "Ah!" he exclaimed with a sigh of delight, "it's gone!"

"Haul in the line, then!" said Josh grimly, while Will, who knew what it meant, touched Dick on the shoulder so that he should watch.

Arthur began to haul in the slack line for a few feet, and then he shouted again:

"Here's another one bigger than the last!" he cried. "I cannot hold it."

"Let it go, then," said Josh; and Arthur once more slackened the line, which ran fast for a yard, and then fell loose.

"He's gone now!" said Arthur, hauling in the line; and then in a tone of voice so despairing that his brother burst into a hearty laugh: "Here's another at it now!"

"I say, what a place this is, Taff!" cried Dick. "Here, let me help you!"

"No, no," cried Josh; "you let him ketch the conger himself. Slacken, my lad."

As if moved by a spring, or disciplined to obey the slightest word of command, Arthur slackened the line.

"Now, then, haul again," cried Josh; and the boy pulled in the line eagerly, as if moved by the idea that the sooner he got the hook out of the water the less likelihood would there be of its being seized by one or other of the monsters that inhabited the rocky hole.

"He has got it again!" cried Arthur in tones of anguish; "he'll pull me in!"

"Oh, no, he won't; you're a-going to pull him out, if he don't mind his eye," said Josh sturdily. "You've got some brains, young gentleman, and he arn't."

"But there must be a swarm there after my bait," pleaded Arthur.

"Not there," cried Josh. "There's one got it."

"But I've had three or four on, and they've gone again."

"Oh, no! you haven't," said Josh; "conger eels often do like that. You pull hard; he pulls hard and tries to get to the bottom. You slack the line, and as there's nobody pulling up, he comes to see what's the matter. Now, slacken!"

Arthur let the line run.

"Now haul again."

The boy drew in the line, and gained nearly twice as much as he had let out before there was a tremendous drag again, and as Arthur held on with both hands his arms quivered.

"Ease him a little—now pull—ease again—now pull!" cried Josh, over and over, till, giving and taking like this, Arthur had drawn the heavy lead nearly to the surface of the water, and for a moment he thought the dark little object going here and there was the eel; but directly after he saw a great wavy blue-black line some feet down, and that all at once turned to one that was creamy white, then dark, then light again, as the conger writhed over and over.

"I've got one too!" cried Dick; and his attention, like that of Will, was taken from what went on upon the starboard side of the boat, leaving Arthur to the care of Josh.

"Josh!—please," faltered Arthur, as he clung to the line in an agony of dread, too much alarmed now even to let go. "Josh—pray—pray cut the line!"

"No, no, no! you don't mean that," whispered back Josh encouragingly. "You mean get my little axe, and kill my gentleman as soon as he's aboard."

"Yes, yes. No, no," whispered Arthur. "Pray, pray, don't bring that horrible thing into the boat!"

"Not till he's dead, you mean," said Josh, in a low voice, so that Dick and Will could not hear. "You're not scared of a gashly old conger like that? You hang on to the line, my lad. You've got plenty of pluck, only you arn't used to it. Now, you see, ease him a bit."

Arthur involuntarily slackened the line, and the eel ceased its backward drag and swam up.

"Now, haul again—just a bit," said Josh, standing there with the gaff in his perfect hand, keen axe in the deformed.

Arthur obeyed and dragged the writhing serpentine creature close to the surface. Then, quick as thought, Josh had the great snaky fish by the head with his short sharp gaff-hook, drew it over the gunwale, and before Arthur could realise what was done the axe had descended with a dull thud, and Josh dragged the quivering half inert conger over the side and forward, clear of the line and away from Arthur.

"There!" cried Josh, as he cleverly extricated the hook with the disgorger; "you come and look at him, Master Arthur. He can't bite now, and I'm holding him down."

There was so much quiet firmness in the fisherman's words that Arthur felt himself constrained to go forward and look at the great snaky fish as it heaved and curved its springy body in the bottom of the boat.

"A reg'lar good fat one," said Josh. "She be a bit ugly, sure enough, and I've seen many a boy in my time scared by the gashly things. It was your first one, Master Arthur, and you caught him, and I say as you warn't a bit scared."

"I—I couldn't help being a little afraid," said Arthur slowly; "but look! look! it's biting the rope."

"Ay, but it has no strength to bite now," said Josh. "There, we'll put um in the well, and let um lie there. You caught um—fine eight-and-thirty pound if it be an ounce. Now you shall catch another."

"What!" gasped Arthur.

"I say, now you shall catch another," said Josh sturdily, as he leaned over the side and washed disgorger, axe, and hook. "You won't mind half so much next time, and then your brother won't be able to crow over you."

"I don't want to catch any more, thank you," said Arthur.

"Oh, yes, you do," said Josh, in his quiet stubborn fashion. "Don't you say you don't. It won't be half so startling ketching the next one, and I've got a tender well-beaten bit of squid for the next bait—one as will tempt the biggest conger that is in the hole."

"No, no!" whispered Arthur. "I don't want to fish any more; I don't indeed."

"Hush!" whispered Josh; "you'll have them hear."

Arthur was silent directly, and just then his fright was at its height with the conger that Dick had hooked, and that Will gaffed and hauled in. For as Will struck at it with the conger-bat or club, instead of there coming a dull thud as the blow fell, there was the sharp tap of wood upon wood.

Will had missed this time, and the conger was apparently starting on a voyage of discovery about the boat.

Arthur shrank back, but before the fish could come his way and tangle the lines Will caught Dick's about a yard above the hook, dragged the fish towards the stern, and gave it four or five paralysing blows in succession, disabling it, so that he soon had the hook out, and he and Dick stood looking at each other and panting with excitement.

"Hor—hor—hor!" laughed Josh quietly as he seated himself on the thwart and leisurely began to pass the hook through the grey piece of tough soft cuttle-fish. "Look at 'em, Master Rawthur, there be a fuss over a conger not above half as big as ourn."

"It was ever so much stronger," cried Dick indignantly.

"Hear him, Mast Rorthur!" cried Josh. "Hor—hor—hor! There, go on, you two. We're going to give you a startler this time. There you are, sir," he whispered, holding up the bait for Arthur to see. "That's one as'll tempt um, and you see we'll have another big one before they know where they are. I say, you won't be scared of the next, will you, now?"

"I'll—I'll try not to be," whispered Arthur, drawing a long breath.

"Then you won't be," whispered Josh. "That's the way: in with the lead. Of course they're awk'ard things for any boy to tackle at first. I was downright frightened first one I hooked, when I was 'bout as old as you, and it warn't above half the size of the one you ketched."

"Were you really frightened of it?" said Arthur in the same low tone.

"Frightened, Master Taffarthur! Why, my cap come off and fell in the water, and I had to up with the killick and row after it."

"But that didn't show you were frightened."

"Didn't it though, sir? Why, it was my hair rose up in such a gashly way it lifted it off. There, now, hold steady, and it won't be long before you have a bite."

It was getting so dark now that Arthur could not see whether Josh was laughing at him or not, though for the matter of that, if it had been noontide, he would not have been able to make out the rough fisherman's thoughts by the expression of his countenance.

A splash from behind them told them that Dick's bait had just gone in, and then they sat—both couples—chatting away in a low tone, and waiting for the next congers, and somehow waiting in vain. The last glow faded out of the sky, and the stars twinkled in the sea, where they were reflected from above. The great black bird rock stood up, looking gigantic against the western sky, and every now and then there was a querulous cry that set a party of the sea-birds scolding and squealing for a few minutes before all was still again.

In the distance across the bay the lights of the harbour shone out faintly at first, then clearly, and the various lamps about the village seemed like dull stars.

Still there was no bite, and Arthur rejoiced in his heart, hoping that they would catch no more, and thinking how horrible it would have been to have one of the monsters on board in the dark.

Josh had changed the position of Arthur's line several times, and at last he took hold of it and began to haul it in.

"Going to leave off?" said Arthur joyously.

"No, my lad, not yet. You won't mind me throwing in for you?"

"Oh no!" cried the boy.

"Then," said Josh, "I'm just going to throw over yonder into the deepest part, and if we don't get one out of there we may give up."

Drawing in and laying the line carefully in rings, he took the weight and threw it some distance from them, the lead falling with a heavy plash. Then Dick and Will followed suit on their side, and Arthur was compelled to take the line again from Josh, for the latter said:

"Oh no! I'm not going to fish. I can have a turn any day, my lad. Go on, and we'll show 'em this time what it is to fish again' us. A mussy me! we'll give 'em a startler directly. We'll show 'em what conger be."

Arthur's hands felt cold and damp as he sat there holding: the line and thinking of what would be the consequences if he hooked a monster and Josh failed to kill it before dragging it on board. It would run all over the boat, and it would be sure to bite him first—he knew it would; and the idea was horrible, making him so nervous that his hands shook as he held the line.

It was quite dark now, but a beautiful transparent darkness, with the sky one glorious arch of glittering points, and the sea a mirror in which those diamond sparks were reflected. The phosphorescence that had been so beautiful on the night when his brother was out with Josh and Will was absent, save a faint pale glow now and then, seen when a wave curled over and broke upon the great bird rock. All was wonderfully still, and they sat for some time listening to the distant singing of some of the fishermen, whose voices sounded deliciously soft and melodious as the tones of the old west-country part-song floated over the heaving sea.

Suddenly Arthur started, for Dick exclaimed:

"This is just lovely. I wish father were here."

"Ay! I wish he weer," said Josh. "I often pity you poor people who come from big towns and don't know what it is to be in such a place as this.

Beautiful, arn't it, Master Rorthur, sir?" "Ye–

es," said Arthur, "it's a beautiful night."

"Ay, it be," assented Josh; "and in a snug harbour like this there's no fear of a steamer or ship coming to run you down."

Arthur shuddered.

"Rather awkward for them among the rocks, eh, Josh?" said Will.

"Awk'ard arn't the word," said Josh. "'Member the Cape packet being wrecked here, my lad?"

"Oh, yes! I recollect it well," said Will. "It was just here, wasn't it?"

"Just yonder," said Josh. "She went on the rocks about ten fathom beyond where our grapnel lies."

"Was anyone hurt?" said Arthur, who shivered at the idea of a wreck having been anywhere near them.

"Hurt, my lad? Why, it was in one of the worst storms I can 'member. Tell him about the poor souls, Will."

"The packet ran right on the rocks, Master Arthur," said Will solemnly. "Where we are is one mass of tossing foam in a storm, and the froth and spray fly over the Mew Rock here. Directly the packet had struck a great wave came in and lifted her right up and then dropped her again across the ridge yonder, and she broke right in two."

"Like a radish," said Josh.

"And one end went down in the deep water one side, the other end the other side."

"Ay," said Josh, "it's very deep water out there, and they used to be at work regular for months and months getting out the cargo and engines when the weather was calm."

"But the people—the people?" cried Arthur. "What became of them?"

"Hah!" ejaculated Josh. "What come o' them?"

"Were they drowned?" said Dick.

"Every poor creature on board," said Will.

"And none of you fishermen went out in your boats to help them?" cried Dick indignantly.

"Just hark at him," cried Josh. "A mussy me! He's never seed the sea in a storm when— Look out, Master Awthur," he whispered.

It was pretty dark, but Josh's eyes were accustomed to that transparent gloom, and he had noted a tremulous motion of the boy's line almost before Arthur started, for there was a gentle, insidious touch at his bait that telegraphed along the line to his fingers, and then drew it softly through them as the fish, whatever it was, took the bait and began to swim away.

Arthur started as Josh whispered to him, and his fingers closed upon the line.

The moment before this latter was moving as if some tiny fish were drawing it from him; but the moment his closing hands checked the line's progress there was a tremendous jerk and a rush; and as, in spite of himself, Arthur held on, it seemed as if a boy a good deal stronger than himself were trying to pull it out of his hands, and after a few furious struggles seated himself, to hang at the end with his whole weight.

"I told you so," said Josh in satisfied tones. "I knowed as well as could be that there would be a big one down yonder, and I think it is a big one, eh, Master Rawthur."

"It's—it's a monster," panted Arthur. "Hadn't we better let it go?"

"Let it do what?" cried Josh. "A mussy me! what do he mean?"

"Oh! I say, Taff, you are a lucky one," cried Dick in genuine disappointed tones. "On! all right, we've got one too."

"Lucky one!" At that moment Arthur was bitterly repenting his want of foresight. Both hands were engaged now or he might have got out his pocketknife and, unseen by Josh in the darkness, have cut the line, which would have been supposed to be broken by the violent struggles of the great eel.

"I'll never come again," he thought to himself, "if ever I get safely back. I would not have come if I had known. Oh! what shall I do?"

These are a specimen or two of the thoughts that ran through Arthur Temple's brains as he clung desperately to the line with the conger or whatever it was at the end tugging and jerking at it hard enough to make the boy's shoulders sore.

"Steady! steady!" cried Josh, interfering. "That's not the way to ketch conger. Give him line, as I showed you afore. There, you see," he continued, as Arthur slackened the cord. "Eh, 'ullo! Why, what's up?"

he exclaimed. "Here, give me hold."

Arthur passed the line to him with a sigh of intense relief, and Josh gave way, hauled, and tried three or four different little plans before passing the line back to Arthur.

"Here, you ketch hold," he cried. "It's a big one and no mistake. He has got his tail twisted round a bit of rock, or he's half in a hole, or something. Don't let him shake you like that, my lad, but give him line when he snatches you. He's half in a hole as sure as can be, and if we hauled we should only break the line."

"What are we to do?" said Arthur, his words coming in pants. "Shall we leave the line and go?"

"Leave the line, my lad!" cried Josh. "Well, that arn't very likely. No, no: lines are too vallerble, and instead of giving the conger the line, we'll get him aboard."

"But how? It won't come," said Arthur peevishly.

"You must coax him same as I showed you before. Fishers wants patience—waiting for what they catches, undoing tangles in nets and lines, and dealing with conger. Don't you see, my lad, if you haul so does the conger: he's frightened, and he fights for his life; but as soon as you leave off hauling, so does he, and begins to uncurve and untwist himself. Then's your time to haul him out of the rocks, before he has time to anchor himself again."

It seemed to Arthur as if he had no power to disobey Josh. Shame, too, supported the fisherman, for the boy had a horror of being supposed a coward, so he acted precisely as Josh told him, giving and taking with the line, but for some time without avail, and Arthur piteously asked if it was of any use to go on.

"Use! I should think so," cried Josh. "Why, he's a big one, and we've got to ketch him. Now haul, my lad, steady."

Arthur obeyed, and the violent jerking of the line began just as if the great eel were making snatches at it.

"Now, give way, quick and sharp," cried Josh.

The boy did so, letting the line run over the side.

"I told you so," cried Josh, as it ran faster and faster. "He's going away now. He's left his hole. Now lay hold, and get him to the top quick as you can. He'll come up now."

Josh was right, for the eel had left the rocks, intending to swim away, and when it felt the line once more it began to struggle, but on the tension being eased it swam upwards. And so on again and again, till the pale under parts of the great fish could be seen below the surface, which was swirling and eddying with the strong motions of the muscular tail.

"He is a big one," cried Josh. "Got yours in, lads?"

"Yes," cried Will.

"Give us room then," cried Josh. "Hold on tight, youngster. No, no, Will: we can do him ourselves."

For Will had changed his position to take the line from Arthur, who felt as if he should have liked to kick the fisherman for interfering at such a time.

Acting like a machine in Josh's hands, Arthur slackened and hauled, and hauled and slackened, until the great eel was right at the surface, and Josh leaning over the gunwale, waiting his opportunity to hook it with the great gaff; but though he made two or three attempts Arthur was so helpless that he rather hindered than aided the capture. At last, though, by a clever stroke Josh hooked the monster, and stretched out his hand for his little axe.

As he did so there was a tremendous beating and splashing of the water, and the eel literally twisted itself into a knot upon the gaff, forming a great writhing bunch upon the shaft, and mingling line and self about the hook in the most confusing manner.

Arthur had behaved as well as he could, but this was too much for him. Dropping the line, he let himself fall backwards over the seat, scrambled forward on hands and knees, rose up, and was getting into the narrow portion of the boat in the bows, when he stepped upon something slippery and fell right upon a living eel, the one Dick had just captured.

"Oh, oh!" yelled Arthur, starting up and bounding back amidships, to fall once more, with his hands upon the huge slimy knot that Josh had just dragged on board.

"A mussy me!" groaned Josh, as he vainly tried to get a stroke at the great eel's head with the axe. "Here, look alive, Will, lad; give him the bat." Dick followed his brother's example and got as far out of the way as he could, while quite an exciting fight went on, if fight it can be called where the offence comes entirely from one side, and the other is winding in and out among legs and seats, fishing-lines and baskets, trying to get away. It was so dark that it was next to impossible to see where the monster was; and though Will struck at it fiercely with the bat, he more often struck the boat than the fish.

Josh, too, made some cuts at it with the axe, but he only missed, and he was afraid to do more for fear he should drive the weapon through the bottom of the boat.

"She's free o' the line now," cried Josh, who was not aware that one chop he had given had divided the stout cord. "Let her go now, Will, lad. She won't get out of the boat."

"All right!" said Will coolly; and Arthur uttered a groan; but just then, to his great relief, Dick spoke out.

"What! are you going to leave that thing crawling about in the boat while we go home?" he said.

"Ay, my lad; she won't hurt."

"Thankye," said Dick. "I'm going overboard then to be towed."

"Hor—hor—hor!" laughed Josh. "Well, all right, my lad, we'll light the lanthorn, and then p'r'aps I can get a cut at her. Where's the matches, Will? Hallo!"

For just then there was a tremendous scuffling in the fore part of the boat, as the great eel forced itself amongst the spare rope and odds and ends of the fishing gear. Then there was a faint gleam seen for a moment on the gunwale, and a splash, and then silence.

"Why, she's gone," cried Josh.

"What! Over the side?" cried Dick.

"Ay, lad, sure enough; and the biggest one we took to-night, and my best conger-hook in her mouth."

Arthur uttered a sigh of relief that was almost a sob, and sitting down very quietly he listened to the talking of his three companions, as the anchor and killick were got up, and the boat was rowed across the starry bay, to reach the landing-place about half an hour before the expected time, Mr Temple being in waiting, and pacing to and fro upon the pier.

"Caught any?" he said.

"Yes, father, lots, but the big one got away," cried Dick.

"How did you get on, Arthur?" said Mr Temple. "Were you very much alarmed?"

Arthur would have honestly said, "Yes;" but before he could speak, Josh exclaimed:

"'Haved hisself like a trump, sir. Him and me got all the big uns; and it's no joke ketching your first conger, as p'r'aps you know."

Chapter Twenty Five.

A Cornish Gale; and Dick Temple takes his First Lesson in Wind.

It can rain in Cornwall, and when it does rain it rains with all its might. The same remark applies to the wind, which blows with all its might sometimes from the west and south-west.

A few days had elapsed since the conger-fishing trip, and it had been arranged with Uncle Abram, who had expressed himself as being highly honoured by a visit from Mr Temple that Josh and Will should be ready with the boat for a long row to three or four of the old mine-shafts and creeks of the bay, where Mr Temple intended making a few investigations, and taking specimens of the different ores.

But when Dick rose, as he thought at daybreak, he found that it was half-past seven, that the rain was streaming down, and that the wind kept striking the side of the house, as it came from over the great Atlantic, with a noise like thunder.

He opened the window, but was glad to shut it again, for the wind snatched it, as it were, from his hand, to send it with a bang against the wall of the house. So shutting it close once more, and giving one of the panes a rub with the towel, he put his nose against it and looked out at the bay.

"Oh, how jolly miserable!" he exclaimed. "Here, Taff, hi! Wake up."

Taff would not wake up, and a second summons had no effect. In fact the nickname Taff had a bad effect upon Arthur Temple, causing a sort of deafness that was only removed by calling him Arthur.

"It rains and it blows, and the sea is one mass of foam. Oh, what waves!"

So impressive were these latter that for some time Dick forgot to dress, but kept watching the huge, dark green banks of water come rolling in and then break upon the shore.

"Here, what a stupid I am!" he said to himself at last; and hastily scrambling on his clothes, he went down-stairs and out on to the cliff, to be almost startled by the heavy thunder of the great billows that came tumbling in, every now and then one of them coming with a tremendous smack upon the pier, when the whole harbour was deluged, the foam and spray flying over the luggers, which were huddled together, as if in alarm, beneath the shelter of the sea wall.

Dick forgot that it was raining heavily, and ran down to the great bed of boulders at the end of the village, where, as the huge waves came in, they drove up the massive stones, which varied in size from that of a man's head to that of a Cheshire cheese, sending them some distance up towards the cliff, and then, as the wave retired, *boomble—roomble —doomble, doomble—doom*, they rolled back again one over the other, as if mockingly defying the retiring wave to come and do that again.

Here was the secret of how pebbles and shingle and boulders were made, grinding one another smooth as were driven one over the other for hundreds and hundreds of years till they were as smooth as the rock upon which they beat.

This was exciting enough for a time, but, regardless of rain and wind, Dick ran along the cliff to a place he knew, a very shelf in the rock which went down perpendicularly to a deep little cove, in which he felt sure that the sea would be beating hard.

"It's just a hundred feet," he said, "because Josh told me, and I shall be able to see how high a wave can come."

He said this, but only to himself, for as he hurried along the cliff there were moments when he could hardly get his breath for the force of the wind which beat full in his face.

Once or twice he hesitated, wondering whether it was safe to proceed in such a storm.

He laughed at his fears, though, as he stood in shelter for a few moments, and then went on again, to, reach the spot he sought, and find to his great delight that the rock bulged out, so that without danger he could look right down upon the sea; while another discovery he made was, that though he seemed to be standing right facing the wind he was in comparative calm.

It paid for the journey, for as he advanced to the edge he could see low down that the waves were churning up foam which the wind caught as it was finished and sent right up in a cloud of flakes and balls light as air in a regular whirl, to come straight up past him, higher and higher above his head, till the very summit of the cliff was reached, when away it went in a drift landward.

Why was it quite calm where he stood, and yet the full force of the Atlantic gale coming full in his face?

It was a puzzle to Dick Temple. The wind was blowing so hard that it was cutting the foamy tops from the waves, and sweeping all along like a storm of tremendous rain. It seemed to him that he should be blown flat against the rock, and held there spread-eagle fashion; but instead of this it was perfectly calm, and the thought came upon him how grand it would be to stand just where the wind was blowing its hardest, and to see what it felt like to be in the full force of an Atlantic gale.

"I'll climb right up to the very top of the cliff," he said. "I wonder whether the wind ever does blow strong enough to knock anyone down."

But there was too much to fascinate him below for him to drag himself away at once. From where he stood he could see all along below the cliffs where he had been rowed by Josh and Will, and that where, then and afterwards, when his father accompanied them searching for some good mineral vein, the sea had heaved gently, and the waves had curled over and broken sparkling on the rocks, all was now one chaos of wildly foaming and tossing waters. The huge green waves ran rolling in to break with a noise like thunder, and when some huge hill of water came in, rose, curled over, and broke, it was with a tremendous boom, and the spray rushed thirty, forty, and fifty feet up the rock before it poured back.

"I wonder what would happen to a boat if it was down there?" said Dick aloud.

"Just the same as would happen to a walnut-shell if you were to throw it down where five hundred hammers were beating about on a pile of stones such as you use to mend the roads."

"Why, I didn't hear you come, Will," cried Dick eagerly.

"I was going to your place to tell you that we could not go out to-day, of course, and I saw you come out, so I followed."

"And so a boat would not get on very well down there, wouldn't it?"

"Get on!" said Will smiling; "why, it would be smashed up."

"And suppose a ship were to be close in there, Will?"

"She would be beaten up into matchwood, all torn and ragged to pieces."

"But is the sea so strong?"

"Look at it," cried Will, pointing to the leaves, "It is awful sometimes."

"Worse than this?"

"Yes: much," replied Will. "But look here, suppose a great ship came driving round the head here and struck?"

"What do you mean by struck?"

"Driven on the rocks. Do you know what would happen then?"

"Well, she would be wrecked, I suppose," said Dick.

"Yes, the waves would come leaping and thundering over her the same as they do over that piece of rock, and sweeping her decks. Then every great wave that came in would lift her up, and then leave her to come down crash upon the rocks, shaking out her masts and loosening her timbers and planks, and keeping this on till she tumbled all to pieces and the sea was strewed with the bits which kept tossing in and out among the rocks."

"Have you ever seen the sea do this?" said Dick eagerly.

"Yes," replied Will solemnly, "often. It's very awful sometimes to live at the sea-side on a rocky coast."

The two lads stood for a few minutes silently gazing down into the wild waste of tossing foam, and then Dick said slowly:

"I think I should like to see a wreck. I shouldn't like for there to be a wreck; but if there was a wreck I should like to see it."

"I don't think you would again," said Will sadly. "I used to think so when I was quite a little fellow; but when I did see one it all seemed so pitiful to know that there were people on board the ship asking you to come and save them."

"Then why didn't you go and save them?" cried Dick excitedly. "You are all good sailors about here, and have boats. You ought to do something to save the poor things."

"We do," said Will sadly. "I mean our men do when they can."

"Haven't you got a life-boat?"

"There is one at Corntown and another at Penillian Sands; but sometimes before a life-boat can be fetched a ship has gone to pieces."

"And all the people drowned?"

"Yes. Come below here," said Will, leading the way down the cliff.

"Is—is it safe?" said Dick.

"I will not take you where there's any danger," said Will.

Dick hesitated for a few moments, and then followed his companion down a path cut in a rift of the rock where a tiny stream trickled down from far inland.

The mouth of the rift was protected by a pile of rocks, against which the wind beat and the waves thundered, but the path was so sheltered that the lads were able to get nearly down to the shore.

"There are lots of paths like this down the cliff all about the coast," said Will quietly. "They are useful for men to get down to their boats in bad weather."

He pointed to one that was drawn right up on rollers twenty feet above the waves and snugly sheltered from the storm.

"There," said Will the next minute, as he stood holding on behind a rock, with Dick by his side. "We're safe enough here; the wind goes by us, you see, and the waves don't bite here. Now, what do you think of that?"

Dick drew a long breath two or three times over before he could speak, for the scene was awful in its grandeur, and, young as he was, he felt what mere pigmies are men in face of the giants of the elements when Nature is in anger and lets loose her storms upon our shores.

Every minute, from amidst the boiling chaos of waves, one bigger than the rest came slowly from seaward with a strange gliding motion, to raise itself up like some crested serpent and curl over, and then, as it was riven in ten thousand streams and sheets of jagged foam, there was a dull roar as of thunder, the wind shrieked and yelled, and, serpent-like, the broken wave hissed, and seethed, and choked, and gurgled horribly amongst the rocks.

"What do you think of that?" said Will again gravely as he placed his lips close to Dick's ear.

"How awful the sea is!" panted Dick as he seemed more than ever to realise its force.

"Yes," said Will quietly, and there was a sad smile on the boy's lip as he spoke. "But you said a little while ago that our men ought to help the shipwrecked men. Shall we get down that boat and have a row?"

"Row!" cried Dick with a horrified look; "why, it couldn't be done."

"Would you like to see your father and some more men get down that boat and put off to sea?"

"It would be impossible," cried Dick. "She would be tossed over by the waves and everybody drowned."

"Hah! Yes," said Will smiling. "You see now the danger. Many people say that fishermen are cowardly for not doing more, when the case is that they know the danger, and those who talk and write about it don't. It isn't everybody who has seen the sea-coast in a storm. Shall we go up?"

"Yes," panted Dick; "it is too awful to stay here. If a wave were to curl round the corner we should be swept away."

"Yes," said Will, "but the waves will not curl round the corner. They can't come here."

He pointed to the rugged path, for it was hard work to speak and make each other hear; and Dick began nervously to climb back, looking down once or twice at the hungry waves, which seemed ready to leap up at him and tear him from the rocks.

"I say," he cried, "I'm glad Taff isn't here."

Will smiled, for he felt that Arthur would never have ventured down the cliff.

"Now," said Dick, as they reached the shelf path once more, and he felt less nervous, "I want to go up right to the top of the cliff and feel the wind."

"Feel the wind?" cried Will.

"Yes; feel how strong it is. Which is the best way?"

"I'll show you," said Will smiling; and leading the way he walked a little back towards the town and then turned into a rift similar to that by which they had descended to the shore.

"This way," he shouted, for the wind caught them here with

tremendous force, and great balls of foam were whirled up over the face of the cliff and then away on the wings of the wind inland.

"What a difference!" cried Dick as soon as they had entered the rift: for there was a perfect lull here, and all seemed comparatively at peace.

"Yes, it is sheltered here," replied Dick; "but wait a few minutes and you will feel the wind again."

"Yes. I want to feel it just as it comes off the sea. I'm going to stand right at the edge. It won't blow me down, will it?"

"No; not there," said Will smiling. "Here we are. Now come and try."

As soon as they emerged from the shelter of the rift and stood upon the storm-swept cliff, Dick had to clap his hand to his head to keep on his hat, for the wind seized it and swept it to the extent of the lanyard by which it was fortunately held, and there it tugged and strained like a queerly-shaped kite.

The wind now was terrific, coming in deafening gusts, and more than once making Dick stagger. In fact if he had set off to run inland it would have almost carried him off his legs.

"Didn't—know—blow—so—hard," he panted, turning his back so that he could breathe more freely, when the wind immediately began to part the boy's hair behind in two or three different ways, but only to alter them directly as if not satisfied with the result.

"Come along," shouted Will. "Let's get to the edge."

Dick turned round, caught at Will's extended hand, and leaning forward, tramped with him step for step towards the edge of the cliff, which went sheer down a couple of hundred feet to the shore.

They had to force their way sturdily along for about a hundred yards with the wind as it came right off the Atlantic shrieking by their ears, and deafening and confusing them. The short wiry grass was all quivering, and it was plain enough to understand why trees found it so hard to grow where they were exposed to the fury of the sea breezes that blew so many months in the year.

Step—step—step by step, the wind seeming really to push them back. Now and then, when it came with its most furious gusts, the lads regularly leaned forward against it as if it were some strange elastic solid; and then, as they nearly reached the edge, it lulled all at once, and right at the verge all was calm.

"Oh, what a pity!" cried Dick, as he stood there panting and regaining his breath; "only to think of it turning so still now that we are here."

"Turning so still!" said Will, laughing; "why, it's blowing harder than ever. Look at the foam-balls."

"Yes; it's blowing there," said Dick; "but it's quite calm here. Never mind; I'll wait. There'll be a regular guster directly."

"No," said Will quietly; "you may stand here all day and you'll hardly feel the wind."

"But why's that?" cried Dick.

"Because we are right at the edge of a tall flat-faced cliff," said Will. "It's generally so."

"But I don't understand it," cried Dick. "It's blowing very hard, and we are not in shelter. Why don't it blow here?"

"Because we are right at the edge of the cliff."

"Don't talk stuff and nonsense, Will," said Dick testily. "How can you be so absurd? Why, that's where the wind would blow hardest."

"No, it isn't," replied Will.

"Now look here," said Dick. "I know that we London chaps are all behind you country fellows over sea-side things—catching fish, and boating, and about winds and tides; but I do know better than you here. The edge of a cliff like this must be the place where the wind blows hardest."

"But you feel for yourself that it doesn't," said Will laughing.

"Not just now," cried Dick, "but it will directly."

"No, it will not."

"But look at the foam flying and the spray going like a storm of rain."

"Yes," said Will, "but not at the edge of the cliff. Look at the grass and wild flowers; they grow longer and better here too. The wind off the sea never blows very hard here."

"Oh, what stuff!" cried Dick; "you're as obstinate as old Taff. It will blow here directly."

"Come along," said Will quietly; and he walked a short distance inland, taking his companion into the full force of the gale once more.

"There!" cried Dick. "I told you so. It has come on to blow again. Let's get back to the edge."

Will made no objection, but walked back quickly with Dick; but before they reached the cliff edge it was nearly calm once more.

"Look at that, now," cried Dick pettishly. "Did you ever see such a stupid, obstinate old wind in your life? It's blowing everywhere but here."

Will smiled so meaningly that Dick turned upon him.

"Why, what do you mean?" he cried.

"I'll try and show you," said Will. "Lie down here. It's quite dry."

Dick threw himself on the short soft turf, and Will pulled out a pocket-book, took the pencil from its loop, and, spreading the book wide, began after a fashion to draw what learned people call a diagram, but which we may more simply speak of as a sketch or figure of what he wished to explain.

It was very roughly done in straight lines, but sufficiently explanatory, especially as Will carefully followed the example of the sign-painter, who wrote underneath his artistic work, "This is a bear."

Will began by drawing a horizontal line, and under it he wrote, "The sea." Then he turned the horizontal line into a right angle by adding to it a perpendicular line, by which he wrote: "The cliff." From the top of that perpendicular he drew another horizontal line, and above that he wrote, "Top of the cliff."

"Now, then," he said, "these little arrows stand for the wind blowing right across the sea till they come to the face of the cliff;" and he drew some horizontal arrows.

"Yes, I see," said Dick, helping with a finger to keep down the fluttering leaves.

"Well; now the wind has got as far as the cliff. It can't go through it, can it?"

"No," said Dick.

"And it can't go down for the sea."

"Of course not."

"It can't go backwards, because the wind is forcing on the wind."

"Yes," said Dick. "Hold still, stupid!" This last to the fluttering leaf.

"Where is the wind to go, then?" asked Will.

"Why, upwards of course," cried Dick.

"To be sure," said Will. "Well, it strikes against the face of the cliff, and that seems to make it so angry like that it rushes straight up to get over the top."

"Of course it does," said Dick; "any stupid could understand that."

"Well," said Will, "the top's like a corner, isn't it?"

"No!" cried Dick; "how can it be?"

"Yes, it is," said Will sturdily; "just like a corner, only lying down instead of standing up."

"Oh! very well; just as you like," cried Dick.

"Now suppose," said Will, "you were running very fast along beside a row of houses like they are at Corntown."

"Very well: what then?"

"And suppose you wanted to run sharp round the edge of the corner, and I was hiding behind it, and you wanted to catch me."

"Well, I should catch you," said Dick.

"No, you would not. You couldn't turn short round, because you were going so fast; and you'd go some distance before you did, and you'd be right beyond me, and you'd make quite a big curve."

"Should I? Well, suppose I should," said Dick, rubbing one ear.

"Well," said Will, making some more arrows up the perpendicular line which represented, the face of the cliff, "that's how the wind does. It goes right up here, and gets some distance before it can stop, and then it curves over and flies right over the land, getting lower as it goes, till it touches the ground once more. There, that's it; and those two dots are you and me."

He drew some more arrows, with Dick looking solemnly on, and the result was that Will's sketch of the wind's action against a cliff was something like the following arrangement of lines and arrows, which illustrate a curious phenomenon of nature, easily noticeable during a gale of wind at the edge of some perpendicular cliff.

Dick felt disposed to dispute his friend's scientific reasoning; but Will showed him by throwing his handkerchief down from the edge of the cliff, when it was caught by the gale before it had gone down a dozen feet, and whisked up above their heads and then away over the land.

A handful of grass was treated the same, and then Dick sent down his own handkerchief, which went down twice as far as Will's before the wind took it and blew it right into a crevice in the face of the cliff, where it stuck fast.

"There's a go," cried Dick. "Oh! I say, how can we get it?"

Will went to the edge of the cliff and looked over before shaking his head.

"We can't get it now," he said. "I'll ask Josh to come with a rope when the wind's gone down, and he'll lower me over."

"What—down there—with a rope?" said Dick, changing colour. "No, don't."

"Why not?" said Will. "That's nothing to going down a mine-shaft."

Dick shuddered.

"Or going down the cliff after eggs as I do sometimes. We have gentlemen here now and then who collect eggs, and I've been down after them often in places where you can't climb."

"But I shouldn't like you to go down for me."

"Why not?"

"You might fall," said Dick.

"I shouldn't like to do that," said Will, smiling. Then in a thoughtful, gloomy way—"It wouldn't matter much. I've no one to care about me."

"How can you say that?" cried Dick sharply. "Why, your uncle seemed to think a deal of you."

"He's very kind to me," said Will sadly; "but I've always been an expense to him."

"Then," cried Dick boldly, "you ought to be ashamed of yourself."

"What—for being an expense to him?" said Will wistfully.

"No; because you couldn't help that when you were a little fellow. Now you have grown, and are getting a big one, you ought to think of letting him be an expense to you, and you keep him. That's what I'm going to do as soon as ever I get old enough."

"That's right," said Will, looking at his companion thoughtfully. "I say, is your father going to open a mine down here?"

"I don't know quite for certain," said Dick; "but I think he's going to try and find something fresh, and work that."

"What—some new metal?"

"I don't know," said Dick, "and I don't think he quite knows yet. It all depends upon what he can find good enough."

"I wish I could find something very valuable," said Will thoughtfully —"something that I could show him; and then he might give me work in it, so that I could be independent."

"Well, let's try and find something good. I'll go with you," said Dick.

"When?"

"Not now. Oh! I say, I must get back; I am so precious hungry."

It was quite time; but they had not far to go, though when Dick did enter the room it was to find his father and Arthur half through their meal.

"Three quarters of an hour late, Dick," said his father. "I waited half an hour for you before I sat down. Where have you been?"

"To look at the sea, father; and up on the cliff to see how the wind blew —how strong, I mean."

"Sit down," said his father rather sternly. "I like punctuality, and would rather know when you are going out."

"Yes, father," said Dick, "I'll try and remember. I'm very sorry."

Mr Temple did not answer, but raised the newspaper he was reading, and this covered his face.

Evidently Arthur thought it covered his ears as well, for he said rather importantly:—

"I was here punctually to the moment."

"Arthur," said his father quietly, "you had better go on with your breakfast, and not talk so much."

Arthur coloured, and the breakfast was eaten during the rest of the time in silence—a state of affairs of which Dick took advantage, for the sea air had a wonderful effect upon his food-assimilating powers, and his performance on this particular morning made his brother leave off to stare.

"My, Dick!" he exclaimed at last as that gentleman made an attack upon a second fried sole, one of several brought in by the trawl-boat on the previous night, "I say, how you are eating!"

"Yes," said Dick, grinning, "I'm a growing boy."

Chapter Twenty Six.

Uncle Abram comes as an Ambassador, and gains his Ends.

"I wanted to make our expedition," said Mr Temple, "but it is impossible, of course, to-day in the face of such a storm. What are you boys going to do?"

"Read, papa," said Arthur. "It is too rough to go out."

"And you, Dick?"

"Ask you to lend me your Mackintosh, father. It's too rough to stay in. The sea's grand."

Arthur had already taken up a book, but he now laid it down.

"I don't think it rains, does it?"

"No; only blows," replied Dick; "but when you get where the spray comes off the sea, it's like a shower."

"I think we'll all go," said Mr Temple. "I want to test a few minerals first. Afterwards I should like to go down and have a look at the waves."

It was settled that the boys should wait, and Mr Temple at once lit a spirit-lamp from a strong box of apparatus he had brought down; and, taking out a blow-pipe, he spent some little time melting, or calcining, different pieces of ore and stone that he had collected, one special piece being of white-looking mineral that took Dick's notice a good deal, for it seemed familiar.

"Isn't that the stone you got in the place Will Marion showed to you, father?"

"Yes, my boy," said Mr Temple; "why?"

"Only I thought it was," said Dick. "Is it valuable?"

"I don't know yet. Perhaps."

"If it is valuable, will it do Will any good?"

"I don't know yet about that either, my inquisitive young friend," said Mr Temple.

"I think it ought if it's any good," said Dick after a pause, during which he had been watching his father attentively.

"Do you?" said Mr Temple coldly; and he went on calcining a piece of the soft white stone, and then placing it in a mortar to grind it up fine.

This done, he took the powder out and spread it upon a small glass slab, where he applied a few drops of water to it, and mixed and mixed till he had formed the white powder into a paste that looked like white clay.

"I say, father," said Dick.

"Yes."

"Will would like to see what you are doing with that stuff. May I tell him?"

"No," said Mr Temple, quietly kneading the white paste in his fingers and then examining it with a powerful lens. "I desire that you say no word about anything that you may see me doing. This is private work that to-day unknown to anyone else may be very valuable. Known to all the world, it might prove to be not very valuable, but absolutely worthless. Wait, my boy, and see."

Waiting was always an unpleasant task for Dick Temple. Time never ran half fast enough for him, and to have to wait in what he called, after some one whom he had heard make use of the term, a state of mental anxiety, was something hard to be borne.

Arthur calmly took a book, after glancing in the glass to see if his collar was quite right and his hair properly brushed. He could sit and read in the most placid manner; but Dick seemed to have quicksilver in his toes and fingers. He could not keep still, but was always on the fret to be doing something.

In his eagerness to help he got into trouble three times with his father, his aid being given invariably at the wrong time, and generally resulting in his knocking over some bottle, disturbing a test, or breaking some delicate piece of apparatus.

"I'm very sorry, father, I am indeed," he would say.

"Nobody doubts your sorrow, Dick," cried Mr Temple; "but what I want is less sorrow and more care. You blunder on at everything instead of making a bit of a calculation first so as to see what you are about to do."

"Well, I will, father, I will really. I'll always in future be as careful as— careful as—careful as Taff."

Dick had been looking round the room for an example of care, and this suggested itself.

Mr Temple smiled, and bent down over his minerals so that his boys should not see his face, as he noticed Arthur's ears turn red and a nervous twitch go through him preparatory to his looking up from his book.

"No," said Mr Temple, "I do not wish you to be as careful as Arthur, my boy, or to take anyone else for a model. Be just your own natural self, and do your best to run straight on your journey through life. Don't try to run like others run; it may not always be in a good style."

Arthur's eyes fell upon his book once more, and his ears became of a very deep crimson as he felt injured and touched in his dignity.

"Papa might have said *yes*, and told Dick to imitate me," thought Arthur; and he went on with his reading, feeling very much ill used.

"Mr Marion would like to speak to you, sir," said the landlord, coming in just then.

"What, Will?" cried Dick eagerly.

"No, Master Richard. I shouldn't have called him Mr Marion," said the landlord, smiling. "It's the old gentleman. May I show him in, sir?"

"Yes, certainly;" and Uncle Abram came in, looking like a Finnan haddock in a glazed hat, for on account of the weather the old man was clothed from head to foot in yellow oilskins, and shone and twinkled with the drops of spray.

"Sarvant, sir," he said, making dabs with his shiny sailor's hat as if to knock the drops off. "Sarvant, young gentleman,"—this was to Arthur, who rose and bowed stiffly—"how do, Master Dick, how do?"

Uncle Abram beamed and shook Dick's hand heartily, seeming loth to loose it again, but he relented and turned to Mr Temple.

"You'll excuse me, sir, for coming when you're busy; but it's to help a neighbour out of a difficulty."

"Subscription?" said Mr Temple.

"Subscription?" said Uncle Abram, dragging a great silk handkerchief from inside his oilskin and wiping the drops of spray from his face. "It was about your lodgings here, sir."

"My lodgings?" said Mr Temple.

"Yes, sir. You see neighbour here didn't like to speak to you 'bout the matter, and I said I would. Fact is, four fish-buyers from London come down here to stay with him every year regular all through the season, and you've got their rooms."

"Oh! I have their rooms?" said Mr Temple.

"That's it, sir, that's it," said Uncle Abram; "and when neighbour let 'em to you he thought you only wanted 'em for a few days."

"And I've been here for a few weeks."

"Toe be sure," said Uncle Abram.

"And he wants me to turn out, eh?" said Mr Temple rather sternly, while Dick's countenance fell.

"Turn out arn't the word, sir," said Uncle Abram. "We don't do that sort o' thing to gentlemen down here in the west countree. Man to man— give and take—do to one another as you'd like one another to do unto you. That's our motter down here, sir. And neighbour he told me his difficulty. 'Nice gentleman, Mr Temple,' he says. 'Master Arthur a bit stiff, but Master Dick—there,' he says, says neighbour, 'you know what Master Dick be.' And I said I did, and I went home and had a chat with my nevvy Will, and then I attacked the missus, and here I be."

"So I see," said Mr Temple rather dryly; "but really, Mr Marion, you haven't explained yourself very clearly."

"I s'pose not," said Uncle Abram in a troubled way. "That's just like me. I never do. Getting old, you see."

"Am I to understand that you are an ambassador from the landlord, and that he wants us to go?"

"Well, something of that sort, sir," replied Uncle Abram, who was very busy wiping drops from his forehead that were not spray.

"When do these fish-buyers come?"

"To-day, sir."

"To-day! Then why did he not speak sooner?"

"Waited like, sir, to see if there might be a change of wind. You might want to go. They mightn't want to come. Things veers about, sir, sometimes."

"I consider it disgraceful," said Mr Temple angrily, rising to touch the bell. "I'll speak to the landlord myself."

"Steady, sir, steady," cried Uncle Abram. "Good neighbour o' mine, you see. Spoke to me 'bout it, and I said yes, and here I be."

"Yes, yes," cried Mr Temple; "but am I to be thrown out without notice just at a time when I want particularly to stay?"

"No, sir, of course not. That's what I keep explaining to you. Neighbour puts the case before me, and I says if the missus is willing nothing would please me better, and here I be."

"But you do not explain matters," said Mr Temple.

"What, not that Mrs Marion and your obedient sarvant to command, Abram Marion, ex Her Majesty's sarvice, would be glad if you'd make shift in our rooms—sittin', best, and two beds?"

"No. You said nothing of the kind."

"Think of that now," said Uncle Abram, smiling broadly. "That's just like me, Master Dick. Gettin' old, you see. But if you could work it round that way, sir, it would be making it pleasant for all parties, and we'd do the best up at the cottage to make you comfortable; and there's my boy Will and our Josh and the boat at your sarvice, and there you are; and neighbour below don't upset his old friends."

"I shall be delighted, Mr Marion, I'm sure," said Mr Temple, holding out his hand, which the old fellow shook heartily, bestowing a solemn wink on Dick at the same time.

"That's a bargain then, sir?" said the old fellow, going to the door, and shouting, "Lan'ord, ahoy!" in a voice of thunder, and then coming back to open the window and yell, "Will, ahoy! Go and tell her as it's settled."

Then he banged to the window, and turned round as the landlord came in smiling and looking greatly relieved.

"Gentleman says it's all right, neighbour," said Uncle Abram.

"Thank ye heartily, neighbour," said the landlord, "and you too, Mr Temple, sir. It's kep' me awake for nights."

The result was that the little party moved bodily to Uncle Abram's that morning, their luggage being conveyed, as soon as possible by Josh and Will; and directly they were in the pleasant sea-side rooms Uncle Abram took Dick round the place to point out various objects about the walls.

"Welcome to 'em as the flowers is to May, my lad," he said with a good many nods and winks; "only wipe 'em dry and put 'em back when done —spy-glass, oilskins, big boots, fishing-lines, nets, and curiosities for a wet day, box o' dominoes for the wet nights. Make yourself at home."

Slap on the back.

This last was a sort of seal to finish the welcome; and then the old man went back to his garden to stand in the rockery, which served as a look-out, and scan the horizon with his glass.

Mr Temple was delighted with the change, for, in spite of the quiet respectability of the Cornish fishermen and their bluff, pleasant ways, a fishing port inn, even in a west-country village, is not always perfect as a place for a sojourn; while Uncle Abram's home was a pattern of neatness, and Aunt Ruth seemed very amiably disposed towards her guests.

Chapter Twenty Seven.

A Terrible Time at Sea.

"Isn't it glorious, Taff?" cried Dick as he stood with his brother in their little low-roofed bed-room, whose window overlooked the sea.

"Can't say that I like it," said Arthur languidly. "The place smells horribly of fish."

"Pooh! That isn't fish. It's the sea-weed. It turns limp, and smells because the weather's moist and stormy. There, come on. Father must be ready now, and I want to go down and see the sea."

Uncle Abram came in just as they were about to start, and insisted upon lending a couple of suits of oilskins, which he brought out of a room in the roof, where he kept his stores, as he called them.

"Was Will's," he explained. "He growed out of 'em. Not much to look at, sir," he added apologetically to Mr Temple, "but they'll keep out the water. We like the sea, but we like to keep dry."

Arthur looked horribly disgusted, for his father gladly accepted the hospitable offer, and he had to submit to being buttoned up in the stiff garb that Will had cast off years before, even to the high boots.

Dick scuffled into his with delight, and tied the sou'-wester under his chin, turning the next minute to see his brother, and stamp on the floor with delight.

"Oh! look at Taff, father; he does look such a Guy Fawkes."

Arthur turned upon him fiercely, and it suddenly occurred to Dick that he was in precisely the same costume; but he only laughed the more as, well equipped to meet the storm, they started for the beach.

"It's ridiculous," said Arthur, in tones of disgust, as they walked down towards the harbour under the lee of the houses. "There was no need to put on these wretched stiff things."

Almost as the words left his lips they passed the last house, and—

Bang!—boom!—swirl!

A large wave struck the shore on a boulder slope and sent a deluge of water across the road, to strike the rock on the other side, and run back like a stream.

Arthur, was sent staggering, and would have fallen but for his father's hand; and all three, but for their shiny garb, would have been soaked from head to foot.

"Oh, here's a game!" cried Dick. "I say, Taff—run—run—here comes another."

They escaped part of the wave, but Dick had his weather ear full, and the sea-water and foam streamed down their backs as they stood in the shelter of a bit of cliff.

"Well, Arthur, what do you say to your oilskins now?" said Mr Temple.

"They're dreadfully stiff, father, and the boots are too large," said Arthur ungraciously. "Hadn't we better get back?"

Poor Arthur repented his words most bitterly as soon as he had spoken them, for there was a hard light going on in the boy's mind. Naturally very conceited, he had had the misfortune to be made the head of a little set at his school—a little set, for they were rather small boys, who looked up to him,—and dressed at him as far as they could, the effect being to make him more conceited still, and think his brother rough and common in his ways.

All this had been pointed out to Mr Temple, who, however, had seen it for himself, and he only said, smiling:

"It will all settle itself. These little spines will get knocked off by contact with the world. Besides which I hope that he will find out for himself the way to grow into a manly man."

Mr Temple was quite right, and Arthur was beginning to discover that, where his brother was met with a genial smile by all whom he encountered, he, who was particular and precise and, as he considered it, gentlemanly in his ways, was either not noticed, or met with merely the coldest reception.

He was learning too that a man—especially an Englishman, whether gentle or simple—born in the lap of luxury, as people call it, or in the humblest cot, must be one who will always keep up the credit of the nation at large by being thoroughly English; and this brings one to the question—while the storm is raging on the Cornish coast, and Arthur Temple is in his glistening oilskins walking stiffly and awkwardly, and wincing beneath his father's look, which said as plainly as look could speak, "If you are afraid you can go back;"—this brings one to the task of stating what one means by being thoroughly English, so let us set down here, something approaching one's ideas of what an English lad should be.

Courageous of course, full of that sturdy determination not to be beaten, and when beaten, so far from being disheartened that he is ready to try again, whether in a fight, a battle with a difficulty, or in any failure.

Honest in his striving for what he knows to be right, and ready to maintain it against all odds, especially of such enemies as banter or ridicule, self-indulgence or selfishness.

That is enough: for so many wonderful little veins will start from those two trunks, that, given a boy who is courageous and honest, or who makes himself so, it would be almost an impossibility for him to turn out a bad, mean, and cowardly man.

And pray don't imagine, you who read this, that by a cowardly man or boy I mean one who is afraid to take off his jacket and roll up his sleeves and fight with his fists. I mean quite a different kind of coward —the one who is afraid of himself and lets self rule him, giving up to every indulgence because it goes a little against the grain, and Arthur Temple is walking uncomfortably in his oilskins because they don't look nice. The storm is raging, and he is still smarting under the belief that his father thinks him contemptible and cowardly, physically cowardly. And all the time, though the tears are rising in his eyes, and the wind is deafening him, and the spray beating in his face so that his tears are not seen, he is proving that, under his varnish, he is made of the right stuff. For even as he battled with self in the boat when conger-fishing, he is fighting the good fight again, has set his teeth, and has made a sort of vow that no one shall say he has not as much pluck as his brother Dick.

There is little work done at a fishing village when a storm comes down. Going to sea is impossible, and men don't care to be mending or making nets when at any moment they may have to be helping to haul up a boat into a safer place, or to drag in a spar, or plank, or timber, that has been washed ashore.

Then, too, there is the look-out kept for ships or boats in distress— perhaps to lend a helping hand; if not, to look on with sympathetic eyes and a thankful prayer at heart that they are in safety, as they think of home, and wife, and child.

Mr Temple was not a violent angry man. His punishments to his boys were conveyed in looks, and one look sufficed. When that look had been given there was an end to the matter; and on this occasion, after Arthur had been made to wince, his petulant display of fear was put back in the past.

"Boys," he cried, "I would not like to have missed this scene. How awful and how grand!"

They were standing in the shelter of a pilchard house, one of the long buildings where these silvery, oily relatives of the herring are salted before being pressed in barrels and sent away to the Mediterranean ports by hundreds of tons every year. The building took the brunt of the roaring wind and spray torn from the huge billows that thundered in and raced up the beach, and pounded the rocks, so that the spectators could gaze at the wild chaos of tossing waves, and watch the heaped-up waters as they dashed in like some savage army, whose aim was to tear down the rocky barriers of our isle and sweep all away.

In the harbour lay the luggers, and a good-sized brig, and a steam-tug that had brought it in after missing Corn town; and as the great waves came with a spang upon the stone pier, and leaped over the lanterns, and poured down tons of spray upon their decks, they rocked and groaned as they rubbed together, and in spite of mooring ropes a sharp crack now and then told of damages to be repaired.

The cliff glistened with oilskin-clad men, many of whom bore long, clumsy telescopes, while others in great high boots, and with their sou'-westers tied beneath their chins, walked amongst the foam, a coil of strong rope upon their shoulders, and a boat-hook in hand, ready for anything in the way of flotsam and jetsam that might come ashore.

Already they had drawn up the mast of a lugger with its ropes and blocks, telling tales of some misfortune at sea.

A barrel or two had come ashore; and as Dick watched, he saw one man run out after a wave, catch at something, miss it, and then get hold of a rope, with which he ran ashore.

Directly after they saw another figure leave a companion and run in after a retiring wave, the foam knee-deep, and catch at something else which came slowly.

"Mind, mind!" cried Dick excitedly; "the wave! the wave!"

Arthur gave a gasp and ran right out towards where the figure, fully a hundred yards away, was clinging to something that looked brown against the white foam, and apparently heedless of the fact that a tremendous wave was racing in.

His comrade saw it though and ran to his help, catching hold of the great brown tangle, and then turning with the other to escape.

They hardly did it, for the huge wave curled over just behind them with a boom like thunder, and swept them up towards the shore amidst the foam.

They would have been carried back, but a dozen hands were outstretched and they and their prize were run up out of danger, where, for the next ten minutes, the little party were busy hauling in what proved to be an immense length of pilchard drift-net, with its corks, and buoys, and ropes, which formed a goodly heap when they had done.

Out seaward there was nothing visible but the tossing waves, and it was with a sense of relief that the boys saw that there was no prospect of any wreck beyond that of the fishing-boat that had been dashed to pieces upon some rock.

"Here! hi!" cried Dick, excitedly. "Why, it's Will! Was it you who ran in after that net?" he continued, as the lad came up.

"Yes, Master Dick; Josh helped me," said Will, smiling. "There's two or three hundred fathom."

"But was it not very risky, my lad?" said Mr Temple, shouting like the others, for the noise made by the sea was deafening.

"Risky, sir? Oh! you mean the waves! There were plenty there to lend a hand, and if we'd been caught they'd have thrown us a rope," said Will, simply.

"Some boat has been lost, hasn't there?" cried Dick, excitedly.

"Saint Ives boat, we think," said Will; "and a timber ship has been wrecked somewhere out Lizard way. There'll be a lot of balks and planks come ashore, the men think."

"I say, Will, is it often as bad as this?" said Arthur eagerly.

"Yes, sir, very often," replied Will. "Old Pollard thinks it will be worse to-night. I should go down to yonder house, sir, if I was you; the young gentlemen would be more in shelter, and you could see the wreck wood come in and the men draw it up, better there, for it's nearer to the sea."

"How do you know it will come there?" said Dick hastily.

"The current. Tide washes it up. We always find wreck come about there."

Will hurried away, his mission being to fetch another boat-hook; and taking the hint, Mr Temple and his boys made a dash across the rock and sand to the pilchard-house further east, the wind blowing in a furious squall now, and just as they were half-way, battling against the spray that cut their faces till they tingled, their numbers were diminished one third, though Mr Temple did not know it, and then two thirds.

He had bidden his boys follow him closely, and then with bent head run forward, Dick and Arthur following as fast as their stiff clumsy garb would allow; but just as they were half-way and were caught by the full force of the gale, Arthur, who was last, made a swerve, gave way a little more and a little more, and then was literally carried shoreward by the gale in a staggering run, for he had found it impossible to resist its force.

"Don't it blow!" panted Dick. "Lean your head over towards it, Taff, and then it won't cut your face. Come along."

He spoke loudly, but every word was swept away by the wind; and if sounds do not melt away, his were taken straight over England and the North Sea to Denmark, and then over the Baltic to the Russ's land.

"Here, give me your hand, Taff," he cried directly after, and turning a little more he held out his hand to lend his brother a little help.

Confused and deafened as he was by the storm himself, he burst out into a roar of laughter at the sight of his brother literally running before the wind in the most comically absurd manner, till, finding a dry spot, he flung himself down in the soft sand, sad clung there with all his might while Dick scudded to him and plumped down at his side.

"Here's a game!" he roared into Arthur's ear.

"A game!" faltered the latter; "very—dread—ful—isn't it?"

"No," shouted Dick. "It's all right. Come along. No, no. Turn your back to it."

"The rain cuts so," panted Arthur.

"'Tain't rain; it's spray. Hook hold tight," cried Dick. "Ahoy! Coming!" he shouted, wasting his breath, for it was impossible for Mr Temple to hear. "Here comes father after us. Now then, stoop down and let's do it. Whoo! Knees."

They threw themselves on their knees to avoid being swept away, for just then a sudden puff came with such violence that, as Dick afterwards described the sensation, it was like being pushed with a big ball of india-rubber.

Mr Temple came with the rush of wind, and as he stopped beside his boys he confessed that it was as much as he could do to keep his legs.

It was only for a few moments that the storm had such tremendous force. Then it lulled a little, and taking advantage of the comparative calm, Mr Temple took hold of his boys' hands, and the three with bended heads trotted towards the shelter on ahead.

They had not been long under the lee of the pilchard-house before they saw Will return and stand with Josh and some more of the fishermen just beyond the reach of the waves. Then first one and then another made a rush at what looked at a distance like a piece of wood, tossed here and there by the great billows. Into this they struck the boat-hook, and ran with it shoreward, the piece of wood which looked so small proving to be a deal that was a pretty good weight for two men to carry.

Quite a stack of these were dragged from the waves, some perfectly uninjured, others snapped in two, others again twisted and torn asunder, leaving long ragged threads of fibre, while others again were regularly beaten by the waves and rocks, so that the ends were like bunches of wood gnawed by some monster into shreds.

They went back to dinner and returned towards evening, Uncle Abram giving it as his opinion that the worst of the gale was not over yet, and pointing to the glass that hung in the passage for corroboration.

"Lower than she's been for months," said the old gentleman. "I hope no ship won't get caught in the bay."

Boom, bom!

"What's that?" cried Mr Temple quickly.

"It's what I hoped would not happen, sir," said the old man, taking off his hat; "a ship in distress, and may—"

He did not finish his sentence aloud, but closed his eyes, and they saw his lips move for a few moments, before, clapping on his hat again, he cried:

"Let's go down to the beach, sir. 'Tisn't likely, but we might be able to do some good. Ah! there she is speaking again."

Boom, bom!

The hoarse echoing report of a large gun heard plainly above the roar of the storm, and hastily putting on his great yellow oilskin coat, old Uncle Abram led the way towards the shore.

Chapter Twenty Eight.

A Brave Act for a Daring Man may be Heroism in a Gallant Boy.

"There she is, Master Dickard, sir," shouted Josh, as the little party reached the shore down by the pilchard-house, and he pointed out over the foaming sea.

"I can see nothing but mist," said Dick excitedly.

"That's the foam," said Josh; "but I can see her plain—three-master—quite a big ship."

"Will she get into the harbour, Josh?" said Dick, with his lips to the fisherman's ear.

Josh looked at him solemnly and then shook his head.

"One of our luggers couldn't do it, Master Dick, with a wind like this, let alone a big ship."

"What will happen then?" cried Dick excitedly.

"Rocks—go on the Six Pins, I should say. That's where the current'll take her—eh, master?"

Uncle Abram was holding his long telescope against the corner of the pilchard-house, and gazing attentively through it at the distant ship.

"No, Josh, my lad," he said; "there's too much water on the Six Pins even for her. She'll come clear o' them and right on to Black Point."

"And then?" said Mr Temple anxiously.

"We shall do what we can with the rocket-line if the masts hold good for a bit, sir."

"But a boat—a life-boat!"

Uncle Abram shrugged his shoulders and shook his head.

"Soon as that first gun was heard, sir, there was a man got on a horse and went over the hills to Corntown, where the life-boat lies, and they'll come over as fast as horses can draw the carriage; but it will take them a long time to get over along the rough road, and when they do get her here, where she's to be launched I can't tell."

Mr Temple and his sons looked about the bay at the tremendous breakers that were forming, as it were, a frame of foam. Even the entrance to the harbour was marked by the waves that leaped against the pier.

"I can't see the ship, father," whispered Dick in an awe-stricken voice, as he handed back the glass, whose bottom was dimmed with spray the moment he put it to his eyes.

"There—there," said Will hoarsely, as he pointed out to sea.

"No, I can't see it," said Dick again.

"Can you see the Bird Rock—the Mew Rock, where we caught the conger?" said Will hastily, and with his lips close to Dick's face.

"Yes."

"Then fix your eyes there, and then look straight from there to the old mine-shaft on the hill."

"Yes—yes," cried Dick. "I can see a mast all amongst the spray; and it's coming on this way."

"To destruction," said Mr Temple to himself, as he too now caught sight of the unfortunate vessel driving towards the rocks slowly and surely, and once more the crew drew attention to their peril by firing a signal-gun.

It is one of the most terribly painful positions in which a man can be placed, to see his fellow-creatures slowly drifting into what is almost certain death without being able to stretch out a hand to save.

There was no need to warn the crew of their danger; they knew that but too well, for the great grey rocks were in front of them with the breakers at their feet; and as the excitement increased Will caught Dick's arm.

"They're getting out the rocket-lines," he said, shouting into Dick's ear. "Come and see."

The wind and spray were forgotten, as the men, headed by a couple of coastguard, drew a truck along the sands and through the pools of water towards a spot to the left of where they stood, and just beyond the place where the seine was drawn in and the shark captured. To Dick it seemed as if the men were going away, from the place where they were likely to be of any help to the crew of the ship; but the fishermen knew what they were about, and old Mr Marion, who was as excited as any one present, came up to shout out his opinions.

"She'll come ashore on the Black Fin," he said. "The other side of the buoy. You watch her, and you'll see."

In spite of the driving foam and the salt rain formed by the spray cut from the tops of the waves, the vessel could now be plainly seen labouring and tossing among the great billows which grew heavier and grander the nearer the unfortunate vessel came to the shore, and Dick began to realise now how a ship could be safer a thousand miles from land in the heaviest hurricane than among the breakers upon our rocky coast.

The beating rain and wind then were forgotten as the rocket-cart came up, and Mr Temple and his sons staggered after it, Josh laying hold of one of Dick's arms, Will of the other, while old Marion and Mr Temple were on either side of Arthur, who wondered how the wind could thunder so heavily in his ears.

Dick had a misty sort of idea that a rope would be shot out to the wreck, and that the men would come along it ashore, but how it was to be done he could not tell. Had the storm been twice as heavy, though, he would have gone to see, and he pressed eagerly forward till, with his companions, he was close up to the cart, waiting for the ship to strike.

On she came through the foam, closer and closer, every mast standing, but the sails that had been set torn to rags, that streamed out like tattered pennons, and whipped and beat about the yards. Men on the shore ran here and there and shouted to each other to do impossibilities. Some got under the lee of rocks to use their glasses, but only to close them again and hurry to gain their excited companions, who were standing with coils of rope over their shoulders, and one arm through the ring, shouting again with their hands to their mouths, and one who had a speaking-trumpet roared some unintelligible order through it to the wind that cast it back into his face.

"Will the life-boat come in time?" said Mr Temple to Josh; but the fisherman did not speak nor turn to the questioner: he only shook his head.

All at once every one stood still. The excitement seemed to be at an end. Heads were bent forward, eyes were shaded, and one impulse seemed to have moved the scattered crowd upon the foaming beach, and those who were standing knee-deep amongst the rushing sea-froth that ran up beyond them to the sand.

"Look!" shouted Josh, without turning his head; and he pointed with his sound arm out to sea.

Dick, Arthur, and Mr Temple strained their eyes to catch signs of what the fisherman meant as they saw the vessel rising and falling, and seeming to glide slowly on, till all at once, in the midst of the dense rain of spray, the vessel rose, as it were, to make a leap, and then charged down a hill of waters, stopped short, and seemed to shiver. Then her tall main-mast fell forward, apparently snapped off close to the deck, carrying with it the fore-mast; while the mizen, that had been sloping slightly backward, now leaned over toward the shore.

"Fast on the Black Fin," cried Josh, with his hands to his mouth, and a shiver of horror ran through Dick and his brother as they realised what all this meant.

There was no time lost on the beach now, for in the midst of the crowd the rocket-cart was run down as far as was possible, the tube laid ready, the case with its line placed in position, and then away with a rush, and a stream of dull, almost invisible sparks sped the rocket with its line, whose destination was the far side of the ill-fated ship.

There was a cry from the men who were watching the flight of the line-bearer.

"Short, short!" And as the boys watched with parted lips, and eyes half-blinded with the spray, they saw the line rapidly hauled in and laid ready for another flight.

It took some time, during which those on shore could just make out the crew of the ship clustering about the stern of the vessel and on the mizen-mast.

All was ready at last, and once more a rocket was sent flying with the same result, its flight too short to reach the ship.

"I knowed it—I knowed it!" roared Josh between his hands. "There's only one way."

A little crowd collected about Josh, and for a short space there was hurried gesticulation, and old Marion seemed to be declaiming to the men.

All at once the boys saw Will back out of the crowd with Josh and wave his hand to them, after which every one set off rapidly round the curve of the bay to where the sands ceased and the shore was piled-up rocks, a reef of which ran right out to the vessel, which was fast on an isolated rock at the end.

They were farther from the ship now than before—probably double the distance; but the reef formed a breakwater, and in its lee, though it seemed almost madness, it was just possible that a boat might live.

"They're going to launch a boat and take out a line," shouted old Marion in Mr Temple's ear. "It breaks my heart, Master Temple, but he's light and strong, and a good rower, and Josh won't go alone."

"Is Will going?" cried Dick excitedly.

"Yes—yes," shouted the old man: "there's fellow-creatures' lives at stake; and at such a time a seafaring man can't say no."

What took place seemed to Dick afterwards like the events in some wild dream; but in the midst of the excitement and confusion he saw a small broad-beamed boat run down a pebbly slope, and that a line was coiled in her. Five men, it seemed, jumped into her as she was thrust off, the men wading out as far as they could to give impetus to the craft before they sprang in. Then the cockle-shell of a boat seemed to be lifted right up to the top of a wave, and then to plunge down out of sight; and as Dick watched for her reappearance, and noted that the line was held by the men ashore, as he had noted that there was some one in the stern of the boat who kept paying out that line, he realised that the boy was Will, and it seemed again more than ever to be a dream.

All that followed in the midst of that horrible din of shrieking wind, beating spray, and thundering seemed to be a confused dream, out of which he kept thinking he should wake, as he sheltered his eyes with his hands and tried to see the boat.

But no. Once it had plunged down that hill of foamy wave it had disappeared into a mist of spray and froth; and though two or three times he fancied that he caught sight of the boat climbing some wave between where they stood and the wreck, he could not be sure.

There was confidence, though, on the part of the men who were holding the line.

"He's paying it out right enough, the lad," shouted one of them to Uncle Abram; and as time went on signals were exchanged that told of the safety of those in the boat.

The distance was not great, and the reef of rocks not only formed a shelter, but produced a kind of eddy, which made the passage of the boat somewhat less perilous; but all the same it was a forlorn hope, and many of the fishermen said to themselves that the next time that they saw Will Marion and Josh it would be beaten and bruised by wave and rock, and cast up upon the shore.

But the signals, jerks of the rope, kept coming, and men perched themselves high up among the rocks to watch the progress of the boat with their glasses, but in vain. All they could see was an occasional glimpse of the mizen of the ship, with a dark patch of clustering humanity.

The life-saving gear had meanwhile been carried to the spot whence the boat was started; and there was hope yet that a connection might be made between the vessel and the rocks.

But time went on—time, confused by the roar of wind and wave, and there was no sign. It had seemed utter madness for that boat to be sent forth into such a chaos of waters; but there are things which some men call mad often adventured by the brave fishers of our coast.

All at once Dick started from his father's side to run to Uncle Abram, who had seated himself slowly upon a block of stone about which the foam floated to and fro on a few inches of water. The old man sank down in a way whose action Dick read at once, for the old fellow let his head go down upon his hands, and these rested upon his knees; and as he saw the air of utter dejection, Dick felt that poor Will must have been lost.

It seemed so horrible, so strange, that as Dick reached Abram Marion's side he sank down on his knees beside the old man, caught at his hands, and literally sobbed out:

"Oh! don't say he's drowned; don't say he's drowned."

There was quite a lull as he spoke; and as the old man felt the touch of the boy's clinging hands he laid his own upon his head with a strange far-off look in his eyes.

"I don't say so; I won't say so!" he cried in a hoarse, passionate way. "My brave, true lad! but I oughtn't to have let him go."

"Hurrah!"

A loud cheer from near the water's edge, and a quick, bustling movement among the men; and then down came the storm again, as if it had been taking breath, and the roar was deafening.

But the boat had reached the ship, of course getting under her lee, and her daring little crew had climbed on board. For there was the proof—the life-gear had been attached to the end of the line, and it was being rapidly dragged from the shore out towards the wreck.

A long, anxious time ensued, during which, while the sea end was being secured to the wreck, the shore end of the life-cable, was carried high up to the top of a cluster of rocks that formed the end of the reef, a flat place thirty feet above the level of the sea.

There were drags at that line, which the men at once knew were given by the waves, but they were mostly sharp twitches, which meant that the daring boatmen, headed by Josh, were making it fast high up somewhere in the vessel's mizen; and at last there was an unmistakable signal which meant, "Make fast," and the shore end was hauled tight round a mass of rock.

Then as Dick and his brother stood in the crowd, which had climbed up to the top of the rock, they saw the block that ran upon the cable set in motion by a thin line that was alongside the thick rope, and there was a burst of cheers as the cradle—that basket-like contrivance of the rocket apparatus—started off, dragged by those upon the rock, to cross the seething waves, which kept leaping up at it as if to snatch it down.

Then came a signal—a twitch of the line, and with a cheer the men on the rock hauled the cradle back—cradle indeed, for it seem to contain a new-born life, saved from inevitable death.

It was the pale, wild face of a woman, speechless with dread and exposure, that greeted the men on the rocks as they hauled in the cradle; and in a minute she was lifted out, and almost before the willing hands had lifted the poor woman down from the rock, the cradle was speeding back.

It returned quickly with a man half dead, and he, amidst rousing cheers, was lifted out, and borne to a place where he would find warmth, welcome, and shelter.

Then four more were dragged ashore over the thundering, roaring waves, as the cradle was merrily hauled to and fro.

Then came another man, but not a storm-beaten exhausted seaman. It was the well-known countenance of one of the crew that went out in the boat, and he was full of activity.

"Back with the cradle!" he shouted, "haul away. The ship won't hold together long."

The cradle began to run back over the swinging rope, while the man who had returned said in reply to questions:

"Those were all. The rest of the poor souls had been beaten off, and these couldn't have lasted many minutes longer. You must look alive."

The men waited anxiously for the signal, and then another mate was hauled over the waves, and the cradle sent back, while Dick stood trembling and wanting to ask why Will, who was a boy, had not been sent first.

Then came another, and still it was not Will.

"This time it must be he," thought Dick; but when the cradle arrived once more, it was the face of Josh that saluted them.

"Haul back quick," the latter said. "She was shivering under my feet when I come away."

"And you left that boy to drown!" roared Uncle Abram, catching Josh by the throat.

Josh did not resent it, but said quietly, in a lull of the storm:

"He wouldn't come first. It was like drowning both him and me to stand gashly arguing at a time like that."

And now every eye was staring wildly, and with an intensity that showed how eagerly all watched for the next freight of the cradle.

"It's hard work for the lad," said Josh hoarsely; "and I'd give anything to be at his side. But he'll do it if the ship hangs together long enough. Oh, pull, pull! Haul away, lads, haul!"

"He made me come—he made me come," he cried frantically. "It was keeping the lad back to say I wouldn't go first. I didn't want to, lads, I didn't want to."

"No, no," came in a sympathetic growl, as once more the wind lulled a little and there were symptoms of the gale being nearly over.

Then there was a groan, for Will made no signal.

"Hooray!" came from the men, as there was a sudden snatch, and the rope they were giving out was drawn rapidly. "He's got it, he's—got—"

The man who was joyfully shouting that stopped short as the rope ceased moving, and one, who was trying to use a telescope, shouted:

"The mizen's over!"

"Then she's gone to pieces, lads," cried another.

"No," cried the man with the glass; "part's standing yet."

"Hooray!" came again, as Dick stood clinging to Uncle Abram's arm, the old man having left the stone, and standing close beside the men who hauled the cradle gear.

Short as the distance was, not a glimpse of the ship could be seen, for every wave that broke upon the rock rose in a fountain of spray, to mingle with the blinding drift and mist of foam. But all the time their eyes were strained towards the rock upon which the ship had struck, and along the reef that the venturesome boat's crew had made the shelter which resulted in the saving of some of the poor creatures upon the wreck.

All at once, when a horrible feeling of despair had settled upon all present, there was a sharp twitch given to the line, the signal for it to be hauled, just at a time too when Josh had turned away, giving Dick a piteous look, and then gone to lean his head upon his arm against the rock.

That cheer which came as the rope was twitched seemed to send life and activity back to Josh, who dashed in among the knot of men at the rope.

"Here, let me come," he shouted; "let me have a hand in bringing him ashore. Hurray! Master Dick, hurray! he's saved, he's saved!"

Was he?

The men hauled as rapidly as was consistent with safety, till the cradle with its occupant was dragged right up on to the rock, where a dozen hands were ready to lift the drooping, insensible figure out, and pour brandy between its lips.

Will opened his eyes at this and stared wildly for a few moments; then a knowledge of his position seemed to come to him, and he smiled and raised one hand.

At that moment there was a shout and the cable of the cradle gear seemed to hang loose, and the sea end to be moving shoreward, while the man with the glass shouted:

"She's gone to pieces, lads; that last wave lifted her, and then she melted right away."

There was no doubt about it, for the cradle gear was floating free, and the men were able to haul it in. The rest of the crew of that unfortunate ship, with twelve passengers beside, were washed ashore with the battered boat that took the line, and fragments of wreck here and there all round the coast for the next ten days or so, long after Will had well recovered from the shock of his adventure. For he had been for long enough beaten about and half drowned by the waves while striving to get the cradle rope clear of a tangle of rigging that had fallen upon it, and threatened to put an end to its further working, till he had run a most perilous risk, climbed over it, hauled the rope from the other side, and had just strength enough left to get into the cradle and give the signal, as a wave came over the doomed ship, and buried him deep beneath tons of water.

He could recollect no more than that he had tried to give the signal to be hauled ashore, and some one had held him up to pour brandy between his teeth.

Yes: there was something else he remembered very well, and that was the way in which Dick held on to him, and how Arthur had shaken hands. He recalled that, and with it especially Mr Temple's manner, for there was a kind, fatherly way in his words and looks as he said to him gently:

"Will Marion, I should have felt very proud if one of my boys had done all this."

Chapter Twenty Nine.

Mr Temple learns more of Will Marion's Character written in Stones.

"Don't say anything about it, my lad, to Will; he don't like it known," said Uncle Abram one day; "and I wouldn't let out about it to his aunt."

"I won't tell anybody but Taff and my father," said Dick.

Uncle Abram took his pipe out of his mouth and scratched the side of his nose with it very softly, as he looked out through the window, and its climbing-roses, to sea.

Mrs Marion had gone into Corntown marketing; Arthur was up the cliff reading in a snug corner he affected; Mr Temple had gone out alone along the cliff "on an exploring trip," he had said with a smile; and Will was down with Josh at the lugger "overhauling," as Josh called it, which meant running over the nets previous to a visit to the pilchard ground.

Dick was just going to join them when Uncle Abram, who was fumigating his rose-trees and enjoying his pipe at the same time, made him a signal, as he called it, and asked him if he would like to see Will's room.

"Well," said the old man, after a good deal of scratching with the red waxed end of his tobacco pipe.

"I s'pose you're right, Master Richard, sir. I say don't tell Will, because he's so modest like, and don't want people to know; and, I say, don't tell his aunt, because she's so particular like with him, and if she know'd all, she'd think he was neglecting his regular work, and that if he could find time, you see, for doing this sort of thing, he could be doing more to the boats. But I don't see why your brother should not know, and I don't hold with a lad keeping anything from his father."

"And who wants to keep anything from his father?" said Mr Temple, who was just passing the window on his return. "What is it?" he continued, entering the room.

"Oh, nothing, sir; only I was going to show Master Richard here our Will's room, and I was asking him to be a bit secret like for the lad's sake. Mrs Marion, you see, is a—"

"Oh, yes, I understand," said Mr Temple. "May I come too?"

"If you please, sir," said the old man smiling. "It's in your way rather, you see, both of you being a bit fond of chip-chopping stones; not that there's many up there now, for you see his aunt makes the lad clear 'em away now and then. Won't have the litter, she says. But I've got 'em all in a box down in my toolshed, where the boy can have 'em when he likes."

"Let's go and see his room, then," said Mr Temple, smiling.

"'Tarn't much of a place, sir, being a garret," said Uncle Abram apologetically; "but lads as goes to sea has snugger quarters sometimes than our Will's."

He put his pipe back in his mouth—it was out now—and held it steady as he led the way to a door in a corner at the end of the passage, and up a very steep flight of stairs to a little room with sloping ceiling, over the kitchen.

"I had this knocked up for the lad o' purpose," said Uncle Abram proudly. "Made it as like a cabin as I could, meaning him to be sea-going, you understand, sir, only he's drifting away from it like. Why, bless your heart, though, Mr Temple, sir, I never find no fault with him, for there's stuff enough in him, I think, to make a real lord-mayor. There: there's our Will's room."

He stood smiling as the visitors had a good look round the scrupulously clean little cabin-like bed-room with lockers and a swinging shelf of books, and everything arranged with a neatness that was most notable.

"Those are his books, sir. Spends a deal of time over 'em."

"Novels and romances, eh?" said Mr Temple, going to the shelf. "Why, hullo! Fowne's *Chemistry*, Smyth's *Mineralogy*, Murchison's *Geology*. Rather serious reading for him, isn't it?"

"Not it, sir," cried Uncle Abram. "He loves it, sir; and look here," he continued, opening one of the lockers; "as full of specimens as can be. All sorts of stones and bits of ore that he gets from the mines. Ah! that's a new net he's making; small meshed seine to catch sand-eels, sir, for bait. That's a new shrimp-net he made for me. Mixes it up like— reads and makes nets together. Once you've got your fingers to know how to make a net, they'll go on while you read."

"What are these?" said Mr Temple, pointing at a series of rough glass bottles and oil flasks.

"Oh, that's his apparatus he made, sir. Does chemistry with them, and there's a little crucible in my tool-house, where he melts down tin and things sometimes, to see what they're made of. I always encourage him, I do, just. Can't do the boy any harm."

"Harm! no," said Mr Temple quietly, as he glanced through Will's treasures with a good deal of curiosity, spending most of the time over a small glass case which was full of glittering pieces of ore.

"He seems to like the pretty bits best," said Mr Temple; but Uncle Abram shook his head.

"Oh no, sir. Those are what his aunt likes best. She won't have the bits of tin and rough copper ore; says they're rubbish, bless her. She don't know what one bit's worth more than another, only goes by the eye, you see. I've got the rough bits hid away for him when he wants 'em."

Mr Temple seemed unusually thoughtful, so it seemed to Dick, who was delighted with the quaintness of the little attic, and declaring to himself that it was just the place he should like for himself; but he wondered a little bit at his father looking so stern.

"Here, quick!" cried Uncle Abram excitedly; "that's my boy's step coming in back way. I don't want him to see us. Looks like spying on him, poor lad, and I want him to enjoy himself when he isn't at work."

"And quite right too," said Mr Temple quietly, as he followed the old man down the steep stairs, and they had just reached the parlour when there was a knock at the door.

"Beg pardon, sir," said Will, who was flushed with hurrying; "but you said you would like the young gentlemen to have a sail in the trawler."

"Sail in the trawler!" cried Dick, bounding across the room excitedly.

"Yes! Well?" said Mr Temple, smiling.

"She's lying off the harbour, sir. I've seen the master, and he says the young gentlemen are welcome, and there's a fine breeze, sir, and it's a lovely day."

Dick turned a look upon his father, such as a prisoner might turn upon a judge as he waited for him to speak.

"I suppose you would not like to go, Dick?" said Mr Temple dryly. "You would miss your dinner."

"Why, father," cried Dick in a tone of reproach, "I can have a dinner

227

every day."

"And a sail in a trawler only once perhaps in your life. Then be off."

Dick bounded to the door and then stopped.

"May Taff come, father?" he cried.

"If he likes; but perhaps he wouldn't care to go. Make him sea-sick perhaps."

"But he may go, father?"

"Yes. But stop. Take something to eat with you in a basket."

"The master of the smack said if the young gentlemen would come in they could have a bit of dinner on board. We could cook some fish, sir."

"Oh!" cried Dick excitedly.

"Come, this is tempting," said Mr Temple. "I'm half disposed to come too."

"Do, father," cried Dick, catching his hand. "Oh, do come."

"No, my boy, I have some important business on hand. There, go and enjoy yourselves. You're going, Will?" he said quietly.

"Yes, sir, if uncle can spare me, and Josh too."

"That's right; take care of my boys—that is, if your uncle can spare you."

"Oh yes, oh yes! They can go. They don't sail for the pilchard ground till sundown."

Arthur was hunted out of his nest, and as soon as he knew of the object in view he displayed plenty of eagerness. The sight of the cutter-rigged smack lying with her bowsprit pointing to the wind, and her white mainsail flapping and quivering in the breeze, which seemed to send mimic waves chasing each other along it from mast to edge, while the jib lay all of a heap waiting to be hoisted, being one that would have roused the most phlegmatic to a desire to have a cruise, and see some of the wonders of the deep dredged up.

The master of the trawler gave the boys a hearty reception, his bronzed face expanding into a smile as he held Dick's hand in his great hard brown heavy paw.

"So you've come a-trawling, have you, my lad? Well, I'm glad to see you, and you too, sir," he added, shaking hands with Arthur in turn. "Going to stop aboard, lads?" he said in a kind of chant to Will and Josh.

"Ay, we're going to stop," said the latter; so the master of the trawler sent one of his own crew ashore with Uncle Abram's boat, telling the man he could stay.

The next minute the master gave the word, and went to the tiller, a couple of men began to haul up the jib, and then Arthur was clinging frantically to Will.

"Quick! The boat!" he cried. "The ship's going over."

Then he turned from deadly pale to scarlet as he saw Will's smile and look of amusement.

"It's all right, Master Arthur," said the latter; "it's the wind taking hold of the mains'l. She only careens a bit."

"But won't it go over?"

"Over! Oh, no!" said Will; "there's too much ballast. There, you see, now we're beginning to move."

"But ought the boat to go side wise like this?" whispered Arthur. "The deck's all of a slope."

"Oh, yes, that's right enough. When we're on the other tack she'll careen over the other side. The stiffer the breeze and the more sail there is, the more she careens. I've been in a smack when we've been nearly lying down in the water, and it's washed right over the deck."

"There, young gents, she's moving now," said the master, as the gaff was hoisted, and the beautifully-shaped cutter began to rush through the water at a rapid rate, leaving two long lines of foam in an ever-widening wake, while, like some gigantic sword-fish, she ploughed her way through the glittering sea. The sails bellied out tense and stiff, and the wind whistled as it seemed to sweep off the three sails.

There was no doubt about it; either the cutter was moving or the pier and shore. To Arthur it seemed as if the latter had suddenly begun to run away from them, and was dancing up and down with joy because it had found the chance.

"Dick," whispered Arthur, after beckoning his brother to his side, where he was holding on by the weather shrouds.

"Hullo!" cried Dick, laughing. "Oh, I say, Taff, isn't it fun? I can't walk."

"I'm sure it isn't safe," whispered Arthur.

"Eh? What? Not safe?"

"No, I'm sure it isn't. We shall be blown over."

"Oh, never mind," said Dick. "They'll turn her round and blow her up again. I say, Taff; don't be afraid. We sha'n't hurt."

"But if we were to be drowned, Dick, what would papa say?"

"Don't know. He wouldn't like it, though. But we sha'n't be drowned. Look at Will. He'd know if there was any danger, and he's as cool as can be. Come, pluck up. Let go of that rope. You'll soon get used to it."

Arthur turned a ghastly face to him.

"I'm trying to master being frightened, Dick," he said humbly; "but I must go home again; I'm going to be sick."

"Nonsense!" cried Dick, laughing. "There, think about something else. There, look, they're going to use the net."

To Arthur's great delight the speed of the smack was checked, and the busy preparations took up his attention, so that the qualm passed off, and he crept to his brother's side and listened as Josh was explaining the use of the trawl-net, which the men were about to lower over the side.

"There you are, you see," said Josh; "here's your net, just like a night-cap with a wide end and a little end, as we calls the bunt. There's pockets to it as well, only you can't very well see 'em now. When she's hauled up with fish in you'll see 'em better then."

"And what's this big piece of wood?"

"Trawl-beam," said Josh; "thirty-footer, to keep the meshes of the net stretched wide open at the top. Bottom's free so as to drag over the bottom. And them's the trawl-irons, to fit on the end of the beam and skate along the sand and keep all down."

"And the rope's tied to them?" said Dick.

"Rope?" said Josh. "You mean the bridle. That's right, my lad, and down she goes."

Over went the huge, cumbersome apparatus of beam, irons, and net, the weighty irons being so arranged as to take the trawl to the bottom in the right position so that the net with its stout edge rope should scrape over the sand as the cutter sailed.

"There you are," said the master, coming up; "now, then, away we go. There's a fine wind this morning, and we shall get some fish."

"Does the wind make you get the fish?" said Dick.

"To be sure, my lad. If we weren't sailing fast, as soon as the flat-fish felt the net being dragged over 'em they'd give a flip and a flap and be out of the way in no time; but the trawl's drawn over 'em so quickly in a brisk breeze like this that they haven't time to escape. They're in the net before they know where they are, and then they get into the pockets, and it's a case of market for them."

"It's all sand under here, isn't it?" asked Dick.

"You may be sure of that, my lad," said the master laughing. "When you see a smack trawling, it's all sand there, says you. 'Cause why? If it was rocks the trawl would catch and be broken before you knowed where you were. Yes; it's all smooth bottom here."

It was wonderfully interesting to see the great strong beam and the thick net, so different in the make to the filmy cobwebs that were used for seine and drift. This was of stout cord, and its edge of a strong over-bound rope. Of course all was out of sight now, the only thing visible being the bridle-rope, by means of which the trawl was being swiftly dragged astern.

"I hope we shall get a good haul or two," said Will, joining the boys as they stood holding on by the bulwarks, with the great mainsail boom over their heads, everything that looked so small and toy-like from the shore being here big and strong.

"What shall we catch?" said Arthur, making an effort to hide the remains of his discomposure.

"Get, sir?" cried Will smiling. "Oh! all sorts of things. If we're lucky, a turbot or two; soles we are sure to have, and some plaice; perhaps a brill; then there'll be a few dabs and whiting, and maybe a red mullet, and along with them the trawl will bring up a lot of all sorts."

"All sorts?" said Dick.

"Yes, sir. Weevers and blennies, and crabs, with oysters and scallops, and sea-weeds of all kinds—a regular mixture if we go over a part that hasn't been much swept lately."

"Here, I say, when are they going to pull up the net?" said Dick eagerly. "I want to see."

"Oh! not yet awhile," said Will smiling.

"But the fish will get out again."

"Oh no! We're going too fast for that," said Will; "and if there are any fish they'll be in the pockets."

"But has a trawl-net got pockets?" said Arthur curiously.

"Oh yes!" said Dick grinning; "two in its trousers, two in its waistcoat, and one in its jacket."

"Don't you mind what he says, Master Arthur," said Will smiling. "The pockets are on each side of the net, where it is sewed up a little, so that if the fish, when once in, try to swim towards the mouth they go instead into some of those sewed-up corners and get no farther. There, you see now, we're going on the other tack so as to sweep back over nearly the same ground again. There are rocks if we go any farther this way."

As he spoke the course of the smack was altered, and the side that had been so low down that at times it was almost possible to touch the water was high up and the other lower down, and the smack rushed through the water, as it seemed, faster than ever.

"She can sail, can't she, young gentlemen?" said the master. "We call her the *Foam*, and she can make foam too. Well, are you ready for the haul?"

"Yes. Are you going to begin?" cried Dick excitedly.

"Soon, my lad, soon," said the master. "Have you got a basket?"

Dick shook his head.

"Oh! you'll want a basket, and you must have a bucket of water. There'll be lots of things you'll like to look at that we should pitch overboard again."

"You lend me a basket and a bucket then," said Dick; "you shall have them back."

"Right, my lad. You tell young Will there to get you what you want. We shall have the trawl aboard soon."

It seemed to Dick almost an age, but at last the master turned his brown, good-humoured face to him and gave him a nod. At the same moment he shouted a few short orders, and Dick rushed to take a pull at the rope as he saw Josh and Will stand by.

"No, no, my lad; you and your brother look on," cried the master good-temperedly.

Dick drew back and glanced at Arthur, whose face was as eager as his own. In fact, a great deal of his London indifference had disappeared of late, and the boy had been growing as natural as his brother.

It was a time of intense excitement though for them, and as they watched they saw a windlass turn, and up came the great trawl-irons and the beam, then, dripping and sparkling in the sun, the foot-rope of the trawl-net, and foot after foot emerged with nothing but dripping water.

"Why, they haven't caught a fish," cried Dick in a disappointed tone of voice.

"You wait till the bunt's aboard," growled Josh just then; and the bunt, as the tassel end of the great net night-cap was called, was hauled on board dripping, and containing something splashing, flapping, and full of life.

"There's something for you to look at, my lads," cried the bluff master smiling. "Let out that draw string, Josh."

The whole of the net was now on the deck, the water streaming from it out at the side; and after Josh had unfastened the string which laced up the small end or bunt, the little crew took hold of the net above the pockets, and by giving it a series of shakes sent the whole of its contents out upon the deck. The net was then drawn away, the bunt fastened up, the end thrown over, and the trawl-beam took all down to scrape once more over the sands and scoop-out the soles and other flat-fish that are so fond of scuffling themselves down in the soft oozy sand, flapping their side-fins about till they are half covered, and very often letting the trawl-rope pass right over their backs.

A good many had, however, failed to be successful this time, for there was a great patch of the deck covered with the contents of the net.

"I never saw such a sight in my life," cried Dick; and then he burst into a roar of laughter as his brother tried to pick up a large sole, which seemed to give a spring and a flap, and darted out of his hands.

It was a sight, certainly; and the master good-humouredly let the men stand aside for a while so that the boys might have a good inspection of the haul before clearance was made.

"Overboard with the rubbish, my lads," he said, "then you can see better."

But the rubbish, a great deal of it, was what Dick and his brother would have liked to keep, as much of it consisted of pieces of heavy black wood pierced by teredo and covered with barnacles. There were curious stones, too, and pieces of weed, all of which had to go overboard though, and then, as Dick called it, the fun began.

It was a good haul. And first and foremost there was a magnificent turbot—a huge round fellow, with his white waistcoat, and mouth awry, apparently, though it was normally placed, and the creature's eyes, like those of the rest of the flat-fish, were screwed round to one side of its head.

Then there was a brill, like the turbot's small first cousin, and a young turbot that might have been its son. There were a dozen or so of plaice, large and small, and, flipping and flapping and gasping, some five-and-twenty soles, from fine fat fellows fifteen inches long to little tiny slips that were thrown overboard.

"Some sends that sort to market," said the master smiling. "I throw 'em in again to get fat."

Arthur's adventures with the conger came back to him as he saw one long lithe fish of some four feet eagerly seized and thrust into one of the many stout boxes on the deck; and he said something to his brother.

"No," said Will, who overheard him. "That's a hake."

There were several whitings, many being of very large size, four times that of the familiar tail-biting gentlemen who are curled up among the parsley upon our tables. No less than a dozen ruddy mullet were there too; and the above-named being the good fish of the haul, the residue was left on deck for the boys to examine and save what they pleased.

Will picked out a small brill and a whiting or two, with a good-sized sole that had been left. These were placed in the basket, and then the basket was dipped full of clean water, and the treasures, as Dick called them, were fished out and dropped in.

Among these were a lovely jelly-fish and a couple of beroes, looking like little oblong balls of the purest crystal; some pieces of stone, with curious barnacles adhering; and a quaint-looking, large-headed fish with prickly weapons about its head and back.

Then Arthur added a baby sole, and Dick an infant turbot, which were entangled amongst the sea-weed that had been dredged up; while everywhere the patch of dredgings upon the deck seemed to be alive with creeping and crawling things, examples of the teeming life of the great ocean.

Then came the master to intimate that the deck must be cleared, for they were going to haul the dredge on board again.

"What—so soon?" cried Dick.

"So soon—eh?" said the master. "Why, you've been stirring that up 'bout half an hour."

"Ah! well, we shall have something more to see," said Dick in a reconciled manner; and he carried his basket astern, while the men swept the remains of the haul—such remains as would have given a naturalist a week's amusement—overboard.

Then once more the ponderous trawl was hauled on board, with its flapping and splashing prisoners, which were nearly as abundant as before; but there was no turbot this time.

"Don't matter," said Dick; "here's the sauce."

As he spoke he pointed laughingly to a great lobster which had been out on its travels away from its home amongst the rocks, and had been swept up, to be turned out upon the smack's deck, to crawl about flapping its tail and opening and closing its pincers, held aloft in the most aggressive way.

"Ah!" said the master thoughtfully, "that won't do. We must have gone a little too near the tail of the rocks when we tacked."

"I thought you was going pretty close," said Josh, "but I said as you know'd best."

The boxes were dragged forward again, and soles and plaice were thrust in, flapping and springing in their captors' hands. Then the whiting were sorted into their home, the sundry fish that were worth saving placed in another box, and once more the visitors were allowed to have their turn in the heap, till, amidst such an embarrassment of riches, as the French call it, Dick stopped short with a laughing, puzzled face, to rub his ear.

"There's such a lot," he cried. "There's so much to see, I don't know what to take first, and what to leave."

It resulted in nearly everything going overboard,—tiny fish entangled in sea-weed, curious stones, dog-fish, and skates' eggs, barnacles, pieces of hard English sponge, bones of cuttle-fish, and scallop and oyster-shells; but one basket was set aside for Mr Temple by Will, who stored in it a fair number of delicious oysters and scallops, whose beautiful shells were bearded with lovely weeds like ferns or plumes of asparagus, while one that gaped open showed his flesh to be of the most brilliant orange scarlet hue.

And so it went on hour after hour, the fresh breeze making the trawling most successful, and at every haul there were so many treasures that at last Dick gave up collecting in despair, confiding his opinion to his brother that the happiest life anybody could lead must be that of the master of a trawler.

Towards four o'clock they were sent ashore with Josh and Will, loaded with bucket and basket of the treasures they had found, including a handsome lot of fish for Mr Temple, with the master's compliments.

"Why, Taff," said Dick suddenly, "you were going to be sea-sick, weren't you, when we started off?"

"Yes," said Arthur uneasily, and then smiling, he added, "I forgot all about it."

"Forgot all about it!" said Dick. "I should think so. Why, it wouldn't matter how bad a fellow were: a day's trawling would make him well."

Chapter Thirty.

Taff objects to Early Rising and being treated as a Seal.

It wanted a perfectly calm day for the visit to the seal-cave, and this was long in coming. There were plenty of fine days when the sun shone brightly and the sea was as clear as crystal; but there was generally a pleasant breeze, and the pleasant breeze that only seemed to ripple the water was sufficient twice over to raise good-sized waves amongst the rocks, and to send a rush of broken water enough to upset a boat, foaming and dashing in at the mouth of the cave.

Failing the success of this enterprise, Mr Temple, who was with them, made Will and Josh row on to the rift in the cliff where the vein of white spar had been found by Will; and leaving all in the boat, Dick's father went up by himself and stayed for long enough, while his sons were rowed to and fro fishing with more or less success.

One morning, though, as Dick was dreaming of being in the green-house at home when the hail was pattering down, there seemed to come three or four such sharp cracks that he awoke and jumped out of bed. The next moment he was at the window pulling up the blind and looking out, to see Will on the rugged pathway waiting for him to open the window.

"Seal-cave to-day," he said. "Look out to sea."

Dick looked out to sea, where there was a dense mist that seemed to wrap everything in its folds. The luggers appeared dim—those that were near shore—while others were completely hidden. Overhead the sky was clear, and the sun was shining brightly, while where its light fell upon the mist it became rosily transparent, and the masts of some of the luggers looked double their usual size.

"Seals, Taff, seals!" cried Dick, shaking his brother's shoulder, with the effect of making him hurriedly scramble out of bed, yawning terribly, and gazing in an ill-used way at his brother, as he sat down and began to rub his feet one over the other.

"Don't sit down, Taff; dress yourself. I'm going to call father."

"Shut that window first," cried Arthur; "it's so horribly cold."

"Cold! Ha! ha! Ha! ha! ha!" laughed Dick. "What a chap you are, Taff! Here, Will, he says it's cold. Go to the pump for a pail of cold water to warm him."

"He had better not," cried Arthur, hurriedly scuffling into his trousers. "If he did I would never forgive him."

"I'm not going to get any water, Master Arthur," cried Will; "but make haste down, it's such a glorious morning!"

"'Tisn't," said Arthur, whose eyes were swelled up with sleepiness. "It's all misty and thick, and the window-sill's wet, and the roses outside look drenched. Heigh, ho, ha, hum!" he yawned. "I shall go to bed for half an hour longer—till the sun comes out."

"No, you sha'n't," cried Dick, seizing the pillow for a weapon of offence. "If you do, I'll bang you out of bed again."

"If you dare to touch me," cried Arthur furiously, "I shall complain to papa."

"And he'll laugh at you," said Dick; "and serve you right."

Arthur snatched off his lower garment with the obstinacy of a half-asleep individual, and scrambled into bed again, dragging the clothes up over his chest, and scowling defiantly at his brother, as if saying,

"Touch me if you dare."

"There's a stupid, obstinate, lazy old pig," cried Dick, throwing the pillow at him and standing rubbing one ear. "Here—hi, Will!" he said, going to the window, "come round and upstairs. Here's a seal in his cave asleep. Come and let's tug him out."

"He had better not dare to come into my bed-room," cried Arthur, punching the pillow thrown at him viciously, and settling down in his place; not that he wanted more rest, but out of dislike to being disturbed, and from a fit of morning ill-temperedness getting the upper hand.

Just then Dick was leaning out of the window half-dressed, and with his braces hanging down as if they were straps to haul him back in case he leaned too far.

Arthur glanced at his brother for a moment and then shouted:

"Here, Dick, shut that window!"

Dick evidently did not hear him, and a low giggling laugh reached his ears.

"They had better not try to play any tricks with me," said Arthur to himself, as he lay frowning and feeling very much dissatisfied, as he thought, with Dick, but really with himself.

Then he heard more laughing, the sound of steps in the garden, and something thump against the wall of the house.

There was no mistake now about Arthur's wakefulness, as he lay with the clothes drawn right above his nose; one eye glanced at the window, and he breathed quickly with indignation as Dick drew a little on one side to make room for Will, who had obtained the short ladder used by his uncle to nail up his creepers, and placed it against the wall, and he was now on the top with his jersey-covered arms resting on the window-sill, and his sun-browned face above them looking in.

"Good-morning, sir!" he said merrily. "Want anybody to help you dress?"

"How dare you!" cried Arthur indignantly. "Go away, and shut that window directly. It's disgraceful. We had no business to come to such a place as this," he continued, forgetting all his good resolves, and giving rein to his anger.

"Why, hullo! what's all this?" said Mr Temple, entering the room, dressed for going out.

"I'm glad you've come, papa," cried Arthur, whose face was scarlet with anger. "These boys have—"

"Oh, I say, Taff, don't be disagreeable," cried Dick. "It was all my doing, father. Taff wouldn't get up, and Will here had come to call us, and I told him to get up the ladder and look in, pretending that there *was* a seal in a cave, and Taff turned cross about it."

"Get up directly, Arthur," said Mr Temple quietly, "and make haste down. How would to-day do to visit the seal-cave?" continued Mr Temple, turning to Will.

"I came to tell the young gentlemen it was just the morning, sir," said Will, who was feeling very uncomfortable. "It is as still as can be, and the tide will suit. I should go, sir, directly after breakfast."

"And so we will," said Mr Temple. "There, finish dressing, Dick," he said, as Will slid down the ladder and took it away. "I thought there was to be no more of this petty anger, Arthur. You are old enough to know better, and yet you behave like a fractious child. Don't tease him, Dick; he can't bear it, I suppose."

Mr Temple left the room, and Dick went on hurriedly dressing, while Arthur, flushed and uncomfortable, sat in his trousers on the edge of the bed, his hair touzled and the pillow creases marked like a map on his right cheek.

"Here, I say, get dressed, Taff," cried Dick, "and let's go down and collect some sea-anemones before breakfast."

"I don't want to dress," said Arthur. "I'm always wrong. I'm a miserable wretch, and nobody understands me. I sha'n't go to the seal-cave to-day."

"Yes, you will," cried Dick, who was very sympathetic but very busy, for he had suddenly awakened to the fact that he had put too much pomatum on his hair. The result was that it looked shiny and greasy, and there was nothing for it but to give it a good rub over with the sponge and then towel it, which he was doing by holding the cloth over his head, and sawing it vigorously to and fro.

"No, I shall not go," said Arthur despondently. "I shall stop at home."

"So shall I then," said Dick panting, and out of breath from his exertions. "It's all right, Taff, I tell you. Get dressed. You'll feel as different as can be when you've had your breakfast. That's what's the matter with you. It makes you feel cross sometimes when you are so precious hungry."

Arthur sat unmoved, making no effort to dress, and Dick, who was nearly complete, wanting only his jacket, turned to him once more.

"Come on, Taff," he cried. "Get dressed, and let's find some anemones, and put in a tub of salt-water. We can feed 'em on shrimps."

"I wish we were back in london," said Arthur bitterly.

"What! to have the fellows shouting 'sweep!' and the girls beating the mats and knocking their brooms against the area railings as you're dressing. No, thank you. I like being here. Oh, I say, how lovely old Mr Marion's flowers smell! Here's a lugger! Hi, Will, what boat's that?"

"The *Grey Gull*, Thomson's boat," came up from the garden. "Been out all night for pilchards. I'll go down and get some for bait."

"I never saw a pilchard," said Arthur, suddenly beginning to dress.

"Look sharp, then, and we'll go down and have a look. Here, I shall go now. You can come on."

"That's always the way," said Arthur bitterly. "You never will wait for me."

"I will now, then," cried Dick. "Look sharp;" and he went and leaned his elbows on the window, to gaze out at the lovely opalescent mist through which, looking huge in proportion, a brown-sailed lugger came creeping over the steely sea, which shone and glanced wherever the sun passed through the heavy mist. The men on the lugger looked huge, and it was evident from the shouts from the pier and the responses that there was some little excitement going on about the new arrival, but what it was Dick was too distant to hear.

"Oh, do make haste, Taff!" he cried, glancing back to see with satisfaction that his brother was now making good speed; "there's no end of fun going on. I've never seen a pilchard yet. There's Will Marion down there, and—oh, I say, what a shame to go down without us! There goes father!"

Arthur's toilet proceeded by big strides now, and it was not long before, looking a good deal more amiable, he declared himself ready, and was in fact so ready that he raced with his brother down to the cliff—rather a breakneck proceeding, considering the steepness of the way; but they got down to the harbour in safety, and to Dick's delight he found that the lugger was not yet in, the progress by means of her sweeps having been very slow, and now for the first time he noticed that she was extremely deep in the water.

"A be glad you've come, Master Diehard," said a voice behind them; and there stood Josh. "*Grey Gull's* coming in with 'bout the gashliest take o' pilchards as never was. Say they could have filled the lugger twice over."

The little pier was pretty well crowded, and the men were in an unwonted state of excitement, but place was made for the boys, and they were soon after standing gazing down into the hold of the lugger, which seemed to be filled with silver whose dust had been scattered all over deck, bulwarks, combings, buoys, ropes, nets, for everything was specked and spangled with silvery scales.

"Here, boys," said Mr Temple, "this is a fresh sight for you. What do you think of these?"

Mr Temple was standing beside Will, who had been on board the lugger and returned with a little basket containing a dozen or two of the little oily fish, which looked like small large-scaled herrings, but richer and fatter and of tenderer skin.

"Wonderful bait," said Will. "We can catch no end to-night with these."

They waited to see the business begin—the said business being the rapid unloading of the pilchards, which were borne along the pier to one of the long low pilchard-houses to be regularly stacked somewhat after the fashion of drying bricks, and salted ready for packing in barrels and sending to the Mediterranean ports.

But after the first inspection the sight of baskets full of silvery pilchard began to grow monotonous, and Dick exclaimed:

"I say, father, it must be breakfast time now."

Breakfast time it was, and after arranging to be back at the pier in an hour, they sought the old purser's cottage, from whose open window the extremely fragrant odour of broiled ham was floating out, ready to act like a magnet upon the sensations of a couple of hungry lads.

Chapter Thirty One.

A Trip to the Seal's Zorn, and a Chip at Metals.

The boat was ready when they returned to the little pier, and the unloading in full swing. Every now and then scraps of damaged fish were thrown overboard to wash about the harbour, but which Josh intimated would have some effect by and by.

"Just you wait till the tide comes and washes them bits o' pilchar' all away about the place. You'll have the fish coming up from sea after 'em, and the whole place 'most alive—eh, Will?"

"Yes," said the latter, who was rowing steadily away. "Some good fishing might be had to-night if the young gentlemen liked to try."

It was decided that if they were not too tired they would try for a few fish after tea.

"Wouldn't the young gents like to go drifting—means all night?" said Josh; "but while the nets is out there's some haking to be done."

"I don't know about that, boys," said Mr Temple; "but I think a good daylight sail with the trawler would be enjoyable. I should like it myself."

"Then jus' you go an' speak to Tom Purnowen, Will, lad," said Josh; "he'll be glad enough to take the gentlemen and pick you out a good day."

They were bound for the seal-cave, but all the same, in spite of the coming excitement, Dick had not forgotten a fishing-line, while Will had ready for him, in a finely-woven basket, a couple of score of silvery sand-eels, which were kept alive by the basket being dragged astern in the sea.

These bright little fellows proved to be a most attractive bait, mackerel, pollack, and bass being taken, only one of the latter, however, which fell to Arthur's share, it being his turn to hold the line; but he did not care to let Will unhook it, and with the usual luck that followed his obstinacy he managed to get a sharp prick from one of the spikes.

Eight or nine fair-sized fish had been placed in the basket before Josh suggested that it would be better to leave off fishing, as the boat was now about to be taken close inshore, and the hooks would be fouled in the floating and anchored weed.

Mr Temple had indicated that he would like to examine the rocks here and there, and hence it was that the boat was taken so far in, where the rowing was more arduous, and the risks greater of being overturned upon some rock that was one minute submerged, the next level with the water.

Josh was too clever a boatman, though, for any such accident to occur, and he ran the little craft here and there most cleverly among the rocks; and, clearing the broken water, backing in for Mr Temple and Dick to land, and rowing out again till they were ready to leap on board once more.

For though, to use Josh's expression, the sea was "like ile" fifty yards out, it was fretting and working incessantly amongst the rocks, and running up rifts and chasms to come back in foam.

One landing of this kind seemed to excite a desire for more, and, hammer in hand, Mr Temple was as busy as could be breaking "the gashly rocks," as Josh expressed it in rather a pitying tone of voice to Will. So search after search was made, Dick scrambling up the most difficult places he could see, and seeming to find the most intense enjoyment in perching upon some narrow ledge, with his feet dangling over the side, though what the pleasure was he would have found it hard to say.

"There," said Mr Temple at last, as he and Dick leaped on board once more, "go on, or we shall see no seals to-day. It is not fair to you boys."

"Oh! I like scrambling about the rocks, father," cried Dick; "it's poor Taff who misses the fun."

"I can enjoy seeing you climb," said Arthur sedately.

"Yes," said his father shortly, "I have no doubt it is pleasant to look on; but is it not rather too ladylike a pursuit for a boy like you?"

Arthur coloured highly, and glanced forward to see if the rowers had heard; but he was relieved, for it was evident that they were too much occupied in circumventing the submerged rocks to pay any heed to the conversation, and the lad heaved a sigh full of content.

A couple of hours' hard rowing brought them to the mouth of the seal-cave, which, as they approached, looked far larger than it had seemed before when the sea was higher, for it generally nearly covered it, and at certain times completely closed it in.

"So now we are to see some seals?" said Dick excitedly.

"I don't know," said Will quietly. "This is the cave they are in sometimes; but one don't know whether there are any here."

"I think I see a little one drop off the rock as we come in sight," said Josh quietly. "Might have been a shag; but there was something on yonder rock; we shall see."

"It looks a rum place," said Dick. "Why, the water goes right in. We shall have to wait till it's dry."

"Then we shall never go in, sir," said Will smiling. "It is never dry, and the water is deep."

"What are we going to do, then?" said Dick.

"Row in—I mean push the boat in. The entrance is wide enough for that."

"What! Are we going to pass right in there?" said Arthur rather excitedly.

"I suppose so," said his father quietly. "Are you afraid?"

"No, I'm not afraid," said Arthur quickly, but colouring a little the while; "only—only it seems so queer—such an awkward place to go in."

"Yes, it will be awkward," said Mr Temple dryly.

"There's lots of room, sir," said Josh. "No fear o' knocking your head. You see, there wouldn't be anything to be afraid of round our coast if there were no rocks."

"I say, Josh, where shall we find the seals?" said Dick as they slowly approached the low arch in the face of the cliff, the boat being backed in so that its rowers could pull strongly away should a dangerous wave come in and threaten to dash them against the rocks—a mishap that occurred sometimes on the calmest days.

"Oh! if there be any, Master Dick, sir, they'll keep going farther and farther away, right into the end of the cave, where it be so small you can't follow unless you wade."

"Will seals bite, Josh?" cried Dick.

"Well, sir, they say they will, and fine and sharp, and fight too; but I never see 'em do it. Only thing I ever see a seal do was try to get away as fast as she could; that's all I ever see."

"But have you ever seen seals in here?" said Arthur, who, in spite of himself, looked rather white.

"Six or seven times, sir," replied Josh. "I've been with gentlemen as come shooting seals, and with a couple of gentlemen who went right in with clubs to kill 'em."

"And did they shoot and kill any?" said Dick eagerly.

"No, sir; not as I see," replied Josh. "One of 'em shot at a seal out on a rock, but I don't think he hit her, for she only looked up at us like a human being and then dived into the water and—but, look!"

Josh, who was about thirty yards from the entrance, ceased rowing; and as Dick and his father followed the direction of his eyes, and Will's pointing hand, they saw a curious, grey-looking creature rise up out of the water and begin to scramble up on to one of the rocks by the cave entrance, but on seeing the boat it gave a wallow, something like a fish, and turning, dived off the rock with a dull plash into the deep water.

"She's gone in," said Josh, propelling the boat towards the rugged arch. "We've seen one. P'r'aps we shall see more seals to-day."

"But won't it be dark?"

"Will's brought the big lantern, sir," said Josh.

"And I," said Mr Temple, "have brought some magnesium wire."

A good-sized wave came in just then, carrying the boat forward upon its swell right up to the archway; and then, as the wave retired, Josh managed to give a touch here and a touch there with his oars, and the next minute the sunshine seemed to have gone, and they glided in beneath a fringe of ferns and into a dark grotto, where the trickling drip of falling water came musically upon the ears.

It was a wonderful change—from the brilliant light outside, to the soft, greenish obscurity of the cave, whose floor was of pellucid water, that looked black beneath the boat, and softly green where some rock came near the surface.

It was of no great size as to width, resembling more a rugged passage or subterranean canal made by nature, regardless of direction or size, than a cavern; but to the boys it was a weird, strange place, full of awe and mystery. Every time oar or boat-hook touched the rocky side, there was a strange, echoing noise. Now and then the keel of the boat grated on some unseen rock, or was lifted by the water and dropped softly, as it were, upon some portion of the stony bottom as the water rose and fell.

The opening was left behind, and it seemed horrible to Arthur that calm coolness with which his father sat still and allowed Josh to thrust the boat along farther and farther till it became too dark for them to see, and Josh laid his boat-hook down. As he did so there was a silence for a few moments, in the midst of which, heard beneath the dripping musical tones of the falling water, came a curious hissing, whispering sound from beyond them farther in the cave.

"What's that?" said Arthur in a low voice as he spasmodically caught at his brother's arm.

Truth to tell, the mystery of the place had impressed Dick, who suffered from a half self-confessed desire to get out into the daylight once more; but now came this evident display of dread on his brother's part, and its effect was to string him up at once.

Laughing at Arthur meant laughing at himself, and he snatched at the opportunity as Arthur whispered once more, "Dick—Dick—what's that?"

"That?" said Dick in the same low tone. "That's the bogle-booby breathing. He's asleep now, but when he wakes he'll roll about so that he'll fill the place with foam."

"Don't you take any notice of him, Master Arthur," said Will gently. "He's making fun of you. That whispering noise is made by the water as it runs gurgling up the cracks of the rock and comes back again."

"Cr–r–r–ack!"

Arthur uttered a shrill cry, and Dick burst out laughing.

"Why, it was only a noisy match, Taff," he exclaimed, as, after a loud cracking scratch, there was a flash of light, and then a clear glow was shed around by the lantern, whose lamp Josh had just lit, its rays showing dimly the rugged walls of granite, all wet with trickling water, while the shadows of the boat and its occupants were cast here and there.

"Now, Master Dick, if you'll take the lantern and hold it up I'll send the boat farther in, so as if there be any seals you'll have a chance of seeing 'em."

"You think there are some then?" said Mr Temple.

"Ay, I do, sir. They won't have got out either. The only way, you see, would be under the boat, and they won't try that way yet so long as there's plenty of room forward."

Dick took the lantern, and as the light spread about the boat and glimmered on the surface of wet rock and water Arthur made a brave effort to master his dread; but all the same he gazed doubtfully forward as the boat was thrust more and more along the waterway among the rocks.

"I don't hear any seals yet," said Mr Temple.

"Oh, you won't hear 'em p'r'aps, sir," said Josh, "till we are close on to them, and then there'll be a splash and a rush. If there be any of 'em they're huddled up together, wondering what this here lantern means."

"Then there is no other way out?"

"Not for them, sir. There's a bit of a hole up towards the end, where a bird might fly out, but there's no way for the fish."

All this time Josh and Will were propelling the boat along with an oar or a boat-hook, and when the way was very narrow and the rocks within reach thrusting it forward with their hands.

"There, there, there's one," cried Dick, as there was a heavy rushing noise which came whispering and echoing past where they were.

"Ay, that be one, Master Richard," cried Josh, mastering the boy's name for once. "She'll go right to the end and come up again."

"How far is it to the end?" said Mr Temple.

"Six or eight fathom," said Josh; "not more, sir. If the light was stronger you could see it."

"Then we'll have a stronger light," said Mr Temple. "Open that lantern, Dick."

The boy obeyed, and his father ignited the end of a piece of magnesium wire, which burst out into a brilliant white light, showing them the roof and sides of the narrow cave, flashing off the water, and, what was of greater interest still, displaying the heads of a couple of seals raised above the surface at the end of the channel, and the dark-grey shiny body of another that had crawled right into a rift but could get no farther, and was now staring timidly at them.

The light sputtered and glowed, and dense white fumes floated in a cloud above their heads, while the boat was urged softly closer and closer towards the seals, the effect being that as the animals saw the light and the curious objects beneath advancing towards them the two in the water swam to the end and began to crawl out upon the rock, forcing themselves towards their companion in the rift.

"Go right on, sir?" said Will in a low voice.

"Yes. Close on, my lad," said Mr Temple. "Have a good look at them, boys, before they go."

"You're not going to catch one, are you, father?"

"Oh no! We'll have a good look at them. Wild creatures are getting far too scarce about the coast as it is."

He kept manipulating the wire as he spoke, sparks and incandescent pieces falling the while with a loud hiss in the water, making Arthur start till he was prepared for what was to come. And as Mr Temple managed the light and stood up in the boat its pale dazzling rays made the cave as light as day; and at last they were within three or four yards of the seals, which suddenly, after gliding and shuffling one over the other in utter astonishment, made Arthur and Dick start back, falling over into the bottom of the boat.

For, evidently frantic with dread, and helpless as far as relief was concerned, the three seals, as if moved by one idea, gave a wallowing movement, and dashed from the rocks together, seeming for the moment as if they were bent on leaping into the boat, but of course falling short and plunging into the water with a tremendous splash, which sent the spray all over those who were nearest; and at the same moment there was a hiss, and they were in total darkness.

"I won't be afraid," said Arthur to himself; and he clenched his teeth as his father said loudly:

"Rather startling. I did not expect that. Dropped my magnesium ribbon. Why, where's the lantern?"

"It's underneath me, father," said Dick in a half-ashamed grumbling tone. "I tumbled back over it and knocked it out."

"Never mind, Master Dick, I've got some matches," said Will; and after a good deal of scratching, which only resulted in long lines of pale light, for every part of the boat seemed to be wet, there was a glow of light once more, and the lantern was lit; but its rays seemed pitiful in the extreme after the brilliant glare of the magnesium.

"And now where are the seals?" said Mr Temple, holding the lantern above his head.

"Out to sea long enough ago, sir," said Josh. "They went under the boat, and I felt one of 'em touch the oar as they went off. You won't see no more seals, sir, to-day."

"Ah well!" said Mr Temple, "we've seen some, boys, at all events. Now let's have a look round here."

He held up the lantern, and as the boat was thrust onward he examined the rock here and there, taking out his little steel-headed hammer and chipping about.

"Granite—quartz—gneiss—quartz," he said in a low voice, as he carefully examined each fresh fracture in the stone. "Why, boys, here's tin here," he said sharply. "This place can never have been worked."

As he was speaking these latter words he held out a fragment of the stone he had broken off to Josh.

"That's good tin, my man," he said.

Josh growled. He had more faith in a net or a bit of rope.

"What do you say to it, Will?" said Mr Temple.

Will took the piece of quartz that was sparkling with tiny black crystals and turned it over several times close to the light. "Good tin ore, and well worth working," he exclaimed readily.

"Yes," said Mr Temple, "you are right, my lad. It is well worth working. Let's look a little farther. Here, you come and stand up and hold the lantern. We can land here."

Will obeyed, and as the boys watched, and Josh solaced himself with cutting a bit of cake tobacco to shreds, Mr Temple and Will climbed from place to place, the boys seeing the dark wet pieces of rock come out clear and sparkling as the blows fell from the hammer.

Now they were here, now there, and the more Mr Temple hammered and chipped the more interested he seemed to grow.

Click, click, click, click rang the hammer, and *splish, splash* went the fragments of rock that fell in the water or were thrown into it; and thus for quite two hours Mr Temple hammered away, and after giving up a fragmentary conversation Dick and Josh grew silent or only spoke at intervals.

Chapter Thirty Two.

How Seals sometimes make those who wax eager stick.

"I say, Dick," said Arthur after a long silence, "I wish we could go out now."

"Not frightened, are you?"

"Not now," said Arthur with simple truthfulness. "I was at first, but I don't mind now."

"It was *unked*, as the people here call it," said Dick, "and gashly. I wondered at first whether there were any sea-serpents or ugly things living in a place like this."

"Sea-monsters," said Arthur. "So did I, but I seem to have got used to it at last."

"Oh, I say," said Dick, "I'm getting so hungry! What a long time father is!"

"He's finding good ore," said Arthur, "he seems to be so interested. Dick—Dick—oh! what's that?"

Snork!

It was not the snarl of a wild beast, but a sound that seemed to be represented by that word.

"Old Josh's fast asleep," said Dick merrily. "It's he snoring. Let's splash him. No; I'll rock the boat."

Suiting the action to the word, Dick gave the boat a rock whose result was to bump it hardly against a rock, and then there was a loud start out of the darkness a few feet away, and then the boat bumped again.

"Why, halloa! what cheer—eh? What?"

"Why, you've been to sleep, Josh."

"No; on'y just closed my eyes," cried Josh; "on'y just shut 'em a moment;" though the fact was Josh had been asleep a long way over an hour. "Master 'most done?"

"I don't know," said Dick; "I know I'm precious tired of waiting."

"Tell 'ee what," said Josh suddenly, as he began to feel about with an oar as the boat swayed more up and down, and was carried a little

250

towards where Mr Temple was standing, and then drawn back; "tide's coming in fast."

"Why, Will," said Mr Temple just at the same moment, "how's this? That ledge was bare—"

"Now it's six inches under water, sir," replied Will. "I think we ought to get out at once."

"Stop a few minutes longer," said Mr Temple; "there is evidently the outcrop of a vein here. Hold the light."

Will obeyed at once, and Mr Temple began chipping at a fresh block of quartz rock which projected from the cave wall at an angle.

"Yes; copper this time," said Mr Temple.

"Father," cried Dick, "Josh thinks we had better get out again now. The tide's rising."

"I'll be done directly," said Mr Temple. "The tide will not run so high that we cannot pull against it."

"Tide's coming in gashly fast," said Josh to himself; "but if he don't mind, I don't."

Twice more Dick spoke to his father about coming, for Josh was muttering very sourly, and seemed disposed to resent this hanging back when he suggested that it would be better to go; but Mr Temple was so deeply interested in his discovery of what seemed to be a promising and, as far as he could for the moment tell, absolutely a new vein, that he forgot everything else in his intense desire to break off as good a specimen of the rock as he could.

"There," he said at last in a tone of triumph, "I think that will do. Steady, Dick, take these pieces. Now, you, my lad, go forward to your place. We'll hold the lanthorn, and—why, how's this? the ceiling seems to be lower."

"But it aren't," growled Josh sourly; "it's the gashly tide come in. There," he said, as he thrust the boat round an angle which had hidden the entrance of the cavern, "the boat won't go through there."

"Through there?" cried Mr Temple, as Dick felt his heart sink at the sight of the little archway in the rock not a foot above the surface of the water and sometimes with that surface going closer still towards the rugged crown of the natural arch.

"Well, there aren't no other way," said Josh, whose long sleep had been the cause of the mishap, for had he been awake he would have known that they were staying longer than was safe.

"But," cried Mr Temple, who felt alarmed now on account of his boys and their companions, "what are we to do? We must leave the boat and wade out."

"Wade!" growled Josh. "Why, there's three fathom o' water under where we sit."

"Then we must swim through," cried Mr Temple excitedly. "There is no time to spare. Man, man, why did you not warn us of the danger?"

"Why—why?" growled Josh. "I didn't know. I never see the tide come up that gashly way afore."

"It was while you were asleep, Josh," said Dick in a whisper; and Josh turned upon him as if he had been stung.

"Now," cried Mr Temple, as he pointed to the low opening through which was the sunshiny sea and safety, while on their side was apparently darkness and death; "now, Dick, you can swim through there; but first try whether by lying down we can force the boat under."

"Oh, I'll try!" said Josh; "but it's of no use, not a bit of use. Be it, Will?"

"No," said the latter decidedly, as he and Josh urged the boat right up to the entrance, and Mr Temple saw at once that it would be an impossibility.

"Then we must swim," said Mr Temple. "You can swim that, Dick?"

"Yes, father," said Dick. "Clothes and all."

"Yes, of course, the distance is so short."

"And you, Arthur, you can swim through there?"

The boy could not speak, for he was battling down the horrible feeling of dread that came over him.

"I say, you can swim that, Arthur?" said Mr Temple sternly.

"Yes, father. I'll try," said the boy quickly.

"That's well. Of course you two can swim?"

"Tidy, sir, tidy," said Josh; "and Will here, he could 'most beat a seal. But there ain't no call to get wetting of ourselves. I'll shove the boat back to where it's highest and where the water never reaches. We can wait there till she goes down again."

"Do you know what you are talking about, man?" cried Mr Temple sternly. "We should be suffocated."

"Josh means put the boat, sir, under the opening in the rock that he spoke about," said Will. "There'll be plenty of air. You can stand up on the rocks, sir, and hear it rush out with a regular roar when the water drives in, and when it goes out again the air sucks in so fast that it will take a piece of paper with it, and sometimes blows it out again."

"There is no time to be lost then if you are sure of this," said Mr Temple anxiously; "but are you sure?"

"Yes, sir, quite sure," cried Will.

"Oh! you may trust Will, sir, that's right enough all as he says. Tide never comes up anything like so high as we shall be."

Mr Temple hesitated, and as he paused, wondering which would be the wisest plan to pursue, there was a wave ready to rise up and completely blot out the faint daylight which streamed through the narrow opening.

This was only for a few moments, and then the daylight streamed in again, but only to be eclipsed by what seemed to be a soft green mass of crystal, that gradually darkened more and more.

Then came sunshine and blue sky again, but a smaller arch than ever, and had the little party not been filled with alarm, nothing could have been more beautiful than the succession of effects.

But in a state of intense excitement Mr Temple was urging Josh and Will to force the boat back to where they would be in safety, if safety it could be called.

Dick was quite as excited as his father, and eagerly seized an oar to help force the boat back, while Arthur, perhaps the most alarmed of the three, sat perfectly still, for, poor boy, he had been fighting for weeks now to master his cowardice, and, as he called it, to make himself more like his brother.

As the boat floated back more and more along the irregular channel they could see the archway entrance open and close—open and close. Now it seemed as if it would not close again, for the water went suddenly lower, and Mr Temple exclaimed:

"Look! the tide is at its height."

"Not it," said Josh. "She's got another two hours to run, I know. But don't you mind, sir, we shall be all right."

Perhaps Josh felt quite confident, but no one else did, as the water rose and fell, giving lovely little views of sea and sky, and then turned into veils of crystal, green and blue, sparkling sometimes like emerald, then changing to amethystine or sapphire hue.

It was surprising what an amount of light seemed to come in when the water sank, and then by contrast the darkness was horrible, and the lanthorn seemed to emit a dismal yellow glow.

They might have stayed for another quarter of an hour watching the light come and go, but there was the danger of their being inclosed in some portion of the cavern where the roof was low, and the boat would be made a prisoner within a prison. So Josh urged the boat forward towards where Mr Temple had been so busy with his researches, and after a little examination he bade Will cover the lanthorn with his jacket.

"It's a long time since I were in here," he said; "but I think as the air-hole ought to be somewhere about here. One moment, Will, lad; hold the light up and lets see the roof."

The rocky summit was in the highest part, some twelve feet above their heads, and satisfied as to this, Josh had the light darkened, and then began to look upward.

"No," he said. "Must be the next. Show the light."

He thrust the boat along once more, grinding and bumping over fragments of rock, till they had passed under another low part of the roof, when this rose once more, and the lanthorn being hidden Josh pointed upward to a narrow crack, through which came a faint light.

"There y'are," he said. "Don't matter how high the water gets, we can get plenty of fresh air. Tide won't get up there."

The position seemed more hopeful now, for the tide would have to rise fourteen or fifteen feet to carry them to the roof; and though in certain places from low water to high water might be perhaps forty feet, they were now so near the height of the tide that it was not likely to rise much farther.

"Don't be frightened, Taff, old chap," said Dick in a whisper; "father's with us, and he'll mind that we don't get hurt."

"I'm not going to be frightened," said Arthur coolly; and then Mr Temple began to talk cheerily as he stood up in the boat and held the lanthorn here and there; but first of all Will noticed that he took his geological hammer and chipped the rock on a level with the water, and soon after he made a clear bright sparkling chip about a foot higher, the granite rock glittering in the feeble rays of the lanthorn.

"I should not be a bit surprised if a good lode of metal were discovered here," said Mr Temple; and he went on chatting lightly about mines and minerals and Cornwall generally, but somehow he could not draw the attention of his companions from that bright mark on the rock, towards which the water was constantly creeping, and then seemed to glide away, as if exhausted with the effort.

And certainly it was a horrible position to sit there with no light but that shed by the yellow lanthorn, the boat heaving up and sinking beneath them, and the sounds of the water dripping and splashing, and now and then making curious sucking and gasping noises, as it ran in and out of cracks and crevices in the rocks.

All at once there was a loud, ringing, echoing blow upon the rock, as the boat approached close to the side, and Mr Temple struck it sharply with his hammer, for one mark had gone and the water was lipping and lapping fast towards the other.

The scraps of granite flew pattering into the water, as blow succeeded blow, Mr Temple making a deep mark on the rock to relieve his pent-up feelings, and to take the attention of his boys, who kept looking at him nervously, as if asking for help in this time of peril.

This done, he made Josh move the boat from side to side of their narrow prison, inviting Dick and Will to help as he chipped here and chipped there, and talked about the different kinds of granite and quartz that he cleared from the dark mossy growth and the film of ages.

But there was the water lapping and lapping and rising, and it was plain now that there would hardly be room to turn beneath the arch-like opening that separated them from the portion where Josh had expected to see the daylight.

It seemed to have grown intensely hot too, for the faint current of cool air that they had felt since entering the place had stopped for some time past, and still the water kept rising, and at last seemed to come through the narrowing opening with so horrible a gurgling rush that it affected even stolid Josh, who took his cap off and said that it was "a gashly ugly noise."

No one spoke, for the attention of all was taken by the increasing sounds made by the water, which seemed forced in now in a way that affected the boat, making it rock and adding so to the horror of the situation that Will leaned towards Josh and whispered for a few moments.

"It's only because there isn't so much room, Master Dick, that's all," he said.

"Yes, that be all," growled Josh; "it don't rise no faster than it did afore. P'r'aps you wouldn't mind making another water-mark, sir. T'other's 'most covered."

But Mr Temple's hammer was already raised as he spoke, and the cave echoed with his blows.

"It sounds different, doesn't it, Will?" said Arthur softly. "It don't echo so much, and seem to run along."

"No," said Will, in the same tone of voice, "there is not so much room. We seem more shut-up like. But it will soon begin to go down now."

"Will it?" whispered Arthur; "or shall we all be shut-up here and drowned?"

"Oh, no, no!" whispered back Will; "don't you get thinking that. The water must begin to go down again soon."

"What time is it high water?" said Mr Temple suddenly.

"Two o'clock, sir," said Josh.

"Why, it must be near that time now," said Mr Temple, laying down his hammer to take out his watch. "Hold the light here, Dick."

Dick caught up the lanthorn, but in doing so caught his foot against one of the bottom boards, stumbled, and there was a splash, and then utter darkness.

The lanthorn had gone overboard, and as the water, disturbed by the fall of the lanthorn and the rocking motion given to the boat, washed and lapped and whispered against the sides, with gasps and suckings and strange sounds, that seemed to be ten times louder in the darkness, Josh growled out:

"Well, you have gone and done it now!"

Then there was utter silence. The water came in with a rush and gurgle that was fearful. The boat heaved and bumped against the side, and it seemed to the prisoners as if the next moment they must be swamped.

But as with breathlessness they listened, the sounds and disturbance died away to whispers, and there was nothing but a feeble lapping.

"It's only noise," said Will, suddenly breaking the silence. "The boat can't hurt."

"Will's right," growled Josh; "but it's a gashly place to be in without a light."

"*Crick, crack!*"

There was a flash, and a little flame for a few moments as Josh, who had taken out his match-box, struck a light, and held it till it was ready to burn his fingers, when he let it fall in the smooth surface of the water, where it was extinguished with a hiss.

"Don't burn any more, my man," said Mr Temple; "we may want them —"

He was about to say, "in a greater emergency," but he checked himself.

"Right, sir," replied Josh.

"Do you think it is high water now?"

"No, sir. 'Nother two hours to flow," replied Josh. "I remember a case once where some chaps was shut-up in a zorn like this, and—"

"Hush!—hold your tongue!" whispered Will excitedly; "don't tell about that."

"Why not?" growled Josh. "We aren't going to be drowned and washed out to sea."

"Are you mad, Josh?" whispered Will. "You'll frighten them."

"Oh! all right, then," growled Josh; "I didn't know."

Mr Temple was silent, and, bending forward, he took hold of Arthur's hand and pressed it.

"Don't be alarmed, my boy," he said. "There is no more danger now than when it was light."

"I'm trying to be brave, papa," said Arthur softly.

"That's as good as being brave," whispered back Mr Temple. "What?" he said, as the boy clung to his hand and leaned forward till his lips nearly touched his father's ear.

"I want to tell you something," whispered Arthur. "I was too great a coward to tell you before. That cigar-case was not Dick's, but mine."

Mr Temple was silent for a few minutes, and then he said:

"Better late than never, my boy. If you had come frankly to me, and not let your brother take that bit of blame, I should have felt that you could not be a coward. Arthur, my boy, you have a good deal to master yet. Well, Dick," he said aloud in a cheery tone, "how are you?"

"Capital, father," said Dick, "but so dreadfully hungry."

"Well, we can't be prisoners much longer."

"Hours yet," growled Josh—"eh, Will?"

"I don't think so, Josh. You must have been asleep a long time, and don't count that."

"G'long," cried Josh. "Don't talk gashly nonsense."

"Strike another light," said Mr Temple after they had listened once more to the horrible gurgling and washing of the incoming water, and the hardly less startling sounds it made as it escaped. "Hand the light to me directly."

Josh struck a match and passed it to Mr Temple, who had just time to see that his last mark was covered, and the boat far higher up the sides of the cave before he had to drop it in the water.

"Still rising," he said quietly. "This will be a curious adventure to talk of, boys, in the future."

Neither Dick nor Arthur spoke, for Dick was wondering whether they would ever get out alive, and Arthur dared not trust himself to utter a word, for he was finding it terribly hard work to be brave at a time like this.

All at once Josh began to whistle an air—a doleful minor melody, that sounded so strange and weird there in the darkness that Will stopped him.

"Don't do that, Josh," he said softly.

"Why not? One must do something."

"It annoys them," whispered Will.

"Ho!" said Josh. Then he was silent, and for quite half an hour all sat listening to the gurgling, hissing, and rushing noises made by the water.

Then, when it seemed to Dick, who had tight hold of his brother's hand, that he could bear it no longer, his father asked for another match.

Josh struck it, and it snapped in two and fell in the bottom of the boat, but burned long enough for him to light another, which was successfully handed to Mr Temple, while Will took the hitcher and forced the boat back to where the marks had been made on the wall by Mr Temple's hammer.

"Strike another, my man, and hand it to me quick," cried Mr Temple excitedly; and as it was done, and the tiny flame burned brightly in the black darkness, he stood holding it close to the wall of rock; and then as he let the little flame fall and extinguish itself, he exclaimed joyfully:

"At last, boys! There's no danger. The tide is falling fast."

"Falling fast a'ready?" cried Josh.

"Yes; it is down a foot."

"Then—well, of all the gashly things! I must ha' been asleep."

It was but a question of waiting now; and though the time seemed long there was plenty to interest the little party, as Mr Temple had the boat kept close up to the rock, and felt his marks, announcing from time to time how much the water had gone down. Then Dick got Will to thrust down the boat-hook to try how deep it was, but to try in vain, though they were more successful with the lead on a fishing-line, Josh measuring the line after the lead had touched bottom, and announcing it as "'bout five fathom."

All at once they noticed that the horrible rushing and gurgling of the water had ceased; and soon after it became plain that it was harder work to keep the boat close to the rock, for, in spite of the returns of the water as the waves beat outside, there was a steady, constant set of the current towards the mouth. So at last the measurement by the rocks had to be given up, for Josh gave it as his opinion that they might as well let the boat drift towards the cave mouth.

This was done; and though they were unable to calculate their progress, as time went on they felt that they must be nearer the entrance.

Josh poked about with a boat-hook, now at the sides, now at the roof; and then, as they were sitting down waiting patiently, there was a peculiar shuffling and splashing noise heard.

259

"What's that?" exclaimed Dick.

"Seal!" cried Will; and as he spoke there was a splash as if the creature had dived off a rock into the water.

But they had something more interesting than the seal to take their attention, for all at once there was a faint greeny transparency right before them. Then it darkened, lightened again, darkened and lightened more or less till, all at once, there was a flash, so short, quick, and brilliant that it dazzled their darkness-becurtained eyes like lightning.

"Hoo-ray!" shouted Dick, stamping his feet on the bottom of the boat. "Now, all together—hip-hip-hip hooray!"

Arthur, Will, and Josh joined in making the cave echo as there was another and another flash of light, and soon after the arch at the mouth of the cave began to open more and more; and at last the boat floated out into the dazzling afternoon sunshine, and was rowed steadily back.

"Been shut-up in a zorn!" cried Mrs Marion, who declared that the dinner was spoiled; "then it was all the fault of that great idle Josh and that stupid, good-for-nothing boy."

"No, Mrs Marion," said Mr Temple gently, "the fault was entirely mine."

Chapter Thirty Three.

Mr Temple takes Will into his Confidence and astonishes Uncle Abram.

"Dick," said Mr Temple one morning, as he looked up from the table covered with specimens of ore and papers.

"Yes, father."

"Is Will Marion at home?"

"Yes, father. Hark!" He held up his hand to command silence, and from the back garden came the sound of a shrill voice scolding, and the deep rumble of Uncle Abram, apparently responding.

"You idle, good-for-nothing, useless creature. I wish we were well rid of you, I do."

"Softly. Steady, old lady, steady," growled Uncle Abram.

"Oh! it's no use for you to take his part. I say he's a lazy, idle, stupid, worthless fellow, and he sha'n't stop here any longer. There: get out of my sight, sir—get out of my sight, and don't come back here till you're asked."

"Easy, old lady, easy," growled Uncle Abram. "What's the lad been doing now?"

"Nothing," cried Aunt Ruth, who was suffering from the effect of what people call getting out of bed the wrong way—"nothing, and that's what he's always doing—nothing. I'm sick of the sight of him—eat, eat, eat, and sleep, sleep, sleep, sleep, and grow, grow, grow, all the year round. I'm sure I don't know what we do having him here. I hate the sight of him."

"Will," said Uncle Abram, "go down and see that the boat's cleaned out; perhaps Mr Temple will want her to-day."

"Eat, eat, eat, and grow, grow, grow," cried Aunt Ruth.

"Which it is the boy's natur' to," said the old man good-humouredly. "There, be off, Will."

"Run out now and you'll catch him before he goes," said Mr Temple.

Dick hurried out by the front to waylay Will, but encountered Uncle Abram.

"Where's Will, my lad? Oh! he's coming. Old lady's been blowing off steam a bit. Busy day with her, you see. Cleaning. Didn't hear, did you?"

"Oh, yes! we could hear every word," said Dick with a comical look.

The old gentleman glanced over his shoulder and then patted Dick on the chest with the back of his hand. "It's all right," he said in a deep bass. "She don't mean nothing by it. Fond o' Will as ever she can be. Feels often, you know, as she must scold something, and sometimes she scolds Will, sometimes it's Amanda the lass, sometimes me. Why," he said cheerfully, "I have known her set to and let the tables and chairs have it for not shining when they were being rubbed. It's all right, my lad, all right. She's awfully fond of our Will, and if you hear her say she aren't don't you believe her. Here he comes."

Will came round from the back just then, with his head hanging, and a look of dejection in his whole aspect; but as he caught sight of Uncle Abram and Dick he made an effort to hide his trouble.

"Here he is," said the old gentleman, clapping Will on the shoulder, "here he is, Master Dick, my nevvy, and as stout and strong a lad of his years as there is in these parts. Your par wants him, does he?"

"My father wants him," said Dick sturdily. "I never call him pa."

"That's right, my lad. I never called my father pa. Wants our Will, do he? Well, I was going to send him down to get the boat ready. Go and see what Master Temple wants, my lad. 'Member what I said, Master Dick, sir."

"All right!" replied Dick; and Will followed him to the door.

"What has my uncle been saying?" he said quickly.

"Oh! only that I wasn't to notice what your aunt said, and that she don't mean all that scolding."

Will drew a long breath, and leaning his arm against the door-post he placed his forehead against it.

"I can't bear it," he groaned; "I can't bear it. I seem to be so poor and dependent, and she is always telling me that I am a beggar and an expense to them. Master Dick, I'd have gone years ago, only it would half break poor old uncle's heart. He is fond of me, I know."

"Oh! I say, Will, don't—please don't!" cried Dick.

"It hurts me, it does indeed. Oh, how I wish I could do something to help you! I tell you what I'll do, and Taff shall help me. I'll save up to help you buy a boat of your own."

"Thank you," said Will gently; "but you must not think of that. No, Master Dick."

"There; don't call me Master Dick; say Dick. I want you to be friends with me, Will. It's all nonsense about you only being a fisher lad. My father said only yesterday to Taff that he should have been very proud to have called you his son."

"Oh!" cried Will, with a deprecatory movement of his hand.

"He did; and that you had the spirit of a true gentleman in your breast. I say, Will Marion," cried Dick, giving him a playful kick, "what a fellow you are! I'm as jealous of you as Taff is."

"Nonsense!" cried Will; "and don't you be so hard on him. Do you know what he did yesterday?"

"Made some disagreeable remark," said Dick bitterly.

"He came up to me when I was alone and shook hands with me, and said he was very sorry that he had been so stuck-up and rude to me as he had been sometimes, and said it was all his ignorance, but he hoped he knew better now."

"Taff did? Taff came and said that to you?" cried Dick excitedly.

"Yes; and we parted the best of friends."

"There's a chap for you!" cried Dick warmly. "There's a brick! I say Taff is a fine fellow after all, only he got made so stuck-up and tall-hat and Eton jacketty at one school he went to. But, I say, my father wants you. Come along."

Dick led the way into the parlour, where the object of their conversation was sitting by the window reading, and Mr Temple busy over some papers.

"Here's Will, father," said Dick.

"I'll attend to him in a moment," said Mr Temple. "Let me finish this letter."

Will stood in the middle of the room in his shabby, well-worn canvas trousers and coarse jersey, his straw hat hanging at full arm's-length by his side, and his clear grey eyes, after a glance at Arthur, fixed almost hungrily upon the specimens of ore and minerals that encumbered the table and window-sill wherever there was a place where a block could be laid.

The sight of these brought up many a hunt that he had had amongst the old mines and rifts and chasms of the rocks round about the shore, and made him long once more to steal away for a few hours in search of some vein that would give him a chance of making himself independent and working his own way in the world.

Dick broke his train of thought by coming behind him and placing a chair for him, but he declined.

"I wish I had thought to do that!" said Arthur to himself. "I never think of those little things."

"That's done," said Mr Temple sharply as he fastened down a large blue envelope and swung round to face Will. "Sit down, my lad," he said quickly.

Will hesitated, and then sat down, wondering what was coming; and so accustomed was he to being taken to task that he began to run over in his mind what he had done lately likely to have displeased Mr Temple. He came to the conclusion at last that he had been encouraging the two lads too much to go out fishing, and that their father was annoyed with them for making a companion of so common a lad.

Mr Temple gazed straight at him in silence for a few moments, and Will met his gaze frankly and well.

"Let me see, my lad," said Mr Temple at last. "You are quite dependent on Mr and Mrs Marion?"

"Yes, sir," said Will with an ill-suppressed sigh.

"And your parents are both dead?"

"Yes, sir."

"You have no other relatives?"

"No, sir;" and Will looked wonderingly at the speaker, who now ceased, and sat nursing one leg over the other.

"Should you like to be master of a boat of your own?"

"Ye–es, sir," said Will slowly.

"You are very fond of the sea?"

"I like the sea, sir."

"And would like to grow up and be a fisherman?"

Will shook his head.

"I don't want to despise the fishermen, sir," said Will; "but I should choose to be a miner and have to do with mines if I could do as I liked."

"And go down into a deep hole and use a pick all your life, eh?"

"No," replied Will; "I should try to rise above doing that. Most of our miners here work with their arms, and they seem to do that always; but here and there one of them works with his head as well, and he gets to be captain of a mine, or an adventurer."

"Ah!" said Mr Temple sternly. "Why, what an idle, discontented dog you must be, sir! I don't wonder at your aunt scolding you so that all the people in the village can hear. Why don't you attend to your work as a fisher lad, and be content with your position?"

"I do attend to my work, sir," said Will firmly; "but I can't feel content with my station."

"Why not, sir? Why, you are well fed and clothed; and if you wait long enough you will perhaps succeed to your uncle's property when he dies, and have a boat or two and a set of nets of your own."

Will flushed up and rose from his chair.

"You have no business to speak to me, sir, like that," he said warmly; "and I am not so mean and contemptible as to be looking forward to getting my poor old uncle's property when he dies."

"Well done, Will!" cried Dick enthusiastically.

"Silence, sir!" cried Mr Temple sternly. "How dare you speak like that! And so, sir, you are so unselfish as to wish to be quite independent, and to wish to get your living yourself free of everybody?"

"Yes, sir," said Will coldly; and he felt that Mr Temple was the most unpleasant, sneering man he had ever seen, and not a bit like Dick.

"Like to discover a copper mine with an abundance of easily got ore?"

"Yes, sir," said Will quickly. "I should, very much."

"I suppose you would," said Mr Temple. "Are you going to do it?"

"I'm afraid not, sir," said Will respectfully; but he was longing for the interview to come to an end. "The place has been too well searched over, sir."

"Try tin, then," said Mr Temple.

"The tin has been all well searched for, sir, I'm afraid," said Will quietly, though he felt that he was being bantered, and that there was a sneer in the voice that galled him almost more than he could bear.

"Why not look then for something else?" continued Mr Temple. "That is what I'd do."

"Because," said Will, "I am not learned enough, sir, to understand such things properly. If I had books I should read and try to learn; but I have very little time, and no learning."

"And yet," said Mr Temple, speaking warmly now and quite changing his tone, "you without your learning have done more than I have with all my years of study and experience."

"I don't understand you, sir."

"I'll tell you then. I have been far and wide about Cornwall for these last three years and done no good this year I thought I would have another search for something fresh, and give my boys a change. I am glad I have come."

265

Will did not reply, but looked at him more wonderingly than ever.

"Suppose, my lad," said Mr Temple, speaking now kindly, "I were to tell you that I have watched you very narrowly for some time past."

"I hope I have done nothing wrong, sir?" said Will.

"Nothing, my lad. I was beginning to form a very pleasant impression of you, and then came the day of the storm."

"If—if you would not mind, sir," said Will uneasily, "I would rather you did not talk about that."

"I will only say, my lad, that it confirmed my agreeable impressions about you. And now, look here, I have paid at least a hundred visits to the vein you showed me—the decomposing felspar vein."

"The vein of white spar, sir?" cried Will.

"Yes, my lad; and I have concluded that it is very valuable."

"Valuable, sir?"

"Yes, far more so than many of the best of the copper and tin mines here."

"I am glad," cried Will.

"Why?" said Mr Temple sharply. "Can you buy the land that contains it?"

Will shook his head.

"Can you get up a company to buy and work it?"

"No, sir," said Will sadly. "I should not understand how to do that, and —"

"Some one else would get hold of it, and you would not benefit in the least."

"No, sir, not in the least," said Will sadly. "I am a fisher lad. That is my business."

"But you discovered the vein," said Mr Temple.

"Yes, sir, I found it when I was hunting about as I have done these two years."

"Then don't you think you have a right to some of the profit from such a vein?"

"I don't know, sir. Of course I should like to have some of it, sir, but I don't see how I could expect it."

"Then I do," said Mr Temple. "Look here, my lad, I will tell you something. I have purchased the whole of the land that contains that vein."

"You've bought it, father?" cried Dick. "Oh, I am glad!"

"Why?" said his father sharply.

"Because we shall come here to live."

"Oh!" said Mr Temple. "Now look here, Marion. You showed me what I hope will prove very valuable to me, and I don't want to be ungrateful in return. Now what should you say if I spent a hundred pounds in a boat expressly for you, and after we had called it *The White Spar*, I presented it to you?"

"I should say it was very generous of you, sir."

"And it would make you very happy, my lad?"

"No, sir," said Will sadly, "I don't think itwould."

"Then suppose I spent two hundred and fifty pounds in a boat and nets. Come, that ought to set you up for life." Will was silent.

"You like that idea?" The lad shook his head.

"Then look here, Marion," said Mr Temple. "Suppose I say to you, I am going to open out and work that vein at once, will you come and help me, and I'll give you five shillings a week?"

"Yes, sir, I'll come," cried Will, with his eyes sparkling; "I'll work so hard for you, I will indeed."

"I know you will, my lad," said Mr Temple, shaking hands with him warmly.

"And you will take me, sir?" said Will excitedly.

"Certainly I will, but not on such terms as that. My good lad, there is honesty in the world, though sometimes it is rather hard to find. Look here. You helped me to the discovery, but it was useless without capital. I found the capital, and so I consider that I and mine have a right to the lion's share. I have worked out my plans, and they are these. We will divide the adventure into four parts, which shall be divided as follows, one part to you, and one each to me and my sons. The only difference will be that you will get your part, and I shall keep Arthur's and Dick's along with mine. Do you think that fair?"

"No!" cried Dick, giving the table a thump with his fist.

"Till my boys come of age and are men," said Mr Temple smiling. "Then they can draw their shares. I think it is a fair arrangement. Come, Marion, what do you say?"

"I don't know what to say, sir," cried the lad, whose lip was working with emotion. "You are not playing with me?"

"Playing, my lad! I never was in more sober earnest in my life," said Mr Temple. "There, I see you agree, and I congratulate you on your success, for it will be a most successful venture—of that I am sure."

"So do I, Will," cried Dick, with his eyes sparkling. "I am glad. Hooray!"

Arthur hesitated. For the last few minutes a feeling of resentment and jealousy had been rising in his breast at the idea of this fisher lad winning to such a successful position and being placed on a level with him and his brother; but he crushed the feeling down, triumphed over it, came forward holding out his hand, and offered his congratulations too. "I am glad, Will Marion," he said, and his words were true and earnest; but in spite of himself the thought would come, "I hope he won't always dress like that."

"Then that matter's settled," said Mr Temple. "Everything necessary has been done. The land is mine, and my solicitor has all the papers. Mr Will Marion, I too congratulate you on being a mine owner and on the road to fortune."

"But look here, father," cried Dick suddenly, "what's the good of your white stone? You can't make tin pots and copper kettles of it."

"No," said Mr Temple smiling; "but don't you know what that stone and the clay beneath it will make?"

"Yes," cried Dick, "of course. Houses of brick made of the clay with white stone facings."

"What do you say, Arthur?" said Mr Temple; but Arthur shook his head.

"Can you tell, Marion?" said Mr Temple.

"No, sir," said Will sadly; "I don't—Yes, I do. It's china-clay."

"Right, my lad. A valuable deposit of china-clay, which we can send off after preparation to the potteries—perhaps start a pottery ourselves, who knows? Yes, it was about the last thing I thought of when I came down. My idea was to get hold of a vein of some little-worked metal, antimony, or nickel, or plumbago perhaps; but I have never found anything to equal this, and I thank you, Will Marion, from my very heart."

Will Marion looked from one to the other as if stunned by the tremendous nature—to him—of the intelligence; then, unable to contain himself, he rushed out of the room to see old Uncle Abram.

"Well, Dick, what do you think of it?" said Mr Temple as soon as they were alone.

"Think, father? Why, I was never so pleased before in my life—at least I don't think I was. Poor old Will! how pleased he is!"

There was not time to say much more, for there was a sharp tap at the door, and Uncle Abram came in to have the matter explained.

"For you see, sir, I can't make neither head nor tail of Will here. Seems to me as if he's been dreaming."

Then after it had all been explained the old man took three or four pulls at an imaginary pipe.

"It's like being took all aback," he said, rubbing his grey head. "I can't understand it like quite. I knew he was always off hunting something, butterflies, or fishing up on the moor, but I didn't think it would turn out like that, sir. And I was always making a fender of myself 'twixt his aunt and him because she was wanting to know where he was, and me pretending he was painting the bottom of the boat and mending nets or something. Well, I've been terrible sorry sometimes at his being away so much; but I feel right down pleased, sir, and—and if you wouldn't mind shaking hands, sir, it would do me a power of good."

Uncle Abram shook hands then with Mr Temple, and then with Dick and Arthur, and next with Will, after which he stared at all in turn, and ended by saying as he went out:

"It's 'most more than I can understand after all."

Chapter Thirty Four.

Winding up with a Dab of Clay.

To enter into the occurrences of the next few years would be to give the business career of young men, when the object of this book was to tell of some of the pleasant adventurous days passed by three boys and their friends in that beautiful rugged county in the far west of

England which the sea wraps so warmly that winter is shorn of half his force.

It is only right to tell, though, that Mrs Marion, upon being taught by Mr Temple's treatment of her nephew that the boy was what some would call a lad of parts, suddenly began to display a deep interest in him—in his clothes—in his linen; and Uncle Abram found her one day scolding poor Amanda the maid till she put her apron over her head and sat down on the floor and cried.

Uncle Abram stood smoking his pipe and sending puffs here and there as Aunt Marion's tirade of bitterness went on.

"What's matter?" he said at last.

"Matter!" cried the old lady fiercely. "Matter enough. Here's this thoughtless, careless hussy actually been throwing away some specimens of ore that Will brought in. I declare it's monstrous—that it is."

Uncle Abram nodded solemnly, sent a puff of smoke to east, another to west, and another due south, and then went out into his garden to tie up an Ayrshire rose that had been blown down by a late gale.

"Wind's changed," he said to himself, "dead astarn; and our boy's v'y'ge through life will be an easy one now."

Uncle Abram was right, for Mr Temple began to make quite a confidant of Will Marion at once, and depended greatly upon him for help in his business transactions over the kaolin and felspar upon his land.

Dick said it was a jolly shame, and Arthur considered it to be a nuisance; but Mr Temple told them it was for their benefit, and to make them more useful to him in time to come, so they had to go to a great school for the next two years, at the end of which time the kaolin works were in full swing, and Mr Temple, as he never forgot to say, thanks to Will Marion, on the high road to fortune.

For while this tin mine proved a failure, and that copper mine had paid no dividend for years, while the fisheries were sometimes successful, sometimes, through storms and loss of gear, carried on at a loss, Mr Temple's kaolin works became yearly more profitable, the vein growing thicker and finer in quality the more it was opened out.

Kaolin—of course you all know what that Chinese word means. Eh? What? A little boy at the back says he doesn't know? Then we must enlighten him, and be a little learned for a minute or two.

Earthenware is of course ware made of earth that was ground into a paste, and after working into shape, baked or burned hard in a kiln. The roughest earthenware is a brick, the red brick of simple clay, the yellow and white bricks of simple clay mixed with more or less chalk. Then we get the flower-pot, again of clay; the common pan, which is glazed by covering the interior with properly prepared minerals, which melt in the baking, and turn into a glaze or glass. Then we have finer clay worked up into crockery; and lastly, the beautiful white clay which, when baked, becomes transparent,—a Chinese discovery, and to this day it bears its name, "china."

This fine white clay the Chinese call *kaolin*, and it is to the discovery of veins of the soft white plastic material in England that the wonderful strides in our china manufactures are due.

And what is this kaolin of which Will had discovered so grand a store? Well, it is easily explained. The rocks of Cornwall are largely of granite, a stone that must be familiar to every one. It is formed of grains of quartz, mica the shiny, and felspar, that soft white creamy stone like our old alley marbles. This vein of granite will be close and hard, and contain a vast preponderance of quartz, the flinty; and that vein of granite will be very soft from containing so much felspar; and this granite, a familiar example of which can be seen in the material of Waterloo Bridge, the learned, who give names, call porphyry.

Such granite as this abounds in Cornwall, and some, too, which is nearly all felspar, and such rock as this in the course of ages forms such a bed of kaolin as Will Marion disclosed to the father of his friends.

For the felspar is soft, and imbibes water; and in the course of time the water causes it to break up, decay, and change from stone to a soft white clay, while where it is hard, burning and pounding will do the work that nature has not quite finished yet.

Mr Temple did not go so far as to commence a pottery, for there was no need, the manufacturers being ready to purchase all the clay that the works could produce; and when Dick and Arthur Temple finally settled down to business, it was to find Will Marion their father's right-hand man.

Later on some further investigations were made of the mineral deposits in the seals' cave; but, good as they were, Will Marion shook his head at them, and Mr Temple took his view. The tin looked promising; but tin and copper mining was so speculative a venture that it was determined to keep only to the china-clay, which brought prosperity to all.

The lads often visited the haunts of their old adventures in company with Josh, who was still venerable Uncle Abram's head man; and it was only necessary to hint at the desire for an evening's fishing to make Josh declare, that as long as there was a gashly boat in the bay, they should never want for a bit of fishing.

But Josh never forgave Will in his heart for deserting the fishing business.

"Oh, yes! I know all about the gashly old clay, Master Rickard, sir," he would say; "and it's made him a sort of gentleman like; but I can't seem to see it, you know. He was getting to be as fine a sailor as ever stepped, and look at him now; why, he wouldn't be satisfied to sail anything commoner than a yacht."

Dick remained the same frank merry fellow as ever; and even when there was a thick crop growing on his cheeks and chin, which he called brown mustard and cress, he was as full of boyish fun as ever.

It was Arthur in whom the greatest changes had taken place. Contact with the world had rubbed off the stiff varnish with which he had coated himself. He had learned, too, that a lad can command more respect from his fellows by treating them with frankness than by a hectoring haw-haw display of consequence, and a metaphorical "going about with a placard on the breast saying what a superior young being I am ism." In fact Arthur Temple's folly had all gone, and he had developed into a true English gentleman, who could be refined to a degree, but in time of need lend a hand in any of the many struggles of life.

Will, too, refined greatly, and one of the Sunday sights down at Peter Churchtown was to see Aunt Ruth Marion waiting at her door, while the bells were going, for Will to come and take her to church, while Uncle Abram in his best blue coat, with crown-and-anchor buttons, smoked his pipe to the last minute and then trotted after them along the cliff path to the pew close under the reading-desk.

"Yes, Abram," she used to say, "our Will has grown to be as fine a gentleman as ever stepped; but you always spoiled him, you did; and I don't know what he would have done if it had not been for me."

The End.